1 - 50   10_
NOVEL SET IN THE   KNS+C
N.C. MOUNTAINS   NCL
BY ED McBAIN'S   (95590)
WIFE

Sassafras

Sassafras

Mary Vann Hunter

NEW AMERICAN LIBRARY

TIMES MIRROR

NAL BOOKS TRADEMARK REG. U.S. PAT. OFF. AND FOREIGN COUNTRIES
REGISTERED TRADEMARK—MARCA REGISTRADA
HECHO EN CRAWFORDSVILLE, INDIANA, U.S.A.

SIGNET, SIGNET CLASSICS, MENTOR, PLUME, MERIDIAN
and NAL BOOKS are published by
The New American Library, Inc.,
1633 Broadway, New York, New York 10019

Designed by Renée Gelman

Library of Congress Cataloging in Publication Data

Hunter, Mary Vann.
Sassafras.

I. Title.
PZ4.H94578Sas [PS3558.U485]   813'.54   79-26716
ISBN 0-453-00376-1

First Printing, April 1980

1   2   3   4   5   6   7   8   9

PRINTED IN THE UNITED STATES OF AMERICA

This is for my grandparents,
Eva Williams Teague
and
William Elvin Teague

Part 1

Grandaddy

*G*randaddy looked very small.

He had shrunk in ninety years to this final diminution of death. This was the thing that all her life she'd feared most, the ultimate horror, the loss that in childhood she'd prayed would not come for a long, long time. She'd been lucky. She'd lived all of forty years before she'd experienced the death of someone she really loved. She'd had a long time to get ready for it.

Grandaddy's death seemed as right as his life had seemed. He and Grandmother had lived lives that were so natural, that so blended with the scheme of the world that death hadn't noticed them and just kept passing them by. She looked at Grandmother sitting in her wheelchair at the end of the pew. She, too, had been diminished. A very large woman she'd been, a strong woman with lots of gumption, one not given to tears till these last years. Grandmother was ninety-three. Her skin, crumpled by age and grief, looked like the flesh of a dried apple. Only the fine bones, barely detectable, suggested the handsome face it once had been.

The church was full. The folding door had been rolled back to make room. She hadn't been in this church since she was a child and occasionally came here with Grandmother. It had seemed staid and dismal compared to the Baptist church where she went with her parents. It did not seem dismal today. The walls were white and sunlight spilled through the stained-glass windows, streaming to a focal point in front of Grandaddy. The front of the church was filled with flowers. The exterior doors were open to a spring day as soft and fresh as spring days can be only in the mountains, the kind of day when you can be content for long minutes sitting alone in new grass thinking of nothing.

The family sat in the second pew. Her daughter Jennifer sat on her left, Daddy on her right, and Mother at the end of the pew next to Grandmother's wheelchair holding Grandmother's frail hand. The third pew was filled with Grandaddy's nephews and nieces from out of town. She noticed that two of Daddy's brothers and their families were sitting near the back of the church. As the family had entered, she'd looked for the faces she associated with this church, the little ladies with their white gloves and dark veiled hats, Sally Smith whom Grandmother had talked about as long as she could remember, Myrtle Haynes who was the most faithful member of Grandmother's Sunday-school class. They weren't here. There were a few faces that she remembered as young which over the past twenty-five years had grown old.

The minister, who was too young to have really known Grandaddy, was reading from the Bible. "So when this corruptible shall have put on incorruption, and this mortal shall have put on immortality, then shall be brought to pass the saying that is written, Death is swallowed up in victory. O death, where is thy sting? O grave, where is thy victory?"

She listened to the words and felt little need for their solace. What she was feeling now was less explored than common grief. The loss she recognized to be something greater than the slipping over the line into death of an old man, and this sense of loss was confused by a joy, a sense of awakening, of discovery, of being near to finding something precious that she hadn't known was lost and hadn't known was precious.

She thought of this town that had been a part of her and would ever be a part of her, though she had left it nearly twenty-five years ago. At last she could begin to see it. She thought of her present home that had been a busy sawmill in a settled community while settlers here were still living in a fort as protection against the Cherokees who filled the mountains and who slaughtered and scalped with the ruthlessness of a fight for survival. It was in 1784 that John Robertson who had founded the fort here had taken his family up the mountain to Linden Creek to build a new homestead only to be scalped by Indians as he was barely finishing the cabin. Less than two hundred years ago. That didn't seem like very long with ninety-three-year-old Grandmother sitting here still alive.

Her daughter Jennifer, sitting on her left, would never know this world that had been the very air surrounding her mother for the first seventeen years of her life. And that world was hardly here anymore to be reviewed. Television, automobiles, shopping centers, governmental largess, and mild prosperity had transformed, were continuing to transform it until there would be nothing left by which she could identify Robertson's Fort or its people, no registry she could go back to and find herself indelibly written on its pages. Soon the blanket of sameness would be tucked neatly into the coves and hollows of these mountains that had resisted it so fiercely for so long.

The pallbearers walked down the aisle. The first two closed the lid on the coffin. Grandmother began to sob.

For a moment she held in her mind the image of Grandaddy's pale, shrunken, dead face under the soft white hair. Then the image began to change. She remembered him as he once was and suddenly she was blinded by tears.

This was the day they were going to kill Big Boy.

Batty had gone to sleep thinking about it and had awakened thinking about it. She was up early, digging around in her chest of drawers looking for her wool socks, when she saw the butcher's old green truck turn into the driveway and head up toward the barn. Just beyond the barn was the pigpen with Grandaddy Terrell's pigs—three ordinary little sows bought from Hiram Brown right here in town, and one very special pig that had been shipped all the way from Indiana. He had a special name, too, but Batty could never remember it. She knew him only as Big Boy. The very first day he arrived, Grandaddy Terrell named him Big Boy, and ever since that's how the whole family had known him. He'd bought Big Boy as a stud to start a brand new line of prizewinning pigs. Big Boy had been here almost a year now and he didn't seem to much like Grandaddy's sows. Mother said he refused to perform.

She and Grandmother had decided that at the age of eight Batty was too young to see the slaughter of Big Boy. Though she didn't want to miss such an important event, she wasn't sure how she felt about the whole thing. Grandaddy had said there was something wrong with him, and he was good for nothing except slaughter. She remembered the day the big truck delivered him in that wooden crate. While Grandaddy pried off the boards, she watched from a position of safety outside the pen. He was the biggest pig she'd ever seen. And he'd come all the way from Indiana. She'd never even been to Indiana. And he was so shiny and clean and so solid gray he almost looked silver, almost as silver as Mother's coffee service that sat on the sideboard in the dining room, unused but kept polished to a high gleam by Virginia. He almost looked like that. But he was big, and Grandaddy had warned that he was mean. Preston had even put another railing around the pen just to make sure he didn't get out. Batty knew she couldn't play with him. She'd once had a pet piglet when one of the sows had farrowed. He'd been the runt. He was warm and pink and wiggly. She'd kept him wrapped in a blue blanket in a cardboard box behind the stove. One morning when she went to get him he was gone. Grandmother told her he'd been sickly and had died during the night. She didn't learn till years later that he'd been born without an anus, and that he'd just filled up with shit and died.

Big Boy was no runt. Though in some respects he was a failure, as far as Batty was concerned he was still King Pig. Though he wasn't a pet exactly, you had to respect him and be proud of him. Even when he turned the ground into deep mud with his rutting and wallowing and the red mud dried and caked on him so he was no longer silver, he was still a handsome fellow. Nobody else in town had a pig like Big Boy.

It was cold this early December morning; it had to be for the killing of hogs, mid-thirties at least, lest the meat go bad while it was seasoning in the smokehouse. Batty was rocking aimlessly in the swing Grandaddy had made for her by tying two ends of a rope to a limb of the maple tree in the side yard and placing a notched board in the loop, when Preston's wagon came up the road raising dust. She pulled her knit cap farther down over her ears.

Preston was a light-skinned black man who sharecropped on the farm. He took care of the crops in the large field across the road from the house and helped Grandaddy with his pigs and with whatever else Grandaddy didn't have time to do; in exchange, Grandaddy let him plant the smaller field on the hill above the house for his own crops. Preston would come with the plow in the wagon behind him. Sometimes his boy William came along to help when he wasn't in school. Preston would take the plow out of the wagon, unhitch the mule, hitch her to the plow and all afternoon you'd hear him talking to her. "Gee haw! Whoa! Okay now, Jesse, giddup!" Batty loved it when Preston was working the upper field talking to his mule. Preston was a small bony man, but she always thought he looked big sitting in his wagon.

"Gee haw," he said now as he pulled on the right rein and led the mule into the driveway. He muttered some other unintelligible things to his mule and angled the wagon on up toward the barn. William and his little sister Caroline were sitting in the back of the wagon on some old burlap bags. Caroline looked small in her large handed-down hooded jacket. Batty could see only her shining brown face grinning at her over the edge of the wagon bed. William hunched into his layers of faded sweaters. He looked serious as always. Mother said he was bashful. He gave a small wave as the wagon disappeared behind the garage.

Batty sprang from the swing and ran into the house through the screened-in back porch, letting the door bang behind her, through the hall and into her mother's bedroom where her mother sat at the dressing table, her marcelled hair in wave clips, putting on her eyebrows. Mother was blond with blue eyes. She didn't look like Batty at all. Everybody said that Batty—with her brown hair and eyes—looked just like her father and all the rest of the Attwood side of the family. Mother's eyebrows were blond, too, and until she painted eyebrows on every morning it looked as though she didn't have any. She looked very pretty, though, when she finished making up her face each morning. She took a towel now and wiped off the excess of brown tint.

"Mother," Batty said, "William and Caroline went up to the barn."

"Well?" Mother said.

"Well, you won't let me go."

"No, not this morning," Mother said.

"But Preston let William and Caroline go."

"Batty, you know you're not allowed to do everything everybody else does."

"But why *can't* I watch the men kill Big Boy?"

"Grandmother and I think you're too young. It would upset you."

"It would not upset me either, and Caroline is eight just like me, and William's only ten."

"I guess Preston thinks it's all right for children to see hogs killed," Mother said.

"I think it's all right, too. Why is it not all right for a child if it's all right for a grown-up?" Batty said.

"Because killing a hog is very unpleasant, and grown-ups are more used to unpleasant things than children are."

"Killing a chicken is unpleasant, too, but you let me watch Grandmother kill chickens."

On days when they were having chicken for dinner, Grandmother would bring a fryer from the chicken house, put its head on the chopping block where Grandaddy split wood for the Warm Morning, and with the ax chop its head off. Then she'd toss it into the backyard to flap around in its last death spasms. It was messy. Blood spattered everywhere. It covered grandmother's legs. Then she'd pick up the chicken, and take it into the room off the garage to pluck it and clean it and singe the last of the feathers before giving it to Virginia to cook. Virginia cooked it brown and crisp. It tasted delicious, as long as you could forget seeing it flapping all over the back yard squirting blood.

"A chicken is just a chicken," Mother said. "Killing Big Boy is going to be much worse. Besides Big Boy is strong and dangerous.

You'd be in the way. Grandaddy is going to have enough to worry about without having to worry about you."

"Then he shouldn't have to worry about William and Caroline," Batty said. "They'll be in the way, too."

"Preston will be the one to worry about William and Caroline," Mother said.

"They should come down here and play with me, the way they always do when Preston brings them on Saturday."

"Why don't you draw with the new artist pencils I bought you?" Mother said.

"I don't want to draw," Batty said. "If I can't watch them kill Big Boy, I want to play with William and Caroline."

Mother looked very serious. She turned from the mirror into which she'd been speaking to Batty's reflection, and said, "I think it's time we had a talk about William and Caroline."

"What about them?"

"You're getting too old to play with them."

"What do you mean I'm getting too old?"

"You know William and Caroline are colored."

"So what?"

"White children and colored children don't play together."

"Why not?"

"They go to different schools and different churches," Mother said.

"Why do they do that?"

"Well . . . colored people are uneducated," Mother said. "Lots of them are dirty. They don't know any better."

"William and Caroline are clean. Virginia's clean. Preston's clean. He always comes to work neat and clean. I've heard Grandmother talking about how clean he is."

"I know Preston is clean and William and Caroline are clean."

"Then why can't I play with them?" Batty said.

In her Sunday School class she'd read with the other children that God loves all the little children. They even sang a song about "Red and yellow, black and white/They're all precious in his sight." She knew Mother was a good person who wouldn't do anything to hurt anything or anybody. Why, Mother was the kindest person in the world! She couldn't even stand to see a stray cat or dog sick or hungry; there were always six or eight cats and a dog or two hanging around the back door to be fed every night after supper. Mother wouldn't tell her to be bad. Everything Mother stood for was good.

"Well, why *can't* I play with them?" Batty asked again.

"Because colored children and white children don't play together," Mother said.

"Why *don't* they?" Batty said.

Mother got up quickly, pulled the belt to her robe very tight and said in a loud voice, "Beatrice Louise, it's just not done."

At that moment she heard him.

There was no mistaking that full-throated rage. Big Boy's loud squalls came right through the walls as though slaughter had been brought into Mother's bedroom to spatter the white rug and ruffled curtains with bloody carnage. It seemed to go on forever, then abated in short, breathless bleats. Then Batty could hear nothing. She stood listening a long moment, Mother not moving, just watching her. Then she bolted from the room, out the back door, slamming it behind her, and took the shortcut over the muddy bank behind the garage toward the barn.

Big Boy was lying on the ground in the middle of the barn, blood pouring from his open mouth and slit throat. He was lying very still. Batty saw Grandaddy's sledgehammer propped against the stable door. A big rope and pulley were hooked over a beam above the place Big Boy lay. She thought he must be dead. When a chicken lay that still you knew it was dead. Grandaddy was down on his haunches looking at Big Boy, who was covered with blood and who didn't look silver at all now. He looked bigger than ever with his fat relaxed all over the ground. Just outside the north door was a big rusty barrel of water supported on two cement blocks. Preston was slipping more wood on the fire under the barrel. The water was hot and steaming, sending up a white vapor into the cold December air. Bill Moody, the butcher at Daddy's store, had set up a big rough wooden table covered with newspapers just outside the barn door near the steaming water. He was a short stocky man who wore his gray hair parted off center. His small mouth was made lopsided by a wad of tobacco always in his right cheek. He had carefully laid out a half-dozen butcher knives of all sizes and was at the spigot a few feet uphill from the barn washing off another one. His legs were spread wide to avoid the stream of water where it splashed to the ground.

Grandaddy just kept squatting there looking at Big Boy.

No one had noticed that she'd come running up in broad daylight. Then she saw William sitting in the hayloft above where Big Boy lay. He was sitting on the edge dangling his legs dangerously over the side, just looking at her. She couldn't tell what he was thinking. She only knew that he'd seen it and she'd missed it. She'd got there only in time to see Big Boy lying there dead and bleeding.

It wasn't over yet, she realized. She walked right by Grandaddy, big as you please, and climbed into the loft on the other side of the barn opposite William. Lowering herself carefully on the edge, she dangled her legs over the side.

Virginia cooked a marvelous supper that evening. At twenty-nine she was the oldest of Preston's four daughters and the best cook of them all. One time when she was sick one of the other daughters had come to take her place. She wasn't the cook Virginia was.

Tonight Virginia had a white linen tablecloth spread on the mahogany dining-room table, the table set, and the house filled with good smells when Mother got home. The dining room was a bright happy place. Mother could turn any house into a bright happy place. When they'd bought the farmhouse before Daddy went off to war, it was drab, Mother said. She had Mr. Duncan, the painter in town, come and knock out the two little windows in the living room and put in a big bay window with lots of little panes which she then hung with crisscrossed and ruffled sheers. She had him put gay wallpaper in all the rooms. Batty's room had blue wallpaper with little white lambs playing in fields of flowers. The dining room had big red roses on a white background. It looked very pretty, especially with Mother's good china and silver sitting on the sideboard. Once in a while, when they had company, Mother used the good silver and china, but most of the time it just sat there looking pretty.

Tonight Virginia had cooked country ham with redeye gravy, mashed potatoes to put the gravy on, green beans that Grandmother had grown in the garden and canned last summer, and thick flaky biscuits. Batty split open a biscuit and spread it with some of the rich butter Grandmother had churned and pressed from Constance's milk. Constance was really Batty's cow, though she let Grandmother Terrell milk her. Grandmother was better at it. She could make the streams fly. When Grandmother was getting the pail and stool ready to milk Constance, several cats would appear out of nowhere and sit silently near Constance's udder. Grandmother, working furiously with both hands, would squirt four streams into the pail and would aim one stream toward the cats, each in turn. The cat toward which it was aimed would open his mouth and catch the milk midair, never missing a drop. The best Batty could do was to squirt one weak stream at a time into the pail. It didn't even make the same clean sharp sound hitting the pail that Grandmother's squirts made.

In addition to Constance, Grandmother also had to take care of the chickens. There were chickens all over the barnyard, most of them just pecking the stony ground aimlessly. Grandmother said they had to get grit into their craws to help them digest their chicken feed. She even opened a craw once to show Batty when she was cleaning a chicken for dinner, and sure enough that's what it was, just a little sack of all that grit. The farm had three big chicken houses. Batty's favorite chicken house was the laying house. Each layer had her own little stall where she sat on her bed of hay till she announced by cackling very loudly that she had laid an egg. Grandmother would reach under the hen's warm belly and bring the egg out and put it into the egg basket. Grandmother even knew the names of all the different kinds of chickens. There were the Leghorns, the Rhode Island Reds, and the Plymouths. To Batty they all looked pretty much the same. They certainly looked the same at first. Grandmother would order five hundred Leghorns and lots of boxes would arrive with little portholes filled with yellow fluff. If the weather was cool, Grandmother would put all the little "biddies" in the incubator house and build a fire in the furnace under it. Batty loved to stand in the middle of them and try to keep her eye on one biddie before it got lost in the roiling mass of yellow fluff.

There was no doubt that Grandmother was queen of the barnyard. No queen commanded such attention as she did when she slung a bucket of cracked corn over her left arm and, from the steps of the incubator building, tossed handfuls to the thick crescent of clucking and squawking chickens before her. She'd stand there, a hefty woman in a cotton dress with her stockings rolled and knotted at the ankle just above her canvas shoes, a helmet-shaped straw hat pulled down over her graying hair and shading her face, and there was no doubt that this woman was regal. Batty always thought that when Grandmother was feeding the chickens she should make a speech.

But she never did. She just went about her work from sunup to sundown, saying only what needed to be said. She saved her talking mostly for the class she taught at the Methodist church Sunday School. Every Saturday night she'd study her Sunday School lesson from the stack of books and little magazines she kept on her night table beside the bed. In the morning she'd get dressed up in her whalebone corset and best dress, her best shoes and hat—it was the only day of the week her stockings weren't rent with runs—and she'd go to teach her Sunday School class. But there wasn't much time for grandiloquence these days, certainly not time for making speeches to chickens.

Batty's father was off fighting the Germans. He'd been thirty-three in 1943, the year he registered, and he didn't really have to go off to war; he'd chosen to go in the name of patriotism. Batty didn't know then about men and wars. She didn't know that the years of the war would be the one great adventure and proving ground of her father's life that would make the rest of it for the most part unnecessary. She didn't know that for years to come, company would be treated to his evening recountings of war experiences. She knew only that her father was a brave man gone to war, and she and her mother knelt beside the bed each night to ask God to bring him back safely. And when, in fact, he did come back safely with his stories of running unharmed through raining German bullets, they were convinced that their prayers had been answered.

But for now he was gone and Grandmother was running the farm, Mother was running the store, and Grandaddy Terrell ran his train. When he came through town, he always gave three long blows and one short so they would know it was him. Then in the late afternoon, he'd come walking home in his sooty overalls and high-top shoes. He was a short man tending toward fat, with bright blue eyes in a round pleasant face and a full head of wavy blond hair. He always carried a paper bag of peppermint sticks for Batty. He'd give her the candy, and then he'd bathe and dress very carefully. Grandmother said he was as prissy as a woman.

When he finished dressing, he'd give Batty all the attention she wanted. He was the only one who wasn't too tired. Grandmother was exhausted from milking Constance, feeding the chickens, canning and churning. Mother was exhausted from working at the store. When Grandaddy was tired he would take a little catnap sitting in his chair. You could hear him snoring all over the house. Then he'd wake up and fix a tricycle, or repair the swing, or make stilts, or just sit for hours letting Batty comb and arrange his thick yellow hair. She'd roll it, braid it, pile it into a pompadour, put hairpins in it. Then she'd stand back and appraise it. Then she'd try another style.

Tonight, in addition to all the other delicious things Virginia had cooked for dinner, she'd also baked a deep-dish blackberry pie from the berries that Batty had helped Grandmother pick last summer—with Grandmother telling her every minute to look out for snakes. Batty ate till she was stuffed. She'd been working up a real appetite. She was lucky no one had said anything about her going up to the barn to watch them butcher Big Boy. She had sort of disobeyed a little bit—well, not exactly. She hadn't, after all, seen them kill Big Boy, but her going to the barn at all could have got her spanked. Nobody in this family put up with much disobedience. She was thankful nothing more had been said about it. She was also a little confused. She kept waiting for Mother or Grandmother to raise Cain, but nobody did. They just pretended it never happened.

During dinner Grandaddy began to cry.

Batty had asked Mother why she had dark hair and eyes like Daddy's side of the family instead of having blond hair and blue eyes like Mother's side. Grandmother pointed out quickly that though Mother and Grandaddy had blond hair and blue eyes *she* had brown eyes and brown hair and she didn't think the Attwoods could take all the credit for Batty's looks. Mother tried to tell her about genes. Batty couldn't understand it at all. Mother said there were dominant traits and recessive traits and, though genetics was very complicated and she couldn't remember it completely, in the making of Batty dark hair and eyes had been dominant.

"If you and Daddy had a baby brother for me," Batty asked, "would he also have brown hair and brown eyes?"

"Maybe not," Mother said. "For him, blond might be dominant."

"You mean we couldn't know till you had me a baby brother?"

"That's right," Mother said.

"Will you and Daddy have a baby brother when he gets home?"

Mother smiled and looked like someone with a secret. "We'll have to wait and see," she said.

"What color hair did your little sister have?" Batty asked, forgetting for a moment Grandmother's warnings.

Grandaddy stopped eating and bent his head over his plate. Everybody got very quiet. He put down his fork, lifted his right haunch from the chair, and dug into this hip pocket for a handkerchief. He took it out and wiped his eyes.

Grandmother watched him for a moment. Then she said, "Andy, don't . . ."

Grandaddy buried his face in his handkerchief and pushed his chair from the table. "I'm sorry," he said, in a voice made high and faint by his crying. He sobbed loudly as he hurried from the room and up the stairs to his bedroom.

"I'm sorry," Batty said, "I didn't mean to make Grandaddy cry. I forgot."

"It's all right," Grandmother said. "He's just a big baby. He's been crying for almost thirty years." Then she sighed. "He'll never get over it," she said with resignation.

Grandmother had given birth to a second daughter when Mother was three. Mary Ann, as Grandmother and Grandaddy had named her, died of pneumonia soon after her first birthday. Grandmother told Batty that for months after the death of his baby daughter, Grandaddy would come home from work every afternoon and throw himself on the bed and cry for hours.

Grandmother didn't have time to cry for hours. She had another daughter to raise, and she had all the cooking and cleaning to do. Grandaddy told her he thought she was hardhearted because she didn't grieve as much as he did, and she told him she thought he was being a baby because he did. Finally, he got over crying every day and cried only when something reminded him of his dead child. "Don't talk about Mother's sister in front of Grandaddy," Grandmother warned repeatedly.

When Grandaddy came back into the dining room, his whole face was red and damp. He sat down and began eating again.

"Would you like some more ham, Andy?" Grandmother asked.

"I don't mind if I do," Grandaddy said, obviously over his spell of grieving.

"I don't want a little brother anyway," Batty said.

"Why don't you want a little brother, Batty?" Grandmother asked.

"Because he'd be everybody's favorite."

"What on earth makes you say that?" Mother asked.

"Because he'd be a boy," Batty said. "I don't want a little brother. I'm enough."

After supper Grandmother went upstairs to her room to study her Sunday-school lesson. Mother began running Batty's bath water and then took Virginia home in the Buick. When she got back, Batty was drying herself getting ready to put on her pajamas. Mother came into the bedroom. "You ready for bed?"

"Almost," Batty said. "Mother, will you read me a story when I'm in bed?"

"No, not tonight," Mother said. "I'm very tired tonight."

Batty was almost relieved. Mother wasn't a good story reader at all. Batty had almost as soon read the story herself as to have Mother read it. She remembered the way Daddy used to read stories. He made them very interesting, his voice getting very loud, then soft, then rising to a high pitch, then falling to a soft low sound. Whether he was reading *Robinson Crusoe* or *Peter Pan* or just telling her favorite story of David and Goliath which she knew by heart, he gave a real performance. Mother tried, but she just couldn't do it as well as Daddy. When Mother read to her, it was very boring.

"Come on now, Batty," Mother said, "are you ready to say your prayers?"

She turned back Batty's bed and fluffed the pillows. Batty got down next to the bed and arranged her hands like a little church steeple.

"I'm ready," she said.

Mother got down on her knees slowly, arranging her skirttail so she wouldn't get it all wrinkled.

"Okay," Mother said softly. "You go first."

Batty took a deep breath and tried to get her mind ready to pray.

"Dear Jesus," she said, "we thank you for all our blessings. We thank you for our food and clothes and our house. Please take care of Mother and Grandmother. Take care of Grandaddy. Take care of Grandmother Attwood and Aunt Harriet. Help me to be a good girl and to help Mother and Grandmother. And please, dear God, take care of Daddy in the war. Don't let him get shot by a German. And bring him home safe and sound. Amen."

Batty hated wearing dresses. She had to wear dresses to school during the week and to church on Sunday mornings, but as soon as she got home she'd change into her corduroy pants. Every morning of the week Grandmother braided her shoulder-length hair into two French braids. She'd start high on her head and pick up sprigs of hair as the braid progressed down her head and then she would braid in a wide satin ribbon to match whatever Batty was wearing. When the hair was braided to the end she would tie the ribbon into a big stiff bow. Then she'd begin on the second braid. Most of the time the ribbon came out of at least one of the braids during the softball game at play period, and Mrs. McAuley would have to braid it again. She'd just do a regular braid since she couldn't make a French braid, and Batty would have one French braid and one regular braid for the rest of the day.

This was Sunday and Batty was wearing one of her hated dresses. It was a blue satin with a gathered skirt and a sash that Mother had tied in a big bow in the back. There were little pink rosebuds embroidered on the bodice. To tie Batty's braids, Grandmother had used pink ribbons that matched the pink rosebuds.

When Mother and Batty walked down the center aisle and slipped into the tenth pew of the Baptist church that morning, everybody turned to look at Mother's new hat. They always did. Even if it had been an old hat, they'd have turned to look. Mother's hats were pretty interesting. Whenever she went to Asheville to buy a new hat, her favorite saleslady at Ivey's or Bon Marché would spend an hour putting hats on Mother and arranging them just right in the mirror. Mother would take the hand mirror and turn from the big mirror to see the hat on her from all sides. Then the saleslady would take it off and put another hat on Mother. When she finally decided on a hat, the lady would put it in a big round box with the name of the store written on it. Mother would take it home and put it on the shelf next to all the other round boxes. Today she had on a tweed suit with a long loose jacket almost to her knees and a hat made of fake cherries that dipped very low onto her face on one side. It had a cloud of green veil that came down just far enough over Mother's face to cover her eyes.

The Attwoods were all Baptists. Before she married, Grandmother Attwood had been a Methodist. She'd been a Carlysle and the Carlysles had been Methodists forever—one of them had been the first child born in the old English fort that once stood next to the river where the community building now stood. When she married Grandaddy Attwood, she became a Baptist. Batty had never seen Grandaddy Attwood. He'd lost his store during the Depression and had died almost immediately afterward, leaving Grandmother Attwood and her six children in a fine pickle. Daddy had been only ten years old. But one thing Grandaddy Attwood was responsible for was that the Attwoods would all be Baptists.

Grandmother Terrell was a Methodist and Grandaddy Terrell went with her to the Methodist church. Batty didn't know whether he was a Christian or not. He never talked about religion the way Grandmother did. Not only that, but when he got real mad at something he said bad words that nobody else in the family said. He never got mad enough at *people* to say bad words, it was only at *things:* a hammer that missed a nail, or a nail that bent instead of going straight, or a piece of wood that split when he was driving a nail into it.

The church was nearly filled this morning. Light streamed through the yellow marbled windows. Someone had placed a large potted azalea on the altar at the front of the church. First Mrs. Gosorn came out in her white robe and sat down at the organ. She opened the book before her and began playing loudly. Then the choir came out in a line and stood in front of two rows of chairs. Mrs. Swann, the minister's wife who led the choir, came in last and stood before them. She looked at Mrs. Gosorn who had stopped playing and she started playing again. Then she lifted her hand and brought it down. The choir began singing the Invocation. When they finished, she gestured and they all sat down at once. Reverend Swann came in from the side door looking stately and very handsome in his blue robe.

"Open your hymnal to page three-twenty-four, and let's all join in singing," he said. It was one of Batty's favorite songs. Everybody sang it very loudly and Mrs. Gosorn played it very loudly, too.

"I've seen the lightning flashing/I've heard the thunder roll/I've heard the voice of Satan/Trying to conquer my soul." They brought the hymn to the last line: "He promised never to leave me/Never to leave me alone."

Reverend Swann waited a minute for everybody to sit down. Then he said, "Brother White, would you please lead us in prayer."

Mr. White was a farmer. He had very gnarled and rough hands. He was a little stooped, too. He looked like a man who worked hard six days a week and who wore a white shirt and tie only on Sundays. He had two sons who helped him on the farm and one son who was away fighting the war. He also had a daughter Batty's age. She loved to visit Sarah in the fall when the Whites were making sorghum molasses. She liked to see the mule going around in a circle to turn the press and squeeze the juice from the cane. She loved the smell of the boiling molasses as Mrs. White kept skimming off the froth from the big tin vat. But most of all, she liked sucking the sweet juice from the pieces of sorghum cane Mr. White cut for her and Sarah.

Mr. White was a very religious man. He came to church every Sunday morning and evening and also for Wednesday-night prayer meeting. He lifted his face and with eyes closed began to talk to God.

"Almighty Father, we thank thee for the privilege of coming to thy house of worship. We praise thee for all thou hast given us, for our families, for our health, for our work. We thank thee for this fine Christian fellowship, for this beautiful day that we have to raise our voices in thanksgiving. Please lift from us our worldly cares. Strike from our hearts envy and greed. Make us worthy of thy love. Give us faith, O God, give us faith. We know that thou taketh care of the birds of the air and the beasts of the fields. How much more bountiful is thy love for us! Please enter every troubled heart today and give it peace. Be in faraway places on the battlefields with our men who are fighting the war in thy name. Bring them home safely to their loved ones. We ask especially that thou be with the family of John Holmes who we all loved and who was killed in action last week. Help them to know that thou hast taken him home to be with thee, and that though we do not always understand thy ways, that thou hast a purpose for everything thou does. Dear God, we beseech thee, give this grieving family thy comfort. Please be with us now. Bring thy presence to this Christian fellowship. Amen."

When Mr. White finished praying, he always took out his large white handkerchief and wiped the tears from his eyes. Everybody sat down. Reverend Swann made a few announcements. The choir stood and sang again. The ushers passed the offering plates into which members of the congregation put white envelopes containing their tithe. Then Reverend Swann stood up and talked for what seemed to Batty a very long time about Faithful Stewardship. She got restless and Mother's gloved hand patted her hand twice, letting her know she had to be still. She thought about Bill Moody hoisting Big Boy on the pulley, and with his big knife slicing him from chin to crotch and taking out all his insides. She thought about that as long as she could and Reverend Swann *still* wasn't finished. She tried to think of something else interesting.

Finally he was finished. The congregation stood up and sang another hymn, the choir sang the benediction, Reverend Swann walked up the aisle and stood at the church door to shake hands with the congregation as they left. Batty always felt good when church was over.

Look at all this rabbit tobacco, Batty thought, running her hand up the stalk, skinning off the leaves. The stalks were about three feet high and were covered with long narrow leaves dried to a furry silver. She rolled them between her palms and held them to her nose. They had a nice pungent aroma. She thought of taking home a handful for Grandaddy to make her a rabbit-tobacco cigarette, but then she figured Grandmother and Mother would probably fuss at him if they saw him making the cigarette. Besides, she surely couldn't *smoke* it in front of them, so even if he did get by with *making* the cigarette, what would be the good of it? She'd better go and bring him up here.

She'd found the clump of rabbit tobacco at the far end of the meadow beyond the barnyard. As she turned to cross the meadow back toward the house, her eye was caught by an apple tree a few feet from the rabbit tobacco. She'd never noticed that tree before. The ground around it was covered with rotten apples, brown and flattened. One brown and oozing apple still clung to the tree. That was an unusual sight on this farm. Grandaddy and Preston usually picked the apples from the trees in the fall, buckets of them. Preston took some home with him. The others Grandaddy took in for Grandmother to can or make into jelly. Grandmother would fuss up a storm about all the apples he expected her to do something with. He'd explain that it was an awful shame to let them go to waste. Batty pressed down one strand of wire and carefully edged herself through the fence so as not to catch her corduroy pants on a barb. She walked through the orchard toward the house. There wasn't a rotten apple anywhere in sight.

Grandaddy was sitting in the living room reading the funny papers.

"Come on," she said. "I've got something to show you."

"What is it, darling? I'm reading the funny papers."

"You can read them later," she said, taking him by the hand and pulling him toward the back door.

Grandaddy laughed tolerantly. "It'd better be good," he said, getting up to follow her.

"It is," Batty said, and led him by the hand up around the barn, taking the long way so Grandaddy could go through the gate and wouldn't have to crawl through the barbed wire.

"Now what is it you want to show me, honey?"

"That," Batty said, pointing. "Look at all that rabbit tobacco, Grandaddy."

"Well, I'll be dad gum! That sure is a healthy stand of rabbit tobacco, isn't it? Why, we could go into the rabbit-tobacco business," Grandaddy said, chuckling.

"Let's have a cigarette," Batty said.

"Okay, suits me," Grandaddy said. "Now don't you tell Grandmother I'm doing this."

"She knows you make me rabbit-tobacco cigarettes."

"Well, I *know* she does," he said, "but if we talk about it much, she'll make me quit."

"Why?" Batty asked. "They're not real cigarettes."

"No, of course they aren't," Grandaddy said. "Now give me some rabbit tobacco."

Batty was lucky. In most cases, a kid had to make his own rabbit-tobacco cigarette. He'd tear a strip from a brown paper bag, put a rolled-up wad of tobacco on it, and roll it into a crude cylinder, licking the edge to make it stick. Then he'd put the cigarette into his mouth and light it with a match. Most of the time, the paper flamed and ruined the cigarette. Besides that problem, the cigarette didn't look very neat.

Grandaddy reached inside his jacket and took from his pocket his little machine. Then he reached into his pocket again and pulled out a little packet of cigarette papers. The cigarette machine was a flat steel box some two inches wide by three inches long. He pressed the edge of it and it opened like a locket. He wet his fingers and separated one of the tissues from the rest and placed the tissue on the machine. Then he took the rabbit tobacco Batty had rolled and put it in the tray next to the paper. He closed the machine and a perfect cigarette rolled out.

"Here, Batty," he said, handing her the cigarette. Then he took out his tobacco pouch and made himself a real cigarette. He put the cigarette in his mouth. Batty put her cigarette in her mouth. Then Grandaddy put his little machine and the tissues into one pocket and reached into another pocket and pulled out a little box of matches. He struck the match on the sandpaper side of the box and held the flame to Batty's cigarette.

"Don't breathe it into your lungs, darling," he said. "Just suck it into your mouth and blow it out."

"Good," Batty said, puffing out a mouthful of smoke.

"Is it good, darling?" Grandaddy said, and laughed. "Now don't say anything about this to Grandmother," he warned again.

"Mine's gone out," Batty said.

Grandaddy took out his matches to light her cigarette again. Then the two of them sat down in the dried grass to enjoy their smokes. It was warm in the sun. Batty unzipped her jacket and lay back on the ground. She thought of all the things that had happened yesterday—the slaughter of Big Boy, Mother's telling her she couldn't play with William and Caroline anymore. She could hardly believe it was only yesterday, today was so peaceful. Occasionally she could hear the pigs grunt. The chickens were making soft clucking noises. From across the meadow the sound was a soft murmur. All at once, she remembered that she wanted to ask Grandaddy about the apple tree. She sat up, took a last puff on her cigarette, and then rubbed it out in the dirt between tufts of grass.

"Grandaddy," she said, "why'd you leave the apples to rot on that tree over there? Why didn't you take them in for Grandmother to can?"

Grandaddy looked at the tree a moment. "You know, Batty," he said, "I never noticed that tree before. It's way up here all by itself instead of being in the orchard with all the other apple trees. It sure is a good bearing tree. Lordy mercy! Look at all those rotten apples!" He took another draw off his cigarette and let the smoke out slowly.

"What a waste," he said. "What an awful waste."

The kids Batty went to school with were divided into the town kids and the country kids. Even though she lived on the outskirts of town, she was still a town kid. She didn't live far enough out to be a country kid. The country kids came from as far as ten or twelve miles out. They came to school on yellow buses. The town kids walked to school. A lot of country kids brought their lunches to school in brown paper bags or tin lunch buckets or old paint cans—delicious things like peanut butter and jelly sandwiches or banana sandwiches made of slices of banana with mayonnaise on white bread. Sometimes they had a chunk of cold corn bread, or some homemade pickles, or a chicken leg. It was always the banana sandwiches that Batty coveted whenever a country kid opened his lunch bucket and unwrapped the waxed paper to lay out his lunch on the long cafeteria table while she was eating the cafeteria food.

The country kids wore denim overalls. The town kids wore dresses or skirts or cotton shirts and washable pants, but not denim. When a country kid got an injury, he came to school with it painted purple. When a town kid got an injury, he came to school with it painted orange. The country kids went to little wooden churches scattered throughout the hills and valleys. The town kids went to one of the three Protestant churches in town. A lot of country kids played the guitar and sang hillbilly music. They took part in all-day sings on Sundays. The town kids took piano lessons from Mrs. LeFevre if they were girls, and, if they were boys, had nothing to do with music at all.

But the biggest difference between the country kids and the town kids was the way they talked. The country kids used words and pronunciations that the town kids knew were incorrect. They said "his'n" for "his,"and "her'n" for "hers," and "your'n" for "yours." They said words like "fetch" and "tote," and pronounced "ate" as "et." Mother said that the people who lived in the mountains were the progeny of sturdy Scotch-Irish, English second sons who didn't inherit their fathers' land, the families of kings who'd lost their thrones; they'd all moved to these mountains for freedom to do as they wished and to be left alone. She said that through the generations, while things were changing in the outside world, they continued to live and talk the way they'd always lived and talked back in England or Ireland. But to Batty they were just snot-nosed country kids who'd never been anywhere, not even to Asheville, and who talked like bumpkins.

There was another kind of kid. That was the kid who lived in town but who came from a trashy family. Maxy McBride was such a kid. Her father did odd jobs for people in town, but you couldn't depend on him. He was usually drunk, and when he was drunk, he wouldn't come to work. He was a lumbering man with sort of straw, no-color hair and a face that seemed not to have energy to give expression to thoughts or feelings. It just hung there like a dirty shirt. There were four kids in the family. Their mama was a knotty little woman who always had her head tied up in a cotton kerchief and who could be seen scurrying around town always looking at the ground.

Maxy could have been a pretty kid. She had light brown hair that was always matted as though she'd never combed it in her life, but her eyes were pretty. They were pale blue and had crinkles around them when she laughed. She wore clothes that someone had given her family. Usually they were much too big, dresses that looked as though they'd once belonged to a grown-up. The worst thing about Maxy was that she was filthy dirty. Her face was gray, and the lines in her neck were black. The grime on her hands had begun to look like a permanent color.

Batty and Maxy got along real well. They were lining up after recess to go in for their geography lesson when Batty got her idea. She had hit the ball past the shortstop and had run to first base. Tommy Laughridge had picked it up near third base and had thrown it to J. C. Marston on first. J.C. picked it up a moment too late but said he'd got it on time and Batty was out. Maxy said she was not so out and if J.C. said it again she'd smack him. She was bigger than him. Batty got to stay on base.

Batty was pretty good at taking care of herself. She often had to fight Charlie Knipe across the creek when they were playing cowboys and Indians. Though she didn't really need anyone to take care of her that way, Maxy's protectiveness was appreciated. Batty decided right then that she could have a good friend in Maxy McBride.

"Maxy, would your mother let you spend the night with me?" she asked.

"She won't keer," Maxy said.

"We could go to the office after school and phone her," Batty said.

"We ain't got no phone," Maxy said. "B'sides, she won't keer."

"If you don't go home, won't she come looking for you?"

"Naw, I'll tell my brother Joe to tell her. She won't keer."

"Where's Joe?"

"He's in Mrs. Bradley's class. I'll git Mrs. McAuley to give me an excuse to go see 'im."

When they walked into the house, Virginia was cutting strips of dough from a circle she'd rolled out in a dusting of flour, lacing them over an apple pie she was making.

"Hi, Virginia, where's Grandmother?" Batty said.

"Upstairs, honey. Hi there, who are you?"

"She's Maxy McBride. She's going to spend the night with me."

"Your mother know you gonna have company?"

"Come on, Maxy, let's go tell Grandmother," Batty said, and dropped her books on the kitchen table. "Grandmother," she called as she bounded up the stairs. "Come on, Maxy, come on up here. Grandmother, Maxy's going to spend the night with me."

Grandmother was darning one of Grandaddy's socks over an electric light bulb. Maxy came around the corner and stood in the doorway with her hands clasped in front of her. Grandmother looked up and stopped her sewing a moment. "Well for Pete's sake," she said, "you girls take your coats off. You're going to burn up in here."

Batty stripped her coat off and tossed it onto Grandmother's other easy chair. Maxy just stood there.

"Batty, help Maxy take her coat off," Grandmother said.

Maxy began unbuttoning her coat. Batty took the coat by the lapels and tried to help Maxy. "Come on, Maxy, pull your arms out."

"Batty, run put your coat in your closet," Grandmother said. "I'll put Maxy's coat away. Just leave it on the trunk there."

When Batty got back, Maxy was standing just where she'd left her. Grandmother was trying to figure out who she was.

"Who's your daddy?" she was asking.

"Jeb McBride," Maxy said, not moving.

"And where do you live?"

"Up by the depot, near the railroad."

Grandmother was quiet for a minute. Then she said, "Okay, what are you young'uns going to do till Mother gets home?"

Maxy and Batty snacked on peanut-butter sandwiches and milk and then spent the rest of the afternoon looking over the barnyard. Maxy was most interested in the guinea hens that Mother called Grandmother's craziness. She'd never seen any of those gray, spotted, hunched-up birds that refused to stay on the ground with the other barnyard fowl, but flew to the top of the highest tree or telephone pole. They spotted two in the top of the oak tree. The others were probably off in the woods somewhere laying eggs. Just as they were giving up hope of finding the other guineas, Batty heard Mother calling her. She took Maxy's hand and began running down the hill to the house. Mother was standing just inside the door waiting for them. When they came into the house, Batty could hear the water running in the bathtub.

"Mother," Batty said, "Maxy's going to spend the night."

"Yes, I know," Mother said, "Grandmother told me. I want you girls cleaned up before supper. Batty, wash your hands and face, and, Maxy, come into the bathroom. We're going to have a bath."

Batty pushed up her sleeves and washed her hands and face. Then she put the top down on the toilet and sat down to watch Maxy take a bath. Mother turned Maxy around gently, unbuttoned her dress, told her to lift her arms, and pulled the dress over her head. Maxy was wearing nothing under it except a pair of dirty panties with the elastic so stretched that Batty wondered how she could keep them from falling down. Mother told Maxy to take off her shoes and socks. She put all of Maxy's clothes in a little pile and called Virginia and told her to soak them in good hot water and then run them through the machine. Mother tested the water, decided it had gotten a little cool and turned on the hot water again.

"Okay, Maxine, get in,"she said, and gave Maxy a hand so she wouldn't slip. "Do you like taking baths?" she asked.

"Yes, ma'am," Maxy said.

"Do you ever take a bath at home?"

"Yes, ma'am."

"But you don't take a bath very often, do you?"

"No, ma'am."

"Do you have a bathtub at home?"

"No, ma'am."

"Well, where do you take a bath?"

"In a pan."

Mother got the washcloth all soapy and bent over Maxy.

"Close your eyes, Maxine," she said. "I don't want to get soap in them."

Mother didn't say a word about how dirty Maxy was. She just scrubbed. She didn't miss a spot. She scrubbed her face and neck, she scrubbed behind her ears, she scrubbed her feet and legs, she scrubbed her hands and fingernails with a brush. Maxy closed her mouth very tight as though she were silently suffering a great indignity. Mother ran the water out of the tub, filled it up once more and started all over again. When she finished bathing Maxy, she wrapped her in a towel and stuck her head in the sink and began washing her hair. Maxy began to whimper.

"It's almost over," Mother said. "You've been very brave."

Maxy continued to whimper softly.

"You're going to feel so good after we finish. And you're going to look so pretty."

Maxy whimpered on.

Mother finished the third lather, rinsed the hair well, and wrapped Maxy's head in a towel.

Batty giggled. "You're all towel," she said.

Maxy just stood there saying nothing while Mother dried her, combed her hair and parted it neatly. Then Mother gave Maxy a pair of Batty's pajamas and told her to put them on.

"That's backward, silly," Batty said. "Here, I'll show you."

Maxy didn't even look like herself; she looked shiny clean and very pretty, and that night she ate supper in pajamas. The next day Mother dressed her in Batty's underwear and socks and one of Batty's old dresses and told Maxy she could keep them. She put Maxy's clothes in a paper bag, gave them back to her, and then drove her and Batty to school on her way to work. Mrs. McAuley told Maxy she looked very pretty. The kids said she sure looked different. Batty never knew whether Maxy liked being clean. She never said.

Batty had decided there weren't many good things in this world about being a girl. Girls had no choices. They couldn't be anything interesting when they grew up, whereas boys could be anything they wanted to be. Sometimes Grandaddy took her to the movies at the Roxy Theater in town on Saturday afternoons. She loved Hopalong Cassidy, Johnny Mack Brown, Kit Carson, and Lash LaRue. Most of all, she liked Red Ryder who always had Little Beaver, his Indian sidekick, with him. There weren't any cowboys who were girls. The girls in the movies Grandaddy took her to see wore long full skirts that they were constantly trying to keep out of the mud. They were often threatened by danger that only the cowboys could protect them from. They spent their time in kitchens doing boring things while the cowboys led exciting lives chasing bad guys and exhibiting skills of all sorts and great courage to boot. Batty wanted more than anything in the world to be a boy.

When she played cowboy with Charlie Knipe, who lived across the river, she always insisted on being Red Ryder and on his being Little Beaver. Sometimes Charlie wanted to be Red Ryder, but though he and Batty were the same age, Batty was bigger than he was and she would never let him. Charlie was a small frail boy with brown hair and blue eyes and a nose that constantly ran. When it was all settled that she would be Red Ryder, they would spend the day looking for bad guys. They knew who the bad guys were and would snoop around waiting to catch them doing something bad.

One day when Batty was walking to the store after school, Gary Reed stopped in his pickup to ask her if she wanted a ride. She said no thank you, she wanted to walk. Mother had told her over and over that bad men tried to pick up little girls and Gary Reed had just now tried to pick her up. She decided right then and there that he was a bad guy. When she told Mother about it, Mother said Gary Reed couldn't possibly be a bad guy. He was an important member of the Baptist church and was so pleasant and soft-spoken besides. Mother's judgment didn't change Batty's mind at all and from then on she and Charlie kept a close watch on Gary Reed's hardware store to make sure he wasn't getting by with doing anything bad.

Every once in a while Charlie would get uppity and *demand* to be Red Ryder. Batty couldn't understand how a little shrimp like him could possibly have any delusions about the appropriateness of his being a Red Ryder. Nevertheless, it always came back to that, and periodically Batty would have to defend her right to the role. One Saturday when they were in the front yard, getting their plans for the day all lined up, Charlie brought it up again.

"You always get to be Red Ryder," he said. "Today, it's my turn. Today, *I'm* going to be Red Ryder."

"No you aren't, either," Batty said. "I'm going to be Red Ryder and you're going to be Little Beaver."

"No," Charlie said, stamping his foot emphatically. "If I can't be Red Ryder today, I'm not going to play. I'll go home."

"You can't be Red Ryder," Batty said loudly. "A little shrimp like you? You don't even *look* like Red Ryder."

"I look as much like Red Ryder as you."

"You don't either," Batty said, clenching her fists.

"Red Ryder's not a girl," Charlie said.

"So what?" Batty said, hunching her shoulders in rage.

"So you shouldn't be Red Ryder. 'Cause you're a girl."

"I'm not a girl," Batty screamed, "I'm *not* a girl. Take it back. You take it back!"

She had him down now. She was sitting on his chest and had his arms pinned to the ground behind his head.

"No," Charlie said.

"Take it back, Charlie, or I'll beat you up."

Charlie was silent.

Batty turned his arms loose and started hitting him. She slapped him on one side of the face. Then on the other. Then she balled up her fists and started hitting his frail, bony chest. Charlie began to whimper, and at that moment Grandaddy swung open the front door and came out onto the porch.

"You children stop this fighting or you're going to have to stop playing together," he said. "Get up, Batty. Let Charlie up."

Batty got off Charlie's chest. He was still whimpering. He stood up and dusted himself off.

"Okay," Charlie said, "you can be Red Ryder today, but tomorrow it's my turn."

"No," Batty said, "I'm *always* going to be Red Ryder."

In January, Batty renamed herself. She decided that Beatrice Louise wasn't an appropriate name for a boy, all due respects to Grandmother's mother who had died a young woman and after whom Batty had been named. Batty was intent upon doing anything possible to be a boy, even if it meant changing the name she was given at birth as a tribute to Grandmother's poor dead mother. Her favorite names were Jimmy and Jack. She took them both. She named herself Jimmy Jack.

"My name isn't Batty anymore," she announced at dinner one night. "From now on my name is Jimmy Jack."

Grandmother laughed.

"Don't laugh," Batty said. "I'm serious. From now on, you've got to call me Jimmy Jack."

"Okay, Jimmy Jack," Grandmother said, amused. "But it's going to be awfully hard to remember, especially since you've been Batty all your life."

"What's wrong with Batty?" Grandaddy asked, puzzled.

"Batty's a girl's name," Batty said.

"But you *are* a girl."

"Yes, but I'm not *supposed* to be a girl. God made a big mistake. I'm supposed to be a boy."

"God doesn't make mistakes," Mother said. "You're just a tomboy. You'll get over it one day and be glad you're a girl."

"He made a mistake *this* time," Batty said. "And I *won't* get over it, either. My name isn't Batty any longer. My name is Jimmy Jack."

Sometimes Batty didn't notice when someone called her Batty and other times she'd get fighting mad. In the daytime when she was playing, she insisted on being called Jimmy Jack. She trained Charlie Knipe immediately, but Mother always forgot and called her Batty, and at last she gave up on her. Grandmother would make a mistake and then, after being corrected, would try for the next little while to remember; she seemed to think it was a funny game, and smiled to herself whenever she called her Jimmy Jack. Grandaddy would remember to call her Jimmy Jack part of the time. The rest of the time he'd call her Batty the way he always had.

The only time Batty didn't expect to be called anything but Batty was at night when she was getting ready for bed. One evening

Grandmother came into Batty's bedroom while she was putting on her pajamas. She sat down on the foot of Batty's bed.

"Batty," she asked, "why do you want to be a boy?"

"Because girls can't be cowboys," Batty said.

"But cowboys aren't real. They're only in the movies. There're no real cowboys."

"Cowboys are, too, real. Besides it's not only cowboys girls can't be. Girls can't be *anything*."

"Sure they can. Girls can be a lot of things."

"What?" Batty asked.

"Well, girls can be teachers," Grandmother said.

"What else?"

"They can go to college and be anything they want to be."

"They can't go to college and be cowboys," Batty said, triumphantly.

Grandmother sat on the end of Batty's bed examining the conversation, thinking about what Batty had said. Batty crawled in between the sheets and pulled the covers to her chin.

Finally Grandmother said, "Well, Batty, I've always thought it would be awfully hard to be a man and to have to go to a job every day—and not be able to have babies. God's greatest blessing to women is motherhood." Her eyes seemed to focus someplace far away. "Of course, it hasn't been all easy, and there've been the heartaches." She sighed and looked down to examine her hands. "But being the mother of a daughter like your mother and the grandmother of a granddaughter like you—that's enough to make me glad I'm a woman." Grandmother's eyes were filled with tears. Batty looked at her over the sheet she'd pulled up to her nose. She had hardly ever seen tears in Grandmother's eyes. Grandmother was usually very strong and unemotional. It was Grandaddy who did all the crying.

"Aren't you sorry I wasn't a boy so you could have had a grandson?" she asked, and waited for Grandmother's response. Grandmother's eyes jerked to Batty's face. Her brow wrinkled deeply.

"No, darling girl," Grandmother said, softly and slowly, moving closer to Batty. "Of course I'm not sorry. I wouldn't want any ragtail little boy for a grandchild. Why I wouldn't trade you for any rats-and-snails boy in the world." She leaned over and kissed Batty gently on the eyelids. "Now you go to sleep and think of all the wonderful things about being a girl."

"Oh, my goodness," Batty said. "I almost forgot to say my prayers."

Grandmother got up and started toward the door.

"I'll send Mother in. Now don't forget to thank God you're a girl," she said, and left the room.

Myrtle and Randy Dillard owned one of the two service stations in Robertson's Fort. They had seven children and every two or three years Myrtle would give birth to another child. It was hard for Batty to keep up with all their names. The oldest two were twelve-year-old twins, a boy named Donnie who worked in the service station on weekends and after school and a quiet soft-spoken girl named Dawn who had long golden hair and who was old at an early age from having to share her mother's maternal responsibilities. The third child was a daughter named Sulie, a feisty little girl of ten who had blond ringlets all over her head and who spoke with the rapidity of machine-gun fire. The fourth child was a daughter Batty's age. Lula Ann was in Batty's class. She was smarter than her sisters and was the only one of the girls who did well in school. She had a pretty, round and cherubic face and soft wavy brown hair. If she hadn't been so chubby, she would have been the prettiest of the Dillard girls.

Often she came to play on the farm with Batty. They would roam the hills looking for wild flowers, or they would play house on mossy floors sheltered by laurel thickets which they entered on their knees, or they would comb the thickets searching for the errant guineas' nests, or they would put an apple in Grandaddy's rabbit gum and return later to see whether they'd caught a rabbit. One day they found a whiskey still.

They'd gone out to play early in the morning after Lula Ann had spent the night, sharing Batty's bed. They'd taken the usual path up through the barnyard and on through the meadow on top of the hill, along the path through the blackberry thicket and to the edge of the property. It was only midmorning and they felt no inclination to turn back. They continued through the hollow above the Morris property and then on across the meadow through the fence and down the dirt road. When they came to the little bridge crossing the stream they forked right, away from the road, moving upstream along the riverbank. They had walked only a few yards pushing aside the tree limbs and the bushes when they came upon a clearing.

"Lordy mercy!" Lula Ann said. "Look at that!"

"Shh," Batty whispered.

"Nobody can hear me," Lula Ann said.

"Shh," Batty said more insistently. "Listen."

Lula Ann cocked her head and listened. The only sound was the monotonous call of a cardinal in a nearby tree. "Richey, Richey, Richey," it intoned endlessly. Then there was a rustling of dried leaves.

"Let's go," Batty said.

"It's nothing," Lula Ann said. "There's nobody here."

"I think this is a still," Batty said, remembering Grandaddy telling her about bootleggers making whiskey in barrels in the woods, hidden from the revenuers. "This is where bootleggers make White Lightning. Bootleggers are outlaws. If they caught us here, they'd probably kill us for finding their still."

"Nobody's going to find us," Lula Ann said. "Nobody uses this still anymore. Can't you see the barrels are old and moldy?"

The main part of the still was a crudely constructed furnace made of large stones chinked with red clay. It was about four feet high and was divided into an upper and a lower chamber. Built into the top of the furnace was a copper container shaped like a milk can, and this was connected by a copper tube to a closed wooden barrel, in turn connected to a second closed barrel. The copper had turned a dark green and was bearded with a white mold. Nearby were two metal drums, one sitting upright and one lying on its side.

Batty cautiously went over to look into the upright drum. A crow winged through the sky above the tops of the pines. She heard his cawing come into range and then move on into the distance. The drum was about a third full of brown and teeming rainwater.

"I wonder whose still it is," she said.

"It could be anybody's," Lula Ann said.

"I'll bet in the fall, when the corn is ripe, the owner'll come back and begin making White Lightning again."

"Probably."

"But the stalks haven't even broken through the ground yet. They won't be back today."

"Unless they want to start cleaning up those rusty barrels."

"I'll bet it belongs to Lonnie Mercer," Batty said.

Lonnie Mercer was married to Bertie Mercer who owned the beauty shop in town and who cut Mother's hair and put in the little finger waves and pin curls. Everybody knew he was a bootlegger. He would be out of prison moonshining all the while, and then the first thing anyone would know he'd be back in prison again. Mother said that when the family used to live in town and the Mercers lived just down the hill from them, the nights were very quiet when Lonnie Mercer was in prison, but as soon as he got out of prison the neighbors could hear the bottles clanking all night long as he made his sales. Then when he went back to prison the nights would be quiet again. Batty thought this had to be his still.

"Maybe," Lula Ann said. "But if it's Lonnie Mercer's, there won't be anyone here for a long time. He's back in prison again."

"How do you know?" Batty asked.

"I heard my daddy say so."

Somewhere a dog started baying, a hound on a rabbit's trail, or on *their* trail, Batty thought.

"Let's go back," Lula Ann said.

"Yeah."

Lula Ann extended her hand. Batty took it. The two of them ran back through the woods the way they'd come, heads lowered, free hands raised, shielding their faces as they went.

Batty hardly ever visited Lula Ann. There were so many children at her house there was hardly any room to play, and certainly no peace and quiet. Besides, when Lula Ann was home there was always work of some kind to be done, some younger child to be fed, some errand to be run. It was much more fun to have Lula Ann visit her. But once in a while, just so Lula Ann wouldn't think she didn't like her family or her house, she'd go there to play.

One day Mother said that Batty could go to Lula Ann's after school and play till she finished work at the store, at which time she'd come by and pick her up. Sulie walked home in front of them with Alexandria Pike, who lived with her grandmother around the corner from the Dillards. When they came through the front door, Sulie had already dumped her books on a chair and was at the piano playing boogie-woogie.

"Lula Ann," she said, over her shoulder and over the noise of her bouncy piano, "Mother said she wants you to wash Susan's diapers and hang them out as soon as you come home so they'll have time to dry before dark."

"They won't have time to dry, anyway," Lula Ann said.

"You'd better do what Mother said."

"Well, Sulie, they'll *never* get dry."

"Just do what Mother said."

"Oh shoot," Lula Ann said, and walked through the curtain that formed the door to the room shared by the four girls in the family, and dumped her books on her cot. "Come on, Batty," she said, and she went into her parents' bedroom. She picked up the white-enameled bucket from the corner of the room next to the crib where the youngest Dillard was sleeping. Batty could see only Susan's blond curls looking moist on the pillow. Lula Ann carried the bucket by its handle to the kitchen and put the diapers in the washing machine. She measured a cup of Ivory Flakes from the box sitting on the shelf above the machine, closed the lid, and turned the dial. The machine started making a quiet splashing sound as water squirted into the tub.

"Nothing more to do till they finish washing," she said.

Dawn—who had come home from school early so her mother could go help her father pump gas—said, "You've got to stay here and keep an eye on Susan. I have to go see Doris."

"You don't have to go *anywhere,*" Lula Ann said. "Mother didn't say I had to watch Susan today. She knows I have company today and I can't stay in the house and watch Susan. *You're* supposed to watch Susan."

Lula Ann went into the bedroom and got down on her knees.

She pulled an old cardboard suitcase from under the cot. With a key she found in her tin jewelry box, she unlocked it and opened it. It was filled with comic books. She took the entire armload and slid the suitcase under the bed again.

"Let's go out to the shed to read," she said.

The shed was a small, rough, unpainted structure used for miscellaneous storage. In the corner was a shovel and a rake. There was an old plastic-covered car seat on the floor, and a naked light bulb hung from the ceiling. There was one small window with no glass. It was both too dark and too cool for comfort.

"Let's go back in where it's warm," Batty said.

"No," Lula Ann said, "there's no privacy in there."

She pulled the cord and turned on the light.

"Sit down," she said to Batty motioning to the old car seat on the floor. Batty zipped up her jacket, pulled her skirt smooth across her behind, and sat down on the car seat. Lula Ann sat down beside her.

"I want *Captain Marvel*," Batty said. "Do you have any *Captain Marvels*?"

"Of course I've got *Captain Marvel*. But I've got something a lot more interesting than *Captain Marvel*."

"What?"

"Just wait a minute while I find it. You'll see."

Lula Ann was not only searching through all her comic books, she was opening each one and holding it up by the spine and shaking it as though she expected something to fall out. All that fell out were the unstapled pages of a well-worn *Batman*. Then a small stapled comic fell out from one of the other books. Batty could see the name *Popeye* on the cover but it was much smaller than the regular comics.

"Take a look at this," Lula Ann said. She sat close to Batty, put the little book on Batty's knees, leaned over, and began turning the pages.

There were pictures of Popeye with a great big penis sticking out of his pants. There were little drawings that told the story of Popeye kidnapping a naked woman with big bosoms and a black triangle for a bottom and carrying her to a house and taking her into the bedroom and taking his big penis out of his pants and touching her triangle with it while all the time she seemed to have fainted for some reason that wasn't made very clear.

"Where'd you get this?" Batty said.

"None of your business."

"Does your mother know you have it?"

"Of course not. She'd beat my tail off."

"Well, where'd you get it?"

"I found it."

"Where'd you find it? Are there any more of them?"

"Somebody gave it to me and I promised I wouldn't tell, so quit pestering me to tell you where I got it, okay?"

"Okay, but aren't you going to show it to your mother?"

"Of course not," Lula Ann said. "Do you think I'm crazy?"

"That's a funny-looking penis," Batty said. "Look how big it is!"

"Penis!" Lula Ann said. "That's a peter. And lots of men have big peters."

"I don't believe it. They couldn't put their pants on if they had big peters like that," Batty said.

"That's why they wear tight underwear, to keep it down so nobody can see it," Lula Ann said. "Look, he's fucking her with that big thing. Oooh, I bet it hurts."

Batty had never heard the word "fucking" before.

"What's fucking?" she asked.

"Don't you know about fucking?" Lula Ann said, sounding very superior. "That's when a man puts his peter into a woman's pussy. It makes her get pregnant and have babies."

"Are you sure?" Batty said, remembering what Mother once told her: that when a mother and daddy loved each other a lot, the mother got pregnant and they had a baby. Lula Ann was trying to tell her that having babies didn't have anything to do with loving each other. It had to do with people doing things they could never admit to anyone.

"Is that the only way to have a baby?" Batty asked, trying to imagine Mr. White putting his peter into Mrs. White four times to have the four children in that family. Then she tried to imagine Reverend Swan putting his peter into Mrs. Swann and figured he would never do it and that was why they didn't have any children. Then she tried to imagine Daddy putting his peter into Mother's pussy. That was just too much. She couldn't even think of that at all. She tried to think of something else very quickly.

"Maureen Wilcox lets boys put their peters into her pussy," Lula Ann said. "She'll let anybody fuck her."

"How do you know that?" Batty said.

"We were on a picnic one time and Sulie and I took a walk in the woods and we saw her fucking Clarence Wilson."

"How did you know that's what they were doing? I mean how did you know they were *fucking?*"

Lula Ann looked at Batty in disgust. "How did we know?" she asked rhetorically. "Well, for one thing he had her blouse off and Clarence was sucking her titties just like a baby and then she pulled her skirt up to her waist and she didn't have any panties on. Clarence took his peter out and put it into her pussy while she was just lying on the ground moaning like it was killing her."

"Does fucking hurt?" Batty asked.

"If a man has a great big peter, of course it hurts," Lula Ann said. "I mean, having that big thing jammed up inside you? But if it's not too big then it feels good."

"Have *you* ever fucked anybody?"

"Only my little brother Howard. I'll get him to fuck you sometime if you want me to."

"Sure," Batty said.

Together they looked at the little book again, very slowly this time. Then they started from the beginning and looked at it again. Batty felt her body growing warm and tingly. It was a very pleasant feeling.

"Give it back to me," Lula Ann said, standing up. She put the little book back into *Superman* and put *Superman* back into the stack of comic books. "Come on," she said, turning out the light and unlocking the door. "I've got to go hang out the diapers."

Every night, Mother sat in the living room with Asphasia the white Persian cat on the arm of her chair, and wrote a letter to Daddy. Mother loved Daddy very much, and when she got a letter from him, which was every two or three days, she would hold it to her chest and jump up and down on her toes like a little girl. Some of the letters were tiny pictures of the letters Daddy had written. Other times they were regular letters. Sometimes he would write Batty letters, telling her how proud he was of her, and that he missed her, and that he was glad she was beginning to take piano lessons from Mrs. LeFevre, and that he couldn't wait to see Constance the cow, and that he thought the war would soon be over so he could come home and have fun with his young lady.

Mother missed Daddy a lot. Life without him was hard. Running the store was more complicated than ever with the war going on. Every week the government put out a list of prices for all the canned food. If a grocer sold something for more than the price ceiling for that week, he could be put in jail. Either Colleen Davidson, a cousin of Daddy's who worked at the store, or Buster Carson would take the list and every Monday go through all the shelves and check the prices. If the price on the list had gone down since the week before, Buster or Colleen would take a red crayon and put the new price on the top of the can.

Another thing Mother had to worry about was the coupons. During the war, almost everything that Americans ate was rationed—sugar, coffee, butter, meat. Everybody received coupons allowing him to buy a certain amount of the rationed products. When Mother sold a person meat, coffee, sugar, butter or cigarettes, she took the coupons from his book and put them in a special box beside the cash register. Once a week Ella Mae Murphy, the inspector for the rationing board, would come around to check the prices of the goods on the shelves and to make sure Mother wasn't charging too much. Then she would take the rationing coupons Mother had collected.

Ella Mae was the daughter of Dr. Murphy and though she was married to Clyde Hempill, everybody still called her Ella Mae Murphy because Dr. Murphy was a much more important man than Clyde Hempill who everybody knew wasn't worth a hill of beans. Ella Mae was a prim and prudish woman whom people didn't like very much. The one thing she had going for her was that she was Dr. Murphy's daughter and that was a lot, because Dr. Murphy had delivered almost everybody in town under the age of thirty and had saved the lives of many more people than that.

Buster Carson was a lot of help to Mother at the store. He was a tall lanky man, slightly stooped, with big hands and feet and a round, almost-baby face. He wore his straight brown hair cut short and slicked back with grease. Most of the time he wore round wire-framed eyeglasses. He had gone off to war with Daddy, but he'd developed a bad knee that kept swelling to twice its normal size and when the army couldn't cure him, they gave him a medical discharge and sent him home. But he'd been in basic training with Daddy, and he and Daddy were good friends; when he got home he began helping Mother with the store.

The store was actually two stores, a dry-goods store in one building and a grocery store in another. The two stores were connected by a big opening in the wall that divided them. They were part of a whole street of old brick stores that looked as though they'd been there forever. They'd certainly been there since Daddy was a little boy; his own father had owned a store in this same building when he lost his money in the Depression and died.

A few people tried to get Mother to let them have more of something than they had coupons for. They thought they deserved special favors. Mother told them these were hard times for everybody and that she had to be fair to all her customers. Not everybody understood. Clyde Hempill, a knotty little man with a tangle of black hair and buck teeth, came in the store one day to buy provisions for a hunting trip. On the counter, he collected bacon, eggs, bread, canned meat, beans and a pound of coffee. Colleen added up the bill and asked Clyde for his coupons. He didn't have a coupon for the coffee, so she told him she was sorry but she couldn't sell it to him. He asked to speak to Mrs. Attwood. Colleen called Mother from the back of the store where she was working on the books. Clyde explained to Mother that he needed the coffee but had used up his coffee coupons and said he thought she ought to sell him the coffee anyway, since he was Dr. Murphy's son-in-law. Mother told him that was against the law and that she couldn't possibly do it. Clyde said he'd go elsewhere to buy his provisions and stormed out of the store.

A few days later Ella Mae came into the store to inspect the prices and collect the coupons. Buster was sorting out the stale and wilting produce from the bins, Colleen was scooping black-eyed peas onto the scale for a little colored girl whose mother had sent her to buy two pounds, and Mother was sitting at the rolltop desk at the back of the store adding up customers' bills on the adding machine. Ella Mae gave the cans an unusually close inspection, holding the list in front of her and picking up every can to check the price written on it. She even borrowed Buster's ladder so she could reach the cans on the top shelf. Buster carried the cardboard box of stale greens out the back door and came back in.

"Why are these tomatoes marked twelve cents for a sixteen-ounce can?" Ella Mae asked. She was off the ladder now. She walked to Buster and stuck the can in his face.

"What?" Buster said.

"I said why are these tomatoes marked twelve cents?"

Buster looked at her. "I don't know," he said. "What are they supposed to be?"

"Didn't you get your price list this week?" Ella Mae said.

"We got it," Buster said. "And we marked the new prices on everything that changed."

"Well, you didn't mark the new price on these tomatoes."

Ella Mae was standing with her feet close together and her mouth looking tense and very small.

"What does the list say the price should be?" Buster asked.

"The ceiling on a sixteen-ounce can of tomatoes is eleven cents this week," Ella Mae said. "This can is marked twelve cents."

"What are the other cans marked?"

"The other cans are marked eleven cents the way they're supposed to be, but *this* can is marked twelve cents."

"I guess we must have missed it when we marked the others," Buster said.

"Well, it's my job to report an infraction, and this is an infraction," Ella Mae said.

Mother had heard the commotion and came up in front of the meat counter now to find out what was the matter. Ella Mae turned to her.

"Mrs. Attwood," she said, "I'm sorry to have to do this but it's my job. I'm afraid you'll have to appear before the county rationing board to explain this violation of the price ceiling."

Buster was a quiet, shy person. Daddy said he was just a good old country boy. Batty couldn't imagine him mad. That day Ella Mae made Buster mad.

"That can of tomatoes was a simple mistake, Ella Mae Murphy," Buster said, "and you know it. Your rationing board changes the prices so damned often it's all we can do to keep up with it. Don't you ever threaten Mrs. Attwood again. Her husband is fighting a war and risking his life every day for this country. That's a hell of a lot more than can be said for yours."

Buster was advancing on Ella Mae. She was backing up right toward the front door. His voice was getting louder and louder.

"And I don't want to hear another word about that can of tomatoes—do you understand that?—not another word. Now get out of here."

Ella Mae darted a look behind her, pulled open the screen door with her left hand, did a fast turn and ran out into the cold January air without her coat. Mother rushed to the back of the store, took Ella Mae's coat from the peg, ran to the front door and called down the street.

"Ella Mae? Ella Mae, you forgot your coat."

One weekend in February, Lula Ann came home with Batty after school on Friday to spend the night. They were sleeping together in Batty's bed on Saturday morning when Batty was awakened by a bad dream. She opened her eyes. Morning light was radiating through the white shades. She got up and reached into the closet for her robe, stuck her arms in the sleeves, and stumbled half-asleep into the kitchen. Grandmother and Grandaddy always got up and had breakfast while everybody else was still asleep. They were sitting at the kitchen table finishing their coffee.

"Well, honey," Grandaddy said, "what on earth are you doing up so early? It's Saturday, you know."

"Grandmother, I've got to talk to you," Batty said. "I had an awful dream."

"What kind of dream, darling?" Grandmother asked, reaching out to catch Batty's robe and pull her close.

"I dreamed I was born a boy and something terrible happened to me. Grandmother, is it true? Was I really born a boy?" Batty stood in front of Grandmother, cracking her knuckles the way she sometimes did when she was nervous.

"No, Batty," Grandmother said, "you've always been a little girl, an adorable little girl."

Batty burst into tears. "Are you *sure*, Grandmother? Are you absolutely sure?"

"I'm absolutely sure," Grandmother said.

"Come here, sweetheart," Grandaddy said. "Come sit on Grandaddy's lap." He held out his arms. Batty went to him and he pulled her onto his lap. "Now, precious girl," he said. "It was just a bad dream, that's all. Stop crying." He took a fresh handkerchief out of his pocket and wiped her eyes. "You'd better *not* have been born a boy," he said lightly. "We don't want any boys in *this* family. We'd have sent you right back where you came from and told them to send us our little girl."

Lula Ann was standing at the kitchen door in her flannel pajamas, her hair touseled in all directions.

"What's wrong, Batty?" she asked.

"Batty just had a bad dream," Grandmother said. "She's all right now. You girls go wash your hands. Grandmother's going to make you a good breakfast."

Grandmother made a big breakfast of oatmeal, bacon and eggs, and toast. Batty finished the meal with a generous helping of sorghum molasses stirred up with a big chunk of fresh butter and then spread on hot toast. Mother said sorghum molasses had lots of iron and made your blood red and strong. Batty thought it must be true. She always felt very strong after eating four or five pieces of toast spread with sorghum. Lula Ann preferred Karo syrup. She spread it all over her toast with no butter at all. Karo syrup wasn't nearly as good for a person as was sorghum. They finished the last swallows of their milk and rushed to the bedroom to dress. As soon as Grandmother had finished Batty's second braid, they grabbed their jackets and ran outside to begin the day.

"Where shall we go today?" Batty asked. "Do you want to walk across the hill to look for the guinea nests?"

"We did that last time," Lula Ann said. "Besides it's kind of cold to be out in the woods."

"Do you want to go look at the chickens or to go pet Constance?"

"Sure, let's go pet Constance."

Constance stood in her stall, her angelic white face projecting out over the door.

"She's sweet, don't you think?" Batty said, rubbing the cow's soft moist chin.

"Yeah, what's she chewing?" Lula Ann asked.

"You see all that hay in the loft up there? She can chew a mouthful for hours."

"Hay sure doesn't look good to eat, does it?" Lula Ann said. "No wonder she chews it for hours. To get it soft enough to go down."

"No, it's nice and soft anyway," Batty said. "Come on, I'll show you." She crossed the barn to the ladder and began climbing. When she got to the top she turned and looked down. "Well, come on, what's the matter?"

"I'm afraid."

"Oh come on, there's nothing to it," Batty said. "Just hold on to the sides very tight and climb on up."

Batty watched Lula Ann slowly begin to climb the ladder.

"That's good. You're almost up," she said. "See? Nothing to it, scaredy-cat."

"Gee, it's nice and warm up here," Lula Ann said. "We should have brought some comic books to read."

"No," Batty said. "It's too dark."

"Do you think your mother would let us sleep up here tonight?" Lula Ann asked, settling down into the hay in the corner of the loft.

"I doubt it," Batty said. "She'd be afraid we'd fall out in our sleep. Or what would we do if we had to go to the bathroom during the night? We'd probably break our necks trying to get down the ladder in the dark. Besides there's no bathroom."

"I guess so, but this sure would be a nice place to sleep," Lula Ann said, stretching herself out in the hay. "It's very comfortable."

Batty lay down beside Lula Ann and propped her head on her elbow.

"You have to watch out for rats up here," she said. "Sometimes there are rats. Grandaddy set some rat traps and caught most of them, I think. But you can't be sure. More may come."

"This would be a good place to play games," Lula Ann said.

"What kind of games?"

"Well . . . we could play house, or we could play doctor."

"How do you play doctor?"

"We take off our pants and examine each other," Lula Ann said.

Batty remembered the time when she was three. She had been behind the sofa playing with herself, discovering herself. She touched herself with her fingers. She held her fingers to her nose. They smelled sharp and fruity. No other part of her body smelled like that. She crawled from behind the sofa and held her fingers to Daddy's nose. He made a face of strong distaste and told her to go wash. Suddenly she felt ashamed.

Or the time she had Donald Grimes pinned to the ground, sitting on his chest, her legs around either side of his head. He had gotten a whiff of her panties and had held his nose and turned his head. She had felt that same shame again. She'd freed him immediately and had gone off to play alone.

And everyone always telling her to keep her dress down and to sit like a lady, to keep well hidden the ugly secret of her femaleness.

"It's too cold to take off our pants," she said.

"It's not cold up here," Lula Ann said.

"You take your pants off first."

"No, you."

"We could both take off our pants at the same time."

"Good idea."

They shuffled around in the hay and took off their pants and underpants.

"Now who's going to be the doctor?" Lula Ann said.

"I'll be the doctor," Batty said.

"Okay. Then I'll be the doctor. We'll take turnabout."

"What do I do?"

"You examine me and touch me."

"Where?" Batty said, not quite daring.

"Right here," Lula Ann said, taking Batty's hand and putting it on her hairless bottom. "Now rub it around a little. Ummm. That feels good. You want me to do you?"

"Yeah," Batty said, lying on her back and spreading her legs.

"Does that feel good?" Lula Ann said. "Shhh." Suddenly she sat straight up. "Listen." They were quiet a few seconds.

"I don't hear anything," Batty said.

"We've got to be careful not to get caught," Lula Ann whispered. "Your grandmother would beat our tails. Will anybody come to the barnyard this morning?"

"Grandaddy will come feed the pigs in a little while."

"We'd better hurry then. And don't talk out loud. You do me one more time."

Batty slowly began to stroke Lula Ann's bottom.

"Let's fuck," Lula Ann whispered.

"Girls can't fuck other girls."

"Sure they can," Lula Ann said. "They just put their pussies together, that's all."

"How are we going to do that?"

"Lie back and I'll show you."

Batty lay back. Lula Ann lay on top of her, head to head, toe to toe.

"I don't think this is fucking," Batty said breathlessly, the weight of fat Lula Ann crushing her. "Get off me."

"Do you want me to pee on your pussy?" Lula Ann asked. "Would that feel good?"

"Yeah, that would feel real good."

"Okay, but don't get it on my shirt," Batty said, pushing her shirt up under her armpits.

Lula Ann squatted over Batty and began peeing on her. It was an uncontrolled stream that seemed to be going everywhere at once. The urine filled her navel and ran in little streams around her body. She felt it making a big puddle under her back. It was making the nice dry hay all wet and stinky.

"Stop it, Lula Ann, stop it," Batty said. "That doesn't feel good at all. You're getting me all wet. Stop it."

Lula Ann couldn't stop it. She just kept on peeing till she was all peed out. Then she got up and sat down in the hay to dry herself before putting on her panties.

"Darn it, Lula Ann, you got my shirt all wet," Batty said. She took a handful of hay and dried herself as well as she could. Then she began putting on her clothes.

"Wipe up that pee with some hay and throw it in the corner so Grandaddy won't find it," Batty said. "Now I have to sneak into the bathroom to wash myself and change my shirt. Darn it, Lula Ann.

Why'd you pee all over me? I thought you said it would feel good. It didn't feel good at all."

Lula Ann shrugged.

"I thought it would feel good," she said.

In the middle of the afternoon Lula Ann's father came for her, and Batty was glad to see her go. After all the things that had gone on today, she needed some privacy to think. She sat in the living room looking through the window of little panes to the blue hills in the distance, thinking about the things she'd done with Lula Ann, things she'd have to keep secret from the whole family. This was the first time she'd ever had a secret from everybody. Sometimes she had a secret from one member of the family which she shared with another—such as when she knew what Grandmother was giving Mother for her birthday before Mother knew—but she'd never had a secret from *everybody*. It made her feel very lonely.

She decided to take a long walk in the woods. When she felt lonely, a walk always helped. She went up through Preston's cornfield and crossed the fence into the woods and took the path across the hill to the other side where she came out into a clearing from where she could look out over Robertson's Fort. Sometime in the afternoon the sky had become overcast. She zipped her jacket snugly to her chin and sat down on a big stone outcropping. From here she could see the old water tank with the ladder climbing to the top crowning the next hill. It had been used for water storage by the tannery before it burned down when Daddy was a little boy. It wasn't used for anything now, but because it was so visible from all over town it was kept painted a metallic silver. She could also see the school and its grounds where she played softball almost every school day that wasn't rainy. She could see the top of the Baptist-church steeple on the other side of town. She just sat there for a long time and thought.

She couldn't quite forget the dream she'd had. It haunted her in some strange way that she'd been half aware of all day. Then she thought of the morning in the hayloft with Lula Ann, and shrank under the burden of guilt and shame. Her walk wasn't making her feel better at all. She sat there in the gray afternoon feeling worse than ever. At last, she got up from the rock ledge and began running back down the path through the woods toward home.

She came in the back door and went quietly down the hall, only glancing into the kitchen where Grandmother was talking to Virginia and didn't notice her.

She went directly into Mother's room and took the scissors from the sewing drawer. Then she went into the bathroom and locked the door. She looked at herself in the mirror; the braids Grandmother had made for her this morning, secured by a rubber band, hung there making her look unmistakably like a girl. If her hair were different, she thought, if she didn't have those hated braids, if it were cut short, she would look just like a boy, certainly as much like a boy as Charlie Knipe. And if she looked like a boy, who was to say she wasn't a boy? She held the left braid straight out and poised the blades of the scissors on either side of it. Then she began to squeeze.

It was harder to cut off a braid than she'd thought it would be. The hair was thick and resistant. She pressed the handles of the scissors more firmly. A few severed hairs popped up from the braid and stuck straight out. She opened the scissors and closed them again. A few more severed hairs popped up. She decided to cut the three strands of the braid separately. She slipped the thinner blade of the scissors behind one of the strands and closed the scissors. She heard the little crackling sounds of tiny hairs breaking. The strand came off neatly. She did the same thing to the other two. Then she lowered the fist holding the severed braid and looked at herself. She didn't look like a boy at all. She just looked like a mess. The remaining hair was all different lengths and was sticking out in all directions as though she'd got her head caught in the corn grinder. She thought that maybe it would look better when the other braid was cut off and when she'd combed it. She was just poising the scissors to start on the second braid when Grandmother knocked on the door.

"Are you in there, Batty?" she asked. Batty froze. "Batty, are you all right?"

"I'm fine, Grandmother. I just had to go to the bathroom."

"Okay, honey, but hurry up. I need to get in there."

Batty just stood there. What on earth was she going to do? Grandmother wasn't going to go away from that door. Besides Grandmother would have to see her hair sooner or later. Batty took some toilet paper and cleaned the pieces of hair from the sink and put the toilet paper with the hair in the toilet. Then she flushed it to get rid of the evidence of what she'd done. She walked slowly to the door and unlocked it. When she opened the door, Grandmother was sitting in the straight-back chair near the wall phone.

"My God, Batty," she said, her hands coming up to her chest. "What on earth have you done?"

"I cut off one of my pigtails," Batty said. "Now I'm going to cut off the other one."

For a moment, Grandmother seemed too stunned for words. Her mouth hung open like a broken sash.

"It'll look better when I've cut the other one off," Batty said reassuringly. "And it needs combing, of course."

"But . . . what on earth made you *do* it?" Grandmother said, finding her tongue. "Come here, honey." Batty walked tentatively to Grandmother. Grandmother examined the damage.

"You cut it off so close to your head, we'll never be able to do a thing with it. This is going to be some mess till it grows out." Grandmother just sat there, shaking her head. "Grandaddy's taking a nap upstairs," she said at last. "Run get him quick while I go to the bathroom."

Batty ran up the stairs and down the hall and pushed open the door to Grandaddy's bedroom. Grandaddy was asleep, lying on his back and snoring loudly.

"Grandaddy, wake up," she said. "Grandmother wants you to come downstairs."

"What . . . what?" Grandaddy said, not awake yet.

"Grandmother wants to see you downstairs."

"Good grief, Batty! What happened to your hair?"

"That's what Grandmother wants to see you about."

He was fully dressed except for his shoes. "Hand me my shoes, honey," he said, looking baffled.

Grandmother and Grandaddy examined the length of Batty's shorn hair. Only one thing to do, they decided, Grandaddy would have to take her to the barbershop. Claude Lavender, Grandaddy's barber, gave her a neat cut all around. Then he put hair tonic on it and slicked her remaining hair back into a ducktail. Batty looked at herself in his big mirror. He swiveled her around and gave her a hand mirror so she could see it in the back too. She thought it looked splendid, just the way she'd wanted it to look when she'd cut off the pigtail. She guessed you had to be a real barber to be able to give a good haircut. She felt very happy.

At least she felt happy until Mother got home from work that evening. Mother took one look at Batty and shrieked.

"Batty!" she said. "What happened? What happened to your beautiful hair? It's all gone! It's all . . . *gone!*"

Grandmother explained that Batty had cut off one of her pigtails and that she and Grandaddy had tried to get it fixed up as much as they could before Mother saw it.

"Oh, Batty," Mother said, "I could blister your bottom! I could really blister your bottom!" She stood looking at Batty, shaking her head for a long time. "It took me forever to get your hair so nice and long. Just look at it! You look just like a boy, Batty. You don't look pretty anymore."

Then Mother went into her bedroom and closed the door. Batty could hear her crying through the walls.

What had been Batty's first experience with sex was to be her first experience with blackmail.

Lula Ann had nothing to lose if her parents found out about the things she'd done. They simply wouldn't care. They let their children do whatever they wanted to; they even let them go to movies on Sunday. Batty, on the other hand, had a lot to lose. Her parents were very strict. If Mother and Grandmother knew what unspeakable things she'd done, they would probably never love her again. Even if they did love her, she would die of shame anyway.

Lula Ann knew she was onto a good thing.

"If you don't let me play first base," Lula Ann said, "I'll spill the beans."

"You played first base yesterday," Batty said, running her fingers through her new ducktail. "It's my turn today."

Lula Ann just gave her head a little toss, narrowed her eyes like a cat and looked very superior.

"Okay," she said, "whatever you want."

Batty played shortstop, which she hated. Lula Ann played first base the whole week it was Batty's turn to be captain.

"If you don't let me use your jump rope at recess, I'm going to spill the beans."

"Lula Ann, this is my brand-new jump rope. I haven't had any time to play with it myself."

"Okay," Lula Ann said, giving her head that little toss. Batty sat glumly on the rock wall, watching, till Lula Ann tired of her jump rope.

"Can I copy your arithmetic homework at recess?" Lula Ann asked. "I had to take care of Susan yesterday and I didn't get to finish mine."

"You know Mrs. McAuley doesn't want us to do that. She said it's cheating and can get us into trouble."

"She won't even know."

"She might. Besides, it's not right."

"If you don't let me copy your homework," Lula Ann said, giving her head that little toss, "I'll spill the beans."

Batty could see no way out of her bondage, till one day Lula Ann went too far.

For Christmas, Mother had given her a little pearl ring that had been Mother's when she was a little girl. On Sunday morning, Batty wore it to Sunday school and church. When she got to her Sunday-school class, Lula Ann was sitting in the back row behind Sarah White. Most of the time the Dillards didn't come to church. She wished Lula Ann would never come. In fact, she wished Lula Ann were dead with her terrible secret so that she wouldn't be tormented anymore.

But Lula Ann wasn't dead, and there wasn't much chance she was going to *be* dead anytime soon. And here she was sitting in Batty's Sunday-school class while Mrs. Carson was teaching a lesson all about taking care of our bodies and keeping them pure so they would be worthy to be vessels of Christ. There sat Lula Ann knowing that Batty had not kept her body a pure vessel at all but had irredeemably defiled it forever. If Lula Ann were to tell all the things in her head, all the grown-ups of the church would chase Batty out the door yelling "Sinner, sinner, get thee from the holy presence of the Lord!" The church bell began to toll. Mrs. Carson excused the class. Batty left quickly and went down the back steps to the ladies' room. She went into the stall and closed and latched the door. She heard someone come in and stand outside the stall to wait for her to finish. She finished peeing and gave the roll of paper a yank. It unrolled too far. She tore off several sheets and left the trail of paper coiled on the floor under the roll. She dried herself, flushed, then unlatched and opened the door.

Lula Ann was propped against the wall.

"Hi," Batty said.

"Hi," Lula Ann said. "What's the matter? Were you running away from me?"

"Of course not. I just had to pee real bad, that's all."

"I'll bet," Lula Ann said.

Batty turned on the water in the sink and began rinsing her hands. She tore a paper towel from the roll and began drying them.

"That's a pretty ring," Lula Ann said.

"Thank you."

"Can I see it?"

Batty extended her hand.

"No, I mean take it off and let me see it."

"No," Batty said.

"I'm not going to hurt it."

"I don't care. I'm not going to take it off."

Lula Ann put one hand on her hip. The other hand she jabbed palm up into the air toward Batty.

"Give it to me," she said in a loud voice.

Batty reached under her skirt and gave her panties a firm yank to make sure they were pulled up well. Then she hurriedly smoothed down her skirt.

"No," she said.

"Okay," Lula Ann said, tilting her head to the side. "If you don't give it to me, I'll spill the beans."

Batty looked her straight in the eye. Then she walked by her and let the door close behind her on its pneumatic hinge.

All day Sunday, Batty—suffering under her burden of guilt—agonized over what she should do about Lula Ann and her terrible secret. That night after she and Mother had said their prayers on their knees, and when she was in bed, she said her own private prayer. "Please dear God, help me get out of this mess and I promise I'll never be bad again. Please, *please,* help me. Amen."

The next morning when she woke up, she knew she had to tell Mother or Grandmother. She couldn't wait for them to learn from someone else. She had to beat Lula Ann to the punch. The thing she had to figure out was which one to tell. Mother would give her a long serious talk that would shame her right into the ground, and Grandmother would probably chase her out of the house with a broom. But it was Monday and Mother would be working at the store until late. Grandmother would be there when she got home from school. She decided to tell Grandmother.

Well, she wouldn't tell Grandmother everything. She could *never* tell Grandmother about touching Lula Ann's bottom and letting Lula Ann touch her bottom. She could never, *ever* tell Grandmother or anyone else about that. But she could tell her about the dirty little book and about Lula Ann making her do whatever she wanted her to do by threatening to tell that Batty looked at dirty books. She could at least tell her that. When she got home from school, Grandmother was sitting on the back porch churning butter. She steadied the wooden churn between her knees and pushed and pulled the plunger with a steady slow rhythm. Batty could hear the buttermilk sloshing inside the churn.

"Grandmother, I've got to talk to you in private," she said. "It's personal."

"Well, go ahead, beautiful," Grandmother said. "There's nobody here."

"Virginia's in the kitchen. She might hear us. I mean *real* private," she said, and began to weep.

Grandmother rolled the churn on its lower edge till it was out of the way. She reached out to Batty.

"Come here, sweetie," she said. "What's the matter, precious?" She held Batty close to her.

"I've done something awful," Batty said. "I've done something very, very bad," she said, and started bawling.

"Now come on, baby. It can't be all that bad," Grandmother said.

"It is. It *is* that bad, too."

"Well, let's go up to my room to talk about it."

Grandmother led the way to her room. She closed the door behind her.

"Come here," she said. "Sit on Grandmother's lap. Now what did you do?"

Batty crawled into Grandmother's lap, and put her head on Grandmother's big bosom. Grandmother began rocking.

"You'll never love me again," Batty said, beginning to cry loudly again.

"I'll always love you no matter what you do."

"You won't love me after this."

"What is it, sweetie?"

"Grandmother, I did something awful with Lula Ann Dillard."

"What did you do that was so awful?" Grandmother said softly.

"Well, I was over at Lula Ann's and we went into the shed to read comic books and Lula Ann was looking through all her comic books looking for something. Then this little comic book fell out. It was about Popeye. And . . . and . . . Lula Ann began turning the pages."

"Yes?"

"And there were awful pictures in it."

"What kind of pictures?"

"Pictures of Popeye with his clothes off doing terrible things to a naked lady," Batty said, and began wailing again.

"Here, here, here," Grandmother cooed, still rocking. "Where did Lula Ann get this book?" she asked patiently.

"She wouldn't tell me. She said someone gave it to her. She wouldn't tell me who," Batty said, beginning to quiet down. "And, Grandmother, we looked at it over and over," she said, and burst into a fresh round of wailing.

"It's all right, Batty," Grandmother said. "Just don't do it again, that's all. Trash like that isn't fit for decent people to see. Now please don't cry anymore and stop worrying about it."

"But Lula Ann's been threatening to tell everybody that I look at dirty books. I had to let her use my new jump rope before I'd even used it, I had to let her be first baseman all week, I even had to let her copy my homework. She said if I didn't, she'd tell everybody."

Grandmother was quiet awhile. Then she said, "Batty, where'd you say you were when you saw this dirty book?"

"At Lula Ann's house. She got it out of a suitcase under her bed."

"I wonder where she got it," Grandmother said, and was quiet for a while. Then she said, "Batty, you tell Lula Ann it's against the law to have a book like that. Tell her if she ever threatens you again you'll call a policeman and have her *and* her daddy put in jail. Now dry your eyes and don't cry anymore. We're going to have some sassafras tea. For a long time now I've been wanting sassafras tea and looking all over the woods for a sassafras tree, and then this morning, Virginia brought me the biggest piece of sassafras root I've ever seen. It's been boiling long enough now."

Batty was beginning to feel better. Grandmother had forgiven her for looking at Lula Ann's dirty book and had told her how to get Lula Ann to stop tormenting her. She dried her eyes and followed Grandmother down the stairs toward the kitchen. Of course, she hadn't been forgiven for everything. She hadn't been forgiven for touching Lula Ann's bottom and letting Lula Ann touch hers. She could never ask Grandmother's forgiveness for that. There were some things that were so awful you just had to bear them yourself.

It was a special occasion when Grandmother made sassafras tea, and she hadn't made it for a long time. The tea smelled delicious. Grandmother took two cups from the cupboard and set them on the counter. Then she took the kitchen tongs and lifted the brown knotty root from the large saucepan, leaving only the steaming golden liquid. She tilted the pan and filled the two cups and handed one to Batty.

"Now let's go into the living room and have our tea," she said. "It'll make you feel a lot better."

Spring comes early in the mountains of North Carolina. Those first gentle days when daffodils—known there as March flowers—break through the ground are harbingers of hot summer days and summer nights cool enough for blankets, of hiking trails winding from steamy sun-filled meadows into cool pine forests sheltering jack-in-the-pulpits and lady slippers, of chilled streams cascading from mountain peaks into rocky swimming holes cold enough on the hottest days to make teeth chatter, of midsummer heat stretching toward horizons of green mountains folding into the blue distance.

The hot summer months were Batty's favorite time, a time filled with pleasures: swimming in the stream across the road with Grandaddy standing by and not taking his eyes off her to make sure she didn't drown; church picnics at the picnic grounds where children played baseball or waded in the stream while women shook out folded cloths, spread them on rustic tables and loaded them with pots of hot chili, cold spicy bean salads, great moist coconut cakes and chocolate cakes, while the smells of the woods mixed with the smells of hot dogs and hamburgers cooking on the fire; and going barefoot, when her feet got to know the ground again, its textures, its temperatures, stony ground over which she'd move gingerly in the spring until her feet had toughened, fresh-cut grass in the morning covered with dew and sticking to her feet, soft wet earth squishing between her toes as she turned stones at the stream's edge searching for crawfish and salamanders, the occasional sharp recognition of the honey bee that she hadn't seen hiding in the clover.

The spring and summer of 1945 came bearing more than the usual blessings. Mother told Batty in the spring that Germany had surrendered and that Daddy would be in the army of occupation; and though the war wasn't over because the Japanese hadn't yet surrendered, at least things were looking better. August came in hotter than usual. Batty had worn almost nothing around the farm all summer except the panties Grandmother made for her on her old Singer foot-pedal machine. The panties were made out of old chicken-feed bags. Grandmother couldn't stand the idea of wasting the cloth so all summer Batty ran around the farm wearing panties that had printed on them in big black and red letters, LAYING MASH or FARMER'S FEDERATION or OPEN OTHER END.

On August 14 she was wearing the panties that read LAYING MASH across the behind. At the stream in front of the house, she was catching red minnows in one of Grandmother's canning jars. She'd tied a string around the neck of the jar and had put pieces of white bread in it. Then she lowered it into the water above a pile of small white stones she knew to be a fish house. She'd never seen so many minnows, and she was having no trouble at all catching them. When she had a jarful of minnows, she pulled it up and emptied it into a big roasting pot she had borrowed from the kitchen. She was standing in the water up to her knees when she heard Grandaddy's voice calling from the top of the bank.

"Batty, come on up here," he said. "Come on now, hurry up."

He seemed very excited about something, sort of jumping up and down from the knees the way she did when she had to pee real bad. She picked up her canning jar and was trying to figure out how to carry the roasting pan at the same time when Grandaddy came down the bank to help. He slid in his hurry. She thought he was going to fall but he didn't. He came on down more carefully now and picked up the pan of fish and started carrying it back.

"Now, let's hurry," he said. "Mother has something important to tell you."

Mother was standing at the edge of the yard when they got to the top of the bank. She was dressed for work in the blue cotton sleeveless dress that matched her eyes. She looked very happy about something, almost like a little girl, the way she looked whenever she got a letter from Daddy.

"Batty," Mother said, "the war is over! Japan has surrendered. Grandaddy just heard it on the radio." She swept up Batty in her arms and did a big pivot as though she could carry her easily. Then she abruptly put her down and told her she was very heavy, and gave her a kiss on the top of her head.

"Come on, let's go to town," Grandaddy said. "Go call Grandmother."

"And, Batty, wash your feet and put on a pinafore," Mother said.

When Batty was ready she went into the kitchen where Grandmother was straining butter from buttermilk she had churned.

"Grandmother," she said, "we're going to town. Grandaddy said for you to come and go with us."

"You children go on and have a good time. I've got things to finish here. Besides the town's going to be plumb crazy this afternoon."

Grandaddy got behind the wheel of the old Buick. Mother got in beside him, and Batty got in the back seat. They had hardly left the driveway and started toward town when the noise started. First they heard the fire whistle. It rose to the highest pitch and dropped slowly, and just as it was about to fade out it rose again. It went on over and over, sounding very excited, the way it had when the Methodist parsonage burned down. Next the church bells started ringing. The Baptist church on the hill was first, the bell ringing over and over, a strong resonant sound. Then it was joined by the Methodist church. The Methodist bell sounded low and throaty, the two of them ringing. Then the Presbyterian bell joined in, a tinny sound, a sort of clank, clank, clank. The three of them ringing at once, having nothing to do with each other in tone or pace, but all ringing, making as joyful a noise as had ever been heard in Robertson's Fort. Then the pealing bell of the colored church on Baptist Side, a high pitch, ringing faster than the others, faster and higher, sounding frantic, a feverish sound. Joy and hysteria pealing across the countryside because the war was over, because we had won. We had won. The bells of the churches ringing and ringing and ringing. The fire whistle climbing and falling, climbing and falling.

When they got to town, the streets were full. Grandaddy inched the Buick slowly up the hill toward John Robertson's monument in the center of town. Everybody who had a car was driving it up and down Main Street and blowing the horn, the cars full of people yelling at each other out the windows. "Hallelujah! We won the war! God be praised! God be praised!" And yelling to each other about family who would be coming home now. Batty had never seen the town in such an uproar in her life. She sat on the edge of the stiff velour seat, looking intently so as not to miss anything.

Every store owner and clerk in town was standing in front of the store, watching the cars and listening to the noise. Buster Carson and Bill Moody were standing in front of Daddy's store wearing their large white aprons. Colleen Davidson was across the street talking to Clara Smith from J and L Variety Store. Maude Nichols was standing in front of Bertie's Beauty Shop with her hair in pin curls. Big fat Harold Mashburn was dancing a silly jig all by himself in front of the fire station. Mr. Shapiro, who made the best milk shakes in town, was standing in front of his drugstore shifting his weight from side to side looking pleased. The four old men who always sat on the curb in front of the barbershop wearing dirty overalls and spitting tobacco juice on the street were standing now, leaning on the railing around the monument, looking confused.

Grandaddy pulled the Buick in front of Daddy's store. "Let's get out a few minutes," he said.

"Batty doesn't have on any shoes," Mother said.

"Victoria," Grandaddy said, "nobody's going to give a gol darn today about whether Batty's wearing shoes. Just be careful, Batty, not to step on any glass."

Buster Carson and Grandaddy shook hands and then Bill Moody and Grandaddy shook hands. Mother laughed and talked a long time with Colleen who came back across the street when she saw Grandaddy park the Buick. Batty asked Mother if she could have a candy bar from the candy counter. Mother said yes. Batty slid open the glass door of the counter and took a Baby Ruth. Then she carefully slid the door closed. The church bells were still ringing, the siren was still wailing. It was beginning to get on her nerves.

She went out the back door and sat down on the rough unpainted steps to eat her Baby Ruth in peace. She could still hear the noise, of course, but at least she was alone back here. She peeled back the paper wrapper and took the first bite. She loved Baby Ruths, the crunchy nuts held together by the sweet chewy caramel. She sat there by herself enjoying eating it slowly. She guessed it wouldn't be long now till Daddy came home, with the war over and all. He'd have to turn in his gun and his uniform and get on a big boat and come across the ocean. That would probably take a while, maybe as long as a month. She tried to remember just what he looked like. She hadn't seen him for over two years. Of course, you don't really forget your daddy, but she was having a little trouble remembering certain things about him, like how big he was. She thought he was bigger than Grandaddy, but she wasn't exactly sure. She remembered that Daddy was stricter than Grandaddy though she couldn't remember *how* strict. Everybody said Grandaddy spoiled her, but she didn't think it was so. Grandaddy was just a *good* grandaddy. Besides if he did spoil her, Mother and Grandmother certainly kept her unspoiled. Maybe Daddy wouldn't let Grandaddy make her any more rabbit-tobacco cigarettes. Daddy might make her quit doing a *lot* of things Grandaddy let her do. She hoped he wasn't too strict, or too big. But she'd worry about that later. After all, she'd already figured out he wouldn't be home for at least a whole month, and that was a long time.

She finished the last bite of her Baby Ruth and wadded up the wrapper and threw it on the ground. Then she licked the chocolate off her fingers and went back into the store to find Mother and Grandaddy.

Daddy came home five months later. Early in the week, Mother and Grandaddy drove to Fort Bragg in the eastern part of the state to get him, and late Friday afternoon the Buick pulled into the yard. Batty was just coming down the hill from the barnyard where she'd been watching Preston slop the hogs, watching them root through the trough of feed, grunting and squealing the way they always did, as though they hadn't been fed in weeks and were starving to death, when she saw the Buick pull into the yard and disappear around the garage. When she got to the foot of the hill and turned the corner, a tall slender man in a soldier's uniform was running toward the house. She could see only his back. He flung open the screen door and ran into the house. She heard him call her name.

"Batty . . . Batty, where are you?"

"Daddy," Batty called. "Here I am, Daddy."

Mother was out of the car by now. "Robert, she's out here."

Daddy came running out the back door right toward her. She'd been right, he *was* bigger than Grandaddy. In fact he was bigger than anybody. As he got closer, he got bigger and bigger. She stood there not moving, just watching him. Suddenly he was upon her. He bent over and had her up in his arms, kissing her over and over and telling her how big she'd got, how much he loved her, how glad he was to be home, how he'd thought about her and pictured her in his mind so many times over the past two years, how knowing he was going to come home to his young lady had kept him going. Batty was silent until in his excitement Daddy knocked his hat off. When last she'd seen him, he'd had a head of thick black hair. Now Daddy's hair was very thin on top. She could see his scalp shining through. Tentatively she reached to touch his head.

"Daddy, you're shedding," she said.

Daddy thought that was very funny. He started laughing and laughing and hugging Batty all over again. Then he put her down and took her by the hand and started walking into the house. Grandmother met them at the back door. She shook Daddy's hand and told him how glad she was that he was home and then her eyes filled with tears and she turned away to blow her nose a little and get her face straight. Batty told Daddy she wanted to take him to show him Constance the cow and let him see how she'd learned to milk. Mother said Daddy was tired from the trip and he could go later. Daddy said he wasn't a bit tired and that he'd just bring his things in and go right with Batty. Grandmother said not to be long because Virginia would have dinner ready in fifteen or twenty minutes.

So Mother stayed behind while Batty had Daddy all to herself for a few minutes. She led him to the barn and showed him Constance. He opened the door to her stall and went in and petted her. He told Batty he'd see her milk Constance tomorrow when Grandmother Terrell was set up for milking. Then she led Daddy on up into the barnyard where she showed him Grandaddy's pigs. She told him about Big Boy, how big he'd been and how he was a lot prettier than the other pigs and how she'd seen Bill Moody cut him up the middle and take out his insides. Then she led Daddy to the incubator to show him the baby chicks. They were just getting stiff feathers and beginning to lose that soft fluffy look, but they were still cute. She chased one around trying to catch it so Daddy could hold it. She had all the chicks in a panic, so Daddy told her that was all right, seeing them was enough, he didn't have to hold one.

Then they walked back down to the house where Virginia had cooked one of Daddy's favorite suppers of fried pork chops, cut-short green beans, black-eyed peas, and corn bread. Daddy ate and ate. Batty watched Daddy butter big pieces of corn bread and devour them. It was a little frightening the way Daddy ate. She sat quietly and listened to Daddy talk about the places he'd been. He liked Germany better than France because the Germans were very clean. Even Paris was filthy. The buildings he'd expected to be beautiful were gray with grime instead. The Germans on the other hand kept everything scrubbed. He talked about the old German couple who'd become his friends during the occupation, who'd somehow, in a time of great need, got together the provisions to make him a birthday cake. He talked about the beauty of the Rhine and his disappointment at seeing the muddy Danube. He talked about the walled cities and the castles he'd been quartered in. He went on and on. Mother said over and over that she'd love to see the things Daddy had seen.

Then after dinner, Mother told Batty it was her bedtime. After she and Mother said their prayers, thanking God for bringing Daddy home, Daddy came in to kiss her good night.

"Daddy, please tell me the story of David and Goliath," she said.

"All right," Daddy said. "Let's see if I remember it. I haven't told that story in a long time." He looked at Mother. "I won't be long," he said.

"Oh goody," Batty said, pulling the cover to her chin, as Mother closed the door behind her.

Daddy sat at the foot of Batty's bed. "Once upon a time," he began, "in the land of Israel there were two armies camped on two hills overlooking a large plain. On one hill was the army of the Israelites led by King Saul, and on the other was the army of the Philistines, who were enemies of the Israelites. They were preparing for a great battle. Now among the Philistines, there was a giant named Goliath. He was dressed in a suit of armor that covered his body completely, and he carried before him a great shield. Goliath walked down to the plain and stood in the center of it and called to the Israelites."

Daddy stood now and spread his legs wide and lifted his head. " 'Send me your strongest warrior to fight,' Goliath said. 'If he slays me, the Philistines will be the slaves of the Israelites. If I slay him, the Israelites will be the slaves of the Philistines.' The Israelites talked among themselves of who might fight this giant, but they were all afraid and did not answer his challenge. Then Goliath called, 'Are you afraid? Are you all cowards?' "

Daddy's voice boomed through the house.

He continued telling the story, playing all the parts, and finally he got to her favorite part. His voice grew soft.

"Then David said to him, 'Thou comest to me with a sword and a spear, and with a shield, but I come to thee in the name of the Lord of hosts, the God of the armies of Israel, whom thou hast defied. This day the Lord will deliver thee into my hands and I will smite thee, and I will give this day the carcass of the host of the Philistines to the fowls of the air and to the wild beasts of the earth: and all the earth will know that there is a God of Israel, and everybody will know that the Lord saveth not by the sword and the spear: for the battle is the Lord's and he will deliver you unto our hands.' "

Daddy was standing in the middle of the room. He reached into the imaginary pouch around his waist. "Then David took a stone from his pouch, and put it into his sling and slung it over his head." Daddy went through the motion with great energy. "The stone flew through the air and hit Goliath on the forehead, the only spot that was not covered by armor, and the stone sank into his forehead and he fell dead on his face in the dust." Daddy spread his arms down toward the fallen Goliath. "David ran to Goliath and took Goliath's own sword and cut off his head. Great shouts of exultation rose from the army of the Israelites, and the Philistines were afraid. They turned and began running away."

When Daddy finished the story, he was quiet for a minute. Then he chuckled.

"That was a good story," Batty said. "I'm glad you didn't forget it, Daddy."

"No, I didn't forget it," Daddy said.

"But why were the Philistines and the Israelites enemies?"

"I don't know exactly," Daddy said. "The Israelites had lots of enemies. Maybe they wanted the same land."

"Where did the Philistines live?"

"They lived in a little country very near Israel on the Mediterranean. I guess they weren't good neighbors."

"I like the story of David and Goliath," Batty said. "Is is true, Daddy?"

"Yes, Batty, it's true. And after Saul died, David became King of Israel. He did something very bad that made God angry at him, but that's a story for another time. Okay now, let's turn out the light and go to sleep."

Mother came in and kissed her good night again and made sure she was still tucked in. Then she turned out the light and she and Daddy went into their bedroom and closed the door. Batty heard the lock slide into place.

The next day was Saturday. Batty had been up for hours, it seemed, waiting forever for Mother and Daddy to get up. Finally Mother came out in her robe and went into the kitchen to start their breakfast. Daddy certainly was a lazybones this morning. He still hadn't got up. Batty peeped through the cracked door. He was still in bed. He must have known she was looking at him because he opened his eyes and looked right back at her.

"When're you going to get up, Daddy?"

Daddy smiled at her.

"I guess I'd better get up now, don't you think?"

"Yeah, it's almost ten-thirty. Everybody else's been up a long time."

It didn't take Daddy long to get dressed. It always took Mother forever. Daddy was dressed in no time. He came out of the bedroom wearing his regular clothes. He looked pretty good though not quite as handsome as he'd looked in his uniform and not quite as big. His pants were a little loose under his belt.

Mother had his bacon and eggs all ready for him. He sat down and began eating. Then Mother fried her own egg and she sat down and ate with him. Batty sat at the table with them and watched them eat.

"Daddy," she asked, "did you fly in an airplane?"

"No, I didn't," Daddy said.

"You mean you weren't in an airplane at all?"

"No, I wasn't in an airplane at all. But I was on several big boats."

"How big?"

"Very big, big enough to carry over two thousand soldiers."

"Did you drive the boat, Daddy?"

"No, I just rode on it."

"Where did you ride to?" Batty said.

Just then Grandmother came in the back door carrying a basket with eggs in it. She put it down on the counter and washed her hands at the sink.

"Batty, why don't you go with Grandmother till Daddy finishes his breakfast?" Mother said.

"I want to stay here," Batty said.

"Don't run off," Daddy said. "As soon as I have another cup of coffee I'm going to unpack and give you the surprises I brought for you."

"What did you bring?" Batty asked.

"I'm not going to tell you. It's a surprise."

When Daddy finished his coffee, he went into the bedroom to unpack while Mother washed their breakfast dishes. Batty followed him. Daddy had two big brown suitcases. He put the first one on the unmade bed and opened it. Inside the suitcase was a strange assortment of things that could belong only to a daddy. There were soldier's khaki clothes—Batty figured he hadn't had to turn in his uniform at all, the way she'd thought he'd have to—and there were some heavy knit sweaters, two sets of false teeth, each with only a few teeth embedded in false gums the color of bubble gum, and two small boxes.

"What're those, Daddy?" Batty asked.

"K rations."

"What're they for?"

"K rations are food."

"Are they good? When do you eat them?"

"The army gives K rations to soldiers to eat when they're out in foxholes and can't get hot meals," Daddy said. "They're not very good."

"What's a foxhole?" Batty asked.

"A big hole, like a ditch, that soldiers get into to hide from the enemy so they won't get shot," Daddy said.

"What're you going to do with them, Daddy?"

"With the foxholes?"

"No, the K rations."

"Nothing," Daddy said. "You can have them if you want them.

There's some canned meat, some beans, a piece of cheese, cigarettes, which you can give to me, and some chocolate."

"That sounds pretty good to me," Batty said. "Can I open one of them now?"

"Sure, if you want to," Daddy said.

Batty immediately started trying to unfold the waxed paper. She was having lots of trouble.

"Here," Daddy said, "let me do that for you."

He took the box and split the paper with his thumbnail and opened it quick as a flash. It was a treasure trove of little tin cans and little packages.

"I'm going to just chew the gum," Batty said, "and save the rest."

Daddy had the suitcase unpacked. He closed it, put it against the wall, picked up the other suitcase, put it on the bed and opened it. There was no gun in either of the suitcases. Batty thought she must have been right at least about that. They'd made him turn in his gun.

"Where's your gun, Daddy?" she asked..

"It wasn't *my* gun," Daddy said. "It was the army's gun. They only let me use it."

"Did you shoot any Germans?"

Daddy didn't answer. He only laughed a little laugh and said nothing. She couldn't figure out why he wouldn't tell her. Was it because he *hadn't* shot a German and was ashamed of it, or was it because he *had* shot a German and was ashamed of it? At any rate, he wasn't saying.

Daddy's second suitcase contained a pair of brown shoes, a brown leather shaving kit, and some underwear. On top of all those things were several little boxes, gift-wrapped in plain white tissue paper and tied with blue satin ribbons. There were no tags on the presents. Daddy seemed to know who they were all for.

As soon as he finished unpacking the second suitcase, he called Mother and Batty into the living room to give them the gifts he'd brought for them. When he gave Batty her present, she immediately tore into it. Inside the box was more tissue paper than the box had been wrapped in. She folded it back and lifted from it a silver bracelet. It was engraved all around with scrollwork and in the middle of the scrollwork in ornate lettering was the name Beatrice.

Batty thought it was the most beautiful thing she'd ever owned. She forgot all about wanting to be called Jimmy Jack. She looked at her name engraved so elegantly. Beatrice. Nobody ever called her Beatrice, unless he was mad at her. She could hardly believe the name belonged to her. But then again this bracelet had much too much dignity to have a silly name like Batty engraved on it. She would probably have this bracelet as long as she lived and when she was a grown woman and everyone called her Beatrice, it would be ridiculous to have BATTY engraved on the bracelet her daddy had brought back from the war. She said, "Thank you very much, Daddy,"and put the bracelet on and continued to look at it. Daddy gave Mother a silver bracelet, too, with VICTORIA engraved on it. It was a bigger bracelet than the one he'd given Batty, as was appropriate since Mother was a grown woman. He gave them other presents as well, but the bracelets were the most important ones.

Then Daddy decided he wanted to go to see the people at the store and then go see Grandmother Attwood. He asked Batty if she'd like to go and, of course, she wasn't about to let him go without her.

Daddy got behind the wheel and Batty sat on the seat beside him. He didn't have any trouble driving the Buick even though he wasn't used to it at all. He drove slowly past the big cornfield looking carefully over the brown stubble. She couldn't figure out what was so interesting about a field of brown stubble, but Daddy just kept looking at it until the car had passed it and crossed the bridge and was in front of Gracie Miller's house. Then he sped up a bit and quit looking so hard. He didn't say anything all the way to town. Finally Batty said, "Boy, Buster is going to be surprised to see you, Daddy! Why don't you slip up on him and really surprise him?"

Daddy chuckled and said, "Oh, I guess he must be expecting me about now."

Buster may not have been very surprised but he sure was happy to see Daddy. He just shook his hand and shook his hand. Batty thought if they hadn't been two men Buster would've hugged and kissed him. But they *were* two men, so Buster just kept shaking his hand, and when he'd finished, Bill Moody shook his hand and welcomed him home. Daddy sure looked handsome next to skinny stooped Buster Carson with his slicked-down hair and Bill Moody with his small crooked mouth with the wad of tobacco in his cheek. Then Colleen shook Daddy's hand. Aunt Harriet had gone home for lunch.

While Daddy was talking to Buster, Batty eyed the candy counter and wondered if Daddy would let her have a Baby Ruth if she asked for one. She might as well ask, the only thing he could do would be to say no. But if he said no she thought she might cry over a silly candy bar in front of Colleen and Buster and Bill Moody. She looked at the box of Baby Ruths again. She could taste the chewy sweetness just looking at it. I'm going to ask him, she thought; after all, he's my own daddy. But she didn't ask him.

Soon Daddy finished talking to everybody at the store and told Batty to come with him to see Grandmother Attwood and Aunt Harriet. He took her hand and led her out the back door of the store and across the parking area. Then, looking both ways to make sure there were no trains coming, they walked across the rails toward Grandmother's.

It was the same house she'd lived in with Grandfather Attwood from the first day they were married until he died. It was an old-fashioned utilitarian house, painted green, just across the railroad tracks from Daddy's store. When Daddy was a little boy, there used to be an outhouse in the backyard, but at some point a bathroom had been built onto the house. To get to it, you had to go outside and cross the small back porch, which was a little bit hard to do on a cold night. When Aunt Harriet or Aunt Caroline—who lived in New York and came to visit—wanted to take a bath, she first heated the bathroom by turning on the small electric heater. Anytime Batty spent the night with Grandmother Attwood, she just washed from a pan of warm water in the kitchen. The nicest thing about the house was the front porch which wrapped halfway around it, had a big swing and several rocking chairs and was covered with a large leaf vine, so that on a summer day when you were sitting on the porch talking to Grandmother and Aunt Harriet and drinking Aunt Harriet's iced tea, it was very cool and very private.

They walked onto the front porch. The floor had been painted recently. It was a smooth gray and it still looked almost sticky. The upper half of the front door contained a window made of squares of colored glass.

When Grandmother Attwood came to the door, her face looked green and wavy through the glass, but Batty could see her recognize them and begin to smile. Then the door was open and Daddy rushed in and lifted Grandmother from the floor and gave her a big hug and kissed her on the forehead. Grandmother giggled and said, "Oh me, oh me, Robert, put me down, for heaven's sake, put me *down*."

Batty couldn't imagine anyone picking up Grandmother. She was such a prim little lady, her brown hair wrapped neatly in a bun at the nape of her neck, her stocking seams always straight, even when she'd just finished scrubbing a linoleum floor on her knees, a look of unruffled dignity that never left her face. There was nothing about Grandmother that suggested playfulness.

Daddy was giggling. "Well, well, well," Grandmother said. "Robert, you look wonderful, maybe a little thin, but look at your hair."

"Daddy's getting bald," Batty said, remembering yesterday, when she'd provoked a big laugh by saying Daddy was shedding.

"He sure is," Grandmother said. "But you look good, Robert." Then she reached down to smooth her dress and remembered the apron she was wearing. She untied it in the back and folded it over her arm.

"Well, give me your coats and come on in," she said, taking their coats and leading them both into the sitting room. "Mrs. Terrell called Buster and asked him to come tell me you'd be home yesterday or today. When did you get here?"

"Last night in time for dinner," Daddy said. "We made good time."

Aunt Harriet was coming from the kitchen. She saw Daddy and ran to him, giggling.

"Well, Robert," she said, giving him a big hug, "it's so good to have you home. It's *so* good." She pushed him away at arm's length and looked him over. "You've gotten thin, but you look good." Then she started giggling again, and reached up to touch his head.

"What's this? My oh my, Robert, if you aren't losing your hair. You sure are."

Daddy chuckled and reached up to stroke his head. "War is enough to make you lose your hair," he said.

"Well, I guess it is at that," Aunt Harriet said. "Well, sit down. Have you had lunch?"

"No," Daddy said, "but we had a late breakfast. I'm not hungry."

"I'm hungry," Batty said, remembering the Baby Ruth.

"I have a big pot of green beans and some corn bread left over and some tomatoes I canned last summer. Are you sure you won't have some, Robert?" she asked, already heading toward the kitchen to put food on the table for Batty.

"I don't think so right now," Daddy said. "I'm not hungry."

"How about a cup of coffee?"

"Yes, thank you. That would be good."

Grandmother Attwood sat in her usual rocker beside the stove in the sitting room. There were two small flat irons on the stove. Daddy sat in the big maple rocker in front of it. Batty sat on the cot under the window.

Grandmother began her gentle rocking. "We've been expecting you for weeks now, Robert," she said. "I know Victoria's been anxious. She said she'd been expecting you to call anytime. I know she's glad to have you back. And, Batty . . . aren't you glad to have Daddy back?"

"Yeah," Batty said.

"Okay," Aunt Harriet called from the kitchen. "Come and eat."

Batty went into the kitchen. Aunt Harriet carried Daddy's coffee into the sitting room. From the kitchen Batty heard her ask Daddy questions about the war. Daddy answered them, but he didn't seem to want to talk about the war. He wanted to talk about Aunt Harriet and Grandmother. He asked them lots of questions about how they were feeling, about the house, about Aunt Harriet's work at the store. He asked them about Aunt Caroline and about his brothers. They laughed loudly several times, so Batty figured it wasn't all serious.

Batty washed down the green beans and corn bread with a big glass of buttermilk. As she was finishing, she heard a train coming into town, blowing its whistle, long loud blows to warn everybody to get out of the way. Then it began to slow down at the station. She liked the train sounds she heard at Grandmother Attwood's, particularly when she spent the night and in her sleep was faintly aware of trains shifting tracks, starting and stopping, backing up, then going forward.

She put her dishes in the sink and went into the sitting room to get the stereoscope and pictures from the bottom shelf of the buffet where Grandmother kept them.

"Do you have any plans, Robert?" Grandmother asked. "Are you going to become a farmer now that you're home?"

Daddy laughed softly. "No, I don't think so," he said. "I don't think I was meant to be a farmer." He was quiet for a moment. When he spoke again, it was in a grave tone that Batty knew meant he was saying something very important.

"I've been thinking we might build a nice modern house right here in town. I've been able to save some money and Victoria has got the store in real good shape while I was gone. I think we could do it."

Batty was looking at the only picture anyone had of Grandaddy Attwood. In the stereoscope he was sitting on a white bench with his straw hat on his lap, in three-dimension, looking very much alive. His hair was parted in the middle and his collar, standing up in the back, looked stiff enough to choke him. He wasn't smiling, just looking stern, his dark eyes focusing on something out of frame. He was about Daddy's age, she thought, though he didn't look very much like Daddy. He looked more like Uncle Junius, Daddy's brother who was the Baptist minister.

"Moving to town would be good for Batty," Grandmother said. "She must get lonely out on the farm. It's kind of a long way from other children."

"Yes," Daddy said, "and it would be a lot easier to walk to school."

Lonely? How could Grandmother think it was lonely on the farm? With all the pigs and chickens, and Constance, not to mention the people. How could *anyone* think it was lonely? Daddy was talking about building a new house and leaving the farm. Batty concentrated very hard on trying to figure out what Grandaddy Attwood must have been like.

"And I was also thinking," Daddy said, "that maybe I'd sell the store and get out of the grocery business. I've been thinking a department store would do very well in Robertson's Fort, a store that carries real good merchandise, not only work clothes and shoes and the dry goods we carry now, but also good ladies' dresses and coats, fashionable shoes, high-priced lingerie. You know, a bigger store than we have now. Something that'd be more fun to run."

"Well, don't overextend yourself, Robert," Grandmother said. "The store you've got now does a good business. You don't want to take any chances."

Daddy laughed again. "Mother," he said gently, "you have to take *some* chances. And, Harriet, you could be head of a department."

Aunt Harriet giggled with pleasure at the idea. Then she asked, "Are you going to buy a different building, Robert?"

"I don't know," Daddy said. "I'm going to find out what the situation is."

Now Batty was looking at a picture of Grandmother Attwood as a young girl. She was standing in a garden surrounded by flowers, wearing a lace dress, full over her bosom and with sleeves puffed from the shoulder to the elbow. Her hair was pinned into a loose soft roll around her head. She was smiling. Batty thought she looked very happy. It was hard to imagine Grandmother young and wearing lace, with her hair looking so soft and pretty.

The train gave a sudden hoot and started moving. Batty heard the couplings carry the jolt all the way from the engine beyond the depot on the western side of town past the house and down the chain to the caboose on the eastern side. Then the train began moving quietly. She heard it clear the house, then the crossing, and begin winding through the valley.

In the distance she heard the long shrill whistle, the waves of the sound of it carrying back to her, as the train began the first gentle incline before the hard steep climb up the mountain.

Part II

Daddy

*G*randaddy's polished-oak coffin was suspended on two wide green belts over the rectangular excavation. Parallel to the excavation was a small marble slab flush with the ground, an inscription chiseled on its surface:

MARY ANN TERRELL

AGE ONE YEAR

BORN NOVEMBER 30, 1914

DIED DECEMBER 14, 1915

DAUGHTER OF

ANDREW W. TERRELL

AND

ELLA MARLOW TERRELL

The modest family plot had been marked for sixty-two years by a black marble stone with the name Terrell chiseled into its surface. Grandaddy's grave would be the second, and Grand-mother, when she died, would complete the small family grouping here in the Asheville cemetery. Mother, Batty felt sure, would be buried back in Robertson's Fort, where Daddy would be buried, in a plot marked ATTWOOD. For a moment she wondered where she herself would be buried when the time came, and thought of how complicated life had become, how fragmented, how beset with conflicts and contradictions. She thought of the families scattered across the face of America, never to be reunited, not even in death, and she glanced at Jennifer standing to her left, her daughter's eyes reddened with crying. At least in death, Grandaddy would lie beside Mary Ann who'd never reached the age of growing away from him.

Daddy pushed Grandmother's wheelchair near the center of the casket and stood behind it. Mother stood on his right and Batty on his left between him and Jennifer. The minister stood at the head of the casket and waited for Grandaddy's nephews and nieces, whose two cars had just pulled into the gravel parking area and who now were hurrying across the grass. He waited for the last members of the family to take positions around the casket. When he spoke his voice sounded thin, stretching away into the green-carpeted silence of the cemetery, where rows of small hummocks lay somnolent in the midday sun.

"Let us now bow our heads in prayer," he said, and hesitated a moment. "Dear God," he said, "we come to you in our grief to ask that you bring us comfort in the time of our great loss. We ask that you bring comfort to this fine woman, who for sixty-five years shared Andrew Terrell's joys and his sorrows, his victories and his defeats, and was to him a loving and faithful wife. We ask that you bring comfort to his daughter and son-in-law who over the years have shown him such selfless devotion, particularly in his old age. And we ask that you bring comfort to his granddaughter whose achievements brought him such pride in his last years. We ask that you bring comfort to his great-granddaughter who is fortunate in having known him, and who will cherish loving memories of him as long as she lives. And we ask that you bring comfort to his nephews and nieces who have come from other parts of the state to share our grief. Andrew Terrell was a man who loved his family and was much loved by his family and who will be missed deeply by every member. Bring this family thy peace. Amen."

Grandmother dabbed at her eyes a little, but for the most part, she was being very strong, much like her old self, Batty thought.

Daddy reached into his pocket and took out his handkerchief. Batty glanced to see that his eyes were brimming with tears. She had never in her life seen Daddy cry. He wiped his eyes and blew his nose. She looked at him a moment. He was beginning to look old and fragile. The heavy muscular structure of his youth had gone, leaving him thin and bony. A ring of gray hair encircled the back of his head, and there were deep creases around his mouth and heavy circles under his eyes. She continued looking at him, surprised at the depth of feeling he was expressing for Grandaddy. For forty-three years Daddy had treated Grandaddy with the strictest formality, calling him Mr. Terrell till the day he died. Batty was struck by what she knew was the enormity of all the unexpressed feelings that had been locked up inside Daddy all these years, and instinctively she moved closer to him and awkwardly put her arm around his waist, leaving it there for a moment while he glanced at her and looked away, a faint and fleeting smile crossing his face.

When the minister finished praying, he opened his Bible and began reading. "'Let not your hearts be troubled: ye believe in God, believe also in me. In my father's house are many mansions: if it were not so I would have told you. I go to prepare a place for you. And if I go to prepare a place for you I will come again, and receive you unto myself; that where I am there ye may be also.'"

He closed the Bible, looked into the faces around the casket, and began speaking in a hushed tone. "We are gathered here," he said, "to give back to the dust this body that is of the dust. Now that the spirit has gone to an eternal home at the side of God and to the eternal life that Christ has promised it has need of this body no longer. This body was but awhile an earthly home and now our loved one has gone on to a much better life, a life free of sickness and of sorrow, a life where death shall be no more. Let us not grieve."

He nodded to the pallbearers who began lowering the casket into the ground. Batty watched it come to rest in the freshly shoveled earth, and the circle of pale faces, sunlit and filtered through her tears, lost focus and softened into a golden haze.

Grandmother held up amazingly well. Only in the car on the way back to Robertson's Fort did she really break down and cry. By the time Daddy pulled into the garage, she'd dried her eyes and had a cheerful face for all the hordes of friends and relatives who came to visit. And she took charge of everything from her favorite chair in the living room just as she would have if she'd been able to get around. She told Batty and Mother exactly where she wanted them to put every bit of food that came into the house—the pies and casseroles, the molded salads and homemade bread, the fried chicken and cooked hams, all brought by neighbors, or members of the Methodist church or the Eastern Star.

When things calmed down a bit, she reminisced with the guests about things that had happened many years ago. She told about the time Grandaddy rode in Uncle Harlow's first car. It was Sunday afternoon and Grandaddy was all dressed up, and as Uncle Harlow was crossing a wooden bridge, a back wheel went off the edge and the car tilted enough for Grandaddy to fall out of the car and into the creek, getting his Sunday clothes all wet except for his straw hat that miraculously was saved. When she'd finished the story, everybody laughed, and then Grandaddy's niece told of the time that Grandaddy had an awful argument with her mother—his sister—because Grandaddy refused to go to church with her till she took off the hat she was wearing and put on one that was more becoming. Grandmother laughed and said that Grandaddy always was particular enough to drive anyone crazy. "And when it came to dressing himself," she said, "he was prissy as a woman." Then Grandmother's lip trembled and Batty thought for a moment she was going to cry, but she didn't. She thought of another story on Grandaddy and began telling it. She didn't get very far into it, though, because the door opened and a pleasant-looking woman, her oval face framed with soft brown curls, came in. She was wearing a pink summer cotton dress and white sandals. Batty noticed the streaks of gray in her hair and the fine lines around her eyes and knew she must be about her own age. The woman walked over to Grandmother and extended her hand.

"Mrs. Terrell, I'm Lula Ann Garland," she said. "I used to be Lula Ann Dillard."

"Well, Lula Ann Dillard," Grandmother said slowly, calling up the memory. "Heaven sakes!"

"I'm so sorry about Mr. Terrell," Lula Ann said, her voice soft and well modulated. "Mother wanted me to tell you how sorry she was that she couldn't come to the funeral, but my father's been very sick, you know, and she couldn't leave him."

Batty involuntarily rose from the straight-backed chair, from which she'd been studying Lula Ann's profile and stood, frozen, flooded with a confusion of feelings, a forty-year-old woman, sophisticated, well educated, well traveled, and at the moment, totally uncertain of herself in the presence of a woman she was convinced had led a more limited life than she. Did she feel a tinge of the shame and self-flagellation that had tainted her childhood because of the things she and Lula Ann had done together— things she'd learned only years later in Psychology 101 were normal childhood sex play? She caught herself quickly and was searching for an appropriate attitude when Lula Ann turned from Grandmother, glanced around the room, spotted Batty, smiled, and pushed through the visitors toward Batty.

She took Batty's hand in both her own and, still smiling, said, "Hello, Batty, I was hoping you'd be here."

Batty was having trouble reconciling this slender, self-possessed woman with the fat and bratty little girl she remembered. There was still the pretty face of the plump child, but slimmed down now, the gray eyes deep set, the wide bones catching the light above delicately hollowed cheeks, her full mouth accentuated with a wine-colored gloss. Her hands felt soft and small.

"Hello, Lula Ann," Batty said. "It's lovely to see you after all these years."

"I've kept up with you over the years through the Cullman *News*," Lula Ann said. "Everybody has. I've read all about your husband's success." She glanced around the room. "I was hoping he'd be here."

Batty smiled and began to relax. "I wish he could've been. I'd love for you to meet him. But this was the one time it was just impossible for him to come."

"Well, next time, maybe," Lula Ann said. "Though I'm afraid I may not be here next time. I'm here for just a few days helping my mother. I live over in Shelby now. My husband is a superintendent in the hosiery mill there. Did you know I have a son who'll be a junior at Chapel Hill next fall?"

"Really? No, I didn't know that. That's wonderful!" Batty said. "And I have a daughter who'll be a freshman at Greensboro."

And Batty knew that Lula Ann was now a grown woman and a different person from the little girl she had known years ago, and she knew that Lula Ann had done very well, very well, indeed, and at that moment she forgave Lula Ann for the dirty comic, and for peeing on her, and for the blackmail, and the years of bearing that awful guilt. She forgave her for everything all at once, and suddenly she was very glad to see her.

"Well, Lula Ann," Batty said, grinning, "that's just terrific."

"And I understand you have a daugher?"

"Yes, she'll be here in a minute. She just ran over to Mother's house to get some cups. I'd love you to meet her."

"I *want* to meet her. Does she look like you?"

"I suppose so. At least everybody says she does."

"She's lucky, then," Lula Ann said. "You're just as pretty as always, Batty. You haven't changed a bit."

"Well . . . thank you," Batty said, surprised by the compliment.

"I understand you're an artist now?" Lula Ann said.

The question threw Batty for a minute, and she paused before she responded. When Jennifer was younger and she was devoting most of her time to doing motherly chores, spending hours in the park, and taking Jennifer all over the city to nursery school, and to dance classes, and to piano lessons, and to doctor and dental appointments; doing domestic chores, cleaning the house, watering the plants, feeding the dog, doing the laundry, shopping, and cooking, and trying to keep both her child and her husband healthy and happy; and when she was, with difficulty, stealing two afternoons a week for herself to go to her painting class, there was one question she was often asked that she hated more than any other. *What do you do?* It was a favorite at cocktail parties. She knew that, translated, it meant what do you do to justify your existence, to prove that you're an intelligent and creative person and not just a dull clod? And rationalize as she would, she could never believe for a minute that the things she was doing at that stage of her life proved her worthy at all. Now that she was forty and Jennifer was older, she no longer hated that question. She welcomed it. When anybody asked her, "What do you do?" she answered firmly and without hesitation, making up for all those years of painful self-effacement—"I paint." It was as simple as that.

Nevertheless, Lula Ann's question, *I understand you're an artist now?* left her a bit rattled. She thought of a few of that venerated group of her favorite artists—de Kooning, O'Keeffe, Chagall—and then she thought of her own brightly colored, childlike primitives, not the New York State and Virginia scenes of Grandma Moses, but scenes of the mountains of North Carolina, her own material. Could she muster up the audacity to cast herself in such elevated company as that of the *artists* of the world? And then she remembered her first show at the Cerberus Gallery six weeks ago. Sixteen out of twenty-seven paintings sold the first two days. Pretty damn good, she thought.

Lula Ann was standing there, smiling gently, waiting for her response.

"Yes," Batty said, "I'm an artist now."

"How exciting!" Lula Ann said, giggling like a child. "What do you paint?"

"I paint . . . simple scenes . . . many from this part of the country. Cornfields. Mountain streams. Barns, orchards, farm animals, villages, and towns. That sort of thing."

"Have you ever painted Robertson's Fort?"

"Oh, yes, it's one of my favorite subjects."

"Do you paint it the way it was when you were here?" Lula Ann asked. "It's changed a lot, you know."

"I paint it mostly from memory," Batty said. "The way it used to be."

The business district of Robertson's Fort was composed of one right angle of streets lined on either side by rows of two-story dirty brick buildings at the apex of which stood a monument, a bronze statue of John Robertson, the founder of the original fort, wearing a coonskin cap, his wide stance braced by the musket he held butt end on the ground, barrel pointing at an angle away from him, skyward. The statue stood on top of a ten-foot pedestal of yellow river rock and mortar, surrounded by a small moat filled with large goldfish. Just west of the monument was the railroad depot. The tracks ran through the center of town, parallel to one of the main streets and intersecting the other. Several times a day trains blocked the intersection for long minutes and cars lined up and waited patiently for the trains to move on and let them pass.

Just south of the tracks was Daddy's store, a large brick building connected to the other buildings on that side of the street. Painted across the front of the building above the display windows in big black lettering was ATTWOOD'S DEPARTMENT STORE. Under the sign was a green awning that Daddy cranked open on sunny days to keep the sun from fading the merchandise displayed in the window.

Now that they were living in town, Batty replaced her friend Charlie Knipe with a girl her own age by the name of Peggy Sue Aldrich. Peggy Sue lived with her mother in a two-story house on the main street east of town. The house was a disgrace to its more aristocratic neighbors, large white Victorians with expanses of green lawns. It sat almost on the sidewalk and so had no lawn at all and bore no evidence that it had ever been painted. It was in such a state of advanced disrepair that it tilted dramatically toward the setting sun. The townspeople had been waiting for years for it to fall, but if the tilt had increased at all it could not be discerned by the naked eye. It held its own at an angle of about eighty degrees to the ground.

Everyone knew that Peggy Sue's mother was a lazy woman who drank a lot. Her house was as big a disgrace on the inside as on the outside. Nobody except Mrs. Aldrich and Peggy Sue entered the house unless it was absolutely necessary. Those who'd been forced to enter it for some reason came away with reports of unequaled filth. Every day or two Mrs. Aldrich walked, head erect, to town. She greeted anyone she passed with an air of condescending beneficence. After a little while she could be seen returning home carrying a large brown bag full of groceries.

Peggy Sue survived on soft drinks, food eaten directly from opened tin cans, and whatever she was fed at somebody else's house. She was a bubbly child of eleven with a plump body, soft blond hair, blue eyes, and a face that was a little too wide to be pretty.

In contrast, Batty at eleven was thin and straight, her only protuberances her bony joints. Her hair had remained short since that day three years ago when she'd cut off her pigtail. Grandaddy's barber still cut it for her, though not quite as short as a boy's. She brushed it away from her face, and it lay in soft natural waves.

Life certainly was a lot more complicated now that Batty was living in town than it had been on the farm. To begin with, there were the little old ladies. After school each day she and Peggy Sue would rush home to change into their pants, cowboy hats, and spurs. Batty would attach to her belt the sheathed knife she was without only for school or church or when she was working at Daddy's store on Saturdays. Then they would get on their bikes and make their rounds because they were the guardians of defenseless old ladies who, they believed, without someone to protect them from the bad guys would be in great danger. There were three of them in Robertson's Fort: Mrs. Seagal, with the sixty steps; old lady Rumfelt, the crazy lady; and Mrs. Ledbetter, the recluse who—rumor had it—lived with a houseful of stuffed animals.

First they pedaled up the back driveway to the house of Mrs. Seagal. She lived in a white house perched on a hill overlooking the monument. The house was approached by a flight of sixty stairs that started at the sidewalk and ascended the hill in sets of ten. After every tenth stair there was a four-foot landing that gave the climber time to rest. When Mr. Seagal was alive and running the telegraph office at the depot, he could be seen coming down those stairs every morning and going back up them every afternoon. Since he died, nobody used those stairs. Mrs. Seagal stayed home all day and had whatever she needed delivered up the long driveway that cut off from the main highway about two hundred yards west of town.

One day when they went to check on her, Mrs. Seagal saw them roaming around her property and invited them in. Batty had never seen such beautiful things as there were in Mrs. Seagal's house—shelves of shining silver tea services and candlesticks, Oriental rugs with patterns of flowers and colorful birds in flight, ornate furniture, family photographs in gilt frames. Mrs. Seagal seemed to like having them visit. She talked on and on, sometimes looking off into the distance, remembering something she was telling them about the past. After that day when she asked them in the first time, they always knocked on the door when they came to check on her and she always gave them a glass of lemonade or a cup of chocolate. Some days Mrs. Seagal liked talking so much that Batty and Peggy Sue were afraid they wouldn't have time to check on their other charges.

After they left Mrs. Seagal they went to check on Mrs. Rumfelt, the crazy lady. They cycled down Mrs. Seagal's long driveway, went through the center of town past the monument, on down the main street east of town, took a left, and pushed their bikes up the hill to old lady Rumfelt's. She was never seen without the same flat-brimmed black hat that she'd worn for years. Nobody paid her much attention except to say hello to her when they passed her on the street or when they met her at the Baptist church which she attended faithfully three times a week, always sitting in the front row. She had a reputation for chasing with a broom any children who approached her property. Because Batty and Peggy Sue understood her eccentricities, they won her friendship. Every day that it wasn't raining they visited her in her yard, never daring to go into her house, for fear she might lock them in or do something else crazy. She had a hard-packed clay yard that she kept swept clean of anything loose. When she swept her yard, she wore her flat-brimmed black hat the same as other times. Spaced evenly around her yard were six large circles of brick around lush and constantly blooming flower beds. When Mrs. Rumfelt wasn't sweeping her yard, she was working in her flower beds. She was in the house only in bad weather and at night.

They saved the best for last. After they had chatted with old lady Rumfelt for a while, they pushed their bikes on up the hill to Mrs. Ledbetter's. Mrs. Ledbetter was a recluse. She lived in a big white house on a hill two blocks above Batty's house. The house was set far back from the road in the middle of spacious heavily planted grounds, and could hardly be seen from the road. When Mrs. Ledbetter's husband was alive, he'd managed the tannery that burned down thirty years ago, when Daddy was still a little boy. Batty had heard Daddy tell of the flames that could be seen in the night sky for miles around. Mr. Ledbetter had been a hunter and had stuffed whatever he killed. At one time he'd had a small museum of his stuffed animals in the middle of town in the building that was now Pyatt's candy store. Daddy said that during the week Mr. Ledbetter would run the tannery and on the weekends when he wasn't hunting he'd open his museum to the public. Daddy said he had stuffed bears, deer, wildcats, great owls and eagles, little brown-spotted birds, all the animals frozen in positions of movement, the fiercer animals frozen in positions of attack, all with their shiny glass eyes looking real and frightening. When Mr. Ledbetter died, Mrs. Ledbetter took the animals to her house. As far as anybody knew they were still there.

Because Mrs. Ledbetter was a recluse and didn't like anyone on her property, they hid their bikes in the bushes on the edge of the property and sneaked through the growth to get a good look at the place. They made a large circle around the house and then hung around for a while to make sure there was no foul play going on. When they were finished with their rounds and were satisfied that their charges were all right, Peggy Sue would go home to her lazy mother and tilting house and Batty would go home to tell Hilda about the day's investigations.

Hilda was as good a cook as Virginia had been on the farm and she could do lots of other things besides. She was a light-skinned black woman in her early forties who had six daughters to raise and a quiet passive husband who neither hurt nor helped her much. She agonized over her daughters. Lots of times Batty could hear her in the kitchen pouring her heart out to Mother about a daughter who was involved with a bad black man, or an unmarried daughter who'd gotten pregnant, or about her oldest daughter who was married to a drunk who couldn't keep a job. When Hilda was upset she stuttered. When she talked about her daughters, she stuttered a lot. She was a very religious woman who went to church every Sunday and read her Bible every day. There was nothing Hilda didn't know about the Bible. There were some things Batty would a lot rather talk to Hilda about than to Grandmother or Mother—the little old ladies, for instance.

Hilda was peeling potatoes in the kitchen sink.

"You should have seen it, Hilda," Batty said. "It's true. She *does* have all those stuffed animals in her house. She has white gauzy curtains and that real dark depressing furniture, and the living room is full of wild animals."

Hilda's knife paused a moment and she turned to Batty. "How do you know that, Batty?" she asked quietly.

"Because Peggy Sue and I got very close to the house. We looked right in the living-room window."

"You'd better be careful," Hilda said, turning to Batty. "What if she caught you?"

"She'd just yell at us the way she always does when she sees us."

"You mean she's caught you sneaking around her property?"

"We weren't *sneaking* around her property. We were checking up on her to make sure she was all right. And there was a wild-cat on a limb. He looked alive just as though he was going to jump on the sofa. And a big bear, standing on his hind legs with his front paws up in the air as though he was going for something."

"Goodness," Hilda said, in her soft gentle voice, "weren't you afraid, Batty?"

"Of course not, Hilda," Batty said, with some disgust. "They're not alive. They're just stuffed. That's all. And there was a big hawk with a crooked beak right up over the door, his wings spread as though he was about to fly away. But he was stuffed so he just sat there with his eyes shining."

"You're going to get in trouble if you're not careful," Hilda said. "What if Mrs. Ledbetter caught you peeping in her windows? I don't think you ought to sneak around her yard, Batty, especially if she's already seen you before. She might call Red Crawford, the policeman, or something."

"Hilda," Batty said impatiently, "how do you think we can be sure everything's all *right* at Mrs. Ledbetter's if we *don't* sneak around to investigate?"

"Are you going to tell your daddy what you saw?" Hilda said.

"I can't," Batty said. "He'd never understand about our taking care of the old ladies."

"Well, why don't you tell your mother then?"

"You know I cant' tell Mother anything I don't want Daddy to know. She tells him everything."

"It seems you ought to tell someone."

"Why?"

"Because it's very interesting, seeing all those wild animals," Hilda said.

"I'm not going to tell a soul except you, Hilda. Peggy Sue and I agreed. You can't protect old ladies from bad people if everybody knows you do it. You've got to keep it a secret, Hilda. You've got to promise you won't tell a soul. Do you promise?"

Hilda swept the potato peelings into the disposal with her hand. Then she looked over her shoulder at Batty, and said, "Okay, I promise."

On Saturdays Batty had to work in Daddy's store.

She unfolded great bolts of material and measured it with a yardstick and cut the required length. She scooped chocolate-covered peppermint kisses onto the scale and adjusted the amount until she had the requested weight. Then she dumped the tray into a brown paper bag. She looked down the stacks of boxes of stockings to find the requested size and shade. She sold ten-cent bottles of olive oil to women who'd put it on their fingernails to make them grow and pomade to colored people who'd put it on their hair to keep it from frizzing. She handed bras in tentlike sizes through the dressing-room curtain till the customer had the right size and style.

She sold Cutex and Dura Gloss fingernail polish in all tones of red, Tangee lipstick in natural, and perfumes that cost ten cents or thirty-six cents and had names like Atom Bomb, Midnight in Paris and Blue Waltz. She sold invisible and visible hairnets, with and without elastic, and nylon and cotton panties—sometimes called step-ins by the country women. She called Daddy or Aunt Harriet whenever a customer wanted to buy shoes and she sent them downstairs to Buster Carson in the men's department if they were looking for men's clothes. On slow days the hours dragged by. She gossiped with the other clerks if Daddy wasn't looking and kept busy dusting shelves or putting price tags on things if he was. On busy days when there were lots of customers, Batty liked working at Daddy's store. She got to see and talk to lots of people. She liked wrapping packages and ringing the cash register and making change. On busy days, the hours went by very fast.

Sometimes she got to help Mother upstairs in the dress department when she had more customers at a time than she could handle. The dress department was Mother's responsibility. She did all the buying and she took great pride in the dresses she sold. Her steady customers bought all their dresses from her. They trusted her to find something for them that was becoming and in good taste. Sometimes Mother convinced a customer to buy something that was more colorful, or more youthful, or more unusual than the dress the customer might have chosen for herself. When a new shipment of dresses came in, Mother was the first one to go through them. She put aside the dresses she thought were appropriate for her regular customers. Then she telephoned the customers and they came and tried on the dresses Mother had put aside.

One or twice a week a salesman came in and spread his merchandise out over the counters. Daddy called Mother and she came to look at the merchandise and help Daddy decide what they should buy. The salesman took the order on a long form with carbons folded into a thick pad. When they'd finished ordering, he had Daddy sign the form. Then he tore off the carbon copy and gave it to him. Mother took it and filed it in the big rolltop desk. Then the salesman folded up his bags and samples and carried them back to his car, shook hands with Daddy and left till he returned with the line for the next season.

If Daddy didn't like a salesman, he went to great lengths to avoid having to spend time with him. The year before he'd bought from the Charlotte Merchandise Show several sets of very convincing false noses and glasses. The noses were soft and rubbery with large pores that made them look real. When Daddy put one of the noses on his face, it sat down over his real nose in a perfect fit, the rubber edges clinging to his face as though the nose had grown there. Daddy had sold all but one of them. That one he kept for himself. One Saturday in October when Batty was working at the store, Daddy saw the salesman from Sweet Dreams Ladies' Nightgowns pull up in front and begin taking his large bags out of the station wagon. Daddy didn't like that salesman. He said the man talked too much. He didn't like his line of merchandise much either.

Batty was thumbing through the Simplicity pattern drawer to find a pattern that Granny Murphy had selected from the book. She glanced up to see Daddy in his false nose and glasses, with his old felt hat pulled low on his head. He was wearing the old gray sweater that had been hanging on a peg behind the shoe shelves for as long as she could remember. It was dirty and stretched completely out of shape. He had taken a cup from the cabinet in the back of the store and was at the stationery counter filling it up with pencils.

"What on earth are you doing, Daddy?" Batty called across the sewing counter.

"Shhh," Daddy whispered. Aunt Harriet and Colleen just went on about their business, ringing up sales, helping customers find the right sizes, as though nothing unusual was going on.

The salesman from Sweet Dreams came in lugging one of his big bags with him.

"Where's Mr. Attwood?" he called to Colleen.

"I'm sorry, he's not here right now," she said.

"Do you know when he'll be back?"

"No, I'm sorry, I don't have any idea."

"Well, he's not out of town or anything, is he?"

"No, he's around here somewhere, I think."

"Would you mind if I waited for him?"

"No, not at all," Colleen said.

The salesman put his bag on the floor and leaned on the candy counter. He stood there looking out the window. Daddy, who had been on the other side of the store, came up to him now and held out his cup of pencils. Then with his other hand he held up first two fingers and then five fingers. The salesman finally figured out that the beggar was trying to sell him two pencils for a nickel. He brushed at Daddy with both his hands as though trying to brush away insects. Daddy continued trying to sell him the pencils. Finally the salesman picked up his bag and moved to the other side of the store. Daddy followed him. The salesman came back to the wrapping counter where Aunt Harriet, Colleen, and Batty were standing watching the show.

"That beggar won't leave me alone," he whispered.

Aunt Harriet giggled nervously.

"I don't know much we can do about it," Colleen whispered. "He's not breaking any laws or anything."

"Sure he's breaking laws," the salesman said. "He's loitering in a public place. You ought to call the police."

"There's no telling where the policeman is right now," Aunt Harriet said. "He's probably sleeping. He works mostly at nights, you know."

The salesman gave up trying to get Colleen or Aunt Harriet to do anything. The store was busy now. He propped himself on the wrapping counter in the center of things to await Daddy's return. The beggar followed him there and continued the effort to sell him pencils. Finally the salesman had all he could take. He picked up his bag and left the store, calling back to Colleen to tell Mr. Attwood he'd see him the next trip around.

When he was gone, Daddy took off his nose and glasses and the old hat, and burst out laughing.

"You do beat all, Mr. Attwood," Colleen said, laughing with him.

Batty looked at Daddy standing there laughing. Then she rolled her eyes heavenward and shook her head.

But most of the time Daddy didn't play such games. He just paced from the front of the store to the back and then to the front again. He usually had a very serious look on his face, as though he was worried about the Gross National Product, or the possibility of war in the Orient. When Daddy was quiet and looked pensive, whether he was pacing the floor or sitting in the living room after dinner with his face buried in his hands, Mother warned Batty that he was thinking and should not be disturbed. Mother said he was a deep thinker: that was her term for anyone who spent a lot of time meditating about timeless and weighty matters. Daddy was a deeper thinker than any of his brothers or sisters. Some preachers were deeper thinkers than others. Mother's shelves were filled with books written by deep thinkers. Batty never doubted that whatever Daddy was thinking about as he paced back and forth in his store was very important.

One Saturday afternoon when Batty came back to the rolltop desk to ask Mother where they were going to have supper that evening, she saw Mother writing out checks for the clerks' salaries. She saw Clemmie Houseman's check for twelve dollars. Clemmie worked only on Saturdays the same as Batty, and Daddy paid Batty only four dollars and a half. She waited till everybody else had gone home. Then she cornered Daddy just as he was turning out the lights and stood facing him between the bras and the panty girdles.

"I should be paid as much as anyone else," she said. "I work just as hard as the other clerks do."

Daddy seemed to think her boldness in demanding fair play was very funny. He was laughing and looking at her out of the corners of his eyes.

"Batty," he said, "you haven't had the experience the women have had."

"I don't care," Batty said. "It's not fair. What's experience got to do with it? I work just as hard as they do and at the end of the day I'm just as tired as they are."

"Well, I know, Batty, but . . ."

"And I have just as much experience as Clemmie. She hasn't been clerking for more than a few months and I've been working here on Saturdays for more than a year now."

"But don't you see, Batty? Clemmie knows more about where everything is and what's out of stock and on order, things you have to ask."

"It's not fair," Batty insisted. "I'm just as much help as Clemmie and you pay her twelve dollars for working on Saturdays and you pay me only four and a half."

"And besides," Daddy said, as a continuation of some point he was making earlier, "you should be working to make a contribution to the family even if I didn't pay you at *all*. You're part of the family. There's nothing wrong with your working to help pay for your food and clothes."

"None of the other girls work to pay for their food and clothes," Batty said. "I don't know why *I* should have to."

"I had to work from the time I was ten years old," Daddy said. "It's good for you to have to work. You need to learn about responsibility and the value of money."

"I already *know* about the value of money," Batty said, "enough to know it's not fair for you to pay the other clerks twelve dollars for working Saturdays and me only four and a half."

"The other clerks have a lot more financial responsibility than you have. They have families to help support."

"That has nothing to do with how much they're worth."

"Well, Batty," Daddy said, no longer smiling but looking very serious now, "I'm not going to pay you twelve dollars. That's out of the question. But I *will* give you a raise. Starting next Saturday I'll pay you *five* dollars."

Batty was quiet for a moment. She stood looking down at her saddle oxfords on the oiled wooden floor. She'd pushed Daddy about as far as she dared, and she certainly didn't want to make him angry because when he got angry he could be pretty fierce. Besides—though a fifty-cent raise wasn't a lot, it really wasn't enough—five dollars *did* sound better than four-fifty. She looked up at Daddy.

"Okay," she said, "but it's still not fair." She turned to walk out the door ahead of Daddy. "I just can't wait till I grow up and get paid what I'm *worth*," she said to him over her shoulder.

Geraldine Kilpatrick had come home.

She was slender as a wraith and had long blond hair that she sometimes wore hanging down her back and sometimes swept on top of her head. Her clothes came from the best shops in Asheville and she looked smart and stunning in them. She'd got an advanced degree in Speech and Dramatic Arts from Northwestern University in Illinois and had gone from there to Briarwood in Virginia to teach. She'd married another teacher there, and now that the marriage had ended in divorce she was back home to stay with her parents while she got herself together again.

Mother was delighted with Geraldine's return. She saw it as a well-timed opportunity for Batty not only to learn elocution but also—now that she was twelve and beginning to be less a little girl and more a young lady—to gain some grace and poise that Batty was so lacking in . . . that Batty, in fact, seemed to consider totally unimportant. Even though she was beginning to round out a little and grow taller, even though her face was taking less childish

planes, Batty still behaved and dressed like the Jimmy Jack she'd
wanted to be four years earlier. Mother had been waiting for Batty
to outgrow her "tomboy stage," as she called it, and decided that
now was the time.

Batty was not at all convinced that she needed development in
any new directions and she was most reluctant to give up the two
afternoons a week she usually devoted to the old ladies or spent
playing basketball in the yard with Peggy Sue and the Hawkins
boys who lived up the street. She wasn't in a very good mood as
Mother drove her up the driveway to the Kilpatricks that first
Monday afternoon.

"Geraldine is a most attractive woman," Mother said. "She'll be
able to teach you a lot. Not only acting and elocution, but also poise
and grace."

"I don't want to learn poise and grace," Batty said sullenly.

"It's a good thing for a girl to learn. When you're a little older
you'll think it's important, too."

"I'll never think it's important," Batty said.

"And Geraldine is a marvelous actress. She's acted with the
Asheville Community Theater, and, they're very good."

"Good for her," Batty said sarcastically.

"Don't be rude now, Batty," Mother said, stopping the car in
front of the house. "I'd be very embarrassed if you were rude."

Batty smirked.

"And call me when you're finished," Mother said.

Batty rang the doorbell and stood there waiting for Geraldine to
open the door, watching the Chrysler wend its way back down the
long driveway.

"Come in, Batty," Geraldine said. "You're right on time." She
smiled so warmly that Batty felt almost ashamed of herself for
being in such a sullen mood. Geraldine was wearing blue slacks
and a white man-style shirt hanging out over the pants and belted
at the waist. She had on straw wedge-heeled sandals and her
toenails were painted bright orange. Her hair was braided in one
long braid that she'd coiled on top of her head like a diadem. Batty
thought she was the most glamorous woman in the world.

"I'm glad your mother called me," Geraldine said. Her speech,
very different from the mountain speech of flat and grating

vowels, rolled from her mouth as smoothly as if on oil. "I've seen you in town several times and said to my mother just last week that Bob Attwood's daughter was getting to be a very pretty young lady. I'm glad I'm going to have the opportunity to work with you." She sat down on the sofa and took a cigarette from the pack lying on the coffee table.

"I'm glad too," Batty said, almost meaning it. She was watching every move Geraldine made.

Geraldine flicked a slender silver lighter and lit her cigarette. In Robertson's Fort everybody thought it was sinful for women to smoke. Batty knew that Mother smoked in the bathroom sometimes, because when she came out the bathroom would be full of smoke. But she would never have dared smoke in front of anyone. Geraldine made smoking seem charming and sophisticated. She inhaled and let the smoke out slowly. She never made a hurried move. She had lots of time to make beautiful creations of every move she made and every sound she uttered.

"I've been thinking about what I hope to accomplish in our time together," she said. "I think the most important thing for now is to work on vowel sounds and try to rid your speech of some of the ugly flat sounds of the speech of this region. A beautiful girl like you should not sound as though she's from Robertson's Fort all her life." Geraldine had called her a beautiful girl. Batty thought she must be teasing her. She looked for any other suggestion of it. Geraldine went right on, sounding dead serious. "Then we'll begin working on some oral interpretation of literature. You know, reading selections aloud." Batty had heard Geraldine reading poems and parts of plays on the radio. She could read a poem so that it would make you cry. She supposed Geraldine was going to teach her to do that too. "And then next year I hope to direct a play to raise money for the P.T.A. at Floral Park High School. Would you like to be in a play?"

Every year a touring company of actors known as the Nodine Players came to Robertson's Fort High School. It was the only time Batty ever got to see live actors onstage. Mr. and Mrs. Nodine were in the play every year. Mrs. Nodine was a rather portly woman with bright yellow hair that she wore lots of different ways. Mr. Nodine was a slender dapper man, graying at the temples, and with a small graying mustache. Every year they acted whatever parts called for a middle-aged actor and actress. They would make themselves up so that they weren't always recognizable until they spoke. But when their voices boomed out across the stage in those deep open-throated tones, and when they swept across the stage in two or three paces taking command not only of the stage but of the audience as well, there was no mistaking them. The audience would clap and shout till all the actors had to stop and wait for quiet before proceeding. The day each year when the Nodine Players came with their brightly colored sets and costumes and their gay romantic plots was one of the best days of the year for Batty.

"Yes," she said, surprising herself, "I'd love to be in a play."

"Good," Geraldine said. "It should be a lot of fun. I'm already getting excited about it. But for now, here's a list of words that are the biggest problems."

Batty looked at the list:

> now, cow, house, follow, borrow, out, spout, drought, without, can't, aunt, band, hand, bland, span, gas, pass, pen, hen, blend, fend, content, rent, men, pin, tin, where, when, whether, high, sky, by, why, eye.

"Read them after me," Geraldine said. "Now." She made the sound, saying the word slowly, opening her mouth and closing it as if she were molding the outside walls of the word as she pushed it through her lips.

"Now," Batty said slowly, imitating the sound, saying it loudly and trying to shape it as Geraldine had done.

They spent the hour working on the words and then Geraldine gave Batty breathing exercises to work on before her Friday lesson. Batty figured that when she finished her speech lessons she'd sound just like Geraldine. It would be a lot of hard work, but it would be worth it. If she could be like Geraldine, maybe it wouldn't be so bad being a girl after all.

At five o'clock, Mother came to take her home. The new house they'd been living in for two years was a block from the town's main street, near the foot of a residential hill. Batty had seen houses like it when Daddy took the family to Florida on vacations, but there certainly weren't any other houses like it in Robertson's Fort. It was a flat-roofed Spanish-style stucco sitting above the intersection of two streets on a terraced lawn. It was almost as interesting as Mother's hats. It wasn't as big as the farmhouse where Grandmother and Grandaddy Terrell still lived, but it was big enough.

Hilda was sitting on the kitchen stool with the Asheville *Citizen-Times* spread out in front of her waiting for the chicken to brown. She had a pencil in her hand and occasionally wrote something on the paper. Batty was searching the refrigerator for something to nibble on to hold her over till supper.

"Hilda, what're you doing?" she asked.

Oh, just working a crossword puzzle," Hilda said.

"You mean you know how to fill in all those little squares? I've tried it and I can hardly get any of them."

"Yeah, I can do it," Hilda said softly, as though it weren't a feat of much importance.

"Let me see," Batty said, looking over her shoulder. "My gosh, you've got almost all of them already."

"This is kind of an easy one," Hilda said with her sweet self-disparaging smile.

"Easy! Look at this one," Batty said. "'A devastating wind.' What did you put for that, Hilda? M-I-S-T-R-A-L. What's that?"

Hilda laughed timidly. "Mistral," she said. "A wind they have overseas that blows down the crops and causes lots of damage."

"Lordy Mercy!" Batty said. "How did you *know* that?"

"Oh, I just read about it somewhere."

"And how about this one, three down, 'Queen of the Olympian Gods.' H-E-R-A. What's that, Hilda?"

"Hera was the wife of Zeus, I mean in ancient Greek religion, before Christianity," Hilda said. "I read about it in one of the books your Mother let me read."

"And you think this puzzle is *easy?*"

"Oh, yeah," Hilda said. "This one's not too hard."

From then on Batty looked through all Mother's magazines and newspapers to find a puzzle too hard for Hilda. Occasionally she found one that gave Hilda a little trouble but nothing she couldn't

finally solve. Hilda had a fine pedigree. Her great-grandfather
had been one of North Carolina's most famous governors. Hilda's
grandmother had been his slave. She'd had a son by him and the
son was Hilda's father. Batty wondered if the great governor had
been as good at crossword puzzles as Hilda.

Everything was going well for Batty.

Sulie Dillard, Lula Ann's older sister and the star of the girls'
basketball team and Batty's idol besides, had been very friendly
lately. She had even spent the night a couple of times, which was a
sure sign of friendship. In addition to that, Batty's speech lessons
were coming along fine. She and Geraldine were working on a
poem she was going to read over the Cullman radio station in a few
weeks. Things were going well, indeed.

Then Sulie invited Batty to her birthday party.

It was the first kissing party she'd ever gone to and Post Office
was the first kissing game she'd ever played. Someone was the
postmaster and someone else went into a room with the lights
turned off. He told the postmaster he had a letter for a particular
girl. Then the girl went into the room and the boy kissed her. Then
the boy came out and the girl told the postmaster she had a letter
for a particular boy. The boy went into the room and they kissed,
and then on and on, till every boy in the room had kissed every girl
and vice versa. Some of the kisses were little platonic kisses that
were just a touching of the lips, but some of the kisses were long,
hot, panting embraces.

The game had been going on for some time when Duane Marley
called her into the dark room. He gave her a little dry kiss on the
lips, which was *enough* touching from anyone as ugly as Duane.
Then Batty called Carl Burnside. He was a large husky senior, new
this year to Robertson's Fort. He wore big metal taps on the heels
and toes of his shoes and walked with a slow rhythmic pace,
clicking his taps as he walked. He was handsome in a dissolute sort
of way.

He came into the room and closed the door. Then he found her
in the dark and crushed her to him. She caught her breath. Carl
Burnside wasn't kissing at all the way Duane Marley had kissed. It

wasn't anywhere close. He was feeling for the bed with his knee now, pushing her back onto it and laying his full weight on top of her. He opened his wet mouth wide upon hers. His tongue pried her lips apart and reached deeply into her mouth. She felt pleasant tingling and swelling sensations where his groin pressed, his full weight upon her.

Someone rapped on the door.

Alexandria Pike said, "Batty, your father's here."

Carl Burnside quickly rolled off her and stood up. Batty felt herself going hot now, not with lust but with terror. How could she have forgotten the time? How could she have forgotten that Daddy would be here to pick her up at ten o'clock? She frantically smoothed out her dress, tried to wipe the smeared lipstick from the lower half of her face, and then in horror and humiliation opened the door of the bedroom and went out. Daddy stood there looking very grave and not saying anything. Everybody was very quiet now.

"Let's go," Daddy said.

She followed him out without looking at anybody.

He didn't speak all the way home. He pulled the car into the basement garage. When they were in the house, he said, "Stay here." Then he went outside.

Mother was taking a bath. Batty could hear the water running in her bathroom. Daddy came in the front door carrying a big switch he'd broken from a tree. He grabbed her by the upper arm and, almost lifting her from the floor, yanked her into her bedroom. She didn't dare utter a sound. He threw her facedown on the bed. She felt the first blow burn into her thighs. Then the next. She choked back her cries. She could hardly breathe. Daddy continued switching her. She knew he was making big red welts. When at last she let escape a sharp breathless cry, Daddy stopped. He took her by the shoulders and yanked her around to face him.

"I will *not* have my daughter behaving like a cheap Dillard," he said, and gave her another violent shake.

"Do you *hear* me?"

Batty sobbed.

"Do you *hear* me?" Daddy demanded again, this time more loudly and emphatically.

"Yes," Batty said in a whisper.

"Let me hear you say it. Do you hear me, Batty?"

"Yes," Batty said firmly.

Daddy released her and turned and left the room.

The next day he went to Randy Dillard's service station and told him he never wanted Sulie associating with his daughter again.

That was when Sulie began making life miserable.

The girls in Sulie's gang were two or three years older than Batty and were in high school and changing classes, while she was still in Mrs. Harman's seventh-grade class being bored to death. Mrs. Harman knew a lot of things, especially math, but she had to spend all her time trying to keep the students quiet and never got very much teaching done. The girls in Sulie's gang constituted the entire Robertson's Fort High School girls' basketball team. They practiced two or three afternoons after school and on Friday nights and some Tuesday nights, they'd play teams from other schools in the county. Sometimes they'd go to the other schools on a big yellow bus, and other times the teams from the other schools came to Robertson's Fort. The girls' teams played first. Then the boys' teams played. The girls wore red basketball uniforms trimmed in white with braid around the edge of the leg and the arm, a stripe down each side, and a big white number on both the chest and the back. Sulie's number was twelve.

When the girls ran onto the court to begin warming up, a cheer rose from the fans in the bleachers. They did layups for a while, each girl running in turn and jumping just as she came under the basket and laying the ball over the rim into the net. The spectators cheered each time a ball fell into the net. Almost everybody in town went to the games. Besides Sulie, the players on the first team were Alexandria Pike, who was so big and fat she scared all her opponents out of her way; Marietta Piercy, who was a steady but not spectacular player; Mamie Dillard, who was Sulie's second cousin; Felicity Harman, who was the daughter of Batty's seventh-grade teacher; and Judy McDaniel, a quiet hardworking girl who was a terrific forward and a follower of Sulie's to the end.

Sulie was the star. She was several inches shorter than the other girls, but she was fast and spunky, her firm legs with their well-rounded thighs moving gracefully as she dribbled and faked, slipped under the arm of her guard, and came out the other side, her lightly freckled face damp with perspiration and her small mouth pinched in determination as she sprang to make a basket before the guard could pivot to keep her covered. And she was cute, her blond ringlets bouncing as she ran easily back to the center of the court to the cheers from the bleachers.

Batty hated Wednesdays. That was the one day a week when the girls' basketball team didn't have either practice in the afternoon or a game in the evening. That was the day Sulie and her gang walked to town after school, always behind Batty, and taunted her all the way. That was the one day a week she often gave up the privilege of stopping to have a fountain Pepsi at Mr. Shapiro's drugstore with Peggy Sue, because on those days Sulie and her gang made sure that every minute she spent drinking her Pepsi was spent in misery.

This Wednesday she and Peggy Sue hung around after school talking with Mrs. Harman, asking her questions about the math she never got around to teaching. They thought if they waited long enough, Sulie and her gang would be long gone and they could walk home in peace. But, somehow, when the school had emptied and it seemed safe to start walking home, she and Peggy Sue had gone less than half a block when they heard the laughter behind them.

"Hey, shake it but don't break it!" she heard Sulie call. More laughter. Boys this time, too. That was unusual. The boys usually stayed out of it.

"Don't turn around," Peggy Sue said. "They're just jealous. That's all that's wrong with them."

"Why on earth would they be jealous of me?"

"Well . . . because your father has a big store and a nice car and you make good grades and . . . and besides you're getting very pretty lately."

"What do you mean, I'm getting pretty?"

"Just what I said."

"Well . . . what do you mean?"

"I mean that since you're getting older and letting your hair grow out, you're getting very pretty."

Batty was silent a moment. Peggy Sue was the second person in as many months to tell her she was pretty. Geraldine had called her *beautiful*, in fact. She'd said, "A *beautiful* girl like you." Before that, nobody had ever called her beautiful, except Grandmother, and that didn't mean anything because Grandmother just called her beautiful the way she called her "honey" or "sweetie."

"You think your daddy's a real big shot, don't you? Just because he owns the biggest store in town!" This time it was Alexandria Pike.

"Slow down, Batty," Peggy Sue said. "Don't let them make you hurry."

They passed the Farmers' Federation with its strong earthy smells of chicken feed and fertilizer and were in front of Reed's Hardware Store just below Daddy's when Sulie dared her last remark.

"You tell your daddy I don't *want* to associate with you. I'd never, *never* associate with you. He doesn't have to worry. You just tell him that, okay?"

Batty was about to dart into Daddy's store when Peggy Sue said, "I want an orange crush from the drugstore."

Batty looked at her.

"That's what I want," Peggy Sue said.

"Well . . ."

"Don't be such a coward, Batty. They can't hurt you. Now come on, let's go to the drugstore."

"Well, okay," Batty said. "I guess."

The gang came into the drugstore right behind them, pushed past them, and spilled into a booth near the back of the room. It was a large room with fans hanging from the white pressed-tin ceiling and a floor of white tiles with a pattern of black squares.

"Let's sit here," Batty said, indicating one of the ice-cream tables near the front.

Lucy, who worked there, came over and took their order.

"An orange crush, and what'll you have, Batty?" Peggy Sue asked.

"Make mine a Pepsi with lemon, please," Batty said.

Suddenly Dawn, the oldest Dillard girl who was a twin, was standing by their table. Batty hadn't seen her walking home from school with the gang. She must have joined them at the drugstore.

"I hear you've been talking about Lula Ann," she said. "I hear you said she wears cheap clothes because we can't afford anything better."

Batty couldn't remember ever having said anything like that about Lula Ann—or *anybody*. In fact, she and Lula Ann got along very well whenever her big sisters weren't around. When they were around, Lula Ann sided with them.

"I didn't say any such thing," Batty said. "I don't care what kind of clothes Lula Ann wears."

"I don't believe you," Dawn said in her soft long-suffering way. "And I don't ever want to hear of you criticizing my family again. We may not have as much money as *your* family, but we're always neat and clean and we're just as good as you Attwoods any day of the week." She turned and went back to the booth where her sister Sulie and the gang were parked, watching.

"What did she say?" Batty heard Marietta Piercy whisper.

Then Dawn said something and there was loud laughter.

Suddenly it was all too much. Batty felt her eyes filling with tears. She brushed them away furiously, angry at herself for letting Sulie's gang upset her so much, angry at herself for crying, and angry—most of all—at Sulie for causing her all this trouble. She got up and threw a dime on the table. It landed on its edge and rolled off. It continued to roll across the checkered tile floor. Peggy Sue scrambled for it. Batty grabbed her books and turned and ran out the door. The last she saw of Peggy Sue was her fat behind under the table where she'd finally brought the dime to rest.

Batty ran up the street, the tears still flowing. Commodore Perkins was sitting just inside the door of his antique shop wearing his navy suit and white bow tie. As she rushed by, she saw him push his weight from the chair and wave toward her. She waved back and rushed on. She heard him calling her from behind.

"Batty, come here a minute, honey."

What? she thought. *What?*

"Come here, I've got something to show you."

Commodore Perkins was an aristocratic old man with a mane of white hair and a handlebar mustache that he kept carefully waxed and twisted on the ends. He'd been a commissioned officer in World War I and had retained the title ever since. In the summer he wore a white linen suit with a navy bow tie and in winter he wore a navy suit with a white bow tie. In the coldest months, he wore a white double-breasted topcoat with large brass buttons. He and his delicate wife came to Robertson's Fort fifty years earlier from New Bern down in the flatlands when, it was rumored, he had an irreconcilable dispute with his father who was the owner of a large tobacco plantation. They'd chosen Robertson's Fort for their home because during several summer vacations in the mountains, they'd come to love the little town. He bought vast tracts of land and got in the lumber business and over the years became quite wealthy. At eighty-two he retired from the business and opened a small antiques shop in the building next to where Daddy's grocery store used to be. In the window were displayed two old clocks, a set of cotton carders with wisps of cotton still caught in the wire teeth, a long brass candlestick, and a silver-mesh bag on a long silver chain.

Batty didn't really want to stop and talk to Commodore Perkins right now. She wanted to go home and lock herself in her room to cry in private. Maybe if she cried she'd feel better. But Commodore Perkins was a man of much veneration, and she owed him respect. She sniffed and took a last swipe at her wet cheeks. She hoped he wouldn't notice that she'd been crying. She'd hate to have to explain it all to him. It was very complicated, and besides, no matter how respected he was, her crying was none of his business. She turned and went back to where he was standing and looking at her just outside the door of his shop. She could see a rag doll with a white porcelain head sitting on one shelf over his shoulder. Its features were so faded it hardly had a face.

"Come on in here, honey," the Commodore said as she approached. "I'm going to show you a pretty little blue light."

"Where?" she said, and stepped through the front door.

"Just come back here with me," the Commodore said. "You can see it only in the dark."

Batty followed him. She was thankful he hadn't noticed she'd been crying. Maybe when you get as old as the Commodore, she thought, you don't see well enough to notice that sort of thing. He led her into the storage room at the back of the shop and closed the door. Now he and Batty were in total darkness.

"Where's the little blue light?" she asked.

"Just look over in the corner," he said, and threw his ancient arms around her and pulled her to him. She smelled the old man's rancid breath. His whiskered cheek brushed hers for a moment. Then she pushed him away with all her strength and groped for the doorknob.

"Come here, honey," he said. "Don't you want to see the little blue light?"

Batty was breathing hard and her hands were shaking. She threw open the door and ran out, grabbing her books from the counter as she passed it. She continued running straight out the door and up the street, beginning to cry harder than ever now. She was crying so hard when she got to the corner that she had to stop running to catch her breath and keep from choking. No one would believe it, she thought, no one! Old Commodore Perkins! Not even Hilda would believe that one. A tear rolled over her lower lid and cleared her vision long enough for her to see Granny Murphy standing across the street with her hands on her hips and her head cocked watching her with interest. Batty turned and ran the rest of the way home. In her room, she locked the door behind her and threw herself on her own bed where at last she could cry in private on this the worst day of her life.

The next day was Thursday and Batty was glad she had the afternoon free to go see Grandmother Terrell. She stopped by the store to tell Mother she was going to ride her bicycle out to the farm. She and Mother and Daddy visited Grandmother and Grandaddy Terrell almost every Sunday, but that wasn't enough for Batty. She liked to visit Grandmother alone, when she could get a lot of attention. She hadn't done that in a long time because she'd been so busy, but today she'd *made* the time. She just had to talk to Grandmother about Sulie. Grandmother had been the one who'd told her what to do when she was in the third grade and Lula Ann was making her life miserable. She'd know what to do about Sulie, Lula Ann's older sister, too.

It was one of those beautiful fall days when the leaves were just beginning to turn, and the sky was a limpid blue and the air was brisk. The yellow had been drained from the sunlight and it fell crisp and white as the meat of a new apple on what it touched, turning houses and trees into vivid contrasts of shadow and light. She was wearing the red cardigan Grandmother had knitted for her birthday. She loved its big wooden buttons and had been waiting for more than a month for the weather to get cool enough to wear it. She passed the Methodist church and took a left going toward the school and then a right heading out the road she used to take to school when they lived on the farm.

From this point on, the road wasn't paved. She rode carefully to avoid big rocks or gulleys. When she crossed the wooden bridge, her bike made a deep rumbling sound on the loose boards. The long stretch of road along the edge of the cornfield was dry. When she looked down, she could see the fine brown dust her tires were raising. As she rounded the curve just before the farm where the stream paralleled the road on one side and the steep red bank rose from the other, she abruptly reversed her weight on the pedals and stopped. Not more than four feet ahead of her was the longest green snake she'd ever seen. He was looping his way across the road, leisurely moving through three knee-high arcs, his head moving into the first arc as his tail came out of the last one. He didn't seem to be in a hurry though she knew he saw her. She stood with one foot on a bike pedal and the other on the ground waiting for him to clear the way. Across the road, he flattened out and disappeared into the thick undergrowth on the bank of the river. She watched a long time. Not a leaf stirred. A shudder ran down her body and her skin pinched into gooseflesh.

Grandmother seemed very happy to see her. She hugged her and kissed her cheek and gave her a big plate of the delicious congealed salad she'd made. When Batty finished eating, she told Grandmother she wanted to talk to her about a problem she was having. In the living room, Grandmother sat down on the sofa and arranged beside her the white bedspread she was crocheting. Batty sat in Grandaddy's favorite rocking chair.

"Well, Batty, what's the problem, honey?" Grandmother asked.

"It's Sulie Dillard, Grandmother. She and her gang are always picking on me. I can't walk home from school when they're around without them making fun of me and laughing at me and yelling mean things." Batty was determined not to cry today. She had cried enough yesterday for the year, she thought, certainly for the week. She was talking to Grandmother in a steady voice.

"Those Dillards sure have given you a lot of trouble, haven't they?" Grandmother said. "It's just plain ole bad luck that those Dillards have to be growing up in this town the same time as you." She shifted her weight and reached for a pillow to put behind her back. Then she began her crocheting again, the hook darting in and out of the pattern, picking up loops, feeding them through other loops. Batty watched the growth of the pattern that Grandmother was spinning with the ease of a spider. "You know," Grandmother said, "those Dillards haven't a chance, not a chance. Their mother has one baby after the other. She doesn't have time or money to take care of the ones she's got and she just keeps having them. How many of them are there now?"

"Eight, I think," Batty said, "counting the one she had last summer."

"That's too many children for any woman to have," Grandmother said, "unless she wants them to grow up like stray cats, which is about what the Dillards are. If I were you, I wouldn't have anything to do with them."

"They're the ones who won't have anything to do with me," Batty said, thinking Grandmother was missing the point.

"I'd make it the other way around," Grandmother said. "They're not going to grow up to be worth the salt in their bread. On the other hand, you're going to grow up to leave Robertson's Fort and go to college and make something of yourself, not just grow up to marry some uneducated man and stay here all your life with a houseful of kids as the Dillards will."

"But how do I get them to leave me alone?" Batty asked.

"Just ignore them," Grandmother said. "Peggy Sue's a good friend, isn't she?"

"Yeah, real good."

"And you stay pretty busy with school and your speech lessons, don't you?"

"Pretty busy, I guess."

"So you don't really need Sulie and her gang very much, do you?"

"I guess not," Batty said dubiously.

"So why don't you just go about your business and ignore them? If they think their picking on you doesn't bother you, they'll stop."

Batty sat and thought about what Grandmother was telling her. She was disappointed. Grandmother wasn't telling her what she wanted to hear. She wanted Grandmother to tell her how she could get even with Sulie and make her stop picking on her that way, and the only thing Grandmother was telling her was to ignore Sulie and pretend not to be hurt. No, not *pretend* not to be hurt. Grandmother was telling her not to *be* hurt.

"You should feel sorry for Sulie," Grandmother said. "And you should feel sorry for Alexandria Pike who doesn't have a mother or a daddy and who has no one to take care of her except her grandmother who's too old to be taking care of anybody. And all the others in that gang . . . they just don't have any backbone, that's all. They just do whatever Sulie wants them to because they haven't got the gumption to decide for themselves what they ought to do."

Grandmother snorted the way she sometimes did when she was feeling very full of gumption herself and laid the bedspread on the sofa beside her. She pushed herself up on the edge of the seat making her back very straight.

"Beatrice Louise," she said, "I'd have too much dignity and pride to be hurt by the likes of them. Now you just hold your head up and go on about your business, and just feel sorry for them, that's all." Grandmother looked at her watch and got up from the sofa. "Come on, Batty," she said, "it's time to feed the chickens. Come help me. You haven't been up to the barnyard in a long time."

In the fall of 1950, soon after Batty's thirteenth birthday, Geraldine began casting her play. *Sun-up* was a folk play about two mountain families who in spite of their ignorance of the reasons for World War I and in spite of their general hostility toward government and the law, became involved and suffered terrible consequences. The hero of the play went off to the war and got killed. When Geraldine first told Batty about the play, she said, "It's a very sad play, I think you'll like it." Batty wondered how Geraldine knew she liked sad things, which she certainly did. She often took down from the bookshelf *The Family Book of Best-Loved Poems* and read her favorites—about the death of a child, or people growing old, or parted lovers.

Batty had grown up a lot during the past year. She was now two inches taller than Mother and at least that much taller than Geraldine, and was beginning to develop a woman's body. When she was twelve she'd worn junior brassieres, not because she had breasts, but because her nipples were just beginning to develop and had poked out and made bumps in all her clothes. She'd thought they looked ridiculous and had worn the little flat bras to keep from being embarrassed. But in just one year her breasts had developed and now she wore regular Maidenform bras like a grown-up woman. Hilda ironed them into sharp little points. Batty loved the way they pushed her sweaters out into little cones.

She no longer went to Grandaddy's barber; Mother took her to Bertie Mercer's Beauty Shop these days. Bertie gave her bangs that came just to her eyebrows. The rest of her hair she cut shoulder length and turned under in a casual pageboy. Batty had just enough natural wave that she never had to set it. In that respect she was pretty lucky. She certainly would hate to have to go to Bertie's every few days and sit there while Bertie put her hair into all those tiny pin curls, and then sit under the dryer for an hour the way Mother did. Her new hairstyle accentuated her slender face with its high cheekbones. Batty felt she might have been very pretty except for her worst flaw, the front teeth that slightly overlapped.

Geraldine believed Batty could easily play the part of the bride of the hero who got killed. She herself was going to play the lead role of the widow who was in a constant battle with the law and who was the hero's mother. She cast the other parts with a strange assortment of people, a few teenagers from Robertson's Fort, the principal from Floral Park High where Geraldine's mother taught history, Earl Oakes—who called the square dances at the teenage club and was one of the town's roughnecks, always red-faced from drinking—and, finally, much to Batty's delight, Geraldine cast Mr. McGinnis in the role of her father. Joel McGinnis was a new eighth-grade teacher, twenty-eight years old, short and sprightly, with light brown hair and a scattering of freckles. Laugh lines around his eyes, and a faint smile that played around his mouth like great good humor barely repressed, gave him a charm that was much appreciated by female students.

The early rehearsals were held in the basement of Geraldine's house, a large finished area divided into rooms and furnished as living quarters. Geraldine chose the largest room for the rehearsals and moved out all of the furniture except the chairs and tables she needed as props. She was on the stage most of the time, acting both her part and coaching everyone else in his. The other actors were on and off, waiting for their cues on the basement steps or upstairs watching the tiny screen of the first television set in town, or disappearing completely to come back later in time for their entrances.

One evening when they'd been in rehearsal for three weeks, Batty and Mr. McGinnis were sitting on the basement steps alone waiting for their cues. Batty was studying her lines, mouthing them with the book turned away and then checking the book to make sure she'd memorized them correctly. Mr. McGinnis was sitting quietly beside her.

"Do you want me to read the cues for you?" he asked.

"Yes, thanks, that would help a lot."

"Where shall I start?"

"Here, please," Batty said, pointing to the line. "I think I know it up to here."

He gave her the cue.

"'Sometimes it just seems I can't stand it,'" she quoted, "'but I kin, cuz other women have stood it and I reckon you ain't no more to me than other women's husbands air to them.'"

"You're supposed to throw your arms around him then," Mr. McGinnis said.

"That's not necessary when I'm just learning the lines."

"But would you mind?" Mr. McGinnis said, sliding toward her

on the step, looking at her out of the corners of his eyes and smiling.

"I don't think this has anything to do with the play," she said.

"No, not much," he said, moving close to her. He took her face between his hands and slowly bent forward and kissed her on the lips. It was a soft gentle kiss. He moved away and looked at her, still holding her face between his hands. She saw the small lines around his blue eyes. She was afraid he could hear her heart pounding. Then he bent to her again, this time kissing her, not gently, but wrapping his arms around her and crushing her to him, enveloping her mouth in a big wet kiss. When he moved away again, she felt weak and quivery.

He slid away from her on the step and looked down at his feet for a long time, saying nothing. In that long silence, Batty felt humiliation ignite and flame upward into her face. Finally he said, still looking at his feet, "How old are you, Batty?"

"Thirteen," she said. Mr. McGinnis just sat there looking down at his feet, and then he began shaking his head slowly from side to side.

From the other room Batty heard Geraldine putting Earl Oakes through the long speech that served as her cue. Geraldine was saying every sentence and making Earl say it after her the way she'd said it. They were coming to the last part of the speech.

"Oh, my gosh," Batty said. "It's almost time for me to go on," and ran down the stairs into the other room to await her cue.

A week after Mr. McGinnis kissed her, Batty was sitting on the steps making sure she knew her lines, and waiting for her cue. Mr. McGinnis was sitting in a straight-backed chair against the wall. He had an artist's pad on his knees and was drawing. He made a few strokes on the paper and then glanced at Batty. He made a few more strokes and glanced at her again.

"You moved," he said.

"Are you drawing me?"

"Uh-huh," he said, cocking his head to one side and looking at the pad with his eyes narrowed.

"Can I see it?"

"When I've finished," he said. "Turn your head a little to the right . . . the way you had it a minute ago."

Batty turned and tried to study her lines without moving. He continued to draw, glancing at her and then looking back at the drawing.

"You're very beautiful, you know," he said, still looking at the drawing.

Batty felt her heart lurch. She'd been hoping all week, ever since he kissed her the first time, that he'd kiss her again. He hadn't made a move since then, hadn't even suggested he remembered it happening.

"Thank you," she said, looking at him now, her script forgotten on her lap.

"It's too bad you're so young," he said. "I'd be robbing the cradle if I were to . . ." He stopped.

"If you were to what?"

"If I were to get serious."

"What do you mean by getting serious?" she asked.

"If I were to care too much . . . or do something I shouldn't. You want to see this?" he said abruptly holding the drawing out to her.

She rose from the steps and walked to where he sat. Over his shoulder she looked at the drawing. It was a picture of a very beautiful girl sitting the way she'd been sitting on the steps. The only thing wrong with it was that it didn't look at all like her. It was so good, though, that it really didn't matter.

"Do you really think that looks like me?" she asked.

He stood up beside her, examining her face and then the drawing. "I think maybe your cheekbones are a little higher," he said, reaching out to touch her face. Then suddenly he put his arms around her and backed her to the wall and pressed his entire body against her. She felt the shape of him fitting into the shape of her. She was beginning to breathe fast again. Then he moved against her, his hips thrusting back and forth. Her excitement turned to fear, and then to disgust. He was moving the way dogs did when sometimes she saw them doing it in the street, one on top of the other pumping away, in and out. Whenever she saw dogs doing it in public, she felt embarrassed and looked away.

"Let me go," she said, "let me *go*."

Mr. McGinnis kept pumping away as though he hadn't heard

her. She twisted her body, trying to keep him from touching her. He rammed his groin into hers, then into her belly, then into her bony hips, it no longer mattered where. He held her pinned to the wall, his head away from hers, his face toward the ceiling, all splotchy and bloated now, his eyes closed as if in a trance.

"Get away," she said as loudly as she dared with the rehearsal going on in the next room. He continued in his trance, humping away. Her arms were pinned to her sides. The only things free were her feet and her legs. She couldn't stand it any longer, this crazed *thing* humping against her and breathing noisily at her. She raised her right knee and kneed him as hard as she could. His eyes popped open and he moved away holding himself between the legs with both hands. He was bent over now and backing up. She ran around him and up the stairs and into the living room where the other actors were intently watching the figures on the tiny television screen.

"Where've you been?" Earl Oakes asked, as she smoothed her skirt and sat down on the sofa.

"Downstairs, learning my lines," Batty said.

He glanced at her quickly and turned away as though he suspected she hadn't been doing that at all.

They gave two performances of the play, one at Floral Park High and one a week later at Robertson's Fort High. It was a big hit. People were amazed to see such convincing sets and costumes and such skillful performances by ordinary townspeople. Batty loved every minute of it. On the evening of the final performance, when the curtain closed and then opened again for the curtain call Geraldine had taught them, Duane Marley—who was an usher—brought a large bouquet of roses onstage and presented them to Geraldine. Everybody clapped very loudly as Geraldine accepted them and then with the roses cascading over her arm took the hem of her skirt and slowly bowed from the waist. The applause continued. Geraldine swept onto the apron of the stage and this time took a slower and even more graceful bow, holding it while everybody clapped. Then she swept back to center stage and held her arms out toward the rest of the cast who'd been standing in a line behind her. They joined hands with Geraldine and everybody bowed. Then Geraldine stepped forward and the curtain closed on her standing in the center of the stage in one long, graceful, sweeping bow.

That evening Batty decided that when she grew up she was going to be a great actress like Geraldine.

Crestview Baptist Assembly was six miles from Robertson's Fort at the top of the mountain beside the highway to Asheville. In the summer, Southern Baptists came from all over the South to spend a week going to classes and inspirational meetings, and to hear—in the evening—the big gun who'd been brought in from one or another of the important Baptist churches. College students were hired to do the menial work: they were the waitresses, the chambermaids, the dishwashers, the office managers; they scooped ice cream in the ice-cream store, lifeguarded at the lake, gave tennis lessons at the courts. They worked long hours every day, all for four dollars and the privilege of being in this inspirational place all summer, doing God's work in the company of thousands of other Christians who were also Baptists.

All her life Batty had seen the assembly grounds every time she'd gone to Asheville. It was an impressive place with its large colonnaded buildings and acres of cabins sitting back in the trees away from the road. Sybil Swann, who was Reverend Swann's younger sister, had spent the previous summer working on the staff at Crestview and had talked one sunday evening at Training Union about her experiences there. She talked a lot about dedicating her life to Christ, quoted scripture with great frequency, and attended church three times a week—not because she had to, but by choice. Batty thought she was one of those pale, placid people who gave religion a bad name.

Nevertheless, the idea of spending next summer in the presence of college students from all over the South was very attractive. The confines of Robertson's Fort were beginning to look very narrow. Batty certainly didn't want to work in Daddy's store all summer long; it was okay to work there on Saturdays, but it would be very boring to be there every day of the week. Most of the people on the Crestview staff were college students, but even though Batty was only thirteen, she thought maybe she could talk the manager of Crestview into hiring her.

One Saturday in April, Grandaddy drove her up the mountain to her appointment with Mr. Parks. Grandaddy pulled into the circular drive and parked in front of the large white administration building. In the summertime there would be vast numbers of people strolling across the expanses of green, walking along the many paths, rocking in the chairs and swinging in the swings on the front porches of the buildings, but today Crestview was deserted. She left Grandaddy on the front porch sitting in a rocking chair with the Asheville *Citizen-Times* spread out before him and opened the white door and went into a room that looked like a comfortable hotel lobby. The floor was covered with a thick mint-green carpet, and white wicker chairs with cushions of green and yellow print were arranged casually in conversational groupings. In the middle of the room was a large rectangular table covered with magazines. Batty glanced at them: *Sunday School Quarterly, The Christian Family, Southern Baptist Convention Report,* obviously all religious or church publications. In the center of the table was a vase filled with dogwood cuttings.

A large white staircase led to the second floor from which Batty heard activity. She climbed the staircase and came out into a narrow, dimly lit hall. A small woman wearing a black skirt, and a man-tailored blouse, her dark hair in a large bun at the nape of her neck, walked briskly down the hall toward her, carrying a piece of stationery by its corner. It crackled as she moved.

"Can you please tell me where I can find Mr. Parks?" Batty asked.

"Yes, certainly," the woman said, turning. "Just at the end of the hall, take a left and his office is the first on the right."

"Thanks a lot."

The door was open. Batty could see that beyond the first small office was a larger office. She could see a wall lined with books and in front of it a dark brown sofa.

"Hello," she called.

Mr. Parks appeared in the doorway. He was a large man in a gray suit. The back of his head was ringed with gray hair, the top bald and shiny. Behind his glasses his eyes crinkled with good humor.

Just seeing his gentle expression put Batty at ease. When he spoke, his voice was low and soft.

"Hello," he said. "You must be Batty Attwood. You're right on time, come in."

"Thank you, sir," Batty said, and followed him into the office.

"Please sit where you like," Mr. Parks said, lowering himself into the swivel chair behind his desk.

"Thank you.

"Mr. Parks, as I mentioned on the phone, I want to work on the staff here next summer. I've heard all about it from Sybil Swann who worked here last summer. Reverend Swann, the minister at our church, said he'd give me a recommendation if you want it."

Mr. Parks listened to Batty, smiling faintly and nodding occasionally. "Are you a Christian?" he asked.

"Yes, sir."

"And are you a member of the Baptist church?"

"Yes, sir."

"How old are you, Batty?"

"I'm thirteen."

"You're pretty young. You sure you wouldn't be homesick?"

"I'm sure," Batty said, "I wouldn't be far enough from home to get homesick."

He looked at her appraisingly for a moment. Then he said, "It's hard work, you know. The young people who come here to work in the summer are the ones who keep this place going. It's not easy—close to eight hours a day of hard work."

"Yes, sir, I know that," Batty said. "I don't mind working. I've always had to work at my daddy's store on Saturdays. I'm a good worker."

"And it's six days a week all summer long."

"Yes, sir, I know."

"Okay, Batty," he said, "here's an application form. Take it home, fill it out, and send it back to me right away. As soon as I get the form and make a call or two, I'll send you a card telling you what I've decided, okay?"

"Yes, sir, thank you," Batty said. "I'll get it in the mail tomorrow." She rose from her seat. Mr. Parks walked from behind his desk and shook her hand.

"Do you think you'll know by next week?" she asked.

Mr. Parks smiled. "I would guess so, Batty. I don't think you have anything to worry about," he said smiling more broadly now.

"Oh, I hope not," Batty said excitedly. "Thank you again, thanks a lot," and ran out of the office and down the stairs and out onto the porch where Grandaddy sat asleep in the sun, his head resting on the back of the chair, his newspaper scattered on the porch around him.

When Batty got home from school Thursday, there was a card from Mr. Parks:

Dear Batty:

It gives me the greatest pleasure to invite you to be among the very special Christian young people who will be working on the staff of Crestview Baptist Assembly for the summer of 1951. Mrs. Parks and I are looking forward to seeing you then and getting to know you better.

Yours in Christ,

DADDY PARKS

In mid-June she moved with fifty other girls into the roughly constructed building that was the dormitory. She was in one of the top bunks in the small cubicle that served as a room for four. Trudy Wall from Julian Marston, a Baptist college in Tennessee, was in the bunk under her. Trudy was a short, fat, and totally shapeless girl who—except for the texture of her skin—looked every bit of fifty. She could have been a German *Frau* hanging her ticking out the windows rather than an eighteen-year-old college girl.

"Get your feet out of my face," she said to Batty the first morning as they were waking up after reveille. Batty was sitting on the top bunk stretching her arms and legs, trying to wake up enough to climb down to the floor. "If there's anything I hate, it's having somebody's feet in my face."

"Sorry, Trudy," Batty said, hanging her feet off the end of the bunk and out of Trudy's face.

"Well, get up, lazybones, you've got to have your station all set up when they open the doors to the dining room and all those hordes come piling in."

Batty couldn't figure Trudy out. She sounded gruff and grumpy as an old witch, but occasionally Batty caught the flicker of a smile that graced the corners of her mouth. Was she teasing her? She crawled down and collected her toothbrush, soap, towel, and washcloth and went to shower.

Thirty minutes later, she came out of the dormitory wearing her green cotton uniform. Everywhere she looked there were green uniforms rushing toward early-morning duties. The boys wore green jackets of the same fabric as the girls' dresses.

"Hi," said a pretty blonde, her hair in pigtails. "I'm Susan Murray."

"Hi, I'm Batty Attwood."

"Nice to meet you, Batty," Susan said. "That's an unusual name. I don't think I've ever heard it before. It it a nickname for something?"

"Yeah," Batty said. "My real name is Beatrice Louise, but everybody calls me Batty. That's a nickname for Beatrice like Bea, except that my great-grandmother was named Beatrice and called Batty. That's how I got it, I guess."

"It's a nice name. I like it," Susan said. "Where're you from?"

"Not far from here. Robertson's Fort."

"Oh," Susan said, laughting pleasantly. "You mean just down the mountain?"

Batty nodded. "Just down the mountain," she said. "Where're you from?"

"Macon, Georgia."

"Where do you go to school?"

"Stetson. How about you?"

"I start high school at Robertson's Fort next year."

"You look older than that," Susan said. "How old are you?"

"I'm thirteen, almost fourteen, really. I'll be fourteen in September. Everybody tells me I look *mature* for my age," Batty said with mock exaggeration.

"You do," Susan said seriously. "You really do."

"Have you worked here before?"

"Yeah, this is my third summer."

"Well, come on," Batty said, "let's get started setting up. Show me what to do."

At exactly eight o'clock, the doors opened and one thousand Southern Baptists, carrying their Bibles and study books, spilled into the huge dining room. Batty carried out platters of scrambled eggs, baskets of toast, platters of bacon. She filled all the cups with coffee and went back for refills.

After breakfast, the busboy cleared off the dishes and she and Susan wiped off the tables, filled the salt and pepper shakers, and stacked the napkins in sufficient numbers for the next feeding of the hordes. Then they were free to go until eleven forty-five when they had to be back to serve lunch.

When Batty got back to the dormitory, Trudy was sitting on her bunk writing a letter.

"I thought you said it took you all morning to make up the rooms," Batty said.

"I'm not finished yet. Laundry was short of towels this morning. I have to go back in a minute. I just wanted to get this letter off in the meantime. No sense standing around wasting time."

"Who're you writing?"

"None of your business. Boy, I can't stand nosy people. You going to hear Gordon Powell's lecture this morning?"

"Who's Gordon Powell?"

"Who's Gordon Powell! Where've *you* been! Gordon Powell is the president of the Southern Baptist Convention from Nashville, Tennessee!"

"What's he going to be lecturing about?"

"The Southern Baptist Convention, I would guess," Trudy said dryly. "I think you ought to go. I'll bet you don't know *anything* about the Southern Baptist Convention."

"It sounds awfully boring," Batty said. "I've got an hour and a half before I have to go back to work. I think I'll walk over to the lake and go swimming."

"Okay, if that's the way you want to spend your time here at Crestview, swimming at the lake and missing all the opportunities to hear the wonderful men of God who'll be here this summer."

"I'd rather go swimming," Batty said.

But Batty wasn't able to continue her secular ways unaffected by the great spiritual atmosphere that pervaded Crestview. After a few days, she found that the most exciting event of the day was the service held in the large assembly hall each evening. She would rush back to the dorm after dinner to shower and change into a cotton dress, pull her hair into a ponytail and go to hear the preacher imported for the week. Sometimes she went with Trudy, sometimes she went with Susan, and sometimes she went with one of the busboys, who wanted to go to the prayer garden afterward to hold hands and pray silently together before walking her back to the dormitory. The prayer garden was a wooded plot with a small stream running through the middle of it. It had benches placed randomly, secluded from each other by gnarled trunks of rhododendron and laurel. Lights were soft and offered barely sufficient illumination to read the Bible. There were always a few people sitting in the shadows, heads bowed to their chests, praying or meditating, and a few people reading scripture to themselves.

After Batty had been at Crestview a few weeks, time began to drag. The work seemed harder and harder. It seemed she'd hardly be finished cleaning up from one meal till she would have to start setting up for the next one. She'd have loved to go home, but two things made that impossible. First, Mr. Parks had let her work on the staff even though she was only thirteen. She certainly couldn't let him think she wasn't mature enough to last the summer. Lots of kids had got tired and gone home early, but they were older and had nothing to prove. Second, she was looking forward to the grand finale when Stewart Simpson from Dallas would come to conduct the services for the last week of the session.

She had heard all about him. Susan had told her that last summer when he was conducting the evening services there were five hundred conversions to Christ in one week. She said he could have converted Attila the Hun. He was a fine preacher, a real man of God. Batty loved to sing those roaring Baptist hymns. She felt herself rise right out of her seat when twenty-six hundred voices were raised in the singing of "Love Lifted Me."

So she waited and worked through that long last month of summer. One evening when she was walking with Susan to the auditorium she was wearing her favorite dress, a paisley-print cotton, lined in crimson and gathered at the waist by a wide fabric belt that tied on the side. It had an elasticized top worn off the shoulder Spanish style. She felt very pretty.

As she and Susan were cutting across the grass, two ministerial students approached her.

"It's a disgrace for you to be exposing yourself like that in this place," one of them said. He was a tall skinny blond with acne scars.

Batty just looked at him. Susan giggled nervously.

"You are a temptation of the flesh in that dress. You are the instrument of the devil. Men come to Crestview as a religious retreat, not to be tempted by girls who indecently expose themselves."

Batty felt herself turn red with embarrassment, and began giggling nervously. She looked down at her pink Capezios against the grass. The other ministerial student looked on saying nothing.

"Now go change that dress," the tall skinny blond said and stepped to the side and briskly walked on past her. Batty turned to watch them cross the lawn.

"Gosh! He sure is narrow-minded," she said. "This is my favorite dress. Mother thinks this dress is all right for me to wear." Then slowly she began to get angry. "The work of the devil! The work of the devil! *My* dress, the work of the devil! I will *not* change it."

"They're ministerial students," Susan said. "Ministerial students are usually very strict."

"Let them be strict if they want to be," Batty said, "but they've got no right to tell me what to wear. It's none of their business."

She didn't change the dress that evening, but she felt uncomfortable wearing it and wondered how many other people in that mammoth hall thought her dress was the work of the devil. She didn't wear it again that summer.

Finally, the second week in August arrived and with it the great Stewart Simpson. Batty went every night to hear him. He was a man of average height, but of something more than average girth. Obviously he'd been fed well by all those Baptists in Dallas. He stood behind the pulpit gripping the sides with his fists and raised his voice so that it reverberated through the balconies to the highest beam of the ceiling. Then he lowered it, speaking softly but spitting the words out forcefully so even his whispers were clear and sharp in the last row. He whispered this way for a while talking about the love of Christ, the *mercy* of Christ, and then when he had the congregation crying about the marvel of Christ's love he surprised them by booming out unexpectedly about the magnitude of their sins. Sitting through one of Stewart Simpson's sermons was a bit like being alternated between the rack and a cold bath. While he was preaching, perspiration ran down his face in rivulets he kept wiping away intermittently with the handkerchief he had lying on the pulpit. He ran his hand back through his hair as though he were trying to dry *that*, too.

Then suddenly he was finished.

He spread his arms wide to welcome all those to whom Christ had been speaking in a small voice, all who had been resisting till now, beseeching them to listen to that voice and come forward, to let Christ change their lives, take from them their burdens, give meaning where there had been only meaninglessness.

Every night, streams of people poured from the balconies, and from the front and back of the auditorium. They streamed by Stewart Simpson, standing in front of the pulpit. The organ played and the choir sang, "'Just as I am without one plea, but that thy blood was shed for me, and that thou bidst me come to thee, O lamb of God, I come, I come.'"

On the last night, Batty went to the service with Trudy. They sat in the front row of the balcony where they could see perfectly everything that was going on. Stewart Simpson opened the service with everybody joining in the singing of "He Leadeth Me." When everybody sat down he laid his handkerchief in its usual place before him and, gripping the edges of the pulpit, looked out at the congregation. There was absolute silence. He continued to look at them without saying a word. Then, suddenly, he lifted a finger and pointed straight to the middle of the auditorium.

"America," he boomed, "you have rejected God!" He was silent. His finger continued to point accusingly. "You have rejected God in your businesses." Pause. "You have rejected God in your schools." Pause. "You have rejected God in the arts." Pause. "You have rejected God in your leisure." Pause. His voice fell in a tone of finality. "And you have rejected God in your personal lives." With that all stated, he shifted his weight and took his handkerchief and dabbed his upper lip.

Then he enumerated all the specifics of how America—and specifically those in the congregation—had rejected God. As he boomed God's disappointment and condemnation, Batty could hear her heart beating. Her breath was coming almost in short gasps now. He spoke for forty minutes, accusing and exhorting. Then his voice softened to soothing tones as once again he offered the opportunity to make amends with God. His eyes looked upward toward the world he envisioned: God accepted in the businesses, the schools, the homes, the lives of the American people. Batty lifted her eyes and looked with Stewart Simpson into that vision, a land of people loving each other and putting God first. Stewart Simpson lifted his arms as the choir began singing softly, "'Just as I am . . .'"

She couldn't sit still any longer. She stood up and walked to the steps, down the steps to the aisle, and down the aisle to join the line already forming, people coming to the front of the auditorium to give their lives to Christ. By the time she got to Stewart Simpson, tears were running down her face. Two girls who had been ahead of her were crying aloud. The front rows, reserved for converts, were filling up, women weeping, men dabbing at the corners of their eyes with white handkerchiefs, some looking transfixed, the line of people now reaching the back door and wrapping around the outside walls, and growing longer as people continued to get up from their seats to join this great army of converts for Christ. Batty had never been more excited. She wanted to give her life to Christ, she wanted to be a missionary and go into darkest Africa carrying the message of Christ, she wanted to help transform the world into a better place, she wanted her sins forgiven, she wanted never to lose this sense of closeness to God, the freedom from the trivial bought at the price of involvement with the Divine, she wanted to stand before thousands of people as Stewart Simpson from Dallas had done and bring them to Christ in tears and on their knees.

She held out her hand to Stewart Simpson. She could hardly see him for the tears that kept filling her eyes as fast as they fell. He took her hand between his two hands and gave her a beneficent look.

"I want to dedicate my life to Christ," Batty said.

"God bless you," Stewart Simpson said.

When Batty got home at the end of the summer, Reverend Swann, who knew about her having dedicated her life to Christ, asked her occasionally to lead the congregation in prayer. She learned to speak to God in "thees" and "thous," to make public her private prayerful conversations, and to lift the subjects of her prayers from personal matters to those that concerned broad segments of mankind. Sometimes she was asked to prepare a Sunday-evening devotional service. From the books on Mother's bookshelves or those in the church library, she found a reading or a poem. She looked through the Broadman Hymnal to find a hymn on the same theme. She'd give her reading, speak a few minutes on the theme, lead the congregation in prayer and close with everybody singing the hymn.

But after carrying on God's work in that manner for several weeks, Batty decided that what she was doing simply wasn't good enough. When she dedicated her life to Christ at Crestview, she'd made a commitment to save the souls of heathens. To do that, she thought, she'd have to be a missionary and go into darkest Africa. It was a little difficult saving souls of heathens here in Robertson's Fort where the only heathens were people a girl couldn't even talk to—the roughnecks who drank whiskey and did God only knew what other terrible things.

She decided the thing she could do that was nearest to going to darkest Africa was to bring the message of Christ to Baptist Side, where, if the colored people weren't exactly heathens, they were at least black. She talked it over with Hilda, never suggesting to Hilda that she thought the colored people in Baptist Side were heathens. She wouldn't think of suggesting that, with Hilda being so close to God and knowing more of the Bible than Batty would know for years if she started studying it regularly that day. Batty figured that most of the colored people on Baptist Side weren't like Hilda. She asked Hilda if she thought the people in the colored church would let her conduct a Sunday-evening devotion for them.

"Of course, Batty," she said. "They'd love to have you come and lead a devotional. I know they would. I'll talk to Reverend Lewis this Sunday."

Hilda set it up and Batty began making her plans. She talked to Reverend Swann of the white church and he thought her plan a good one. He suggested that the three young women of the choir who sang as a trio go along to conclude her service.

On the Sunday evening of her missionary journey to Baptist Side Batty was well prepared. She and the trio—June Hendricks and the Matthews twins—met at the Baptist church and from there June drove them through East Fort toward the colored church. Just beyond East Fort, the pavement ended and they drove the rest of the way on a rutted dirt road. When they got to the church, there were only two vehicles in the parking lot, a shiny black pickup truck and an old blue Ford with a fender smashed and rusting. June pulled into the red clay lot, the car bouncing over the gullies, and parked close to the building. The twins, in their early twenties, looked beautiful with their blond curly hair framing their pale faces like halos. They were wearing dark green jumpers and white blouses with ruffles circling the neck. June, the same age as the twins, was long and gangling with a thin face and mousy hair that she'd pulled back with a rubber band. She was wearing a pink cotton dress that fit snugly at the waist and flared at the bottom. Beside the twins she looked homely.

When they came in, Hilda and Reverend Lewis were at the front door waiting for them. Hilda was dressed in a black dress with a round neckline trimmed with black lace. She looked very stiff and straight in it, as though she were wearing one of Grandmother's corsets. Her hair stood in stiff black curls all over her head. She was wearing a deep rose-colored lipstick, and she smelled of the lilac talcum powder Batty sold at Daddy's store. Batty had never seen Hilda look so pretty. Hilda smiled broadly at her.

"Good evening," Reverend Lewis said, bowing slightly from the waist. "We're mighty glad to have you this evening, mighty glad."

"Come this way," Hilda said, still smiling broadly.

The twins went first, followed by Batty and then June. Hilda led them to the front row right of the pulpit. Batty let June sit next to the twins and she sat on the end of the bench next to the center aisle. Bertha Lewis, the minister's wife, sat down at the black upright piano to the left of the pulpit and began playing by ear. Batty recognized the melody; they sang "Standing on the Promises" at her own church. She took a few deep breaths to relax and looked around as far as she could see without craning her neck and being obvious. In spite of the familiarity of the hymn, she felt very much out of place at Hilda's church.

The room smelled strange. It was not a smell of uncleanliness, the church was very clean, the walls freshly painted, the plain wooden floors swept, the wooden straight-backed benches dusted. But it was a definite smell that was different from the smell of her own church. She searched to find the strangeness she sensed. The church was plainer than her own, no stained-glass windows, ten plain wooden straight-backed chairs for the choir sharing the platform with the pulpit instead of the rows of folding seats attached to the floor like those in her own church. The only adornment she saw was a small print of Christ in Gethsemane in a wooden frame that was almost lost hanging on the side wall. There was no painted lake scene on the back wall of the baptistry, just an arched cutout in the wall behind which she knew would be a tin-lined basin to be filled with water for baptismal services when those who were born again were immersed by the preacher to have their sins washed away as Christ had washed away the sins of his disciples in the River Jordan. Those differences didn't account for the feeling that she was out of place, that she didn't belong here, that she was somehow an alien.

Bertha continued to play. Now she was playing "Nearer My God to Thee." She played it loud and fast, her right hand not quite in synch with her left, half a beat away, giving her playing a sort of cut time. Reverend Lewis came to the front of the church and stood behind the pulpit. He was wearing a chocolate-brown suit almost the color of his skin, a white shirt and a mustard tie. His black kinky hair, mixed with gray, was cropped close to his head. Lights hanging from the ceiling on either side of the pulpit shone down on his face, making his forehead and cheekbones glisten.

"Let's open our hymnals to page two-oh-six and sing together 'Shall We Gather at the River,' " he said. The twins shared a book. Batty could see their red nail polish on the white page. June had found her place and was resting her hymnal on the back of the bench in front of them. Bertha played the opening bars and then the singing began. Batty began singing softly. She couldn't hear the trio beside her at all, only the strong force of the colored people singing, a body of sound that welled up from an undertone into a cadence they knew and she didn't. It burst and fragmented into fireworks of sound, falling out, parts sung on one side of the congregation and echoed on the other, a lone voice carrying the melody against the background of chanting, then dropping it to be picked up by another voice, nobody waiting to be called upon to sing, just singing when his time came, knowing the time had come, and taking over. She heard Ida Bell's beautiful voice loud and clear. It rang through the room and out the windows. Batty knew it could be heard all over Baptist Side. The others let her carry it. Her voice moved off to someplace Batty had never been. She turned to see Ida's shoulders hunched and her eyes closed as though she were in a trance. Then her voice began to work its way back, coming in now, back to the hymn and the room, she rode the melody easily like a track till she came to rest in the final lines. Then Tom Jameson, Hilda's husband, echoed the last phrase in a soft low bass and the congregation brought it all back together with an "Amen" at the end. When they finished singing, there was a rustle of hymnbooks closing. Batty put hers in the rack on the back of the pew in front of her.

"Tonight we are happy to have with us visitors from the white community to lead us in a devotional. Miss Batty Attwood will share the devotional to be followed by Miss Sharon Matthews, Miss Karen Matthews, and Miss June Hendricks who will sing for us." Reverend Lewis smiled beneficently and nodded toward Batty. Then he stepped down from the platform and sat in the front row across the room from Batty. Batty stood up and opened *Christ and the Fine Arts,* flipping to the reading she'd selected. She'd read it over so many times in preparation that she hardly needed the book at all. It was about an imagined hall of heroes, of various sorts, concluding with the greatest heroes, the heroes of love, with Christ in the center of the hall as the greatest hero of all. She cleared her throat and looked around the room. Hilda sat in the third row, her big chest held high, looking proud and possessive of Batty. Tom, her husband, sat beside her, wearing a pin-striped suit that Batty recognized as being one of Daddy's old suits. He looked very small beside Hilda, all folded in on himself, not even looking at Batty but looking down at something. Next to Tom was Gussy, Hilda's daughter who was married to the alcoholic who couldn't keep a job, and next to her was Florine, Hilda's granddaughter. Florine was about Batty's age and looked very pretty in a pink cotton dress with little puffed sleeves and a big pink ribbon around her head. In the middle of the congregation she saw Hattie Norris, her black face lifted toward Batty expectantly. She knew Hattie from Daddy's store, a wizened little woman with a deep voice like a man's. She talked a lot and could be heard all over the store and was always in good humor. Myrtle Brown who'd worked for Mother for a while was sitting on the left. In the back row, she saw John Souther, the cook at the Steak House where Daddy took them for dinner almost every Sunday. John was an excellent cook. He made delicious dinner rolls and fruit cobblers. People came from all over the county to eat his Sunday dinners. He and his wife were very light-skinned, and lived almost like white people. Their house was a neat little brick structure with a green lawn and lots of flowers. You wouldn't know from looking at it that it belonged to colored people, except that it was on the edge of Baptist Side.

Batty glanced at the book and began reading slowly, looking at the brown faces with their polite smiles. She paused at dramatic points to let what she had read soak in. She got louder on the parts she thought were most important. The faces continued to look at her with those same polite smiles. She brought the reading to a finish and closed the book and laid it on the bench in front of her. Then she began the little speech she'd prepared about the love of Christ who'd died on the cross and the responsibility of people to accept that love and respond to it by giving their lives to Christ in return. There was a little shifting in the seats as the wooden benches became uncomfortable. Hilda didn't stir. She continued to give Batty her undivided attention. When Batty had finished her talk, she said, "Let us pray." She bowed her head and closed her eyes and waited a minute till everybody got in a praying mood. Then she thanked God for having sent his only son, she beseeched God to make her and the others present worthy of that gift, and finally she asked God to help them all be good Christians and resist daily temptations. When she finished, she sat down and the trio got up to sing. Karen stood in the middle. She was slightly prettier than

Sharon though they were both very pretty. She opened her mouth into a perfect circle and made the first sound. Then Sharon and June joined in. They sang in perfect harmony, but Batty felt it was a bit lifeless after the singing she'd heard earlier. They finished and sat down, and Reverend Lewis went back to the pulpit again. He thanked Batty and the trio for coming to lead a service for them, and then he made several announcements—about meetings during the week, about somebody who was sick and in the hospital. When he finished, the congregation sang another hymn, and Reverend Lewis prayed one last time and the service was over.

"That was very nice," Hilda said, coming up to Batty. "You read real good, honey."

"Thanks, Hilda," Batty said. "Do you think it did any good? I mean do you think people got the message?"

"Of course it did good," Hilda said. "It always does good for people to think about God."

She and Hilda were walking toward the door. At the end of one of the pews, Hattie was waiting for them. Her shriveled face was turned up, beaming at Batty.

"Well, honey, that sure was a nice service," she said. "You'll have to come back and lead another one for us."

"Thanks, Hattie, maybe I'll do that sometime."

"That was very nice, Miss Attwood, very nice," Reverend Lewis said as she and Hilda got to the back door.

"It sure was, wasn't it?" Hilda said, nodding at Reverend Lewis. "How do you like my girl, Reverend?"

"She's a good Christian girl," Reverend Lewis said, nodding. "Yes, a good Christian girl."

When she'd said good-bye to Hilda, Batty and the trio got into June's car. June started the engine and began backing out over the ruts.

"I thought it went well," Karen said. "Batty, I liked that reading you chose a lot."

"Thanks," Batty said.

"And you read it so well," Sharon said.

"You sure did," June said.

"You all sang beautifully, of course. Just as always," Batty said.

"It smelled funny in there, didn't it?" Karen said.

"It just smelled like colored people, that's all," Batty said.

"Have you ever been in a colored person's house?" June asked.

"Uh-uh, have you?" the twins said, almost in unison.

"I have," Batty said. "Lots of times."

"I never have," June said.

"You know what?" Batty said slowly.

They turned to her.

"No, what?" Karen said.

"I don't think they needed us."

"What do you mean?" June said.

"I don't think they needed us to come hold a service for them."

June pulled up in front of the Baptist church. The evening worship service was just letting out. At the top of the steps Ken Larson was opening the doors and putting stops under them.

"I think you have to really leave home to be a missionary," Batty said. "When you're in Robertson's Fort, you should mind your own business. That's what I think."

At the top of the steps Reverend Swann was shaking hands with the people coming out of the church, the men in their suits and ties, the women in their Sunday dresses. The twins and June were on the church steps now, greeting friends. Batty didn't feel like talking to anybody. She turned her back to the people and started walking home.

Hilda knew all the time, Batty thought. She knew all the time that the colored people on Baptist Side didn't need a missionary—but she let me come hold a service for her church anyway. Batty walked on, thinking about it.

That was really very nice of her, she thought.

The Teenage Club met every Thursday evening in the community building down next to Mill Creek where the old fort had been. The building had been on that spot as long as anyone could remember. It was built of the yellow rocks that came from the river and looked as though it had been put there by some natural phenomenon as an extension of all those rocks lining the creek. A wide porch stretched across the entire facade. Between the porch and the creek was an outdoor cooking area with fireplaces and grills and a circular counter—all this under a round peaked roof. Batty remembered picnics there with fires blazing and hamburgers cooking. But that had been some time ago. These days the community building wasn't used for much of anything except the Teenage Club dances. It was in a state of some disrepair, having no hot water and two johns that were stopped up half the time.

But on Thursday evenings the old building came alive. The piano player was a man in his twenties named Perry Stevens. Nobody had much respect for him because he came from a family of people who drank whiskey. The old piano he played was an upright that had been modified by having thumbtacks put into its hammers so it made a plinky sound. Perry had a natural gift; never having taken piano lessons in his life, he could play that old piano so that it made the building bounce. When Perry Stevens played the piano, it was almost impossible not to dance. Earl Oakes, who'd been in Geraldine's play with Batty, called the dances.

All the teenagers in town came to the dances. In fact, the dances on Thursday nights were so successful that word of them got all the way to Cullman, twelve miles away. Cullman had a population of about twelve thousand people, which was about eleven thousand five hundred more than the population of Robertson's Fort. Cullman considered itself a metropolis compared to the backwoods of Robertson's Fort. It even had a residential section named Nob Hill where all the rich people lived. Some of them had second homes on Lake Susquot ten miles from town on a back road that wound up the mountain to the Blue Ridge Parkway.

Batty was at the Teenage Club one Thursday evening in September just three days after her fourteenth birthday when what looked like half the boys in Cullman visited. The dance was just getting warmed up. Batty was dancing with Paul Marley, one of the basketball players. Peggy Sue was dancing with Matty Grimes who of course was clicking his taps more loudly than anybody, coming down on the heels and toes at every beat with intense concentration and a forcefulness reserved for big fat loudmouths. Peggy Sue was discreetly making faces at Batty every time they crossed over to let her know she didn't like dancing with Matty.

The foreign contingent came in the door and formed a line against the wall; with their hands clasped behind their backs, they stood watching. Batty counted eight of them.

She knew they were from Cullman because three of them were members of the Cullman basketball team that had defeated Robertson's Fort when they played them earlier in the year. The tall blond one walked over to the tub of ice and sodas and bought a Coke from Susannah Pearson who had the drink concession. The others followed. Then they went back to form the line around the wall again and stood watching and drinking their Cokes. Batty tried to decide which one she wanted to ask her to dance, the tall blond one, or the dark one with the baby face. The one she hoped would not ask her to dance was the short heavy one with the limp. She concentrated on her dancing. Maybe they were watching her, maybe the tall handsome blond would ask her to dance. She thought he was watching her. If she danced well maybe he would think she was pretty. Boys from Cullman, she'd heard, were not at all bashful. The dance ended. She went over to the windowsill and took a nickel from her wallet. Then she went to the bucket and took out a Pepsi. Susannah shook off the dripping water and opened the bottle with the church key. Then she handed it to Batty.

"Who are those boys?" she asked.

"They're from Cullman," Sulie said from behind her. Sulie was unpredictable. Sometimes she could make Batty's life miserable, and other times—like right now—she would talk to Batty as though she were just any other person. Batty didn't understand it at all but she appreciated whatever kindness she got from Sulie.

"That cute blond one is Tommy Wilson," Sulie said. "His father owns the Wilson Insurance Agency in Cullman. He has lots of money. The tall athletic-looking one is the star of the Cullman basketball team. His name is Steve Walker. His daddy is the Presbyterian preacher in Cullman. That short stocky one, the one in the blue pants with the nice teeth, is Vance Hollifield. His father is a judge in the state supreme court. I don't know who the others are."

"Who's that tall dark-haired one with the round babyish face?" Batty asked.

"I don't know," Sulie said. "Why don't you ask him?"

"Why don't *you* ask him?"

"Maybe I will," Sulie said and walked off toward Alexandria Pike who was already talking to several of the Cullman boys.

"Want to dance the next one with me?" someone at Batty's elbow said. It was the tall baby-faced one. He stood there in his white pants and white bucks and navy blazer, looking almost handsome.

"Yes, thank you," she said. "Is it about to start again?"

"The piano player is back at the piano. It looks as though he's about to begin. I'm Gus Oliver," he said, extending his hand.

Batty was caught by surprise. She wasn't used to manners from boys. The boys in Robertson's Fort would never introduce themselves and offer to shake hands. She thrust her hand out a little too quickly.

"I'm Batty Attwood," she said. "It's nice to meet you."

"Do you come to these dances every Thursday?" Gus said.

"Most of the time," Batty said. "I love to square dance."

The couples were beginning to file out onto the floor. Perry was playing the piano softly till everybody was ready to dance.

"We'd better get into place," Batty said, extending her hand, and suddenly the piano cut loose.

"*O-kay,*" Earl Oakes chanted, "take *your partner and a-way we go.*"

The taps began to click in rhythm.

"*Join hands and cir-cle to the right.*"

The taps picked up the beat of Perry's piano.

"*And now to the left.*"

The circle reversed, the beat growing louder.

"*Break into fours and join hands.*
Bird-y in the cage. Now cir-cle to the left,
and cir-cle to the right.
Bird-y out and old crow in."

Gus stood in the circle, smiling sheepishly and looking silly with nothing to do.

"*Put your arm a-round that lit-tle la-dy*
and prom-en-ade to the left."

"Can I take you home when this is over?" Gus shouted over the noise.

"I guess so," Batty shouted back. "You mean walking?"

"No, I've got my daddy's car."

"What about everybody else who came with you? You didn't get them all in one car, did you?"

"No, Steven has a car, too."

"We'll have to walk," Batty said. "I'm not allowed to ride in cars with people Daddy doesn't know."

"Now la-dies in the mid-dle. Join hands.
Lad-ies to the left. Gents to the right.
Re-turn to your part-ner and put your right
arm o-ver her left shoulder.
Now cir-cle to the left. . . ."

"That's silly, Batty, having to walk when I've got a car. I'll look like a fool," Gus shouted.

"And cir-cle to the right."

"I can't help it, Gus. Daddy's very strict."

"O-kay now, let's wind that clock."

Clarence Stuart on Batty's right dropped her hand and started the spiral with her and Gus in the center. The beat of the piano was faster, the taps were clicking in perfect rhythm, the circle tightening. Batty could hear nothing but the piano and the taps clicking, faster now, the circle winding tighter, she in the center, Gus being wrapped in with her, their bodies pressed together by Mamie Dillard and Carl Burnside who were now part of the knot around them, the bodies of Lula Ann Dillard and Vance Hollifield squeezing them tighter. Clarence Stuart and Sulie now in the knot and the knot growing tighter, Batty knowing that when this was over, her yellow dotted swiss was going to look like a cleaning rag. Then the last of the rope making the final turn. Perry banging out the final refrain, then ending it with a long arpeggio up the piano keys. Then down the piano keys. Then the right hand going up, and the left hand down. Plonk! The last note. Laughter and squealing. The dancers fell away.

"If we've got to walk," Gus said, "we'd better get started."

"Yeah," Batty said.

She took her sweater from one of the straight-backed chairs that lined the outside walls. Gus spoke quietly to a boy named Mark Padgett, and then he and Batty headed toward the door. Mark Padgett called over the din, "Hey, Gus, don't do anything I wouldn't do, you hear now?" The Cullman contingent laughed. Batty felt the blood rise hot to her face.

"Don't worry," Gus called back, grinning a silly boy grin. Then he looked serious. "I'll be right back," he said.

"Yeah, I'll bet," the blond one said.

"Are they good friends of yours?" Batty asked when they were outside.

"Pretty good," Gus said. "As good as any, I guess."

"Why don't you play on the basketball team?" Batty said. "Some of the others do."

"I can't. I had hepatitis last year and I'm not completely well. I have to take it easy and get a lot of rest."

"Is it contagious?" Batty asked, moving farther away from him on the sidewalk.

"Naw, not now," Gus said, dismissing it.

"Where on earth did you get hepatitis? Don't you have to be in a foreign country to get hepatitis?"

"You don't have to be," Gus said, "but it helps." He laughed. "Daddy doesn't know exactly where I got it. He thinks maybe he brought it home from the hospital. But at any rate, I got it and that's that."

"Your father's a doctor?"

"Uh-huh," Gus said. "A good one."

"Dr. Oliver," Batty said. "I think I've heard of him. He's a surgeon, isn't he?"

"Uh-huh."

"Lots of people from Robertson's Fort go to Cullman specialists. We don't have any specialists here." They were leaving the hardware store and approaching Attwood's Department Store.

"This is my daddy's store," Batty said. "I have to work here on Saturdays."

"It's a nice store," Gus said, pressing his nose to the glass. "There's a light on in the back."

"Yeah, Daddy leaves a light on so it'll be easier for Red Crawford to see if anyone's broken in."

"Has anybody ever broken in?"

"Not our store. But someone broke into the J and L Variety up the street last year."

"Did they ever catch them?"

"No, we've got only one policeman," Batty said, "but he's not much good at catching people. You see that car over near the monument with its lights off?"

"Yeah. Who's that?"

"That's him, Red Crawford, the policeman, keeping an eye on things."

"We have twelve policemen in Cullman."

"Well, I should hope so," Batty said. "With all the mean people in Cullman, you probably need more than that." She was looking at him out of the corners of her eyes. When he glanced at her to see if she was teasing him, she burst out laughing.

"Come on now," she said. "Let's get across the tracks before the train comes." In the distance they heard the train whistle. The southern signal light was red. They turned the corner next to Miss Teal's Tea Room and started up the hill, and heard the train speeding through town. "It's a freight train," Batty said. "It doesn't stop here. It just comes through on its way to somewhere else."

When they got home, Daddy was sitting alone in the living room, reading a Zane Grey.

"Daddy, this is Gus Oliver from Cullman," Batty said.

Daddy looked very pleased. "Oh, yes," he said, offering Gus his hand. "I think I know your daddy. Is Dr. Richard Oliver your daddy?"

"Yes, sir," Gus said.

"I met him at a meeting of the county town boards last year. Nice man," Daddy said, smiling. "A real nice man. Well, Mother's in bed, reading. If you'll excuse me, I think I'll join her." He took his Zane Grey with him.

"Do you mind if I play the piano?" Gus asked.

"You play the piano?" Batty asked.

Mr. Green, her piano teacher, came every Tuesday evening to give her a lesson. They had been working for weeks, two lines at a time, on a piece Batty liked a lot but found difficult. The sheet music for "Kamennoi-Ostrow" was opened on the piano rack. Gus sat down, looked at the notation a moment and began sight-reading it. He played beautifully. Besides Mr. Green, Perry was the only man Batty knew who played the piano, and he didn't play classical music. In Robertson's Fort, playing the piano was not considered appropriate for boys.

"You play beautifully," she said when he'd finished and closed the sheet music.

"Not really," he said self-disparagingly. "My little sister Annette plays a lot better than I do. She gives recitals all the time and she's only twelve."

"Wow! She must be a prodigy."

"I guess so," Gus said. "She wants to be a concert pianist when she grows up."

"What do you want to be when you grow up?" Batty asked.

"A doctor," Gus said. "I've always wanted to be a doctor."

"Like your father," Batty said.

"No, not exactly like my father. The study of medicine will have changed a lot when I'm a doctor from the way it was when he studied. They'll probably have cures for all sorts of things they didn't have cures for when he was in school."

"You may catch hepatitis again," Batty said and laughed.

"Not very likely," Gus said. "When you're a doctor, you develop an immunity to all sorts of things."

"Do you want to practice in Cullman or do you want to go to someplace else to practice?"

"I haven't thought about that yet," Gus said. "I wouldn't mind practicing in Cullman, though. It's a nice place to live."

"I wouldn't want to live there," Batty said thoughtfully. "I wouldn't want to live anywhere around here. When I grow up I want to live in New York."

"Why on earth would you want to live in New York?" Gus asked. "I'd be afraid. It's so big and everything."

"Because New York is exciting, with lots of things going on all the time—plays, symphonies, poetry readings. I read about it all the time in Mother's magazines. There're beautiful restaurants and stores. People get all dressed up in beautiful clothes and go to fancy parties with maids and butlers. I'd like to live there, that's all. And besides, I'm going to be a professional actress, and to be a professional actress, you have to live in New York."

"Have you ever been to New York?"

"Once when I visited Mother's cousin in Connecticut. She took me to New York for the day."

Batty looked at Gus a moment. He had slipped off his white

bucks and had his stockinged feet resting on Mother's coffee table. He certainly had made himself comfortable in a hurry. She couldn't put the things she was learning about him together in any way that made sense. He looked very handsome, the blue of his eyes picked up by his blue sweater, his dark wavy hair falling on his forehead. He certainly didn't look like a sissy.

"What else do you like to do, Gus?" she asked. "I mean besides playing the piano."

"Cooking," he said, breaking into a broad smile. "I *love* to cook. I'm the best cook I know."

"Really?"

"Yes, and I'll prove it to you sometime. I'll cook dinner for us. Would you like that?"

"Sure."

Not only did Gus play the piano but he had just admitted that he loved to cook. She was beginning to be disappointed in him. Even though he didn't look like a sissy, she was becoming more and more convinced that he was one. Besides that, he didn't seem to have much ambition, even if he was planning to be a doctor. With a whole world of exciting places out there, he thought Cullman was a nice place to live.

Daddy stuck his head around the door. "Tomorrow's a school day," he said. "You'd better get ready for bed."

"Can I call you sometime soon?" Gus said.

"Sure," Batty said, not exactly delighted with the idea. "And thanks for walking me home."

"What time is it?" Gus asked, looking at his watch. "My God!" he said, slapping the side of his head. "Those guys are going to kill me."

He sprinted down the walk and on down the street and disappeared behind the shrubs that bordered the Mercers' while Batty watched. Through the trees she could see the red blinking of the traffic light on Main Street.

The whole family liked Gus Oliver. Daddy liked him a lot. Gus could get by with all sorts of things with Daddy that nobody else could—like keeping Batty out sometimes past her usual ten-thirty deadline. Batty liked Gus, too. He was intelligent and had so many interests. He read a lot and knew about lots of things, but most of all, she was fascinated by how different he was from the other boys she knew. In addition to playing the piano and cooking, he was different in that he had such strong *feelings* about things, such definite *opinions*—and he always knew just what his feelings and opinions were. He didn't mind telling you about them either. Most boys—or men, too, for that matter—kept their feelings pretty much to themselves. Daddy did. Mother said it was because he'd had an authoritarian father who didn't think it was appropriate for boys to express wishes, or longings, or to complain when they were in pain, or felt sad or disappointed about something. Boys were supposed to take care of those feelings by themselves. Only the weaker sex was allowed to cry, to have and express longings, sadnesses, and fears. Batty couldn't remember ever hearing Daddy say that anything hurt him. She'd never even heard him say he had a headache. Sometimes when he went to bed earlier than usual while Mother was sitting in the living room doing some mending, her eyes would watch him thoughtfully as he left the room. When he was gone she would say, almost to herself, "Daddy mustn't be feeling well today. He ate almost no supper and he usually loves collard greens and corn bread." Gus wasn't like that at all. Batty wondered if that had anything to do with Daddy's liking him so much.

Sometimes Gus would come and have dinner with the family. Other times, when Hilda was off, Gus would cook. He'd go to the supermarket and buy the things he needed—including strange herbs Hilda never used—and go into Mother's kitchen and make marvelous things: stews with thick brown sauces, fried chicken and biscuits that were better than Hilda's, thick red spaghetti sauces that he poured on spaghetti still firm and steaming hot.

When he went off to college at Chapel Hill in the fall of 1952, he learned to make some new and exotic dishes, and one Saturday when he was home for the weekend he called Daddy at the store and told him he'd like to come up and cook dinner for the family. Daddy chuckled with pleasure, the way he chuckled with pleasure over almost anything Gus did, and told him that would be very nice. Gus came on up in the afternoon and when everybody got home from work, he had the table set and the house filled with strange and delicious smells. When everybody was seated, he served Malayan shrimp curry on rice with slices of banana and chutney on the side. Whenever Daddy ate anything spicy, the top of his bald head perspired. When he ate the curry, he had to keep wiping the top of his head with his handkerchief. Daddy ate with great concentration leaning over his plate. It was hard to believe he could like such an unusual dish since Mother was always saying he was so set in his ways when it came to eating.

One weekend in November, Batty looked up from where she was crouched searching for an empty box under the lingerie counter to see Gus leaning on the counter not three feet from her and smiling at her.

"Hi," he said softly, no other word than that, just saying he was glad to see her with his eyes, the softness of them.

"Oh, hi, Gus," Batty said, glad to see him, thinking he looked handsome in his blue turtleneck sweater. "I'll be through here in a minute."

"I'll take care of that," Aunt Harriet said softly, coming up from behind Batty. "You talk to Gus. Hello, Gus," she said, "how are you today?"

"Fine, thank you, Miss Attwood," Gus said. "Do you think Batty could come out and get a hamburger with me? I'm starved."

"I think so," Aunt Harriet said. "We're not very busy right now."

"Didn't you eat any lunch, Gus?" Batty asked, thinking of the pimento-cheese sandwich she'd eaten an hour and a half earlier at the drugstore.

"Not yet. I've been too busy this morning."

Batty went to get her jacket from the rack at the back of the store. They went across the street to the café where Gus ordered a hamburger and a glass of milk.

'What have you been doing that you've been too busy to eat lunch until two o'clock?" Batty asked.

"I've been to Asheville to get some things I'm going to need for tonight," he said without further explanation.

"Why?" Batty asked, looking at him intently, wondering why he was being so mysterious. "What's going on tonight?"

"I'm cooking dinner for just you and me at the lake house. A

candlelight dinner for two. How's that?" he said, smiling at her.
"You sure do take me for granted, don't you?" Batty said. "How
do you know I don't have something else to do?"

"Well, do you?" Gus asked, a flicker of concern crossing his face.

"Well, no, but . . ."

"But what?" He looked at her a moment. "Don't you *want* to have
dinner with me?"

"Well, yes, of course I do," Batty said. "It's just that I don't want
you to think I have nothing to do but wait for you to call me when
you're home or to appear the way you do out of the blue. What if I
were busy?"

"But you aren't," Gus said, smiling, "so let's not worry about it.
And about taking you for granted," he said, taking the top of the
roll from his hamburger and pouring catsup on the meat, "when a
person offers to do something for another person, or invites
another person to spend time with him, or to enjoy something with
him, it's silly for him to have to play silly games to make the other
person feel important when if she weren't important to him he
wouldn't have offered the gift, or extended the invitation in the
first place. Isn't that true?"

Batty was quietly watching Gus eat his hamburger and thinking
that he was the strangest boy she knew and that his strangeness
somehow made him special.

She left the store early that evening to be ready when Gus came
to pick her up at seven o'clock. She'd decided to get a little dressed
up for the occasion and was wearing her blue angora sweater and
matching skirt with her black patent pumps when he came to pick
her up. She had brushed her hair back and gathered it in a rubber
band at the crown of her head. It fell in a dark wavy ponytail. Her
mouth was painted crimson; if Daddy were here he'd have told her
she had on too much lipstick. When she opened the door, Gus was
standing there smiling at her.

"Well, don't we look pretty all dressed up," he said.

"I'm not very dressed up," Batty said. "Wait a minute till I get my
coat."

It was dark when they got to Lake Susquot. The water stretched
between the trees lining its shores, a mirror to the blackness of the
night sky. The sparse lights of houses scattered around the lake

flickered through thick matted vegetation and shot in rippled streaks across the dark water. They turned off the main road and onto the dirt road that wound around the edge of the lake. Gus looked ahead intently. Batty didn't recognize the driveway when they came to it. Gus had brought her here once before in the daytime when his parents and Annette were here. It was in the spring and she and Gus took the small motorboat out of the boathouse for the first time of the season. He had worked over it a long time to get it started and when they got out in the middle of the lake, it died. He couldn't get it started again and they had to row all the way back to the boathouse.

They walked up the back steps now and entered the house through the kitchen. The lake house was built of dark natural wood. In the daytime it looked very much at home sitting in the trees and shrubs, just as if it had grown there in the middle of the foliage. The interior was a dark-stained pine. Two walls were lined with books. The living room, dining room and kitchen were one large space, the living room a step lower than the dining room and kitchen. The kitchen was defined on two sides by counters, over one of which was a large copper hood covering a grill. Copper-bottomed pots and pans hung from the ceiling over the counters. The focus of the living room was a large stone fireplace, stretched in front of which was a large, rough, loosely woven wool rug. Several stuffed chairs and a black leather sofa were arranged in a comfortable square before it. The living room opened onto a wide screened-in porch that stretched across the front of the house overlooking the lake. A fire had been laid. Gus went to the fireplace and lighted the paper under the logs.

"See what a nice fire I laid for us?" he said. "The secret of a good fire is to have enough kindling and to leave enough room between the logs for the air to circulate."

The paper blazed and the kindling began to crackle as it caught. Gus took their coats into the bedroom. When he got back, Batty had turned up the three-way lamp on the corner table and was thumbing through a home magazine she'd found.

"I really love this house, Gus," she said.

The dining-room table was set for two. Two red candles in crystal holders flanked a bud vase containing one crimson rosebud just beginning to open. Batty leaned over the table to smell it.

"Where did you get this gorgeous rose?" she said.

"I bought it from the florist," Gus said. "Now help me get set up. We're having something I bet you've never had before."

"What?"

"Shabu shabu."

'What?" Batty said again, thinking she hadn't heard right.

"It's a Japanese dish," Gus said. "First we put this burner on the table and plug it in. Then we get a big pot of water and put some kelp in it."

By the time the water was boiling, Gus had put a tray of thinly sliced, red, and well-marbled beef on one end of the table. On the other end were a large bowl of chopped vegetables and a bowl of noodles that looked like very thin spaghetti. Between the two plates was a small bowl of dark and pungent sauce.

When they sat down, Gus said, "Now you just watch what I do." He took his fork and rolled a thin slice of beef around it. Then he held it for a few seconds in the boiling water. When it was no longer red, he took it out, dipped it in the dark sauce, and ate it. "Ummm, good," he said.

Batty imitated him. "It *is* good," she said. "Gus, it's absolutely delicious."

Gus put the vegetables into the same pot of boiling broth in which they'd cooked the meat and let them cook a few minutes. When they'd eaten the vegetables, he dumped the noodles into the same broth, explaining that as more things were cooked in the broth it became more and more flavorsome.

"I can't eat another bite," Batty said, as he forked noodles onto her plate.

Gus continued to eat.

"I just can't *believe* you do all this terrific cooking," Batty said. "It's so strange."

"I don't think it's strange at all." Gus said. "Preparing food is one of the most basic of man's activities."

"Usually the most basic of *woman's* activities," Batty said.

"Women cook because most of the time they have to. When a man cooks, it's because he enjoys it. That's why the men who cook are better cooks than the women."

"I'd sure hate to have to cook all the time."

"How do you know you'd hate it?" Gus asked. "I'll bet you've never cooked anything in your life."

"That's not so," Batty said. "I cook fudge very often. My fudge is almost as good as Aunt Harriet's."

"That's nothing. You can't live on fudge, at least not very well and not for very long."

"But I'd sure hate to have to cook for a husband and squalling kids every day. Gosh! That would be depressing. You'd no sooner get one meal cleaned up than you'd have to start another one."

"That wouldn't be any worse than it is for a man to have to go to a job he hates every day, the way lots of men do."

"Like who?" Batty asked, challenging him. "What men do you know who go to jobs they hate?"

"I'm sure the men who work in the mills and have to run machines every day hate their work."

"But the people who work in factories aren't people like you and me," Batty said. "What doctors, or lawyers, or businessmen do you know who hate going to work every day? You're not going to hate going to work every day when you're a doctor. You've told me lots of times how much you want to be a doctor."

"Maybe most women don't mind cooking every day, either," Gus said. "What makes you think they hate it?"

"I just think any woman would have to hate it," Batty said. "Besides, I'm not talking about most women. I'm talking about me. I would hate, hate, *hate* having to cook three meals a day every day for a husband and snot-nosed kids."

"You probably wouldn't have to do much of that sort of stuff anyway," Gus said. "Your mother doesn't do much cooking."

"I know she doesn't," Batty said. "But most women do. That's why I'm not going to get married for a long time—maybe never. Because I want to have my own career." She looked at Gus teasingly. "Unless I should marry you and you'd do all the cooking."

"I won't do *all* the cooking when I get married," Gus said. "Just on special occasions, when I want to. I'll expect my wife to do the cooking and housework so I can concentrate on being a good doctor."

"I'm glad I'm not going to be your wife."

"How do you know you're not?"

"Because I wouldn't marry anybody who expected me to do all the boring things while he had an interesting career."

"Well, you wouldn't be above giving me a hand with these dishes, would you?"

"No, not at all," Batty said. "In fact, you cooked such a good dinner, I'll do the dishes all by myself. You just go sit by the fire."

"No, I'd rather help you so we can be finished earlier. I don't want to sit by the fire alone."

When the last of the dishes had been put away, Gus and Batty sat on the sofa by the fire. "We'll have to leave in about forty-five minutes," she said. "I promised Daddy I'd be home by eleven."

"Okay," Gus said. "Then we'll have to hurry." He slid over close to Batty on the sofa and put his arm around her. She'd let him kiss her on the lips lots of times, just little dry kisses; she hoped he wasn't expecting more than that tonight, but she suspected he was. The way he'd arranged everything so perfectly—right down to the red rose—made it look as though he was planning on a real hot necking session. When it came to necking, she'd a lot rather neck with Paul Marley who was one of the star basketball players than with Gus, though Gus was a lot smarter and more talented than Paul. Whenever Paul walked her home after a game, he took her to a spot on the walk just below the hedge where Daddy couldn't see them from the living room, and he held her tight and kissed her, his tongue exploring deep inside her mouth. When he kissed her like that, she felt her pants get wet. She always had to go into the bathroom and wash before she went to bed. She didn't want *Gus* to kiss her like that.

Gus was a good friend—almost like a girlfriend, but better than a girlfriend. He paid attention to her feelings and understood them, even shared them sometimes. She couldn't think of such a good friend as a boyfriend. Somehow the two kinds of friends were different things, had to be. He wrapped his arm firmly around her neck now and pulled her face to him and kissed her on the lips, his lips moving over hers hungrily as his hand came to rest on her breast over her sweater.

It was almost incestuous—like kissing a brother.

"No, Gus, no," she said, pushing him away.

Gus moved away from her and sat looking at her silently. She got up and went to the bedroom and got the coats. When she came back, Gus was still sitting on the end of the sofa, one arm dangling over the back and one arm dangling off the armrest. He was watching her intently, a hurt look on his face.

Suddenly she felt confused. She felt sorry for what she couldn't feel for him and yet convinced she shouldn't feel sorry for not having a particular kind of feeling for him when the feeling she *did* have was so strong.

"I'm sorry, Gus," she said. "I just can't. I mean . . . you're such a good friend. . . . I just can't think of you like that."

"Can't think of me like what?" he asked, blinking with hurt.

"Like a boyfriend. It just wouldn't be right, Gus."

"Who can you think of as a boyfriend?" he asked, an edge to his voice now, his face flashing hurt and anger.

"I don't know anyone yet," Batty said.

He got up and went around turning off the lights. "Let's go, Batty," he said. "We don't want to get you home late."

He drove the miles home in total silence. When they got there, he walked her to the door.

"Gus, please don't be mad at me," she said.

"I'm not mad at you," he said, his head tilted to the side. He shrugged. "See you around sometime," he said and turned and walked back to the car. She stood on the porch and watched as he turned on the ignition. The beams of the headlights flashed up the hill onto the steps of the Baptist church. She watched the car pull away from the curb and shoot up the hill and screech around the corner, the headlights throwing the colonnaded facade of the church into full illumination for a moment. Then the car disappeared around the parsonage and everything was dark again.

Batty was bored to death with school. At fifteen when she was in the tenth grade, Robertson's Fort High School hit a new low. A few teachers struggled to do their jobs but others, Korean War veterans newly returned to civilian life, made no attempt at all. Mr. Honeycutt who taught biology came to class the first day and listed on the board the nine phyla and their characteristics. That was the last thing he did all year that had anything to do with teaching. From then on he came to class and propped himself on his desk and told war stories. Mr. Stockton, another new teacher, who taught English stayed with it a little longer than Mr. Honeycutt. His instruction lasted about two weeks before he announced one day that from then on the students were to bring to class something to keep them busy and out of his hair for the hour. Though Batty told Mother and Daddy that some of the teachers weren't doing their jobs, neither of them wanted to make a fuss because they thought making a fuss was bad manners.

One afternoon when Batty was at the piano practicing her Hanon for Mr. Green, Geraldine called. "Hi, honey," she said. "How are you?"

"Fine, thank you, Geraldine. How's your new job?"

"To tell you the truth, I like everything about it except the drive to Asheville. It's a long commute."

"I suppose so," Batty said.

"I like my students. And working hard again is good for me. But I miss working with you. You've got a very special talent, honey—more than any of my other students—and you mustn't let it go to waste."

"I won't, Geraldine. When I go to college . . . "

"I'm talking about *now*. College is a long time away, honey, you should be doing something with it right *now*."

"Well, I guess so, Geraldine, but . . ."

"My mother was telling me about a national speech contest the American Legion is sponsoring. You'd have to write a speech about the Constitution—your mother and daddy could help you with it—and learn to give it really well. I'd help you on the delivery. You'd have to compete in the county contest, and then if you won you'd go on to other contests—all the way to the national contest—if you keep winning. And I think you can, if you really put your mind to it. Does it interest you?"

"Well yes, but . . ."

"I'll have Mother make the arrangements or I might even talk to

Mr. Collins myself. At any rate, I'll take care of getting you entered if you're willing to try."

"Sure," Batty said. "Why not? I could use something interesting to do."

"Good, honey, that's my girl. Now you talk to your mother and daddy and see what they think. I'll call tomorrow to see what's been decided."

The writing of the speech became a family effort. Mother and Daddy and Batty sat in the living room after dinner every evening and worked on it. First they worked out the outline. Then they began to fill in the details, Mother writing all the time. Mother was the expert on history. Daddy provided some facts about history, too, but he was mainly for rhetoric. Mother would give him the facts and he would organize the facts into sentences that built to climaxes. He would make sure he varied the sentence structure, but wherever possible he'd put the long detailed subordinate clause first and then punch the idea home with a short strong main clause. Then he'd put his sentences into order building them to the final sentence that punched home the main idea. Batty sat in the middle and supervised. After all, she was the one who had to *give* the speech; she certainly had the right to make sure it was good. At the end of each session, Mother gave Batty the paper on which she'd written and Batty copied it all over to make sure it was neat and legible for her to memorize. As soon as Batty memorized her speech, Geraldine came to the house to help her work on the delivery.

On a cold day in February, Daddy drove her to Cullman High where the contest was to be held. It was midafternoon and the last of the school buses was pulling out of the driveway just as they got there. There was only a scattering of cars left in the lot. Daddy pulled in close to the school building beside an old blue Chevrolet. He opened the heavy front door and he and Batty entered a large foyer. Across a wide expanse of polished vinyl floor was a long counter behind which a gray-haired woman sat talking on the telephone. When Batty and Daddy approached, she put the phone on her shoulder.

"Can I help you?" she asked in a pleasant voice.

"My daughter is in the speech contest here this afternoon," Daddy said.

"Oh, yes, just a minute, I'll page Mr. Buckhorn. He's in charge of the contest." She excused herself to the person on the phone, laid the receiver on the desk, and went to page Mr. Buckhorn. Batty was fidgeting with the zipper of the folder she carried with her. She felt her legs quivering. She thought if she didn't calm down, her voice would sound high and weak. She took several deep breaths and tried to relax.

Mr. Buckhorn came around the corner and immediately extended his hand to Daddy. He was a small man who radiated energy. He smiled as though he were glad to see them.

"Hello," he said, "I'm Paul Buckhorn."

"How are you?" Daddy said. "I'm Robert Attwood, and this is my daughter Batty."

Mr. Buckhorn shook hands with Batty, and led them down the hall to a classroom. There were four rows of desk-chairs facing a larger teacher's desk. Several middle-aged men dressed in business suits were sitting in the third row talking loudly. At the other end of the second and third rows were another man and three women who were talking quietly. One of the women was checking papers with a red pencil while she talked. A scrawny boy with wire-framed glasses sat in the front row. He was wearing a blue dress suit and a white shirt and dark tie. Batty, still wearing her school saddle oxfords and skirt and sweater, wondered if she was supposed to have dressed up.

Daddy whispered to her to sit in the front row—she sat several seats away from the scrawny boy—and then went to the back of the room and sat in the middle of the last row. She knew she was on her own now. She looked around at everybody, trying to find friendly faces to dispel her continuing nervousness. Soon the door opened again and a man came in and sat next to the scrawny boy and whispered something in his ear. The scrawny boy nodded. Mr. Buckhorn, who had directed them to the classroom came in with a large blond girl. He led the girl over to Batty.

"This is Alice Marsh," he said. "She's our contestant from Cullman High. Alice, this is Batty Attwood from Robertson's Fort."

Alice Marsh seemed completely relaxed. She smiled warmly at Batty and offered her hand. "It's a pleasure to meet you," she said.

"Same here," Batty said. "Good luck to both of us."

Alice seemed to think that was funny. She giggled. "I'll second that," she said, and sat down and began riffling through some papers. Batty looked at her watch. It was five minutes till three. Just as she was wondering if there were going to be only three contestants, the door opened and a tall thin boy, his dark hair greased back, came in, followed by a very pretty dark-haired woman who Betty thought must be his mother. Mr. Buckhorn rose to meet them and said a few words to them. Then the boy sat in the front row next to Batty, and the woman sat several rows back. He sat there, clasping and unclasping his hands between his knees, and stared straight ahead at the blackboard. Batty thought he must be as nervous as she was.

She looked at her watch. They were five minutes late starting. One of the middle-aged men got up from the third row and walked to the front of the room. He was fat and gray-haired and was wearing a brown pin-striped suit that fit him more approximately than precisely. He was carrying with him a white sheet of paper. He glanced at it and then, with the paper still in his right hand, clasped his hands behind him and rocked on his heels.

"Ladies and gentlemen," he began, nodding slightly toward the two sides of the room, "and student contestants," nodding now to the four of them in the front row, "the American Legion has always stood for love of country and loyalty to country and for instilling in our young people that same love and loyalty. For that reason we decided this year to have a nationwide speaking contest on the subject of the Constitution of the United States. The student who wins the contest today will go on to the division contest to be held in Asheville next week and that winner will go to the state contest and from there to the contest for the whole Southeast of this great country and so on right up to the final national contest.

"Speaking first today will be Alice Marsh representing Cullman High, followed by Steve Cavanaugh from Floral Park High, then Malcolm Cambridge from Pine Rocks, and last, Beatrice Louise Attwood from Robertson's Fort. Each of the contestants will speak approximately ten minutes. After the main speech, each of them will be given a topic and will be allowed five minutes to organize his thoughts before we go on to the final part of the contest which will be the extemporaneous speeches. These, I believe, are to be four to five minutes long. It gives me pleasure now to introduce the first of our contestants, Miss Alice Marsh from Cullman High." He sat down and Alice got up and went to the front of the room. If she felt nervous, Batty couldn't tell it. She looked very comfortable and when she spoke her voice was well modulated.

"Ladies and gentlemen," she began, "in the year 1787, the leading statesmen of our young nation came together in Philadelphia with the intention of redrafting the Articles of the Confederacy in order to solve problems of a rather grand magnitude that were beginning to be troublesome among the sovereign states involved. They had no intention at that time of drafting an entrely new document. . . ."

The audience clapped as Alice returned to her seat. The man in the brown suit got up and introduced Steve Cavanaugh from Floral Park. Batty thought that unless he sounded a lot better than he looked, she didn't have anything to worry about. He took a position next to the desk, and, before he began speaking, pushed his glasses up on his nose. His face was damp with perspiration. When he began his speech, his arms flew up from his side in a grand gesture toward his listeners. Batty was so startled at the suddenness of it she almost giggled. Then one of his arms came back down to his side and the one that remained extended tensed as he balled his hand into a fist. He flung the fist skyward and punctuated the next three sentences with it. His voice was high and twangy. Batty was so busy watching his arms, she didn't hear a word he was saying. She doubted that anyone else did either. Then he smoothed the air in front of him with both his hands just before he fell onto one knee and quick as a flash was up again. After a while his hands began to wind down. His speech was finished. Everyone clapped again as he sat down.

The man in the brown suit introduced Malcolm Cambridge from Pine Rocks High. The tall thin boy with his dark hair slicked back with grease stood in front of the audience with his hands clasped behind his back. Several strands of hair on the crown of his head had come unglued and stuck straight up. He began speaking in a monotone as though he were reading his speech when, in fact, he had it memorized.

"Ladies and gentlemen," he said, "the Constitutional Convention was held in Philadelphia in May of 1787. Among the representatives who attended that convention were James Madison, George Washington, Alexander Hamilton, Benjamin Franklin, Edmund Randolph. . . ." He continued to reel off lists of facts and figures, and then spent three minutes listing the powers given by the Constitution to each of the branches of the government. When he finished, Batty knew that her only possible competition was Alice Marsh.

The man in the brown suit got up and said, "Our next contestant is Beatrice Louise Attwood from Robertson's Fort."

Batty felt her body flash hot and cold, the way she often felt when she was suddenly frightened. She walked to the front of the room and stood for a moment looking at her audience as Geraldine had taught her. She saw a roomful of friendy faces. The only face that didn't look pleasant belonged to one of the men in the American Legion group. He was a very fat man, his glasses down on his nose, his chin lost in layers of jowl as he looked at her, apathetically, if attentively, over the top of his glasses. She decided to think about the encouraging face of the slender brown-haired woman in the second row. Daddy was looking at her expectantly, a pleasant smile on his face, and leaning forward in his chair, his elbows propped on his knees.

She began speaking slowly, concentrating on every word the way Geraldine had taught her to do, so she would register the right emotions in her face and in her voice.

"Ladies and gentlemen," she said, "one hundred and sixty-six years ago, our forefathers signed the document declared by that great English statesman William Gladstone to be the most wonderful work ever struck off at a given time by the brain and purpose of man, the Constitution of the United States.

"This is not to suggest that the ideas on which the system of government drawn up by those wise men gathered at that convention suddenly came to birth overnight. They did not. They had been developing over centuries in the minds of great political philosophers and in the laboratories of English law. The concept of a system of law the purpose of which was to serve the people and of inalienable individual rights had been strongly advanced in a document signed by King John at Runymede as early as 1215—the Magna Carta, certainly an ancestor of that very important part of our Constitution, the Bill of Rights."

The pitch of the voice she heard, higher than she expected it to be or wanted it to be, was the only thing that gave away her fright. She worked to get it down. And then she began to think only of her speech. She continued speaking about the history of the Constitution, the roots of it in English law, all the facts that Mother had contributed and that Daddy had shaped into speech. Everybody was listening intently. Then she started speaking about the protections the Constitution gave the citizenry. She was beginning to enjoy herself, and by the time she got to the part about Ellis Island and the poor oppressed immigrant she knew she had everything under control, the speech, her voice, her audience. She relaxed and began to work on the last half. As she got to the final paragraph, she hated to let it go. The jowly old man who was looking at her over his glasses took out his pocket handkerchief and wiped a tear from his eye as she finished on Daddy's final line: "And so, ladies and gentlemen, over the years the Constitution of this great country has proven to be strong enough to protect the weakest of its citizens and, at the same time, flexible enough to provide an unrestrictive framework within which the strongest can live and work to his fullest potential." She stood a moment after she had delivered that line and held the gaze of her audience. Then, quietly and quickly, she dropped her eyes and took her seat.

After each of the contestants had spoken extemporaneously on the topics they'd been given, three of the American Legion members excused themselves and left the room to make their decision. When they came back the fat one who'd introduced the contestants went to stand behind the teacher's desk. He seemed to be carrying the same sheet of paper he'd had with him earlier.

"Ladies and gentlemen," he said, "we've heard four fine speeches today made by four fine young people whose schools can be proud of them. We wish they could all win the contest"—here he paused a moment and made a gesture of resignation—"but, of course, contests wouldn't be contests without winners and losers, and today we can have only one winner. We've made a difficult decision. The winner is"—and here he stopped to look at his sheet of white paper—"Miss Beatrice Louise Attwood from Robertson's Fort High School." Everybody clapped. "Miss Attwood, would you please come up to receive the medal?"

Batty went to the front of the room. He gave her the medal and shook her hand. Everybody clapped again, but more faintly this time, as though they thought maybe they'd clapped enough. Then it was all over. People began talking to each other. The other contestants congratulated Batty. Then they collected their coats and the sheaves of paper they'd brought with them and left. Daddy got into a conversation with the men from the American Legion. After he and the men had found out who they all were, who they were related to, what business they were in, or in Daddy's case what store he owned, they shook hands and said good-bye.

Daddy grinned all the way to the car.

"Well, you won," he said, "how does it feel?"

"It feels wonderful," Batty said, grinning as broadly as Daddy.

The second contest was held in Asheville, at the school Mother had attended before Grandaddy Terrell was transferred to the new job at Robertson's Fort. Though the competition was tougher and the audience larger and more sophisticated, Batty breezed through and was unanimously declared the winner again. Her picture was on the front page of the Asheville *Citizen-Times* the next day with the story of her winning the contest. In Robertson's Fort where everybody read the Asheville newspaper, she was a celebrity. Now she would go to the state contest to be held in early March at McBee in the Piedmont section of the state.

Batty knew her speech so well she could have recited it backward. Nevertheless, every few days, just to keep it fresh in her mind, she went over it from beginning to end while Mother or Daddy followed the written speech and nodded approval. "Let us imagine for a moment the feelings of the poor oppressed immigrant coming into New York Harbor when first he caught sight of that grand old lady lifting her torch of freedom, welcoming him with the inscription: 'Give me your tired, your poor,/Your huddled masses yearning to breathe free,/The wretched refuse of your teeming shore,/Send these, the homeless, tempest-tossed, to me:/I lift my lamp beside the golden door. . . .' "

On the day of the contest, Daddy and Mother took the day off from the store and drove Batty to McBee. They had dinner at a Howard Johnson's and got to the high school at seven-thirty. Two women behind a desk welcomed them and gave Batty a sticker with her name and the name of her high school lettered on it, and then one of them ushered her and Mother and Daddy to the teachers' lounge where the other contestants and the men from the American Legion were gathering. A tall, slender man with silver hair, wearing a trim-fitting steel-gray suit introduced Batty to the other four contestants—a small wiry dark-haired girl from Lumberton, a tall athletic-looking blond boy from Moorehead City, a fat and very knock-kneed boy from Greensboro, and a short brown-haired boy with a big smile and two dimples that made his face light up when he smiled at her.

In a few minutes the silver-haired man led them through the back doors of the auditorium, down the aisle, and up onto the stage where there were five chairs behind the podium. The auditorium was filled. It looked very much like the auditorium at Robertson's Fort. There were the same windows high on the wall where you couldn't see out of them and the same hooked poles for opening them leaning in the corners. There were the same big light bulbs hanging on chains from the ceiling, the same United States flag and the same state flag on either side of the stage.

Batty was to be the first to speak. She was glad for that. She could get the speech over with and sit back and relax while the other contestants were still sweating it out. She wasn't at all nervous this time. So many people from the two other contests had told her she was wonderful that she was beginning to feel invincible. When the silver-haired man introduced her, she walked to the apron of the stage and looked at the audience, making eye contact before she began. From the first sentence, she squeezed from the speech everything that was in it.

"Ladies and gentlemen, one hundred and sixty-six years ago, our forefathers signed the document declared by that great English statesman William Gladstone to be the most wonderful work ever struck off at a given time by the brain and purpose of man, the Constitution of the United States. . . ."

The audience was very attentive. By the time she got to the part about a man's home being his castle they were spellbound. She knew the speech so well, she hardly had to think of it anymore. It spilled from her mouth like a beautiful river on which floated the barks of pure wisdom and true emotion. She quit thinking about the speech and let it issue forth in its greatness, watching her audience and realizing what her speech was doing to them, loving it, thinking the great mission of her life was to rally masses of people to great causes by her speaking. Maybe one day she would be the small-town maiden who leads her country to greatness like Joan of Arc. Or maybe, even though she was a girl, she would be another Winston Churchill. She decided she could be as moving as Winston Churchill.

"Let us imagine for a moment the feelings of the poor oppressed immigrant coming into New York Harbor when he first caught sight of that grand old lady lifting her torch of freedom, welcoming him with the inscription . . ."

And that was when she lost her place.

Her last word had fallen from her mouth cleanly and left not a trace. There was no echo of it in her memory. She knew she hadn't finished the speech, that she was somewhere in the middle—but she didn't know where. Had she been speaking about innocent Europeans languishing for years in jails and our right guaranteed by the Constitution to a fair and speedy trial? She hadn't a clue. She felt her heart begin to pound through her rib cage. She looked for Mother who was sitting in the third row and following her speech, the sheets of paper turning in her hand. Mother knew she had forgotten. Mother's lips were forming words. Batty couldn't read them. Mother's lips kept moving: "'Give me your tired, your poor . . .'" Mother said over and over again.

Suddenly nothing but panic, sheer terrifying panic. She stood there. The audience, aware that something was wrong, began to buzz softly. Batty turned and walked from the stage in rigid humiliation to the nearest privacy she could find, a small dressing room near the exit. She was the only person backstage. How to get home before someone sees me, she thought, how to get Daddy to drive the Chrysler to the back door and let me in and leave quickly. Her hands were sweating. She rubbed them together.

Suddenly Daddy was standing quietly in the doorway.

"Daddy, let's get out of here," she said, "let's go home." She was crying now. "Bring the car up to the back door and let me get in and take me home."

"No, we can't do that," Daddy said softly.

"But, Daddy, I'm so embarrassed. Please take me home. Please."

Daddy stood there looking at her. Then he put his hands on her shoulders and stood facing her squarely.

"Beatrice Louise," he said, "you've got to go back out there. You've got to go back out there and finish your speech."

"Oh, no, Daddy," she said, shaking her head violently. "I couldn't. I just couldn't."

"You've got to," Daddy said. "You can't run away."

"That's what I want to do. I want to run away quick before anybody sees us."

"You must never run away in shame," Daddy said, "or you'll never quit running. You'd never get over this if you ran away, Batty. You've got to go back out there and finish your speech."

She began drying her eyes. She was quiet for a long moment while Daddy held her in his steady gaze. Finally she said, "How do you know they'll let me have another chance?"

"I think they will," Daddy said, "I'll have to go talk to them. You stay here till I get back, okay?"

"Okay," Batty said, tentatively.

She sat in the straight-backed wooden chair and waited for what seemed like forever before Daddy returned.

"You can finish your main speech during the time that would have been used for your extemporaneous speech," he said.

"When will I give my extemporaneous speech?"

"The judges are still talking about that. They're trying to work something out. The important thing now is that you go out and finish your speech."

Batty walked back onto the stage and took her seat just before it was her turn to make an extemporaneous speech. She walked to the front of the stage and looked at her audience. "Ladies and gentlemen," she said, "I don't know why I forgot my speech. I've never forgotten it before. But to prove to myself and to you that I can do it, I'm going to finish it now." Then she started where she had left off and finished the speech. She felt a lot humbler about the whole thing now, thinking of every line to make sure she didn't forget again. When she finished, the audience clapped very hard. She didn't know whether they were clapping because they liked her speech so much or because they liked that she'd got up the nerve to come back and finish it. At any rate, they liked something.

The next moring back in Robertson's Fort, Batty and Mother and Daddy were discussing the contest over breakfast while Hilda kept the coffee cups filled.

"I don't know why on earth you forgot it," Mother said in disappointment. "If you hadn't forgotten it, you'd probably have gone all the way to the national contest."

"Well, Victoria," Daddy said, "I don't think we should be too disappointed. In a way Batty *did* win. She won the respect and admiration of everybody there by going back out onstage and finishing her speech. After it was over, one of the judges told me confidentially that they all wanted to give Batty the prize, but that the rules wouldn't allow it. And I think Batty learned an important lesson she won't forget soon."

Hilda brought a plate of hot buttered toast from the kitchen and put it on the table.

"Batty learned an important lesson all right," she said. "Sometimes no matter how bad you want to run away, you just have to stay and face the music. That's all. You just have to stay and face the music."

Christmas was the busiest time of the year at the store and the time Batty loved most. The interior was decorated with garlands of evergreen that smelled like all the sixteen Christmases she'd lived through. She and Mother wore little corsages that had small bells worked into them and tinkled when they moved. There were lots of special things Mother and Daddy bought just for Christmas— lacy panties and nightgowns, dolls with shiny yellow hair, fire trucks which when you wound them up ran along the corridors between the aisles, their sirens screaming. There was a section of

Christmas tree ornaments, shiny garlands and icicles, and another one of wrapping paper and ribbon. Batty loved wrapping the packages in the bright Christmas paper Daddy put on the roll. She'd wrap a neat package and tie a big bow in no time at all, before handing the customer the package and ringing up the sale. At the end of the day, Daddy would add up all the sales on the cash register and look very pleased. Another thing she liked about working at the store before the holidays was that she got to see everybody in town to wish them a merry Christmas.

This evening when the store closed, she and Mother and Daddy were going to have dinner at the Steak House and go to the Baptist church in Cullman to hear Handel's *Messiah*. It was to be sung by the combined choirs of the Protestant churches who had been working on it for several weeks with a guest director from Asheville. She loved the parts of the *Messiah* that she'd sung with the choir at her own church every Christmas. She especially liked "For unto us a child is born," and the hallelujah chorus. She couldn't wait to hear them sung by three choirs all at the same time.

By the time they got to Cullman, the parking lot was filled and cars were parking on the street. Daddy parked about a block from the church, a large red brick building of a sort of modified Gothic design. Ivy covered the outside walls almost up the windows. As they approached, Batty could see the light shining through the stained glass. There were three ushers in the vestibule and one very fat old lady whose husband was, with great effort, helping her take off a fur coat. He carried it over his arm as one of the ushers handed each of them a program and led them into the auditorium. Another usher led Batty, Mother and Daddy to a pew and handed them programs.

The organ was loudly playing "Joy to the World." Batty felt suddenly flooded with happiness. She looked around to see who was there. She saw Mr. and Mrs. Piercy from her own church sitting a few rows in front of them and, on the other side of the sanctuary, Mary Carson and Betty Hempill from Grandmother's church.

And then she saw Gus.

She'd seen him less frequently since that evening at the lake house more than a year ago. She'd gone to summer school since then and had skipped a grade and now at sixteen was a senior. The last time she'd seen him was at the end of the summer when he'd invited her to a cookout at the lake house. There were lots of people at the cookout and she and Gus hadn't talked privately at all. She'd sort of lost touch with him—and she missed him.

And now he was being ushered to a seat on the other side of the auditorium, several rows in front of her. He was wearing a dark blue suit and a crimson tie. He looked more mature than she remembered him. He almost looked sophisticated, she thought. Then she saw the redheaded young man beside him, and wondered who he could be. She thought she knew all of Gus's friends. His red hair curled around his ears and over the top of his collar. Gus turned to look around the auditorium. She kept staring at him and wondering if he would see her. When finally he did see her, he smiled and gave a little wave. She smiled and waved back.

"There's Gus," Daddy whispered.

"Yes, I know," Batty said.

Gus said something to his friend and his friend turned to look. Batty saw the most perfect masculine features and the greenest eyes she'd ever seen in her life. Those green eyes held hers for a moment and then turned away. She continued looking at him as he turned and whispered something to Gus.

The *Messiah* was a terrible disappointment. There were a few stirring parts when the chorus sang parts of the oratorio that were familiar, but most of the time one person sang the same line over and over again and then someone else sang another line over and over again. She thought it would never be finished. Daddy squirmed a lot, which was not surprising, and before the intermission Mother was squirming, too. At the intermission, while Daddy was having a cigarette outside the church and trying to convince Mother to go home, Gus pushed his way through the crowd with the redheaded fellow following him. He was very slender and a little taller than Gus; at least six two, Batty guessed.

"Hello, Batty," Gus said.

"Hi, Gus, how've you been?"

"Terrific. Hello, Mr. Attwood," he said, shaking hands with Daddy, "Mrs. Attwood," shaking hands with Mother. "I'd like you all to meet a friend of mine, Plum Bradley. Plum, this is Mr. and Mrs. Attwood." Plum shook hands with Daddy and Mother. "And this is Batty. Plum is home on vacation from Davidson."

"Hello, Batty," Plum said, not smiling. "It's nice to meet you. Gus has told me a lot about you."

"Oh, really," Batty said. "I hope it was good."

"It was," Plum said.

"Plum's an unusual name," Daddy said. "Is it a nickname?"

"Yes, sir," Plum said. "It's a nickname for Pelham. I was named for my great-grandfather Pelham who was killed at the Battle of Bull Run."

"That's interesting," Daddy said. "It's a nice name. I like it."

"Isn't this a bore!" Gus said, motioning toward the church with his shoulder.

Daddy giggled. "It sure is too long-hair for me. I think we're going home."

"I would, too, but my friend here is enjoying it," Gus said rolling his eyes heavenward.

"I like it a lot," Plum said. "Did you know that in addition to his oratorios, Handel wrote forty-six operas?"

"Did he really!" Mother said. "I always thought he wrote only religious music."

"Lots of people think that. In fact, most people never heard anything of Handel's except the *Messiah* that's done every Christmas. It's a shame."

"We'd better go back in if we're staying," Gus said. He smiled at Batty and Mother and Daddy. "See you around," he said and began pushing his way back through the crowd.

"Nice to have met you," Plum said to Mother and Daddy.

"Yes, same here," Daddy said.

"And I'll see you," he said looking at Batty a long moment. She felt her heart lurch; she knew he was, in that moment, looking for confirmation.

"Yes, okay, I'll see you," she blurted out.

She watched as he turned and pushed his way through the crowd behind Gus toward the front door.

Batty didn't hear from Plum till New Year's Eve when she was working at Daddy's store. She had worked since Christmas helping mark down the merchandise for the after-Christmas sale. As soon as Christmas was over, Daddy put everything on sale, to reduce the inventory before January, when the clerks had to count every item in the store.

New Year's wasn't a very important event in Robertson's Fort. All the Christmas trees came down the day after Christmas and the holidays were over. To have them up any longer was like having a corpse in the living room. New Year's Eve was to most people like any other day of the year. If you were still awake at midnight, you might hear a few firecrackers go off someplace across town. Other than those firecrackers, nothing marked the changing. The next day everybody marveled at how quickly the year had passed and asked each other about resolutions nobody made.

Batty was sitting on the stool near the sock counter, putting the sale pin tickets on each pair of socks, trying to keep from puncturing herself with every ticket, when Plum came in. She looked up to see him standing there looking at her, his perfect features framed by his red curly hair and a green turtleneck the same color as his eyes.

"Hi," he said, smiling at her.

"Hello," she said. "I was wondering what happened to you."

He laughed and then she laughed.

"I had to do some work for Mother this week. She's kept me pretty busy."

"You have to work on vacation? That's terrible."

"It's not so bad. Anyway, I finished the work yesterday. Now I'm free till I go back to school. Do you want to go to a movie tonight?"

"Sure, I'd love to," Batty said. "Is there anything good playing in Cullman?"

"I'll find out. Suppose I pick you up about seven-thirty. Okay?"

"Okay. By the way, what did Gus tell you about me?"

"I'll tell you later," he said, and smiled as though he enjoyed frustrating her curiosity.

Batty was ready at seven-thirty, but Plum wasn't there. She sat down at the piano and began playing to pass the time. At eight o'clock, she decided she'd been stood up. She kept playing more and more loudly. Daddy and Mother had gone to the Steak House for dinner and she had stayed at home and made herself a hamburger. By eight-thirty when she heard the car pull into the garage, she was furious.

"Batty, quit banging that piano," Mother said when she came into the living room. "I thought you had a date at seven-thirty."

"I did, but he isn't here yet. I think I've been stood up."

Just then the doorbell chimed.

She looked at her watch. He was exactly an hour late. Nobody in the whole *world* was an hour late without calling and explaining.

"It looks like you haven't been stood up after all," Daddy said.

"He sure is late enough," Batty said, still sitting on the piano bench.

"Well, answer the door," Mother said, going to the coat closet in the hall to hang up her coat.

The doorbell chimed a second time. Batty got up from the bench and went to answer it.

"Sorry I'm late," Plum said.

"Where *were* you?" Batty asked.

"I got held up," he said, without further explanation. "Are you ready to go?"

"Sure," she said, "but *where*? Isn't it too late for the movie?"

"I'm afraid so. We'll go for a drive up the mountain."

"Be careful driving," Mother said. "There might be ice."

"I'll be very careful, I promise," Plum said as though he were reassuring a child.

"We'll be back by eleven," Batty said.

The dashboard lights illuminated Plum's hands and face as he turned onto the old road up the mountain, the road that had made her carsick for as long as she could remember. She had *walked* as many miles of it as she had ridden, Daddy always stopping the car and letting her out to walk a way till her stomach stopped heaving, and she got back in to go a few more miles before she had to get out and walk again. She'd been happier than anyone in Robertson's Fort when the new road was built and she no longer had to wind up the mountain, near death in an automobile. She didn't tell this to Plum. She would *not* get sick tonight. She would *not*.

"What year are you at Davidson?" she asked.

"I'm a senior. I graduate in June."

"How old are you?"

"Twenty-one."

Batty was sixteen. Gus was three years older than she. Plum was five years older. That seemed pretty old, even though people had been telling her for years she was mature for her age.

As soon as Plum started winding up the mountain he started talking. He didn't talk about himself. First he talked about the political situation in Korea since the war had ended. Then he explained to Batty all about the United States weaponry system. She listened intently as he went on and on telling her about things she knew nothing of. He talked about the economy, first talking about Adam Smith, and classical economics and going on to somebody by the name of Keynes who he said introduced neo-classical economics, which was what everybody believed in today.

Batty decided Plum was a genius.

Gus was very smart, but he didn't know half as much as Plum. He was just beginning an explanation of why the stars looked as though they were twinkling when Batty felt it coming on, that unmistakable misery, that sickness that was unlike any other, that rose up from the pit of her stomach and sat in her chest like a piece of poisoned meat. She knew she was turning green. Please, dear God, she thought, not now. Don't let me get sick now. He was explaining about the light-waves traveling through the atmosphere as she was breathing slowly and deeply, trying to keep down the poisoned meat. She slid lower in her seat and cracked the window. If she could just get around the next five curves—she knew them by heart—she would have it made. Just five more curves. He was telling her that the stars were balls of burning gas millions of light-years away. She felt the poison come dislodged and rise into the back of her throat. Oh, dear God, she thought, I'm going to be sick in front of him. And then the sickness became so great that it flooded over the embarrassment.

"Stop!" she said. "Stop the car! I'm going to throw up! Let me out!"

He turned to look at her. She thought only of keeping the poison down, of holding it there another moment, while he pulled off the road. The headlights flashed across an overlook on the next curve. He pulled into it quickly.

"Are you all right?" he asked, as she threw open the door, and rushed to the side of the mountain, and leaned over the darkness, and heaved. When there was nothing left to heave, she stood there breathing the fresh air. He was out of the car and behind her now.

"Get my handkerchief from my purse, please," she said, and stood there taking deep gulps of air, waiting for him. She was beginning to feel a little better. She thought of him, that he had seen her sick, that maybe she smelled of vomit. She hoped she hadn't spattered herself.

She wiped her face with her handkerchief. "I'm sorry," she said. "I always get sick on this road. I hoped I wouldn't this time."

He was standing there looking clumsy, his hands in his pockets, as though he didn't know what he should do, the moonlight lifting from his shadowed face the lines of concern. "You should have told me," he said. "We could've taken the new road up the mountain. I just thought this one would be nice with no one else on it."

"It would be," she said, "if I didn't get so carsick." She looked at him a moment standing there waiting for something from her. "But I'm all right now. We're almost to the top. We can take the new road back."

"Okay," he said. "Are you sure you're all right?"

"Yes, I'm sure."

They got back in the car and Plum drove on toward Asheville. He was telling her now about the engineering marvels of the new road that had been built up the mountain with no curve sharper than thirty degrees. He explained about how the tops of peaks had been brushed off into the valleys to build the road. It had been written up in all the engineering magazines. When they came to the turn for the Blue Ridge Parkway, he took it, driving past the sign that said the road was closed for the winter. When he was all talked out, Plum turned on the radio and tuned in to the Mount Monmouth station, the only station that played classical music. He turned the volume up very high and drove along the parkway in the dark listening to it. She wondered what he was thinking.

She could see the lights from the city of Asheville flickering in the valley below. A few curves later, she could see off the other side of the mountain. There were only a few lights from this side. In the distance she could see the faint flickering lights of the town of Black Point just up the mountain from Robertson's Fort. She was beginning to feel very sad. She thought maybe it was the effect of the music. Or maybe it was just being up here on the parkway in the dark when it was closed for the winter, the utter aloneness of it. Plum hadn't spoken a word for the past ten minutes.

"We'd better go back," she said. "I have to be home by eleven."

Plum turned the car in the next lookout and started driving back down the mountain, the music still playing.

When they were almost home, he turned the radio down. "Can I see you again next time I'm home?" he asked.

"Sure," Batty said. "When do you think that'll be?"

"I don't know. Probably not too long," he said, and smiled. "I'll make sure it's soon."

Batty was convinced that the reason Plum had stopped talking and had listened to music for a solid hour was that he was a deep thinker. Just the way Batty believed that Daddy was pondering very important matters whenever he paced from the back of the store to the front and back again, so she believed that Plum's long meditation to music represented the distinction of those rare special deep thinkers from common humanity. Oh, if she could only tap the soul of this young man, what riches she would find!

"How did you like him?" Mother asked when she came in.

"I like him a lot," Batty said. "He's a deep thinker."

"What's he studying at college?" Mother asked, sitting on Batty's bed while Batty undressed.

"I don't know. We didn't talk about that."

"What did you talk about?"

"He just told me all about weaponry systems and economics and things like that. Then he turned on the radio and listened to classical music the rest of the time."

"Aren't you curious about what he's studying in college?" Mother asked.

"I guess so. I'll ask him next time I see him."

"Okay, dear," Mother said, kissing her on the forehead. "I'm glad you like him. Now get a good night's sleep."

She went to bed thinking about Plum, the way his eyes looked so green in the green turtleneck, the way he looked so pensive listening to classical music, the dashboard lights illuminating his clean, even profile. Somewhere in the distance a firecracker exploded, and then another. It was midnight, the beginning of the first day of 1954. A dog somewhere up the hill began to bark and then another joined in. She heard a third firecracker. The firecrackers stopped and now the dogs whined.

She still felt the profound sadness that had overtaken her on the parkway, and she still couldn't figure out what on earth she felt so sad about.

In a little while, she slipped from the plane of that sadness into sleep.

Part III

Plum

After the visitors left, Mother helped Grandmother get into bed to rest while Hilda's oldest daughter straightened up Grandmother's living room and cleaned the kitchen. Then Mother went home and changed into a pair of slacks and sat in the living room smoking a cigarette and talking to Hilda about what she'd do with all of Grandmother's things now that Grandmother was to be moved into Mother's guest room. Over the years Mother had got fat. Her hair was cut short and lay in soft gray curls all over her head. Even though Hilda was too old to work anymore, she often came to visit and spend long hours talking to Mother and drinking tea. Batty thought she'd changed less than anybody over the years. She certainly didn't look like a woman in her seventies. She was still wearing the black crepe dress and fake pearls that she'd worn to the funeral. Now that her hair had turned white, she kept it dyed black as it had been naturally when she was younger, and today it was arranged around her head in tight glistening curls. Her skin was as smooth and as wrinkle-free as a girl's. Jennifer had changed into her jeans and lay on the sofa looking at a fashion magazine.

Batty sat for a few minutes listening to Mother and Hilda and decided there wasn't much she could contribute to that conversation. She was beginning to feel a little restless anyway. For three days she'd given up her individuality to share with the family a communal grief, and now that Grandaddy was buried and the last guest gone home, she felt relieved, as though it were appropriate now to withdraw from that larger family circle and claim herself again.

"I think I'll take a little walk," she said, getting up from the chair and stretching her arms over her head.

"Where are you going, Mom?" Jennifer asked, looking up from her magazine.

"I think I'll walk downtown, maybe over to the school and back."

"What if Dad calls?" Jennifer asked.

"He won't call till after dinner," Batty said.

"Then I'll come with you," Jennifer said, getting up and putting on her shoes.

"My oh my," Hilda said, "Jenny, honey, you get taller every time I see you. You're soon going to be tall as your daddy if you don't quit growing. The first time I saw you in that hospital up North when I came up to take care of you and your mother, I *never* would have thought you'd get tall enough that we'd all have to look up at you."

"She turned out pretty well, didn't she, Hilda?" Batty said, putting her arm around Jennifer's waist. Jennifer smiled weakly and looked at the floor.

"She sure did, God bless her," Hilda said.

Outside the air was becoming refreshingly cool as the light softened and the sun moved into the western sky, sending long shadows across the landscape. It was the time when "the ploughman homeward plods his weary way," the time for solitude, for reflection.

"Do you think I'll need a sweater?" Jennifer asked, as they cut across the lawn down toward the old Mercer house.

"You might," Batty said. "It gets cool here when the sun goes down. Hurry, I'll wait for you."

She stood looking at the Mercer house where Lonnie Mercer used to sell his White Lightning at night. It was a rooming house now and looked run down and in need of painting. Lonnie had died of a heart attack years ago. She didn't know what had happened to Bertie.

When Jennifer returned, they walked on down past the post office to Main Street. Before they turned right to go through town, Batty's eye scanned South Main Street. There were three gas stations, an overgrown lot, and three square brick buildings that were a bank, a doctor's office, and an insurance office.

"It isn't very pretty, is it?" Jennifer said.

"No, it isn't," Batty said. "You don't remember when that street was lined with big white Victorians. It was *very* pretty then."

"They shouldn't have torn them down," Jennifer said.

"Big old houses like that are expensive to take care of," Batty said. "Nobody can afford them anymore."

The old Chrysler place where Daddy had bought his first car after the war and that had been closed and boarded up about the time Batty graduated from high school looked as though nothing had been done to it in all those years. It was still boarded up, though some of the boards had rotted and fallen from the windows and the windows had been broken. A large section of the glass of the main display window had fallen out leaving an oblique and jagged edge of broken glass from one side of the frame to the other. The building hadn't been painted in all those years. It was still that raucous shade of yellow, but quieted now by years of fading and soot stains. Across the street the old Roxy Theater where Grandaddy had taken Batty every Saturday to see cowboy movies had been renovated and now housed a bright and shiny hardware store. Batty read the lettering above the door: REED'S HARDWARE STORE. So Gary Reed is still running a hardware store in this town after all these years, she thought, and decided that hardware stores must be a little like cockroaches—they can survive under the most inhospitable conditions. The hardware store and the pharmacy next to it looked very prosperous in contrast to all the empty and soot-stained buildings that surrounded them. When they passed the building where Daddy's grocery store had been, Batty stopped to press her nose against the glass. The room contained only three empty counters and a litter of scattered papers on the floor. The glass candy counter, where at one time the Baby Ruths had been lined up in their display box, was still there, pushed up against the wall. Above the shelves, where once groceries had been stacked, there were large brown water stains on the walls, and sections of the tin ceiling overhead had come loose and hung into the room.

"The town gets uglier every time we come," Jennifer said.

"Yes," Batty said.

"I just can't imagine you growing up here, Mom," Jennifer said. "I mean . . . I know how much you *hate* things that are ugly."

"Well . . . the town never was beautiful," Batty said, as they passed the empty building that had once been Commodore Perkins' antiques shop, "but it used to look a lot better than this. And it certainly was livelier." She glanced around at the nearly empty streets. A red pickup truck came around the corner under the blinking yellow light and drove down Main Street. Up the street she could see two old men sitting on the curb in front of the café. "There were a lot more people. On Saturdays when everybody did his shopping, the town was packed. And when I was a child, all these empty stores were thriving little businesses."

"Why did they close?" Jennifer asked.

"Because the town's dying," Batty said, "like a lot of other little towns in this country. People all have cars now . . . they build houses out in the country . . . they drive miles to big new shopping centers. They don't need the little towns anymore."

"Will Grandaddy Attwood have to close his store, too?"

"I'm afraid so," Batty said. "I think he's just barely hanging on."

"They shouldn't let the little towns die," Jennifer said with a sudden strength of feeling. "Somebody should do something."

"I don't think much can be done," Batty said, as they approached the monument to John Robertson. "It's just the direction of the country. It's . . . progress, I guess."

She examined the statue carefully. John Robertson stood there yet with the same fierce determination she remembered, ready to build a fort and start a new settlement in the wilderness, ready to vanquish savages and carry on a tradition of forging a great nation reaching across the continent and built on the unshakable foundation of every person's individuality and self-reliance, unaware that his dream was as anachronistic as he was, standing there in the middle of what was rapidly becoming a ghost town, clinging to his musket.

"Daddy says that statue's the only good thing about this town," Jennifer said.

"I've always liked that statue, too," Batty said.

"He says it's as good as a Remington."

"Yes," Batty said, "I think it is."

When they turned the corner, Batty stopped abruptly and drew her breath in sharply. A familiar figure was coming across the railroad tracks, carrying a brown paper bag full of groceries. For a moment Batty thought it was Mrs. Aldrich and wondered if Peggy Sue was off on her bicycle taking care of the little old ladies all by herself. But it can't be Mrs. Aldrich, she thought. She'd be a very old woman now. Yet it was the same heavy frame, the same careful and controlled walk, the same feigned pride of a head held high.

"What's the matter, Mom?" Jennifer asked.

The woman was wearing a wraparound cotton housedress of a large floral print and her hair was dyed a hard black with an inch of dull copper-gray coming out at the roots. She had on a heavy pale makeup spread over skin that looked tissue-thin, loose around the eyes, and lifeless, small lines radiating from a mouth that was carelessly smeared with orange lipstick. As she drew near, her eyes met Batty's and flicked away, then darted back, and suddenly Batty knew who she was.

"Peggy Sue?" she said.

Through the hard makeup, Peggy Sue's face became soft as a caress when she recognized Batty. She smiled, and her whole face crinkled, and the mischievous and merry child appeared—but only for a moment. "Oh, Batty," she said, a little thickly, "I *thought* it was you." She bent down awkwardly, put the bag of groceries on the asphalt between the railroad tracks, and stood up and patted her hair. "I . . . I didn't want you to see me this way," she said, looking down at her dress. "I mean . . . if I'd known I was going to . . ."

"You look just fine," Batty said.

And then there were tears in Peggy Sue's eyes and suddenly she gave Batty a big hug. Batty smelled whiskey and thought of Peggy Sue's mother who'd been a drunk. Peggy Sue pulled away and took a tissue out of her pocket and wiped her eyes, laughing nervously. "I'm so glad to see you," she said, smiling. Then her face clouded over. "Batty . . . I'm awfully sorry about your grandfather . . . and that I didn't get to the funeral. It was just that . . ."

"That's all right, Peggy Sue," Batty said quickly. "I know you would have come if you could have."

"I've had . . . a lot of trouble lately. John left me and . . ."

"John?" Batty asked.

"My husband. And I lost my job at the plant."

"Oh, I'm so sorry," Batty said, feeling clumsy and inadequate.

"I'm just staying home now and . . ." Her voice strayed off and her eyes wandered away. In a moment, she caught herself, inhaled and lifted her shoulders and turned to Jennifer. "Is this your daughter?" she asked, smiling too broadly.

"Yes, Jennifer, this is Mrs.—I'm sorry, I don't remember your married name."

"Brown," Peggy Sue said with an air of dignity, and offered her hand.

"It's nice to meet you," Jennifer said.

"She's beautiful," Peggy Sue said. "You're lucky,"and she enclosed Jennifer's hand in both her own and for a long moment continued holding it while fixing Jennifer with a syrupy smile. In the distance, the train whistle blew. Jennifer glanced at Batty imploringly, and took her hand from Peggy Sue's. "Come on, Mom, we've got to get off the tracks," she said insistently as the train came around the corner and into sight.

Peggy Sue bent over stiffly from the waist and picked up her groceries. "Good-bye, now," she said, smiling and regaining the composure the meeting had cost her. "I'm glad I saw you, Batty." She turned and began walking on across the tracks, her head held high, carrying the bag of groceries. Batty stood a moment watching her, then turned and rushed on across the tracks, clearing the way for the train that was now screaming relentlessly as it came down the straight stretch into town.

When the train had passed on through, Jennifer asked, "Who was that lady, Mom?"

"She and I used to play together when we were little girls," Batty said. "We rode our bicycles all over town, visiting some little old ladies. We had a lot of fun together."

Suddenly she felt chilled all over and her palms began to sweat.

What if *she* had stayed in Robertson's Fort? What if *she* had ended up like Peggy Sue? And then she remembered that from the time she was a little girl she'd been told she'd grow up to go away to college, and learn a lot of things, and get to know interesting and educated people, and make a good life for herself some place *away* from Robertson's Fort. She took Jennifer's hand as they passed Daddy's store, closed and with a white wreath on the door, the barrenness inside hidden behind the opacity of sheets of glass transformed into glowing reflectors of the late-day sun.

Her fading summer tan was pinched into gooseflesh above the sheared top of her white organdy formal, the skirt of which was spread around her on the crepe paper. She shivered both with cold and with excitement and glanced down at her arms to make sure they weren't turning blue. Then she raised her face and smiled her most beautiful smile and waved to the crowds lining the main street of Hillsborough.

Above her on the float was Sally Clark, the homecoming queen, a tall slender blonde wearing a pale blue organdy dress with a single wisp looped over her shoulder and snapped to the bodice of the dress above each breast. Sally was not only pretty; she was also president of the Baptist Student Union. Batty remembered the inspirational talk she'd given at vespers just the week before, about God in campus life. On a lower level of the float was Mary Ann Poteat who wore a big diamond engagement ring from a senior at Lowell Hall. The skirt of her crimson dress was spread around her like an inverted rose, and she wore draped over her shoulders a dark fur jacket the same color as her hair. She smiled easily, looking far more comfortable than the other girls. Below her was Clara Barnes from the sophomore class, a very sweet but mousy girl who was neither pretty nor accomplished. Batty thought the only reason she'd been elected class representative was that the sophomore class was short on beauties. The pale skin of her arms was mottled purple against her mint-green dress. She beamed a congealed smile and waved a white-gloved arm mechanically.

Batty was on the lowest tier of the float because she was the freshman representative—a "rat" she'd been for the first weeks of school, Rat Batty Attwood. She'd had to wear that orange beanie with the cardboard ears till she thought she'd go bald. If it hadn't been for the good sense and equanimity of her roommate, Laura Jessup, she'd probably have had a run-in with some of the sophomore girls who gave the freshmen so much trouble, especially at the initiation ceremony when in addition to wearing the beanies and ears, each of the freshmen had to wear paper whiskers, a tail made from a coat hanger, and a big sign with her name on it preceded by the word "Rat." She'd really got fighting mad when Jenny Matthews—the sophomore who took all this nonsense most seriously—made Batty push a peanut across the room with her nose in front of the entire sophomore class, who laughed as though they thought she was the funniest sight they'd ever seen. If Laura hadn't been there whispering to Batty behind her hands at every opportunity that initiation would soon be over and she shouldn't get into trouble now, she was afraid she might have got in a real tangle with Jenny. But thank God for Laura and her calming presence. There was one thing Batty knew already, and this was only November: she was awfully lucky to have Laura Jessup for a roommate.

When the freshman class elected its representative for homecoming, Batty had been the strong favorite. That was because there were twice as many boys on the men's campus as there were girls at the "Zoo," and they'd voted for her because they'd seen her around and decided she was the prettiest girl in the freshman class. She could hear the school band in front of her playing "Oh! My Papa." She wished she could see the major with his tall plumed hat but the only thing she could see in front of her was a mountain of fluted and stapled crepe paper.

She scoured the crowds hoping to see Plum's face. She couldn't help thinking that if he missed her as much as she missed him, he'd surely come today, even though when he'd called on Monday he'd told her he had other plans. He would, in fact, be going into the swamp collecting cypress knees with a friend of his who was a captain in the Air Force stationed with him at the base in Charleston. Although Plum was only a lieutenant, he had several friends who were captains; Batty figured this was because the captains recognized, just as she did, that Plum was brilliant and special and appreciated his fine qualities enough to think they were more important than his lower rank. She had hoped that this weekend, when she'd be riding a float down the main street of Hillsborough, South Carolina, and being presented flowers at halftime in the Lowell Hall–Citadel football game with everybody clapping and cheering, he'd have wanted to come see it all. When he said he was going collecting cypress knees instead, she'd let it go at that. She didn't want to seem too eager—even though she was.

It was wrong for a girl to seem more eager to see a boy than the boy was to see her. She'd always known that was the quickest way in the world to make him lose interest. And besides, with Plum, you just couldn't get too eager. His cool manner, the totally sensible approach he had to everything, didn't encourage you to get all enthusiastic and excited about something that probably wasn't worth it in the first place and make a fool of yourself. One of the nicest things about him was that he never got so excited about anything that he failed to make the right decision. He thought about things unemotionally, and his decisions were based on nothing but good sense. If he decided not to come today but to go into the swamp collecting cypress knees instead, she was sure he had a good reason for it. He'd probably figured that since this was her first year in college and since she was getting a lot of attention for being pretty and a good student—she'd even got a part in the first play of the year—he ought to give her the freedom to enjoy it and date other boys and get involved in campus life and do all the other things girls were *supposed* to do in their first year at college. If he wasn't here today, that was probably the reason.

It was very exciting being the most popular girl in the freshman class and riding a float wearing a formal, while crowds of people lining the streets watched and waved. She only wished it weren't so cold. The crowds were composed mostly of Hillsborough residents who had nothing to do with Lowell Hall. In the front row were tow-headed twin boys of about three, she guessed. They tugged at the arms of their mother, a slender exhausted-looking blonde with her hair in a French twist. On the bank steps above the crowd, an old man in a baggy suit, the jacket unbuttoned, stood with his arms folded, the broad brim of his hat shadowing his expressionless face, and watched the float go by. A group of town boys, their hair slicked back with grease, congregated around an old Ford parked on the street. One of them, wearing a black leather jacket, sat on the hood of the Ford playing a harmonica along with the band. Two of them were laughing and pointing at the Theater Guild float following her float. She could see only the back wall of the float now, but she'd seen the whole thing earlier. It was a replica of a stage put together in the scenery shop with a real proscenium, a red velvet Victorian sofa and chair, and six members of the Guild dressed as supposedly recognizable characters from famous plays—Lady Macbeth dressed in a long nightgown and holding a candle; Laura Wingfield, looking a bit dazed, examining and reexamining an assortment of little glass animals; Saint Joan, tied to the stake; Cassius, wearing a toga, a plastic wreath around his head, and brandishing a rubber dagger menacingly; and two cardboard robots from some Czechoslovakian play. The townies around the Ford were quiet now, watching the float move by. There was only a scattering of students in the crowd.

The float turned off Main Street and moved up the hill toward the men's campus. The side street was lined with boys who waved and called to the girls on the float. The other girls knew the boys and called back to them. To Batty they were still mostly strangers. Now the float was passing the Sigma Alpha Epsilon house. A group of about twenty SAEs were standing out front chatting and watching the parade go by. The SAEs were the biggest fraternity on campus. They were also the nicest boys, mostly serious students, several ministerial students, no football players, just real clean-cut fellows. Marion Dawson, who'd taken her to the fraternity party last week, was in the group. He was short and nice-looking with brown hair and blue eyes and a ready smile, brightened by big dimples. Marion was looking at her now and grinning broadly. One of the boys leaned over and said something to another, at which point they both looked at her. Then all the SAEs were looking at her. She felt embarrassed. She smiled and waved, but she knew her smile looked wooden.

The float moved on up the hill. She was beginning to get tired and very cold. She had almost forgotten till this minute how cold she was. She looked at her shoulders and saw that she was beginning to turn blue. She wrapped her arms around herself, shivered, and forgot for a moment trying to look pretty. The band had quit playing and the float was coming to a stop at the top of the hill. Ahead of her the parade was beginning to disperse. The float moved ahead slowly now and pulled to the edge of the green at the center of the men's campus. The square was filled with people, rushing about busily, shouting directions about where to put the floats, carrying props from the floats to truck beds, chatting with great excitement. The band members in their orange-and-blue uniforms, still carrying their instruments, were scattering across the green.

Out of the crowd, Laura rushed toward the float, holding Batty's coat by the shoulders. She was a tall big-boned girl with big blue eyes in a round sunflower face. Her short curly blond hair glistened in the sun.

"For God's sake, Batty," she said, "put this on before you turn into an icicle. You must be freezing to death."

"Laura, what would I ever do without you?" Batty said, briskly putting on the coat. She moved to the edge of the float where Miss Fletcher, the dean of women, had placed a step and was helping Sally down. Batty followed her off and stood a minute, pulling the coat around her tightly for warmth and looking around at all the activity.

The men's campus with its large green square, its bell tower, and buildings dispersed across the hill was very different from the women's campus, a series of connected brick buildings with wide porches fronted by a great lawn with huge old trees that were probably as old as the buildings themselves, which had been used as a hospital during the Civil War.

The bells from the tower began to peal out the college alma mater slowly and majestically. Batty started, then looked at her watch. It was twelve noon. The bell tower in the center of the green was built of large blocks of gray stone and was about a story taller than the classroom buildings forming the square. It had three levels of elongated arched windows from the base to about two-thirds of the way up its height and was covered with a thick growth of ivy. The top two levels were open arches behind which were two clusters of large brass bells, swinging now, each in its turn ringing out the music that spread across the green and over the classroom buildings to the dorms on the perimeter of the campus and to the football field and bleachers down the hill behind the Administration Building.

Batty stood very still, listening to the alma mater, and thinking about Lowell Hall. This was the first semester of four years she'd be here studying drama with Dr. Barrow, and taking other interesting courses, and being in plays, and meeting lots of interesting boys, and being the most popular girl in her class besides. Four whole years!

Suddenly she gave Laura a big hug.

"Laura," she shouted over the sound of the bells, "isn't this the most exciting place in the world?"

Batty knew she was a real pain in the neck and that no one except Laura would put up with her. She hadn't taken very well to dormitory living, trudging down the hall with her soap dish, towel, washcloth and razor whenever she had to take a shower, having intruders burst into her room without warning, having to be quiet when someone else was sleeping or having to put up with their nose when *she* was trying to sleep. Whenever Batty studied late, which wasn't very often, Laura went to sleep with the light on. But whenever she finished studying early, which she usually did, and was ready for sleep by ten o'clock, Laura had to go off down the hall to find an empty desk in a lighted room, because Batty couldn't sleep with the light on. Laura never complained. She just made some good-humored remark about Batty having to get her beauty sleep and left, closing the door behind her.

Bedtime hadn't been a problem for the past week, though, because Batty had been in the final week of rehearsal of *The Importance of Being Earnest*, the first performance of which was being given tonight. The final dress rehearsal last night had gone really well, all the technical cues coming right on time, the costumes and props in place right down to the last shoe and handbag, everybody remembering his lines. She hoped such a good final dress rehearsal wasn't *truly* a bad omen for opening night. All week long, she'd come in at midnight just as Laura was finishing her studying and they'd both been ready for bed at the same time. Batty didn't understand how on earth she was getting by on so little sleep. She figured she must be running on nervous energy and that when the play was over she'd have a lot of catching up to do.

All afternoon she'd been writing a paper on "The Advantages of a Liberal-Arts Education" for Mrs. Muller. She killed herself for that woman and, while she was getting B + and A in her other courses, the best she could get from her was a B − . For the first writing assignment in September, Mrs. Muller had given the students the freedom to choose their own topics. Batty had written her paper on "Why I'm Glad to Be an American." She'd taken a lot of the language directly from the speech she'd used in the American Legion contest two years earlier. In fact, she'd used some of Daddy's best sentences. She knew the speech was good enough to get a favorable response from the severest critic, but Mrs. Muller had given it an F, and had written a terse sentence at the bottom: *"Too much fine writing."* And she didn't mean by "fine writing" what Batty wished she meant. What she meant was that many of the sentences sounded flowery and dramatic but upon close examination had very little meaning. For Batty to have to write for Mrs. Muller while avoiding "fine writing" was a bit like running a race in a potato sack.

She'd been working on her new paper all afternoon. She'd written and then gone back and struck out anything she thought Mrs. Muller could judge "fine" and then had discovered she had very little left and had gone on to add to that, and then strike from it, and add to it again, and on and on and on. It was a little difficult to have the additions exceed in length the deletions so that in fact the paper wouldn't spend more time getting short than it spent getting long. Finally, she ended up with about a thousand words—which was five hundred words short of the assignment but the best she could do. She put her name in the upper right-hand corner of each page, closed her notebook, and pushed it back to the corner of her desk.

Laura was studying biology for a test she would have on Monday. She was learning the parts of the circulatory and the nervous systems. For two hours she'd been at it. She'd look at her notes for a while and then raise her eyes and look out the window, mouthing silently what she could remember. Batty had taken the same test earlier in the week, and thought it was the biggest waste of time imaginable. Mrs. Turnbull couldn't see the forest for the trees, and she refused to have her students looking for the forest when, according to her, what they should be looking for was the trees. Batty had been looking forward all the years she was in Robertson's Fort High School to going to college where she could learn a lot of interesting things, broad concepts that would help her in judging the nature of God and Man, and when she finally got to college and had an important course like biology, Mrs. Turnbull had her spending all her time looking at cells through a microscope and learning their parts—one time she discovered she'd been working for more than an hour and didn't even know what it was a cell *of*—and learning the names of all the trillions of components of a whole spectrum of systems. Mrs. Turnbull obviously was not a deep thinker. She was much too preoccupied with trivia.

Batty pinned her hair on top of her head and pulled her pink plastic shower cap down over it to just above her ears. She stripped to her panties and bra and walked to the closet and hung up her skirt. Then she folded her sweater and laid it in the bottom drawer of her chest. She took her red terry-cloth robe from the hook on the back of the door, slipped it on, and picked up her soap dish, washcloth and towel.

"I'm going to take a bath, Laura," she said. "I'll be back in a few minutes. I've got to eat early tonight because Dr. Barrow wants us there by six o'clock."

"Okay, honey," Laura said and turned her attention back to her notes.

The phone on the wall began to ring just as Batty was turning the corner to the bathroom. She knew it would be for someone down the hall and if she answered it, she would have to run find the girl and maybe even write a message if the girl wasn't in. She had to answer it, though, because there she was right next to it. She put her soap dish and washcloth in the pocket of her robe and picked up the receiver.

"Women's College," she said. "West Dorm."

"Would you please get Batty Attwood to the phone?" the voice on the other end of the line said.

She recognized his voice as soon as he said her name.

"This is Batty," she said. "Plum?"

"Yeah, how are you, Batty?"

"I'm just fine. How are you?"

"Fine. I just called to wish you luck tonight. Break a leg, as they say." He laughed. "Not really. For God's sake, *don't* break a leg. Are you nervous?"

"I haven't had time to be nervous yet," Batty said. "But I'm afraid I will be."

"Do you know your lines well?"

"I know them backward and forward. I just hope I won't panic and forget everything."

"Oh, you won't," Plum said. "I guess all actors worry about that before going on the stage. Just have a good time, that's all."

Batty was quiet for a minute. "I was hoping you'd come to see me in it," she said finally and a bit timidly.

"It's a long drive, Batty," he said, "and after I got there, I wouldn't be able to be with you. You'd be too busy to have time for me. I'll see you over the Christmas holidays."

"It's almost four months since I've seen you. Charleston isn't so far away that you can't come up sometimes on weekends, you know."

"Well, I suppose so, Batty," he said. "But if I *did* come, what would we do? There's not much to do in Hillsborough. It seems especially silly for me to come see you this semester when you have to sign in so early in the evening."

"I didn't even see you over Thanksgiving."

"Batty, I called to talk to you *now* and all you can talk about is how I don't come to see you. Let's talk about something other than how I'm neglecting you when I've been attentive enough to call."

"I miss you, that's all," Batty said.

"I miss you, too," Plum said. "We'll have lots of time together over the Christmas holidays."

"That'll be nice. Thanks for calling, Plum. Thanks a lot."

"Yeah," Plum said. "And good luck tonight."

When Batty hung up the phone, she went directly to the bathroom, passed the shower stalls and opened the door to the bathtub enclosure at the farthest corner of the room. Usually she took a shower because it was faster and she hated having to scour out the tub, which she did before taking a bath whether it needed it or not; but occasionally, when she had more time and wanted to relax, she took a bath. She pushed up her sleeves, took the sponge from where it was wedged between the wall and the pipe behind the tub, and washed out the tub. It was a long old-fashioned tub, raised on claw feet, and the enamel was stained a permanent yellow. She turned on the hot water, waited a minute, tempered it with cold and waited until she had a couple of inches before taking off her robe, hanging it on the hook on the back of the door, and easing herself into the water.

The tub was so long that, when she braced herself with her feet in the front, her head rested low on the back. She lay there as the water rose over her shoulders to the edge of her cap. She didn't have a lot of time to relax, but she figured she had at least a few minutes. She thought of the phone conversation she'd just had with Plum. She hated herself for having sounded so whiny. She was not a whiny person, but she *had* missed Plum a lot and whereas many of the other girls had boyfriends who were in school at Lowell Hall or who lived nearby and came to visit or take them home on weekends, Plum hadn't come to see her even once since school started. That was hard to understand considering that he'd told her he was thinking very serious thoughts about her, that he was thinking of marriage, in fact—which was a whole lot ahead of what Batty herself was thinking. All *she* was thinking was that he was about the most beautiful person she'd ever seen of either sex, with his perfect features, sculptured nose, those green eyes and hair as red as a brushfire, and that she wished he'd kiss her, *really* kiss her, not one of those short tight-lipped kisses he'd been handing out so stingily all summer.

He'd told her how serious he was the evening they went to Lake

James for a picnic with Plum's best friend Sully Sparks and his girlfriend. They'd found an enclave of picnic tables in a tall stand of pine trees near the edge of the lake. There was only one other group of picnickers, a family of five people, three grown-ups and two children, and they seemed to be minding their own business. Sparky's girlfriend had brought a tablecloth in her picnic basket. She spread it out on the table and then she and Batty unpacked their baskets. Hilda had packed potato salad, fried chicken and deviled eggs for Batty. Plum had brought a cooler of soft drinks. When they'd finished eating and had cleaned up the scraps and put the baskets back in Plum's Chevrolet, Sparky and his girl disappeared with a blanket, walking hand in hand into a thicket of trees.

She and Plum just sat there on the splintery picnic table, talking, while the shadows of the pine trees lengthened and the grove darkened. Occasionally they heard laughter from the picnickers at the other side of the site until, when it was almost dark, they packed up and left. Plum did most of the talking, more talking about himself than Batty had ever heard from him. He told her how he felt about having to go into the Air Force for two years. He said he'd be a communications engineer which he thought would be fun and that Charleston, where he'd be stationed, was an interesting city and he really didn't mind very much losing those two years. He said two years would go by quickly and he was planning what he'd do when he got out. He wanted to go to Harvard Business School and get an advanced degree, because it was the best business school in the country, and he wanted to get a good job in a big company—he even had one in mind, United American Chemicals—where he would work his way up the executive ladder.

Batty sat and listened, stopping him only occasionally to ask a question. She could just see Plum dressed up in a business suit and tie behind a big desk in an office with his name on the door. She was sure that before any time at all he'd be right at the top. He'd probably be the youngest president in the history of United American. He told her he'd already talked to the people at the company and thought it was a good company with a good future and that it treated employees well. He said he thought the company would grow a lot bigger and that the importance of his job would grow with the company. It was almost dark when he finished telling her all this. He took her hand and moved closer to her on the picnic table.

"The headquarters of United American is in White Plains, New York," he said. He took her by the shoulder and turned her face toward his. His own face was in the dark but she knew that hers was lit by the distant light from the parking lot. Almost in a whisper he asked, "Batty, do you think you'd like to live in White Plains?"

"I . . . I don't know," she said. "I mean . . . I want to live in New York City."

"White Plains is very close to New York City," he said.

"But I want to live *in* New York City, not very close to it."

"Maybe you'll like White Plains," he said, turning away from her, and then getting down off the table. "Wait here a minute," he said and ran off toward the parking lot. She could see him weaving through the black shadows of the pines. The trunk lid of the Chevrolet slammed shut, and in a moment, he returned carrying a flashlight and a rolled blanket.

"Come on," he said, and took her by the hand and moved down toward the beach, directing the beam of the flashlight on the ground, leading their footsteps. She thought of snakes and remembered Grandmother's warning to look out for them around water because snakes, too, liked water. The pine needles crackled underfoot and she thought the crackling sounded like a rattler coiled in the dark, shaking his tail in warning. Moving by where he was poised there, vulnerable in her strap sandals, she waited for the fangs to sink into her heel. But there were no snakes, just the needles crackling.

Plum spread the blanket on the dry sand above where the little waves were slapping the stony shore. He swept the light around to make sure everything was okay and then sat down on the blanket and turned off the flashlight.

"Sit down," he said.

She sat beside him. For a long time he didn't say anything. He just sat there. She could hear his breathing in the dark. She knew he was thinking about important things.

"Batty," he said finally, "I have much more serious thoughts about you than you know." She felt his arm across her back and his hand on her shoulder. She waited for him to continue.

"Batty," he said, "I'm thinking of marriage."

She drew in her breath sharply and felt her body losing solidity. He leaned over her and pushed her back on the sand and kissed her, his mouth open and wet. She knew that if she ever married anyone it would be Plum. There was no doubt about that. He was lying pressed very close to her now. She felt the hard bulge in his pants pressing against her thigh. Then he moved away from her and took her hand and placed it where he was hard, his hand over hers, holding it there. She began to tingle with excitement and remembered looking at Lula Ann's dirty comic and Popeye with his peter out of his pants, big and hard, and was ashamed to be feeling this way, to be remembering Lula Ann's dirty comic. She was glad it was dark and Plum couldn't look into her eyes and see her guilt. Through his jeans she could feel the very shape of him. He gripped her hand more tightly and began moving it back and forth, the fabric of his clothes moving with her hand. He cupped his free hand over her breast and began kneading it through her T-shirt. The pleasant tingling she'd felt down there was now a swelling ache. Suddenly Plum moved away and sat up. She heard his zipper opening and knew he was taking out his penis.

"No," she whispered.

But he rolled back to her and wrapped her fingers around the warm sticky skin that over its firm core was as thin and veiny as the skin of a new bird. She wanted to take her hand away but Plum's grip was firm and relentless. He moved her hand slowly up and down the shaft, the thin slippery tissue of him moving with her hand over veins and tendons, like the goose-pimpled skin of a plucked chicken neck not even the cat would eat.

"Bring me off, Batty," he said, taking his hand away.

And she, half knowing what he wanted, said, "I can't, Plum, I can't," and took her hand away and wiped it on her shorts, afraid she was going to cry. She blinked her eyelids furiously to clear away the tears. She didn't want him to think she was a child when she was supposed to be so mature for sixteen. The ache down there had gone away. She felt embarrassed for having touched him and guilty for having encouraged him and then failed him somehow. It was all her fault. Plum would never have tried to make her go so far if she hadn't led him on to the point where he couldn't help it.

She heard his zipper again and then he stood up and turned the flashlight on her face.

"Are you all right?" he asked.

"Yes," she said.

"It's time to go." He took two corners of the blanket and lifted them. "We'd better shake the sand out of this," he said. "How about taking the other side?"

They went back to the car to find Sparky and his girl in the backseat, not wasting any time. As Batty and Plum approached, their heads popped up and they squirmed around a lot while Plum opened the trunk and put the blanket in on top of one of the baskets. Batty wondered if Sparky's girl held his naked penis in her hand. Plum closed the trunk and came around and opened the door for Batty. He drove Sparky and his girl to the girl's house and left them there before driving Batty to Robertson's Fort. He didn't talk all the way home. Batty didn't know whether that was because he was a little bit mad at her for what happened at the lake or whether he was just all talked out, having talked to her more this afternoon than he'd ever talked to her before. When he parked in front of the house, he gave her one of his tight-lipped kisses and walked her to the door and said good night. He didn't even come in to say good-bye to Mother and Daddy, though he knew he wouldn't see them before he left for the Air Force two days later. That was the last time she'd seen him. He called to say good-bye the evening before he left—and that was that. He hadn't called again until two weeks after she'd got to school. Since then, every two or three weeks when she was least expecting it, she'd get a call. Well, at least she wouldn't have to worry about making a fool of herself in front of Plum tonight since he wouldn't be there. She hoped to heaven she wouldn't make a fool of herself in front of *anybody*.

She'd been amazingly calm about tonight's performance until she'd finished the last line of the paper she was writing for Mrs. Muller. Then, almost immediately, she'd begun to think about the play, wondering if she knew all her lines, then being sure she couldn't *possibly* have them all stored away in her head, remembering the time at McBee when she'd forgotten her speech, or forgotten where she was in her speech, which was the same thing. Thinking of all this while she was lying there in the tub, she began to feel very jittery. She took a few deep breaths to relax the way Mother had taught her, and started going over her lines from the beginning. She got through the first scene, which was the best she could do with no one there to give her the cues. She decided she knew it well enough and hoped she wouldn't panic.

Mother and Daddy would be there tonight. They'd drive down from Robertson's Fort—which would take them only a couple of hours—and then they'd drive back home after the performance. She figured most of the students would come see the play tonight, rather than tomorrow night, because on Saturday night they had dates and liked to go to places more romantic than a college play. They went to drive-in movies, or out on back country roads where they could neck, or to private parties at the fraternity houses. Some of them went to the Hide-A-Way to dance. The Hide-A-Way was off-limits because beer was served and dancing was an activity many of the trustees of the Baptist college considered to be evil because it provoked Lustful Longings, particularly in the more uncontrollable male, which could lead from there to Inflammatory Fondling, and end up in Sinful Sex that might produce Illegitimate Offspring who would be the Eternal Shame of both of the new parents as well as of their families—especially of the girl and *her* family. Nevertheless, some of the students of Lowell Hall went to the Hide-A-Way on Saturday nights and took their chances. She knew Marion Dawson was coming to the play tonight. He'd called her earlier to wish her good luck. She was going with him to a movie on Sunday afternoon and then out to a Chinese restaurant for supper. That was why she'd done her English paper this afternoon instead of waiting till Sunday.

The water in the tub began to cool. She turned on the hot water again. It was time to finish her bath and get ready for dinner. She turned off the water and began to wash herself. Dr. Barrow wanted her at the theater by six o'clock, and though she didn't think it would take her two hours to get into costume and makeup, she didn't want to anger Dr. Barrow. He'd taken a big interest in her, giving her a big part in the first play she tried out for and spending lots of time helping her with scenes in his acting class. She was his star pupil, and she wanted to make sure she deserved all that attention. She finished washing herself, climbed out of the tub, pulled out the rubber stopper, began drying herself as the water swirled around the drain and disappeared down the pipe making obscene noises. She slipped on her robe, wrung out her washcloth, picked up her soap and towel and went to dress for an early dinner.

Batty had wrung into a lifeless rag the white lace handkerchief that was one of her props. She had paced from the prop room to the edge of the stage and back again, sweeping her skirt around at every turn, till Dr. Barrow—sitting on a stool just behind the curtain and following the script in case someone forgot a line—told her to *please* keep still. Now she stood next to the wall with her hands behind her. Lady Bracknell, stiffly corseted, sitting just inside the prop room, looked at her script a few moments, then raised her head, eyes closed, and looked at the script again. She repeated this process a few times, then closed the script and laid it on a corner of the prop table.

Dr. Barrow was very pleased that the house was more than half full. He said that was very good. Batty had looked through the opening at the edge of the curtain before the play began—and before Dr. Barrow yelled at her that it was very unprofessional to peep through the curtain—and saw Mother and Daddy sitting about halfway back in the middle. There were many people in the audience whom she'd never seen before; she supposed they were Hillsborough residents. Almost all her teachers were there. Mrs. Muller was sitting in the third row center, dressed in black and wearing rouge and lipstick. Batty figured Mrs. Muller had two selves: a classroom self dressed plainly and without makeup, her gray hair in a small knot at the nape of her neck; and a social self, dressed up and wearing makeup, her hair in an elegant French twist. Most of the students were sitting near the front. Laura was sitting in the second row, chatting with two other girls. Batty wished she could catch her eye just for good luck. And Marion Dawson was sitting right in the middle of the front row surrounded by several fraternity brothers. He looked very nice in a suit and tie—not exactly handsome, but very cute.

She heard Jack Worthington's line about being Earnest in town and Jack in the country and knew it was getting close to time. She flashed hot and then cold. She tried to remember her first line. What was her first line? Her first line?

Now Jack was saying the line about washing one's own clean linen in public. She had to walk onstage in a moment, because if she didn't, Dr. Barrow would get off his stool and *push* her on. She would stand there sputtering because she couldn't remember her line and make a great fool of herself. Lady Bracknell who made the entrance with her was now standing behind the door, plumping herself up. And then the cue: "I hate people who aren't serious about meals. It's so shallow of them."

She looked desperately toward Dr. Barrow, but his head was hidden behind the teaser and she could see only his rump on the stool.

Then suddenly, she found herself onstage.

Everything was the same as the night before, the Victorian costumes, the heavy makeup, the gaudy furniture, and blinding lights. The only difference was the faces beyond the footlights. All those faces!

And here she was. She had automatically walked on as the charming Lady Gwendolyn, the nervous Batty left behind.

Algernon turned to her. "Dear me," he said, "you are smart!"

She turned flirtatiously toward Jack, the line rolling out all by itself: "I'm always smart. Aren't I, Mr. Worthington?"

Batty didn't go to church that Sunday morning. She slept till noon, bathed and dressed in time for lunch, and did her French translation before Marion Dawson called for her at two-thirty. It was a gray cold day with the promise of rain in the air. She bundled up in her red belted coat to walk the four blocks to the movie theater on Main Street. She was looking forward to seeing *White Christmas* with Bing Crosby. He was one of her favorites. Besides, it was just before the holidays, which was a perfect time to see a movie about Christmas.

As soon as the houselights dimmed Marion reached over and took her hand. She didn't mind so much as long as his hand didn't sweat. As she watched the movie, she wondered why it never snowed very much anymore. She hadn't seen a white Christmas since she was a little girl. She remembered a wonderful Christmas before Daddy went to the war, when the family walked all the way from the farm to Grandmother Attwood's in town on Christmas afternoon with the snow so deep it came above the tops of her golashes. It never snowed like that anymore. She wished that this year, when the Christmas tree was decorated and Mother and Daddy closed the store on Christmas Eve, it would snow knee-deep the way it used to and make this a *real* Christmas again like the old Christmases she remembered.

When the movie was over, Marion helped her with her coat.

"I like Bing Crosby, don't you?" he said.

"Everybody likes Bing Crosby," she said. "It *was* good, wasn't it? This is the first time this year I've felt any Christmas spirit at all."

"Me, too. You want to take a walk to Bon Marché and look at the Christmas windows? It's kind of early to eat."

"Sure," she said, "if it's not raining. Maybe we'll get some ideas for Christmas. I haven't even *thought* about what I'm going to give people, and I've got only a little over two weeks left."

It wasn't raining outside, but the air felt as miserable and damp as it had all day. Even though it was only a little past five o'clock, it was beginning to get dark already. To Batty, stepping out into gray Hillsborough after seeing *White Christmas* was a big letdown.

"I always do my Christmas shopping at the last minute," Marion said, "the way I do everything else." He laughed and she noticed how cute he was when his dimples showed. He was about the same height as she, maybe a fraction taller, but not enough to make any real difference. As they were walking, he took her hand. She wished she could tell him she didn't want to walk down the street holding hands with him, that it made her feel silly, but she didn't know how to do that without hurting his feelings.

"You really were good in the play," he said.

"Thanks," she said, "that's very sweet of you. Allgood Bryan wrote in his review for the *Gadfly* that I 'made a charming Gwendolyn whose classic beauty could captivate any man' and that

I was 'excellent of voice but a bit distracting of bodily action.' I wonder what he meant by that. Did *you* think my bodily action was distracting?"

"No, not at all. I thought you were perfect."

"If my bodily action was distracting, I don't know why Dr. Barrow didn't tell me about it *before* the play so I could have changed it. He *should* have told me. After all, that's his job. He shouldn't have let me go onstage with distracting bodily action. He really shouldn't have."

"I wouldn't worry about it," Marion said. "I'm sure most people didn't notice it. I didn't."

The windows of Bon Marché, Hillsborough's only big department store, were decorated for Christmas and filled with things she'd have loved to buy the very next day—not as gifts for other people, but for herself. One window was a fantasy in white, the floor covered with sparkling white powder, a white stylized tree without leaves, the branches loaded with lamb's-wool sweaters, leather gloves, colorful scarves, belts, handbags. Batty never got much chance to shop because she got all her clothes from Daddy's store where they cost much less than in a big department store. Sometimes she wished she could go to Bon Marché to shop for clothes the way the other girls did.

"What do you want for Christmas?" Marion asked.

"I really don't know," Batty said. "I never have to think much about it. Mother just decides what I need."

They started walking back uptown.

"I hope you like Chinese food," he said.

"I've never had it. I like almost anything, though, except the food at Women's College. But I won't know what to order."

"I'll help you. My family goes out for Chinese food in Columbia a lot. My brother's still living at home. He's coming to Lowell Hall next year. People say we look alike, but he's a lot different from me. More serious about everything. And a very good student."

"Aren't you a good student?" Batty asked.

"Fair, I guess, I make B's and C's."

To Batty, that was a record of abject mediocrity. She thought of Plum. She was sure *he* hadn't made C's in college. He was brilliant. He'd probably made all A's.

"What're you majoring in?" she asked.

"Bible. I'm going to be a minister."

"You mean a Baptist preacher?" she asked incredulously.

"Yes, a Baptist preacher," he said, smiling at her.

"You don't seem the type," she said. "Baptist preachers are supposed to be very straitlaced and holy. They don't spend much time dating girls and having fun the way you do." She shook her head slowly. "I never thought of you as a ministerial student. And if you're going to be a Baptist preacher, what are you doing going to the *movies* on Sunday? All the Baptist preachers I've known think going to the movies on Sunday is a *sin*."

"I guess they're a little more straightlaced and holy than I am," Marion said, chuckling, and put his hand in her coat pocket and took hers.

The Chinese restaurant was a small room with about a dozen tables. The cream-colored walls were dark with grease. In the front window was a plastic orange tree with plastic oranges under a red-and-black Chinese lantern with a long black tassel. On the walls were Chinese prints of grotesquely shaped mountains etched in white on black backgrounds.

"I love sweet-and-sour shrimp," he said. "Tell me whether you prefer fish, chicken, beef, or pork, and I'll tell you what's good."

They began with hot-and-sour soup swirling with streaks of egg, followed by egg rolls, a mixture of finely chopped vegetables, pork, and shrimp dipped in egg batter and fired golden-brown. When the main course came, Marion served them both, heaping steaming rice on the plates, then spooning onto them the shrimp in a delicious sauce with big chunks of pineapple, pea pods and other Chinese vegetables Batty had never seen before. The dish she liked best was the one Marion had helped her choose—bite-sized pieces of chicken and chewy cashews in a delicate brown sauce. When they finished eating, the waiter cleared away the plates and put between them a dish containing two little folded cookies.

"They're fortune cookies," Marion said, refilling the teacups. "There're fortunes inside. You have to crack them open." He broke open one of the little cookies and left the pieces on the plate, taking out a thin strip of paper and then reading it.

" 'He who wastes not, wants not.' " He laughed and looked up at

Batty. "That's not a fortune," he said, "that's a proverb. Go ahead and read yours."

Batty cracked open the cookie and left the pieces as Marion had done. " 'Pride cometh before a fall,' " she read. "Do you know what I think?" she said, laughing. "I think the fortunes for Chinese fortune cookies are written by Baptist preachers." She put the strip of paper on the plate with the pieces of the cookie and looked at him, growing more serious. "Why do you want to be a minister?" she asked.

"Because I've been called," he said.

"What do you mean by that? You mean God spoke to you and told you he wanted you to be a minister?"

"No, not exactly. God didn't actually talk to me *that* way."

"Well, then what *did* God do that makes you think you've been called?"

"I can't exactly explain it," Marion said. "It's just a very strong feeling I have. Sometimes God communicates with us that way. We pray for an answer to a question and then suddenly we know the answer. It just comes to us. That's because God made the answer clear."

"If you're going to be a preacher, that means you have to give up everything else, the way Christ said. Are you willing to do that?"

"Yes. Nothing else has any meaning or gives any real satisfaction. If you spend your life chasing goods or worldly success, you'll always be miserable."

"Maybe," Batty said. "But that's what I want, wordly goods and worldly success."

"Then you'll probably be miserable."

"I hope that's a mere prophecy and not a curse," Batty said, and laughed.

It was drizzling when they left the restaurant.

"We'd better walk fast," Marion said.

Batty knew that before they reached Women's College, her hair would be a mess. She turned up her coat collar and put her hands in her pockets. It was a dark night. The only illumination was from the street lamps, haloed by the drizzle, and the few cars that sent yellow streaks along the shiny black pavement. When they turned and started up the long front walk, there were three other couples saying lingering good-nights below the dormitory porch. Marion tugged at her hand, signaling her to stop.

"I've had a good time," he said. "Thanks."

"So have I," Batty said. "Thanks for supper and the movie."

He smiled and his dimples appeared. On his forehead she could see small drops of water reflecting the distant porch light. He leaned toward her and closed his eyes. She met him halfway.

It was a soft dry kiss.

On the last day of classes before the holidays, the sun was shining and the sky was an unblemished blue, though it was cold, in the low forties. When Daddy's car pulled into the circular drive in the early afternoon, she was on the porch waiting for him. She rushed into the foyer, signed out, grabbed her suitcase and dirty-laundry bag, and before Daddy got halfway up the walk, met him, gave him a quick peck on the cheek, fled past him to the car, and threw her suitcase and laundry bag onto the backseat. As they pulled out of the drive and into the street she could suppress her misery no longer. She leaned over her lap and, covering her face with her hands, wordlessly, she sobbed.

It embarrassed her to cry in front of Daddy. He should think of her as being very strong as he was very strong. Besides, he didn't know what to do when she cried. She could tell he felt embarrassed, too.

"Well, Batty," he said, with a tone of surprise, "what on earth's the matter?" He watched the road ahead, flicking glances at her.

"I've been so homesick, Daddy," she said. "I can't stand living in a dormitory and not being at home. It's so lonely and sad."

"How can you be lonely with so many girls around?" Daddy asked softly.

"It's not the same as being at home. It just isn't."

Daddy glanced at her again, looking concerned. A truck pulled out of a side street in front of him. He braked to give it room, then followed it closely, waiting for a chance to pass.

"This week I was so miserable and homesick, I talked Laura into taking a walk with me through a residential neighborhood behind the campus. We just walked and looked at all the little houses decorated for Christmas, watching the children playing in the yards, and I just *wished* so very much that I was home again."

"Is Laura homesick, too?" Daddy asked.

"A little, but not as much as I am. I just hate not having a home anymore. I just hate it." She began sobbing again.

"You still have a home, Batty," Daddy said.

"Not really," she said, shaking her head. "I can never come back to Robertson's Fort to live again, never, only to visit. Oh, it makes me so sad." She turned and rested her face in her arms on the back of the seat and after a while, her sobbing subsided.

"Cheer up, Batty," Daddy said. "I thought you'd be very happy with all the honors you've had your first semester. I thought you'd be proud of yourself."

"I am proud, I guess," she said, "but the honors don't make up for everything. They just don't."

By the time they got home she'd cried herself out and was beginning to feel better. She wanted to see Grandmother and Grandaddy in their new home next door. Earlier in the year, Grandaddy had retired from the railroad, and he and Grandmother had decided to sell the farm. Preston had died four years earlier, and the fields hadn't been planted in all that time. Grandmother and Grandaddy were in their sixties and that was too old to be going to the barnyard every morning and evening to feed chickens, collect eggs, and take care of pigs. The farm had been sold in September while Batty was at school, but the new owners hadn't taken possession till after Thanksgiving. The last time Batty had seen it was during Thanksgiving vacation. Over the years the hundreds of chickens Grandmother once had were reduced to fewer than a dozen, and Grandaddy had only one very ordinary pig. The farm was beginning to look a little run down, too, with the fields uncultivated and the buildings not as clean and freshly painted as they once had been when she was a little girl, living on the farm and playing in the barnyard. If she hadn't been so busy at school when the farm was sold, she thought she might have grieved more. She wondered now if the sadness she was feeling might be, at least in part, the delayed grief inexorably finding its way to the surface.

Of course, she'd seen the little white house next door ever since she'd lived in Robertson's Fort. The Plemmonses had always been good neighbors till he died at the age of eighty-two and she went across town to live with her daughter. Grandaddy and Grandmother had the house freshly painted and wallpapered before moving in, and she was eager to see it.

As soon as Daddy got out of the car to open the garage door, Batty bounded out, torn between her desire to rush into the house to see Mother and her desire to run next door to see Grandmother and Grandaddy. When Daddy lifted the garage door, Mother was standing behind it. She was wearing brown wool pants and a beige wool sweater. Batty thought she looked as though she'd gained weight since Thanksgiving. Mother ran to her with her arms outstretched and Batty met her halfway.

"Darling girl," Mother said, "I'm so glad you're home."

"I'm glad to be home," Batty said. She felt her eyes filling with tears again but she was determined not to cry. That was all over for now. She certainly couldn't cry in front of Grandaddy or he'd start crying, too, and then she'd cry more and he'd cry more and they'd *never* stop.

"Well, honey, what's the matter?" Mother asked, holding her at arm's length and looking into her face.

"She's been homesick," Daddy said, smiling tolerantly as if to suggest that the subject should be treated cautiously for the moment, lest more tears erupt.

A door slammed and Granddaddy came across the lawn. His once-yellow hair was almost white and he walked slowly and carefully. Batty ran to meet him.

"Well, hello, sugar," he said, and gave her a big hug and reached up to kiss her on the cheek. She thought he'd got shorter. "We've been so anxious for you to get here, it seems we've been waiting forever." He gave her another kiss. "Come on now, Grandmother wants to see you, too."

Grandmother was at the screen door of the back porch. Her face was beaming as she pushed the door open and held it for them to enter. She was wearing a brown wool skirt and one of Grandaddy's blue flannel shirts hanging out. Her hair, cut short and brushed back from her face in natural waves as long as Batty could remember, was getting very silver.

"Come in, beautiful," she said. "It seems I've been looking out the window every two minutes just waiting for you to get here. Excuse the way I look. I've been doing some work around here, getting things ready for Christmas. Come on in and see our little house."

Grandmother led Batty first into the kitchen, Grandaddy following. The wallpaper had a pattern of large brightly colored vegetables—big green peppers, red tomatoes, yellow squash, brown potatoes—on a white background. The crisscross curtains were white muslin with green fringe. The new sink, stove and refrigerator were gleaming white.

"Kinda cute, isn't it?" Grandmother said and snorted the way she did when she was feeling proud.

"It's adorable," Batty said. "It's just adorable."

Then Grandmother led her into the living room where she'd put all the furniture that had been in the living room on the farm: the comfortable brown sofa, the orange recliner, the mahogany drop-leaf table, now folded against the wall and adorned with an arrangement of plastic flowers in a fluted carnival-glass bowl. The painting of an Indian playing a flute that Mother had done years ago when she was an art student hung on the wall next to the front door. A van Gogh print in a heavy gilt frame hung on a wall across the room.

"It's lovely," Batty said. "And I'm so glad that every time I come home you'll be right next door and I can run over and see you anytime I want. How do *you* like it?" she asked Grandmother and Grandaddy.

"I like it a lot," Grandmother said. "I was good and ready to give up all those chickens." She paused for a moment. "Of course, we had a lot of good times on the farm, and I'll miss it." For a brief moment Batty thought Grandmother fought to keep back tears, but then she went on. "Things are going to be a lot easier here. You know it's getting time your grandaddy and I took things a little easy."

"Oh, yeah," Grandaddy said. "And we can walk downtown in no time at all. Grandmother can send me to the supermarket for eggs, which is a lot easier than having to go up the hill and steal them from the chickens. Isn't it, Ella?" Grandaddy said, and laughed.

"When you get *back* with eggs," Grandmother said, "and not *lemons*." She turned to Batty. "I swear he's the biggest child. I have to write everything down for him. I sent him downtown for a dozen eggs. He called from the supermarket to ask if I wanted a dozen *onions*. I said no, I wanted a dozen *eggs* and he came home with a dozen *lemons*. Can you imagine that? He's just like a child."

Grandaddy laughed again. "How am I supposed to remember that sort of thing?" he asked, and winked at Batty. "I've got a lot of important things on my mind."

"Like what?" Grandmother said. "Just name one."

Grandaddy looked at Batty, his eyes twinkling.

"One of these days I'm going to tell her," he said. "Then she'll be sorry."

"Oh, Andy," Grandmother said, dismissing him.

"Sugar, I was in the garage washing the car," Grandaddy said. "I'm going back out and finish. I'll see you in a few minutes."

"Okay, Grandaddy," Batty said.

"It's awfully nice to have you home. It sure is," Grandaddy said and went out the back door.

"You want some hot tea?" Grandmother asked.

"Yes, thank you. That would be good," Batty said.

Grandmother filled the whistling teakettle and put it on the burner and turned the electricity on under it.

"Grandmother, I want to talk to you about something," Batty said.

"Okay," Grandmother said. She took a box of tea bags from the cabinet and pulled out two bags and placed them in white porcelain cups with the little paper tabs hanging over the rims.

"You know I've always planned to be an actress," Batty said.

"Yes," Grandmother said.

"My acting teacher at Lowell Hall thinks I'm very talented. He says I can be a successful actress if I'm willing to work hard. He says I should be in as many plays as I can while I'm in college, and I ought to take all the courses the school has to offer in acting and directing and literature of the theater and Shakespeare. He says that's all part of an actor's preparation. And after college, I'd go to New York."

"Uh-huh," Grandmother said noncommittally.

"But Mother thinks I ought to take lots of education courses and get my teaching certificate just in case I need it. Well, Grandmother, I just don't see how I can do both."

The water was boiling and the kettle began its shrill whistle.

Grandmother poured the water into the cups with the tea bags and placed the cups and saucers on the table.

"Well, Batty," she said, "now that we know what your *acting* teacher thinks you should do and what your *mother* thinks you should do, what about you? What do *you* want to do?"

"I want to be an actress. I've wanted to be an actress ever since I was in Geraldine's play."

"But have you ever thought of anything else?" Grandmother said. "There are lots of things you could be that I'll bet you've never thought of."

"Like what?" Batty asked, looking at Grandmother suspiciously.

"Well . . . like *anything*. Like a doctor, or a lawyer, or a businesswoman. You could own a store like your daddy. Maybe in Asheville or Charlotte. Or—"

"Grandmother, you know I can't be any of those things," Batty said, interrupting her. "I don't know *any* girls who're going to be those things. At Lowell Hall they don't even *teach* you to be those things."

"If they don't teach you what you need to learn at Lowell Hall, you can always go somewhere else," Grandmother said. She sipped the hot tea carefully. "Batty, I told you a long time ago, when you were a little girl, that girls could be whatever they wanted to be. You answered—and I'll never forget it—that girls couldn't be cowboys." Grandmother chuckled at the memory. "Well, Batty, I'm still telling you, girls can be cowboys if they want it badly enough. They just have to work harder at it than boys. That's all."

"How could I be a doctor or a lawyer or any of those other things and have a family at the same time? Lots of famous actresses have families and careers at the same time. Take Helen Hayes and Jessica Tandy, for instance." Batty stopped talking long enough to take a drink of her tea. Grandmother waited for her to go on.

"I don't plan to get married for a long time yet," she said. "But someday I think I may want to. I don't want to be all by myself for the rest of my life."

"Well, it's going to be hard to do *whatever* you do and have a family at the same time," Grandmother said. "You may even decide when the time comes that you just want to stay home and take care of your house and your family the way lots of other women have done."

"No, what I want to do is become an actress. That's what I want to do." Batty was thoughtful a moment. Finally she said, "I'll decide later whether I want to get married."

"Well, honey, I sure hope you *do* get married," Grandaddy said behind her, startling her. She hadn't heard him come in from the garage. "There's nothing in the world sadder than an old maid. Nothing. Every time I see an old maid, it's all I can do to keep from crying. I sure hope you get married." He began washing his hands in the kitchen sink.

"But not anytime soon," Grandmother said.

"Oh, heavens, no! Not anytime soon. When you're old enough." He dried his hands on the towel and turned to Grandmother. "How about fixing *me* a cup of tea, Ella?"

Grandmother got up to fix Grandaddy's tea and Grandaddy sat down at the table.

"I guess I'd better go talk to Mother," Batty said, beginning to feel restless. She didn't feel her conversation with Grandmother was finished, there were still some important things she wanted to talk to her about—such as her fear of going to New York all alone to become an actress. New York was the biggest and most frightening city in the world, and she didn't know a soul there. How would she manage? Dr. Barrow had told her that the competition would be very tough and that it would be a long time before she got a part in a play. Who would give her encouragement and support when she needed it? She'd have to talk to Grandmother about these things later, because she couldn't talk to her now with Grandaddy around. There were some things Grandaddy knew nothing about, and being an actress in New York was one of them.

She took her coat from the living room and started out the back door.

"Hurry back and see us," Grandmother said over her shoulder as she put Grandaddy's tea on the table in front of him.

The next morning Batty slept late. She woke up just in time to say good-bye to Mother before she left for work at the store.

Mother didn't usually rush to the store in the mornings, but this was next to the last week before Christmas and the store would be very busy. Batty ate her breakfast leisurely and talked to Hilda over her coffee. Then she got dressed and started walking to the store. There was a chill in the air and the sky was a little overcast with just a hint of snow in the air. She cut across the street and walked down the hill past the Mercer house.

When she got to the post office, she went in, from years of habit, and looked inside the family's box. It was empty. Mother probably had picked up the mail already on her way down to the store. Batty turned the little arrow through the numbers of the combination and opened the box just to be sure she still remembered. She closed the little brass door and continued on downtown. Main Street was festooned with heavy green-and-red garlands and ropes of Christmas lights looped across the street from lamp post to lamp post.

She thought for the first time that Robertson's Fort looked a little shabby. The old Roxy Theater that Grandaddy had taken her to on Saturday afternoons had been closed for years and the building, once a bright pink stucco, was now faded and soot-stained. Across the street, the Chrysler place, where Daddy had bought his big new car at the end of the war, was empty, its plate-glass window—behind which shiny new cars used to sit in display—now boarded up. She continued walking. Thank God, Daddy's old grocery store was still there though someone else had owned it for eight years. She glanced in as she passed and spotted the glass candy counter from which she used to take Baby Ruths. Mr. Shapiro's drugstore was still there, but Mr. Shapiro wasn't in it anymore. Now that he'd retired, his sons ran it.

One thing that hadn't changed at all over the years was the cluster of old men who hung around in front of the barbershop. They sat there on the curb, chewing and spitting tobacco, and watched her pass. She pretended they weren't there, just as she'd always done. When she got to the railroad tracks, she looked both ways. The old water spout where coal-burning engines used to fill up before heading up the mountain was still there but it hadn't been used since the diesels came in years ago. She remembered the days when the fireman on the engine would swivel the big spigot till it was over the water tank and then turn the control on top, opening the faucet and releasing a frightening volume of water. Three Southern Railroad boxcars sat on a sidetrack. The lights in both directions were green. She crossed carefully so she wouldn't get her shoes caught in the tracks.

One of the windows of Daddy's store had the usual plastic Santa sitting on a step covered with white cotton. He waved mechanically, his head bobbing as though he were "ho-ho-ho-ing." Surrounding him were toy trucks, dolls, tea sets, scooters, and teddy bears. In the other window on a terrace of white cotton was displayed a haphazard arrangement of clothes—sweaters, gloves, lingerie, ties, and shirts. Sprigs of holly were scattered among the merchandise. Christmas balls, hanging from foot-long ribbons, fringed the top of the glass.

Even before Batty opened the door, she heard the music from the record player. Daddy continued to use the same records he'd used for the past several Christmases and some of them were scratched badly enough to get stuck in places. Batty had heard the records so many times she knew when a record would get stuck and start repeating before it actually did. "Silent Night" was playing. She stepped inside and looked around. The store was filled with people and all the clerks were busy. Colleen was wrapping a package for Hattie Norris who was leaning against the counter talking about how much she had to do to get ready for Christmas. Her loud voice could be heard all over the store. When she saw Batty, her black face beamed.

"Hello, honey," she called from the distance. "Come on in and stay awhile." Then she burst out laughing. Batty was embarrassed having everybody's attention called to her that way.

"Hi, Hattie. Merry Christmas," she said, walking up the aisle and taking off her coat.

"Well, honey, you sure do look good. You sure do," Hattie said.

"Thank you," Batty said, wishing Hattie wouldn't talk so loud.

"Thanks a lot," Hattie said as Colleen handed her the package. "That's just beautiful." She took the package and headed for the door. "I'll be back later, honey. I'll be back," she said again and closed the door behind her.

Batty hung her coat up at the back of the store. Colleen was helping a country woman buy a small rubber doll that wet its pants. Aunt Harriet was helping two customers buy shoes. Mother was putting Christmas wrapping in a bag for a fat woman with bleached hair. Batty figured the woman must be from somewhere else.

"Pretty busy, huh?" she asked Mother.

"Not as busy as we'll be next week."

"Need some help?"

"You don't have to help. This is your vacation. We can manage just fine."

Batty went over to the lingerie counter and looked at the lacy nightgowns Daddy had got in especially for Christmas. She unfolded a pink one with a white lace top, held it up, then folded it again and put it back in the box. She looked at the lamb's-wool sweaters and wondered what she'd do all afternoon. Then she wondered what she'd do till next week when Plum came home. Maybe one afternoon Daddy could do without Mother at the store and they could go to Asheville together to finish their Christmas shopping. But that would be only one day. There weren't many people for her to visit in Robertson's Fort. Her old friend, Peggy Sue Aldrich, was working at the plant now—and besides, the last several times she'd seen her, they hadn't had much to talk about. Of Sulie's old gang, the only one who was still in town was Marietta Piercy who had a job as secretary to the manager of the hosiery mill. Sulie had married someone Batty didn't know from Cullman, and they'd opened a sporting-goods store there. Mother said Sulie hardly ever came to Robertson's Fort. Alexandria Pike lived with a cousin in Asheville and had a job as a hostess in a restaurant.

"God Rest Ye Merry Gentlemen" got stuck on ". . . mas day." It repeated ". . . mas day . . . mas day . . . mas day . . ." Batty quickly lifted the arm and put it down again: ". . . let nothing ye dis-may."

Bertie Mercer rushed in and closed the door behind her. She was wearing her white beautician's's uniform, a black coat thrown over her shoulders.

"Batty, honey," she said. "Can you help me real *quick*? I just need some white thread. I split a seam in my uniform."

Batty started to tell Bertie she wasn't working today, but she didn't.

"Sure," she said, "what do you need? About sixty gauge?" She led Bertie over to the thread chest and pulled out the drawer of whites and off-whites. She picked out a spool of sixty-gauge white.

"That should be just fine," Bertie said, reaching into her pocket for her wallet. "How much do you need?"

"That'll be twenty-six cents with tax," Batty said. "Do you have needles?"

"I have needles," Bertie said.

Bertie handed her the exact change. "Thanks a lot," she said, turning toward the door. "If I don't see you, have a Merry Christmas."

"Thanks, and you, too," Batty said, ringing up the sale.

Mother was standing behind her, waiting to get to the cash register.

"I think it's awfully busy," Batty said. "Maybe I'll help out awhile, at least through the lunch hour."

"You don't have to, but it *would* help," Mother said.

"Why don't we have Christmas corsages this Christmas, the way we used to?" Batty asked, and went over to the toy counter to wait on an old man in overalls who was examining a fire truck.

Plum told her he'd be home on Wednesday three days before Christmas and Batty counted the days. When Wednesday arrived, she rushed to the store in the morning and rushed back home in the afternoon, so as not to be away from the phone for a minute longer than was necessary. It was nine o'clock in the evening and she was just getting out of the tub when he called. Mother answered the phone.

"It's Plum," she said as Batty came out of the bathroom holding a towel around her.

"Hello," Batty said, trying to keep the phone braced between her head and her shoulder so she'd have both hands free to keep the towel in place.

"Hi," Plum said, "how are you?"

"Fine, thank you, how're you?"

"Fine."

"When did you get home?" She pulled the towel firmly around her breasts and turned the top down twice to hold it in place. It felt secure.

"Just a couple of hours ago. Mother wouldn't let me do anything before I'd eaten. Actually I hadn't eaten since morning and I was pretty hungry."

"I should think so."

"Would you like to go to a Christmas dance with me tomorrow night at the Cullman Hotel?"

"I'd love to," she said, "but won't I see you before then?"

"I'm afraid not," he said. "I'm exhausted right now and I plan to go to bed early tonight. And Mother has chores to keep me pretty busy all day tomorrow."

Batty thought about how she'd waited for hours by the phone because she'd been so eager to see him. She wouldn't tell him she'd been counting the days. She just wouldn't tell him.

"Is the dance formal?" she asked.

"Yeah," he said. "You'll have to wear an evening dress, I guess."

"I wish I'd known sooner. My evening dress is dirty. I brought it home just to be cleaned."

"I'm sorry," he said, "I should have let you know sooner. I just wasn't sure I wanted to go."

"Why not?"

"I wasn't sure I wanted to bother with all that fuss, you know, getting all dressed up. I thought maybe I'd rather take it easy."

"Well, I guess the dress'll be okay," she said. "In any case, it'll have to do. I just didn't expect I'd have to wear it over the holidays. Who's giving the party?"

"A couple of girls who are home from Saint Mary's."

Batty thought a moment. "I guess I don't know them," she said. "I don't know many girls who go to Saint Mary's."

"I'll pick you up about seven-thirty. I'll be awfully glad to see you. It's been a long time."

"It sure has," she said.

After he hung up, Batty went to the closet to examine the dress. Well, at least he'd said he'd be glad to see her, and she guessed he would. He wasn't coming tonight because he'd probably worked at the base part of the day, and then driven for five or six hours. No wonder he was tired. If he weren't so tired, she was sure he'd come to see her, even if only for a few minutes, and not wait till tomorrow night. The white organdy was pretty dirty around the hem but it looked clean everywhere else. She figured no one would notice the grayness of the hem at night, but she *did* wish Plum had made up his mind sooner and hadn't given her such short notice.

The next day she slept late and worked at Daddy's store only during the lunch hour, when they needed her most. Then she came home and spent the afternoon washing her hair, setting it around big wire rollers which she did sometimes when she wanted to look especially pretty, and painting her nails as red as holly berries. Mother came home from the store at seven-thirty, just in time to go to the closet and bring out her fur coat for Batty to wear. Batty's hair was fluffy around her face and long rhinestone earrings hung almost to her bare shoulders. She looked at herself in the mirror, decided no one would notice that her shirttail was dirty, sat stiffly on one of the dining-room chairs, trying not to crush her dress or flatten her crinoline, and waited for Plum.

She sat there for half an hour and Plum still hadn't arrived. She wondered why she continued to be always ready on time in spite of the fact that he was invariably late, often as much as an hour. She would fume the whole time she had to wait and then become perfectly placid when he finally arrived. She couldn't imagine expressing anger to him. At five past eight she heard his Chevrolet pull up in front of the house and stop. When she heard him step onto the porch she opened the door immediately, not waiting for the doorbell to ring.

She froze for a moment and looked at him. She'd never seen him in a tuxedo. Above his white ruffled shirtfront and black bow tie, the red hair that usually curled wildly around his collar was brushed neatly into place. His face seemed thinner, the good bone structure more defined, his green eyes appearing larger.

"Aren't you going to invite me in?" he asked.

"Yes, of course," Batty said. "It's just that you look so . . . handsome in your tuxedo. I mean . . . well . . . you look *terrific*, just terrific." She pushed the screen door open for him. "Come on in. I'll get my coat."

Mother came in from the kitchen where she was making hamburgers.

"How're you, Plum?" she said. "Come here and let me take a look at you."

Plum did a little model's turn, looking very silly.

"You surely do look handsome," Mother said. "The Air Force must be treating you pretty well."

"Not bad, thank you," he said and bowed from the waist.

"You haven't said a word about how I look," Batty said.

"You look beautiful," he said hurriedly. "You really do. Are you ready to go now?"

The Indian Head Room at the Cullman Hotel was peculiarly lush in a hotel the rest of which was strictly utilitarian. Plum led her up some steps with rubber treads and down a hall with a worn solid green runner on a wood-grained linoleum floor. At the end of the hall was a heavy varnished door that looked as though it might be the entrance to Ali Baba's cave. When Plum opened the door, and followed Batty in, the party was in full swing. The room was paneled in rich dark wood, the floor a shiny parquet. At one end of the room four musicians played "I'm Dreaming of a White Christmas." They played it slowly while a large crowd of young people danced close in the dim light from ornate sconces on the walls. Next to the musicians was a huge tree decorated with large outdoor Christmas lights. At the other end of the room was a long table with a punch bowl on one end and trays of food on the other. A tall slender blonde with her hair swept up on top of her head came over to Plum and Batty. Her exposed neck was long and swanlike. She looked very fragile.

"Hello, Plum," she said, offering her hand. "It's lovely of you to come."

"It's our pleasure," Plum said. "Sarah Bridges, this is Batty Attwood from Robertson's Fort. Batty goes to school at Lowell Hall in Hillsborough, South Carolina."

"It's nice to meet you, Batty," Sarah said. "I'm glad you could come."

"So am I," Batty said, meaning it. "It looks like a great party."

"It's only begun," Sarah said and rolled her eyes. "Plum, put

Batty's coat in the coat room over there," she said, pointing, "and help yourself to refreshments."

"Thanks," Plum said. When he returned from hanging up Batty's coat, he asked, "Do you want to dance or do you want to have refreshments first?"

"I'm not hungry now, are you?"

"No, not really."

"Well, then, why don't we dance?"

"Okay, suits me."

Plum wasn't a great dancer but as long as they stuck to the regular old dip that anybody could do they got along just fine. Batty looked over his shoulder when they began dancing to see if there was anybody there she knew. She saw several of the boys who used to come to the Teenage Club square dances on Thursday evenings. She didn't know any of the girls. Plum must have been looking over her shoulder too.

"Sparky," he said dramatically, "how *elegant* we look tonight!"

Batty turned to face Sparky and his girl, still in an embrace and swaying to the music of "Three Coins in the Fountain."

Sparky's face crinkled with merriment. "Yes," he said. "I borrowed these togs from DeWitt's Funeral Home. Do you like them?"

"They're right for you," Plum said and winked, trying to match Sparky's wit.

Batty and Sparky's girl smiled graciously in appreciation of the boys, and nodded quiet "hellos." The couples dipped away from each other into the crowd of dancers.

One of the boys went over to the rheostat on the wall and dimmed the lights a shade more, making the lights on the Christmas tree the brightest in the room. Batty was beginning to have a very good time. The room was festive and romantic, she felt Plum's arm around her tighten, and moved in closer, and rested her head on his shoulder. The musicians began to play "I'll Be Home for Christmas." Batty closed her eyes and felt Plum's closeness.

"Mind if I cut in?" someone asked over her shoulder.

She turned to see Gus standing there. She hadn't seen him in ages, not since he introduced her and Plum at the *Messiah* last

Christmas. He hadn't changed very much. The ingenuousness of his expression was in sharp contrast to the sophistication of his perfectly cut pin-striped tuxedo.

"After all, Plum, I *did* introduce you. I think you owe me this one," he said dramatically, and laughed.

Plum smiled, extended his arm in a grand gesture of offering Batty, and walked to the refreshment table.

"You look great, Batty," Gus said. "How've you been?"

"Fine. You look good, too," Batty said, feeling surprisingly comfortable with Gus after such a long time. Almost immediately they fell into perfect step, and both realizing it, were silent a few moments, enjoying the dancing. He began to lead her through longer strides, and then he was spinning her in circles. She grew dizzy, but didn't miss a step. They realized they were dangerously close to their limit and to awkwardness and laughed and began dancing normally. "I didn't know you were such a good dancer," he said.

"Neither did I," she said, her laughter dying. "Are you still at Chapel Hill?"

"Yes, my third year," he said. "After next year, I'll be in medical school."

"Where?"

"I'll be staying at Chapel Hill. The medical school's terrific, and anyway I love it there."

"It's really good, huh?" Batty asked.

"It's great. It's a beautiful little town and a real cultural oasis. You're at Lowell Hall, I hear."

"Yes, I like it, too, except that I get homesick. I don't like living in a dorm. It seems so . . . unnatural."

"What're you planning to major in?"

"I'm still going to major in drama."

"Oh, yes, of course. How could I forget?" They danced silently a few minutes. Then he said, as if with sudden inspiration, "After next year, you ought to come to Chapel Hill, Batty. Women aren't admitted till their junior year, but you'd love it there. They have a really good drama department. The Carolina Playmakers are famous. Andy Griffith went there, and lots of other successful actors and actresses."

"I've heard of the Playmakers," Batty said. "But I'm not sure Mother and Daddy would let me go to such a big university. They want me to be at a school that has lots of rules."

"They won't feel that way two years from now. How old will you be then?"

"Nineteen."

"Heavens!" Gus said. "That's almost grown."

"I guess so," Batty said.

The music was coming to an end. Batty felt Gus's hand pressing on her back, forcing her to drop her weight on his arm. He held her there a moment, then lifted her with a flourish and ended with a grand dip. When she was back in an upright position, he bowed deeply before her and they burst out laughing. Then he took her by the hand and led her back to the refreshment table where Plum stood watching them.

"He's some fancy dancer," Plum said a little bitterly when they were back on the floor. He was dancing stiffly now, holding her at a distance.

"Not so fancy," Batty said. "He just *finished* fancy, that's all."

"Did you have a good time?"

"What?"

"Did you have a good time dancing with Gus?"

"Sure I had a good time," Batty said, pleased that Plum sounded jealous. "But not as good a time as I have dancing with you." She snuggled closer to him, trying to make him dance the way he'd been dancing before Gus cut in.

"Umm," he said, noncommittally.

The musicians began to play "Deep Purple," which was the most romantic song in the world. Batty rested her head on Plum's shoulder. She felt his arm tighten around her as he began to relax. They danced awhile without saying anything, Batty entranced by the music, the Christmas-tree lights and Plum's closeness.

"Are you having a good time?" he asked.

"Yes, I'm having a *very* good time. Why?"

"We've been doing nothing but dancing for the past hour and a half. I thought you might be ready to go."

"Where do you want to go? There aren't many places I can go dressed like this."

"We could go to my house. There's no one home," he said. "Mother won't be home till after midnight."

"Well, okay, if you want to," Batty said.

It was very cold outside, somewhere in the thirties, she guessed. She knew Plum would freeze, wearing only his tuxedo. He walked briskly, huffing out puffs of frost. She turned the collar of Mother's fur coat up around her neck, and they walked in silence down the street to where his car was parked. At ten o'clock, the town was deserted. There was a light on in the drugstore across the street. A car sat at the traffic light waiting for it to turn green. Then it made a right turn and disappeared down the hill going away from them. Plum rushed ahead of her and opened the car door.

"It's gotten colder," she said.

"I think it's probably close to freezing right now," he said.

"I wouldn't be surprised. It sure feels like it."

He pulled into the white cement driveway and drove to the back of the house, parking the car outside the closed garage door. The house was a large brick Victorian set back on an expanse of green lawn. A front porch with a swing and white metal furniture with green plastic cushions stretched across the facade. In the summertime, green awnings projected over the upstairs windows above the porch. Batty had always thought the Bradley house was one of the prettiest in Cullman. Plum led the way onto the small screened-in back porch and reached under the doormat for the key.

Mrs. Bradley was the town librarian and every table and chair in the house was covered with books dangling fringed bookmarks and little magazines that she read faithfully to keep up with the new books being published. With all that involvement in books, she didn't have time to keep her house very well organized. There were enough things out of place to give Mother apoplexy. The kitchen was a busy place with teapots, vases, salt and pepper shakers, syrup jars all sitting out in view. Dishes were stacked in the drain beside the sink.

"Would you like some coffee or anything?" Plum asked.

"I'd like a glass of water, that's all," Batty said.

Plum ran the water a few minutes to let it get cold. Then he took a glass from the cupboard, filled it, and handed it to her. She drank it and put the glass down in the sink.

"Here, let me take your coat," Plum said. "Have a seat in the living room while I hang it up and put on some records."

Batty walked through the dining room with its two sideboards filled with sparkling silver and crystal, and its long mahogany table. Her steps were hushed by the thick Persian carpet. The living room was scarcely larger than the dining room and was furnished with a sofa upholstered in a tapestry-like fabric, a matching chair, two red velvet chairs, and a large cabinet-style record player. The focal point of the room was a grand piano which Plum had explained was played by his father when he was alive. His father had been a lawyer, who, according to Plum, was a lot older than his mother and had worked himself to death. He'd died of a heart attack at the age of forty-two when Plum was only five. Though no one played the piano anymore, Plum's mother kept it tuned just as she had when Mr. Bradley was alive. When Batty asked Plum why his mother kept the piano if no one ever played it, Plum said he didn't know. He'd never asked her.

She turned up a floor lamp that had been left on dim, picked up *The Library Journal* from the magazine rack, sat down, and began to thumb through it. Plum came into the room, turned on the light above the phonograph, and squatted to look at the records stored vertically in the cabinet below the turntable. He had taken off his jacket and bow tie and opened his shirt at the collar.

"Do you like Dvořák?" he asked.

"I don't know," she said. "I don't think I've ever heard him."

"You should get to know him," he said, taking the record out of its sleeve and putting it on the turntable. "This is from the New World Symphony, his most popular work. You'll hear themes from Negro spirituals running through it. He spent a lot of time in America and was very much impressed by Negro spirituals."

"Where was he from?" Batty asked.

"He was Bohemian," Plum said. "In fact, he was the first Bohemian composer to gain worldwide fame."

The symphony began quietly. Batty wondered if she should tell Plum she had no idea where Bohemia was. The only time she'd ever heard the word "Bohemian" used was in reference to a strange college out in the woods near Black Point, very close to Robertson's Fort, where the students were sometimes called beatniks and sometimes called Bohemians. She was embarrassed to have Plum know how ignorant she really was. She didn't have time to think about it long, though, because Plum turned up the volume so loud he couldn't have heard her even if she'd told him. He stood in front of the record player, his eyes closed, fingers straight as blades, cutting great squares out of the air in front of him. He continued conducting for several minutes, his face set in a trance-like expression, beads of perspiration rising to his forehead while he struggled to keep the music under control as it rose to a crescendo, then victoriously brought it to rest as it slid from the peak into a trough of sound, a faint smile softening his expression, his face blissful now. He opened his eyes, looked at Batty, smiled, and turned the sound down. He dimmed the light above Batty and took her by the hand.

"Why don't you come over here?" he said leading her to the sofa. "You should try to sit where you get the stereo effect from the speakers."

Batty sat on the end of the sofa, with her crinoline spread out around her, and Plum sat down as close to her as the crinoline allowed. For a few minutes, he sat there listening to the music, his eyes half closed, and Batty sat, hands folded in her lap, waiting to see what he had in mind. Surely, if he took her away from such a beautiful party he must have had something in mind other than just sitting here on the sofa listening to records she was certain he must have heard dozens of times. After a few minutes, Plum edged closer, picking up the fabric of her skirt and sliding under it, laying it on his lap. He put his hand behind her head and pulled her face to his and kissed her long and hard on the lips. With his left hand he reached under her and lifted her hips and laid her lengthwise on the sofa and lay beside her and kissed her on the mouth again. While he was kissing her he moved a leg over her thighs and moved in tight, the bulge in his pants pressing against her; then he took his mouth away from hers and buried it in her neck as he slid on top of her, fitting the shape of his body into the shape of hers through the fabric. A hoop in her crinoline was digging painfully into her thigh.

"Plum," she said, "my crinoline's pinching. Get up a minute."

He pushed himself up on one elbow and sat on the edge of the sofa.

"Why don't you take off your dress, Batty?" he said.

"Take off my dress!" she said, shocked. "You know I can't take it off. I'd be lying here in my underwear."

"Wait a minute," he said and disappeared into the hall. In a minute he returned, carrying a red flannel robe.

"You could put this on," he said.

Batty looked at the robe a minute. It was so short, she suspected it wouldn't come to her knees.

"Is it your mother's?" she asked.

"Yes," Plum said and held the robe up to him. "You didn't think it was mine, did you?" he asked and fell into a feminine pose.

Batty laughed and then turned serious. "What if your mother comes home and finds me with my dress off and wearing her robe?"

Plum looked at his watch. "Mother won't be home for at least an hour and a half," he said.

She wanted him to hold her and kiss her and lie close to her, his body touching hers, more than she wanted anything, and she knew that her dress and crinoline were going to make that very difficult. At the same time, she'd never been so intimate with a boy as to wear only a robe in front of him. She knew she had to keep enough clothes on to stay out of trouble. Sometimes, the only thing between safety and a ruined life was a forbidding piece of fabric.

"You can keep on your underwear," Plum said, sensing her reluctance. He held the robe out to her.

"Of *course*, I'll keep on my underwear."

"Why don't you give me your dress to hang in the bathroom? I'll turn the shower on and steam it. The wrinkles we got in it'll fall out and when you're ready to put it on again, it'll look good as new."

Batty looked at Plum standing there, holding the robe, and remembered how handsome he'd looked tonight when she opened the front door and saw him standing there.

"Okay, I guess," she said at last. "But turn off the music so we can hear your mother if she comes home early. And I don't want to take off my dress in front of you."

Plum walked over to the record player and switched it off. "Come change in Mother's room," he said. "Give me the dress when you're changed and I'll begin steaming it."

When she closed the door, she unzipped the dress and let it fall to the floor. Then she stepped out of her crinoline with its three hoops and looked at herself in Mrs. Bradley's long mirror. Her legs were long and slender and her breasts swelled deceptively over her merry widow, which hooked all the way up from two inches below the waist to the crease between her breasts. Four elastic straps from the bottom of the garment hooked into the dark bands around the tops of her flesh-colored stockings. The robe barely covered the tops of her stockings. She examined herself, decided she was just over the line of decency, and opened the bedroom door, her dress over her arm. Plum was standing there, leaning on the rail of the stairs, waiting for her.

"Give me that," he said, reaching for the dress and ignoring the fact that she was wearing the robe. He put the dress on a hanger, took it into the bathroom and turned on the shower. When he came into the living room where she was sitting on the sofa, he turned off the light, throwing the room into darkness except for the front-porch light that sifted in through the sheer curtains. He came to her and leaned down to kiss her. She could hear the shower running in the bathroom.

"Lie down," he said in the dark and waited for her to finish shifting. He lay beside her and put his right arm under her head and kissed her firmly while his left hand played with her breasts through the armor of the merry widow. He found the soft flesh bulging from the top and stroked it, and in a moment lifted himself on one elbow and thrust his hand under the merry widow and cupped her naked breast. She felt light enough to fly. Plum sat up now, straddling her hips and in the dark began to struggle to unhook the front of her merry widow.

"I'll do it," she said breathlessly and unhooked it halfway down, exposing her breasts. He lay beside her and stroked her, then took her hand and put it on the bulge in his pants. She'd thought about this a long time and had resolved long ago that if he wanted her to touch his naked penis again she would and she'd not flinch with disgust as she'd done the first time. She'd have to worry only if he wanted to touch her there where he shouldn't, where he'd put his hand in the shame of her wetness and discover everything. When he unzipped his fly and took out his penis, she was ready for it. She held it in the dark, trying not to think of chicken necks. He took her hand and moved it up and down and she felt his penis growing bigger and harder. Then he took his hand away and threw his head back.

"Don't stop," he said, "don't stop," and she didn't. He cupped her breasts in both hands and put his mouth on one of her nipples and began sucking, making her wetter and wetter. Then he sucked the other nipple. She was so excited now, she had trouble keeping her hand moving steadily on his penis. Suddenly Plum opened her robe in the dark and moved fiercely on top of her, spreading her legs with his knees. She opened easily and he put his penis against her where she lifted herself to him with only the wet nylon of her panties between them.

"Batty, let me in, for God's *sake*, Batty," he whispered desperately in the dark.

"I can't, Plum," she said, panting.

"Why not? You *know* I'm going to marry you. You *must* know that." He was almost whining now.

"I can't, Plum, I'd get pregnant. You know I can't."

He was pumping harder against her now. In the dark silent room, there was only the sound of his labored breathing and the muffled sound of the shower running in the bathroom.

"Oh, please, Batty. I promise I won't come."

She wondered what he meant. She knew quite well that if he put his penis inside her, she'd get pregnant; she knew she was close to letting him do it and if he did, her life would be ruined forever. She was dangerously close to slipping her wet panties down over her garter belt and offering herself to him, wet and aching, for him to enter hot and hard.

"No, Plum! *No!*" she said loudly, her voice breaking the silence. She tried to push him away.

Suddenly Plum quit breathing. His eyes opened wide. His whole body stiffened. After a long moment, he exhaled loudly and dropped his head on her shoulder, breathing more calmly now.

"What's wrong?" Batty asked. "What's *wrong?*"

He shook his head weakly on her shoulder.

She reached down to where he lay still hard against her thigh and touched a wet mess that she knew had come from him and all at once she understood what he'd meant when he said he wouldn't come.

"My God, Plum," she said. "Oh my *God!* Get off!" He rolled off and she sprang from the sofa and ran to the bathroom where the shower was still running. She opened the door and felt around and found the wall switch and turned on the light. The bathroom was filled with a cloud of steam. She found the lavatory and washed her thigh. Then she washed her hands and face and wiped away the wetness between her legs, and flushed the tissue down the toilet.

When she felt clean again, she turned to look at her dress hanging on the shower rod in the cloud of steam. Plum had been right. It hung there wrinkle-free, the tiers of organdy cascading gracefully, one over the other, as fresh and pristine as the day she'd bought it.

The next day, when Mother asked Batty about the party, Batty told her about the Indian Head room and the beautiful decorations and about dancing with Gus. She told Mother it was a beautiful party. What she didn't tell her was that she and Plum had left the party after only an hour and a half and gone to Plum's house where she took off her dress and he made a mess on her leg. She didn't tell Mother that he wasn't a bit embarrassed about it though she'd expected him to be, or that he wore a silly grin for the rest of the evening and kissed her over and over, or that he didn't turn on the radio even once when he drove her home, that he just hummed the entire time while she sat there puzzling over his strange behavior.

What she said to Mother was, "Mother, he makes me lust."

To which Mother replied, with a mouth so tight she could hardly get the words out before she turned away, "Then, Batty, you'll have to quit seeing him."

That was when Batty knew that when it came to unraveling certain mysteries, she would get no help from Mother.

May Day celebration was held in the amphitheater on the men's campus. Sally Clark, who had also been homecoming queen, was

May queen. She was attended by three girls from each class, and Batty was one of the three from the freshman class. The girls formed an arc across the narrow stage, each organdy skirt forming a bell, the queen in white, the seniors in lavender, the juniors in pink, the sophomores in mint green, and the freshmen in yellow, which wasn't Batty's favorite color. The dresses were strapless and tight around the bodice, and below the waist a puff of organdy sat on the bell of the skirt, high up on the left side and dropping lower on the right.

The theme chosen for May Day was "Snow White and the Seven Dwarfs" and for the past hour the girls had been standing and smiling while being entertained by ballet dancers, folk dancers, acrobats dressed as dwarfs, and even fencing duelists, performing in the grassy circle in front of the stage. An *a cappella* choir was finishing its program of medieval songs as the Lowell Hall Band sat in two rows of folding chairs on the edge of the circle and waited till time for them to play again. The stone benches of the bowl-shaped amphitheater were filled with faculty and students and some townspeople who had come to watch the celebration.

The choir finished singing and filed out of the circle and took seats at the side of the bowl-shaped seating area. Seven dwarfs entered from behind the proscenium wall, three of them carrying the ten-foot Maypole and the other four carrying the attached satin streamers that were folded and tied in little packages. They placed the pole in the center of the grassy circle and unwrapped the folded streamers, which were divided into the colors of the girls' dresses, and laid them out on the grass in a star pattern from the pole. When they had arranged the streamers to suit them, they turned to the audience, bowed quickly and playfully, and tripped behind the proscenium from which they had come. The band began shuffling the sheet music on the stands before them, lifted their instruments and prepared to play while the bandleader stood before them, baton poised. Batty lifted her shoulders and shifted her weight and got ready.

The bandleader punctuated the air with his baton and the band began playing a Strauss waltz. The girls filed toward the pole and took their places at the ends of the long satin streamers. The bandleader brought the phrase to a close and held his baton aloft as the girls stooped, bending at the knees so the bell skirts crushed like bellows to the ground and then released as they picked up the satin streamers and stood up, alternate girls turning to face each other in pairs. With a flourish of his baton, the bandleader started the music again and the girls began moving in a waltz step—one, two, three—weaving in and out of the flashing streamers, covering the pole with a braided pattern, the streamer each girl carried the color of her dress, the colors catching the sun and like light through rain, breaking into the spectrum, the streamers winding shorter, the circle of girls tightening, dropping their heads now and bending at the knees to move under the streamers as the bandleader brought the music to a final phrase, dropped to a minor key, and ended it. The girls laid the tails of the streamers on the grass and stepped back from the pole, clasped hands in a circle, and curtsied together.

The sound of the spectators clapping in the open air was as thin as the rustling of new leaves.

In the fall when Batty was a sophomore, Plum picked her up on his way home for the Thanksgiving holidays. It was a beautiful crisp day with a lot of sunshine. She was wearing her new rust-plaid skirt, rust sweater and brown suede jacket when she came down the stairs carrying her suitcase to meet him. He was leaning against the banister wearing pants with a small black check and a black turtleneck sweater that made his skin look as pale as ivory. He had a tan wool zip-up jacket thrown over his arm.

He just stood there smiling at her as she came down the stairs. She smiled back.

"Hi," she said when she was within arm's length.

"Hello," he said, reaching to take the suitcase. "Ready to go?"

She nodded. It was always an awkward moment when she saw Plum after not having seen him for a while. She felt somehow they should do more than just say hello. Maybe they should kiss or something, but neither of them knew quite what to do, so they just smiled and said hello as though they had seen each other just the day before.

She had a lot of things to tell Plum. She told him about all the interesting things she'd been reading in sophomore lit, about the fact that she was working as stage manager on the fall production because Dr. Barrow thought she should get more understanding of all the aspects of producing a play, about being asked to give a dramatic reading at the Baptist church. She talked on and on as he concentrated on driving the Chevrolet around the sharp mountain curves.

"The only thing I don't like about school," she said, "is living in a dormitory. Laura's a wonderful roommate and I like her a lot, but I hate living in a dorm. It's not like home at all."

They were just coming out of the curve on the top of the mountain. Plum accelerated and passed a gasoline truck they'd been trapped behind for miles and pulled into the lane in front of it on a straight stretch of road.

"I've been doing a lot of thinking, Batty," he said, "and I want to talk to you about it. I've done some investigating. You know I've been planning to go to Harvard Business School to get my master's."

"Yes."

"The University of North Carolina has a good business school, too. Not as good as Harvard's, but pretty good. I've talked to some people about it and they say that once you start working with a big company, after the first weeks it doesn't make any difference *where* you went to school. After that, the only thing that matters is how well you do on the job. I've been thinking we could get married and you could transfer to Chapel Hill and finish your last two years of college there while I get my MBA."

"Do you mean next year?" she asked almost in a whisper.

"Yes. Next year."

She was silent for a moment. Finally she said, barely audibly, "But that means we'd have to get married next summer."

"Yes."

She looked at Plum. His eyes were on the road ahead, she could see his perfect profile, the thick lashes, the black turtleneck outlining the clean line of his jaw.

"I . . . I don't know," she said, "I mean . . . how would we manage it? Where would we live?"

"When Daddy died, he left me some money in trust. Not a lot but enough to take care of us for a couple of years in school. And I'll get the GI bill, of course, which will help. I've figured it all out." He took his eyes off the road for a moment and glanced at her. "We'll rent an apartment and you won't have to live in a dormitory anymore. How would you like that?"

"I . . . don't know. I haven't thought about it."

"Well, Batty," he said. "Why don't you start thinking about it?"

Batty *did* start to think about it. When Plum came up after Thanksgiving dinner that Thursday, she had things she wanted to discuss with him. Hilda was cleaning up in the kitchen, and Mother and Daddy and Grandaddy and Grandmother were sitting in the living room. Daddy was trying to talk Mother into taking a long walk, but Mother didn't seem about to budge. When Plum came, Daddy tried to talk Plum and Batty into taking a walk with him. Batty said she had lots of things to talk to Plum about in private and they'd take a walk with Daddy another time. Mother finally said she'd take a *short* walk as long as Daddy found someplace to walk that was flat. She didn't want to walk up any hills. Batty and Plum decided to take a drive out into the country so they could be by themselves.

At Batty's suggestion, Plum drove several miles out of town and parked the car beside the road on the edge of the property where Grandmother Attwood had grown up. The property was a large green stretch of meadow at the far side of which was an old stone chimney with a fireplace on either side—all that was left of what had been the farmhouse. They got out of the car and walked along the trail that led into the center of the property. Though it was only the middle of the afternoon, the air that had been so pleasantly warm earlier in the day was beginning to chill. The shadow of the stone chimney stretched across the grass toward them.

"Shall we sit down on the hearth?" she asked as they approached it.

"I wonder if there's any danger of its falling on us," Plum said almost to himself.

"I don't think so," Batty said. "It's been here a long time."

They sat down side by side with their legs stretched out on the grass in front of them. For a while neither of them spoke.

"Plum," she said finally, and almost in desperation, "how can you be so happy?"

He turned to look at her.

"What do you mean?" he asked.

"I mean . . . nothing ever seems to bother you. You're just always so content. I'm always worrying about one thing or another, or I'm depressed about something. I mean . . . you never seem to be worried about anything . . . you never seem depressed."

"Well . . . I don't know, Batty," he said. "I never think about it. I guess I'm just *naturally* content, that's all."

She thought of the way he seemed to be content no matter what he was doing. If he spent the weekend in the swamp collecting cypress knees, he was content. If he spent a vacation doing chores for his mother, he was content. If they were driving through the mountains listening to the car radio, which most of the time bored her to death, he was content. Mother always said a person had within him the seeds of content or discontent and that happiness had nothing to do with what was going on in the world *around* the person. She said Batty would always be unhappy because she had within her the seeds of discontent. Batty thought Plum must have within him the seeds of contentment. She wondered if his contentment would rub off on her. If she married him and moved into his contented life, would she be as content as he was?

"Plum," she said, "are you still planning to work for that company near New York City?"

"You mean United American Chemicals in White Plains?" he asked.

"Yes, that's the one."

"Uh-huh," he said sleepily.

"How far did you say that is from New York City?"

"Not very far. Half an hour by train, I'd guess."

Batty though awhile. "Plum, you know I want to be an actress," she said at last. "I've wanted to be an actress for a long time."

"Uh-huh."

"And I don't see any reason I couldn't get married and still be an actress, do you? I mean there are lots of actresses who're married."

"You ought to do what makes you happy," Plum said. "I think it's important that you have something to do to keep you busy until we're ready to have children."

"Well, I wouldn't *be* ready to have children anytime soon. Not until I've got a good start on an acting career."

"No, of course not," he said.

"And it seems to me that if you're going to be working in White Plains and if White Plains is so close to New York, I could work in New York if we were married, don't you think so?"

"I see no reason you couldn't," Plum said. "White Plains would be an excellent location for you. A lot of professional performers have homes in Westchester."

Batty thought of all the fears she'd had of going to New York alone. Then she thought of having Plum, an apartment in White Plains, and an acting career besides. It sounded almost too good to be true.

Plum was leaning back against the chimney with the late-afternoon sun on his face. His eyelids were half closed. She couldn't tell whether it was because the sun was in his eyes or whether he was just sleepy.

"I'm very happy, Plum," she said and moved closer to him.

He smiled weakly, his eyes completely closed now. She leaned back against the chimney and thought of living in White Plains and trying out for parts in New York every day, and of *getting* a part one day, and rushing home to tell Plum the good news, or maybe calling him on the telephone because she couldn't wait. And he'd be thrilled and congratulate her. And he'd be so proud when he saw her, *his wife*, on Broadway.

The sun was beginning to set and she began to feel cold. She sat up and pulled her jacket around her tightly. Plum sat up and zipped his jacket to the throat. A dark-haired boy of about ten led a cow by a rope around her neck along a path at the foot of the hill in front of them. Batty waved, and he waved back. The cow's udder was so full it almost dragged on the ground.

Plum was the first to get up from the hearthstone.

"I guess we'd better go before it gets dark," he said.

"I guess so," Batty said.

The sun had long since disappeared behind the hill and the rosy glow was rapidly draining from the western sky.

In January, when the students came back to school after the Christmas holidays, Batty was only one of many girls who returned wearing sparkling diamonds on the ring finger of the left hand. The diamonds were for the most part small, mounted in Tiffany settings, and each was individually admired and appraised by all the other girls, those with rings and those without. During the first few days in January, a large percentage of the female students spent much of their time with the left hand extended for the examination of their diamonds while the remaining percentage spent the same amount of time examining. There were many hugs and kisses, some gay laughter, and bucketsful of joyful tears. The only person who was displeased with Batty's engagement was Dr. Barrow.

He kept her after class the day he found out about her plans and let her know just how he felt. He was a dapper little man with a trim mustache and a lean body, who could look tired and disheveled and all of his fifty years and yet retain at all times an air of worldly sophistication. He spoke with the slightest hint of an English accent even though he was from Chicago. Batty thought he looked as though he should wear an ascot though he never did.

"How could you do this to me, Batty?" he said. "You *know* you've been my star pupil, you *know* I've had big hopes for your future. You *know* I've spent a lot of my time and energy working with you to develop your talent, and now you're going to throw it all away."

"Well, I'm not really throwing—"

"If you were going to get married you should have told me so, and I wouldn't have invested so much in you."

"But, Dr. Barrow," Batty said, meekly, "I don't think anything's going to be wasted. I mean . . . just because I'm getting married doesn't mean I won't be able to—"

"No," Dr. Barrow said, somewhat sharply. "You simply won't be able to make the commitment that professional theater requires. You'll end up joining the ranks of all those untalented, inadequately trained dilettantes whose lives revolve around the mediocrity of community theater. No, Batty. Good theater demands *all* or nothing."

"Well, I'm sorry, Dr. Barrow, but—"

Dr. Barrow snapped his briefcase closed, pivoted, and walked out the door, leaving her standing there in mid-sentence. And in February when she tried out for *What Every Woman Knows,* he assigned her to the scenery crew. He never again mentioned her plans to get married, but one thing was clear: she was no longer his star pupil.

Two weeks after Batty returned to school, she received a gift from Plum. She'd just got out of her English class with Mrs. Muller and had stopped by her mailbox before she went up to her room to study biology during her free period, when she found the yellow slip indicating she had a package. The package was wrapped in brown paper and her name and college address were written on it in Plum's stiff style of half printing and half writing. When she tore away the paper she discovered that Plum had sent her a book entitled *Perfect Marriage.* The title was printed in white letters on a brown background and under the title was printed in smaller white letters the name of the author, Dr. Harvey Finkelstein. Batty opened the book.

On the first blank page Plum had written her name under his. She turned to the table of contents. "Sex in Marriage" was the first chapter, followed by "Female Physiology," then "Male Physiology." There was a chapter on birth control, a chapter on the honeymoon, a chapter on hygiene, and a chapter on scents and sexology. She flipped through the book and looked at the diagrams. There was a drawing of the female organs with all the parts labeled. She learned that what she had always called her bottom was, in fact, her *pudenda,* that the little opening she peed through was just in front of the larger opening to her vagina which was enclosed in the *labia minora,* which were in turn enclosed in the *labia majora.* She looked through the book and found the diagram of the male sexual organs, the penis hanging in front of the little sack, the little tubes leading from the prostate to the testicles where they made a few loops then led on through the penis to the opening at the end. When she finished examining the book, she opened it again to the front page where Plum had written her name under his. This book, with both their names written in Plum's handwriting, was the most intimate thing he could possibly have sent her. It was as great a testament to the specialness of their relationship as the diamond on her finger.

That evening after supper she went down the hall to talk to Mary Ann Poteat. Mary Ann was one of the beauties of the senior class and was engaged to be married as soon as she graduated in the spring. She was an art major, and Batty found her working on a still life.

"Mary Ann," she said, handing her the book, "have you read this?"

Mary Ann looked at the book. "No, I haven't," she said, "but it's supposed to be the best. I have *The Marriage Manual.*" She thumbed through the book. "It's similar to mine," she said. She stopped thumbing to examine a diagram of the male sexual organs, then continued thumbing. "Have you read it?"

"I just got it today," Batty said, sitting on the bed. "I've read parts of it and skimmed through the rest."

"What do you think of it?" Mary Ann asked.

"I don't have anything to compare it to," Batty said, "but as far as I can tell, it's okay. It sure makes sex sound dull, though—sort of like dissecting a frog. Can you imagine having sex while reading the directions from a book? Or can you imagine saying to your husband, 'Honey, last night we did position four, tonight why don't we do position five? I'm bored with four already.' "

Mary Ann laughed. "I sure can't," she said. "The thing *I* don't understand is the part about contraception. I mean, first you have to put in the diaphragm with all the jelly, then your husband ejaculates his semen inside you. What I don't understand is where does all that stuff *go?*"

They were quiet for a moment. Finally Batty said, "It must be an awful mess. And another thing that sounded funny to me was the part where it gives advice to husbands, you know, where it tells them how to get their wives excited. It says wives are very excited when the husband uses dirty words. I can just hear *Plum* using dirty words."

"Yeah," Mary Ann said. "If George started using dirty words while we were having sex, I'd burst out laughing."

"Which I suppose would ruin everything," Batty said.

"I guess so," Mary Ann said. "Sex is no laughing matter."

"It sure isn't," Batty said and picked up the book and opened it to the chapter on the honeymoon. "See you later," she said, going to the door, "I've got some more reading to do."

"Now *this* is the vagina," Laura said pointing to the diagram from the box of Tampax, and exaggerating the instructional tone of her voice, "and *this* is the opening to the vagina. All you have to do is take the paper off the Tampax and push the end without the string into this opening, with the string hanging out. Then you push this little cardboard tube into the outside tube to push the Tampax out. Then you pull the cardboard out, leaving the string hanging so you can pull the Tampax out with the string when it's time to change. Okay? You got it?"

"I think so," Batty said. "It sounds simple enough." In the bathroom Batty closed and latched the door to the stall and spoke to Laura through the door. "Okay, now tell me again, Laura, what do I do?"

"Well *first* you have to take off your panties," Laura said.

Batty took off her panties and hung them on the hook on the door. Then she took the Tampax out of the paper wrapper.

"It makes it easier to get it in if you put one leg up on the toilet seat," Laura said.

Batty lifted her skirt and put her leg on the toilet seat and aimed the stringless end of the Tampax toward the spot that corresponded to the place where she'd seen Laura's string hanging when Laura had her period.

"Okay," she said, "I'm all set, now what do I do?"

"Just push it in," Laura said.

Batty pushed the Tampax between her *labia majora* where she knew there must be an opening, but the Tampax met firm resistance. She moved it forward a bit and tried again. Still no luck. Then she tried moving it back a bit. No luck. She didn't know exactly where her vagina was, but she felt pretty sure it must be somewhere in the middle and she was sure that by now she'd tried everywhere.

"Let me see that diagram again, Laura," she said.

Laura handed her the folded sheet under the door. Batty unfolded it and looked at it. Then she tried the Tampax again and again she met resistance.

"Where do you *put* it, Laura?" she asked.

"Batty, you just put it *in,* that's all. Just push it *in.*"

"I can't find the hole, Laura. How do you find the hole?" She looked at the Tampax she'd been trying to get in. "This one's coming apart," she said, "the cardboard's all mashed. Can I have a fresh one?"

"Sure," Laura said patiently, and handed her another tampax under the door.

"Thanks," Batty said.

Three Tampaxes later, Laura began to be concerned about her dwindling supply.

"This is the last one, Batty," she said as she handed it under the door.

Batty peeled away the paper and looked at the fresh uncrushed cylinder. This one should be a lot easier to get in than those others she'd shoved at herself till they were flat and blunted. She tried one last time.

"I still can't find the hole," she said. "I haven't even got one *started.* I guess I'll have to give up till I can find the hole."

Batty got the book Plum had sent her and read the chapter on the honeymoon again. The book said that one important thing for the bride to do in preparation for the honeymoon was to sit regularly in a hot tub of water and put two fingers in her vagina and gently stretch so coitus would be less painful the first time. The next time Batty took a bath, she tried desperately to find the opening to her vagina so she could put her fingers in. She knew there had to be a hole there somewhere, because when she and Plum had been necking a lot and touching each other, and she got excited and wanted to take off her panties, a lot of slippery wetness came from somewhere down there; but she couldn't find anything she could get even one finger in.

The next afternoon, when there were no other girls in the bathroom, Batty took her book and her hand mirror and locked herself in the bathtub enclosure. She propped the book on the chair, the pages open to the diagram of the female sexual organs, and, sitting on the edge of the tub and using her hand mirror, compared herself with the diagram and was pleased to see that she corresponded perfectly in every part. She was especially relieved to see the opening between her *labia*. Reassured, she carefully folded the mirror inside her towel before she walked back to her room. She certainly didn't want the other girls in the hall to know she'd been in the bathroom looking for her vagina.

"Batty," Mrs. Muller said, being her social self, rather than her classroom self, "I want to congratulate you on your engagement."

"Thank you," Batty said, a little awed as she always was in Mrs. Muller's presence.

Mrs. Muller raised her eyes toward the ceiling, took a deep breath, and lifted her chest, the way she did when she was about to say something profound.

"Young people today are very courageous," she said. "In spite of the uncertainties we must live with about the future of the human race, they have the courage to marry . . . and to have children . . . to go on with their lives." She lowered her eyes to Batty's face, took another breath, lifted her eyes again and continued. "It's as though they are saying we will allow *nothing* to interfere with our lives. We *will* go on in spite of it all." She lowered her eyes and again smiled beneficently at Batty. "Dear, I want to wish you the best of everything."

"Thank you very much, Mrs. Muller," Batty said.

Mrs. Muller lifted her eyes again as though she had something else important to say. "Young people always expect so much of their lives." She lowered her eyes and looked at Batty. "You must accept that you won't get everything you want. If you get seventy-five percent of what you want, you'll be fortunate. Seventy-five percent is very good." Then she tossed her head, turned abruptly, and walked purposefully back down the hall the way she had come.

The church was packed.

She'd known when she saw the cars lining the streets as far as she could see in every direction that her wedding was the most important thing to happen in Robertson's Fort in a long time. And when she saw the interior of the church she knew her wedding was very special indeed. All day long, while Mother and Hilda had been getting the house ready for the reception, and while the baker was building the most exquisite colonnaded cake she'd ever seen, and while the confectioner was delivering mints and petits fours all the way from Asheville, and while friends were dropping by to deliver gifts, the florist had been busy turning the sanctuary of the church into a spring garden. Across the front of the church, against a background of white fabric, were banks of ferns fronted by lush arrangements of the most delicate spring flowers—sunny daisies and fragile narcissus, sprays of heather and stephanotis, long bell-covered stalks of delphinium, and small shadowlike violets, all suspended in clouds of baby's breath. The white background covered the altar and spilled over the edge of the platform and down the aisle all the way to the church door.

Eight candelabra, each with seven tall candles, stood in front of a forest of ferns and flowers. The ushers seated Mother in the second row next to Grandmother and Grandaddy, leaving Daddy in the back to take Batty down the aisle. With Batty and Daddy in the back of the church were Laura—the maid of honor—four bridesmaids, and Mrs. Piercy, whose job it was to see that each of them went down the aisle at the right time, just as they'd rehearsed.

Batty watched anxiously as two ushers lit the fifty-six candles, watching each wick begin to burn independently before the usher moved on to the next one. When the candles were lit, the church lights dimmed and Batty heard a murmur of approval from the guests. Robertson's Fort Baptist Church had never looked so beautiful.

As Laura and Mrs. Piercy were spreading her train on the white runner behind her, and Daddy was checking to make sure his carnation was secure, Plum and Sparky—the best man—entered from the front of the sanctuary and stood looking up the aisle, over the heads of the guests packed in the pews, to where she stood. She thought Plum would have looked very handsome in his white dinner jacket if only he weren't wearing such a grave expression. His mouth was in that tight little circle she hated. Even from the back of the church, she could see the beads of perspiration on his upper lip catching the light from the candles. She wished he'd smile so the guests would think he was happy about getting married. She smiled at him trying to get him to smile back. He didn't respond. It was as though he didn't see her, but she knew he was looking straight at her.

Mrs. Gosorn finished the selection she was playing and began rearranging the music on the piano stand in front of her. Suddenly she began playing "Here Comes the Bride" very loudly. Mrs. Piercy touched the first bridesmaid lightly on the shoulder and the procession began. When the bridesmaids were lining up at the front of the church and Laura was the proper distance down the aisle, Daddy smiled at her and offered her his arm. She thought he looked handsome in his tuxedo and she felt proud of him. Mrs. Piercy smiled and nodded, and they began to move down the aisle toward the new minister, standing at the front of the church with his white Bible open before him.

At the altar, Plum stepped up to the right of Daddy who was now between him and Batty.

"And who gives this woman away?" the minister asked.

"I do," Daddy said loudly, the way Mother had told him to. He turned and took his seat in the second row beside Mother, and Plum moved into his place.

"If anyone knows any reason,"the minister said, "why these two should not be joined in matrimony, let him speak now or forever hold his peace."

There was a moment of silence. Then the minister said a few things about marriage being a sacred institution ordained by God. While he spoke the church was dead silent. He turned to Plum.

"Do you, Pelham Harding Bradley, take this woman to be your lawful wedded wife? To love, honor, and cherish her in sickness and in health, prosperity and adversity, and forsaking all others cling to her till death do you part?"

"I do," Plum said, so softly Batty was afraid he couldn't be heard beyond the first row.

The minister turned to her. "And do you, Beatrice Louise Attwood, take this man to be your lawful wedded husband? To love, honor, and cherish him, in sickness and in health, in prosperity and adversity, and forsaking all others cling to him till death do you part?"

"I do," Batty said, so loudly it could be heard in the last row.

"The ring is the outward symbol of this union, and is as God's love, having no beginning nor end but continuing always. Pelham, you may now place the ring on her finger."

Sparky produced the ring quickly and Batty extended her left hand. Plum took the ring, tried to put it on her middle finger, and discovered it wouldn't go over the second knuckle. She tried to withdraw her hand so she could curl up all except the proper ring finger but Plum had a firm grip on it and was working hard to get the ring on. She remembered the time a fly had lit on the preacher's nose and she had laughed out loud in church. She didn't want to laugh at her own wedding. She looked at Plum's face, the intensity of the expression, the way he kept trying to push the ring over the knuckle of the wrong finger and she couldn't hold it any longer. It was just a giggle, but a giggle that could be heard to the back of the church. She took a deep breath and swallowed the giggle as the minister stepped in and guided Plum's hand to the proper finger. The ring slid on easily. The minister turned to her.

"Now, Batty," he said, "you may place the ring on Pelham's finger."

Laura handed her the ring and she slipped it easily on Plum's finger and smiled at him. He didn't smile back.

"And now by the laws vested in me by the church and the state of North Carolina, I pronounce you man and wife. Pelham, you may now kiss the bride."

Batty knew in advance that Plum wasn't going to give her one of those long romantic kisses she saw at the end of weddings in movies, so when he gave her one of his usual dry little kisses, even shorter this time, she wasn't disappointed. When Mrs. Gosorn burst out with the Recessional, Plum stood there looking dazed. She took him by the hand and pulled him running up the aisle toward the church door.

It was not until the end of the reception, when she was in the bedroom changing into her suit, that she realized the wedding was the first time she'd ever seen Plum nervous. And it was the first time she'd seen him when he wasn't in perfect control of a situation. She thought of him doggedly trying to push the ring onto the wrong finger and she burst out laughing all over again.

For the honeymoon Plum had planned a week at the Shoals, a hotel on the Outer Banks. It would be a hard day's drive to the Shoals, so for the first night he'd reserved a room at a motel about an hour from Robertson's Fort. They arrived at the motel shortly before midnight. Plum checked in and carried the luggage into the room. Then he sat in the one chair and watched Batty open her suitcase. Mother made sure that Batty's trousseau included several long and fancy gowns unlike anything Batty had ever slept in before. One of them Mother had bought especially for Batty's wedding night. It was sheer white nylon with a fitted bodice and lace trim through which was threaded blue satin ribbon. It had a matching peignoir that tied at the neck and fell loose and free to the floor. While Plum watched, Batty took the gown and peignoir out of her suitcase, went into the bathroom, locked the door, and began filling the tub.

As she bathed, she could hear Plum moving around in the other room. She wondered if he was taking off his clothes and would be standing there with nothing on when she went back in. She finished bathing and got out of the tub and let the water out. She dried herself well, took the gown off the back of the bathroom door, slipped it over her head, and pulled it down around her waist. She looked down at herself and felt embarrassed. She could see the black triangle of her pubic hair perfectly through the sheer fabric. She wished Mother hadn't chosen something so sheer for the first night. She slipped her arms into the peignoir and tied the blue ribbon at the neck. The extra fabric helped to conceal her a little but not nearly enough. She picked up the skirt and blouse she'd taken off and held it in front of her as she opened the door and stepped out of the bathroom.

Plum had taken the spread off the bed and turned the cover back neatly. He was sitting in the chair just as she had left him. His eyes followed her as she hung the clothes in the closet and quickly got into bed and pulled the cover up over her. Plum got up, turned his back to her and began undressing. When he'd taken off his pants and undershorts, she could see his ugly goose-pimpled testicles swinging between his legs as he carefully lined up the seams of his pant legs,and folded the garment over the hanger. He laid the hanger on the back of the chair, took a pair of blue cotton pajamas from his suitcase, and put them on. Dressed in his pajamas, he took the pants over to the closet and hung them up. Then he got into bed next to her and strained to reach up under the lampshade on the bedstand to switch off the light.

He turned to her and fumbled for her breasts through the gown and kissed her firmly on the mouth as he edged in close. She wrapped her arms around him and he moved in closer and threw a leg over her. She could feel his penis hardening against her thigh. She knew this was the moment she'd been saving herself for, the moment for which she'd been waiting such a long time. She no longer had to make Plum stop when she desperately wanted him not to stop. She no longer had to worry that someone would walk in and find them doing things they shouldn't. She no longer had to worry about whether someone—or everyone—would find out and make judgments about the kind of girl she was. She no longer had to worry about sinning before God. She didn't even have to worry tonight about getting pregnant, because she knew from the way Dr. Murphy had explained it that this was her safe time. Plum threw back the cover, took off his pajama bottoms, lifted her gown to her waist and lay on top of her, spreading her legs with his knees. She felt his hard penis lying against her slit. He searched for her mouth, found it, and kissed her again. She felt nothing. She tried to remember all the times when they'd been parked on the mountain touching each other, the times there'd been only her panties between them, and she'd wanted to take them off and let him enter, and he'd begged her to take them off, and she wouldn't—couldn't. She tried to recall how much she'd wanted him then, to bring it forward to the present, to make her want him now. Plum lifted himself on his knees and took his penis in his hand and directed it toward her. He was pushing it against her trying to get it in. She thought of the time after the Christmas dance when he drove her to his house and she took off her dress and put on his mother's robe, the time she was dripping wet and swollen and ready for him. She remembered how she wanted him so much it had hurt down there. Plum was beginning to hurt her now—a different kind of hurt. She took a deep breath and tried to relax. He kept pushing.

"Let me rest a minute, Plum," she said.

He moved away from her, and she took a deep breath and lay flat on her back looking up into the blackness. She was as dry as a desert down there. She wanted to save all this till later. Tomorrow maybe. But this was their wedding night. Tonight it was very important that he enter her and break the hymen membrane and that they both have orgasms at the same time and achieve great peace of soul the way the book said they should.

"Okay, Plum," she said, "I'm ready."

He moved onto her again and again began pushing at her where she was so sore now. She knew she couldn't stand it. She was afraid Plum would think there was something wrong with her, or that he would be impatient with her for not letting him keep trying to get it in. She didn't want to cry on her wedding night, but the tears filled her eyes and the back of her nose. She swallowed hard and choked them back.

"Plum, let's wait till tomorrow, please," she whispered. "I'm exhausted."

"Okay, Batty," he said and rolled away from her. She lay there a moment wondering if he was angry with her. Then she heard his deep, even breathing and knew he was already asleep. She hoped Plum wouldn't mind waiting till she got over being sore down there before trying again. She touched herself and felt the pain shoot through her groin. It wouldn't be tomorrow. No, it certainly wouldn't be tomorrow. She turned onto her side, pulled her knees up to her chest, and fell asleep.

In the four days they'd been at the Shoals, Plum hadn't tanned at all. He'd just turned red and freckled. His nose had already peeled once and was red and almost ready to peel again. Batty, on the other hand, almost never burned in the sun, and had turned a golden brown.

The Outer Banks were miles and miles of wild and unpeopled beach, littered with rotting hulks of old shipwrecks. After the first two days of swimming in the surf and sitting in the beach chairs in front of the hotel and reading or looking out to sea, Batty had begun to get bored and had suggested they go for a walk. Yesterday they'd gone north along the beach and had found one of the old shipwrecks. Today they decided to explore in the other direction.

In addition to his swimming trunks, Plum was wearing a wide-brimmed straw hat he'd bought at the gift shop and a white long-sleeved dress shirt, turned up at the cuffs to protect him from the sun. Anywhere his skin was exposed, he was covered with a thick and gleaming coat of suntan oil. Batty loved the way it smelled. It recalled the two weeks each summer when she was a child that she and Mother and Daddy used to spend at Myrtle Beach. Those weeks were always the best weeks of the year as far as she was concerned—sleeping in wood-frame beach apartments with the windows open to the sea breeze, and everything smelling musty and damp and salty, and in the morning walking long miles with Daddy while Mother sat under the beach umbrella. Weeks of being browner than almost anybody else except Daddy, and always ravenous at meal times, particularly on the evenings they drove to the old rice plantation converted to a restaurant where they ate fried shrimp, flounder, and crabs with baskets of hush puppies and drank tall glasses of iced tea, and then finished with thick slices of homemade pecan pie a la mode. And Mother, being a blonde, coated all day in the cream that smelled just like the cream Plum was wearing now.

As soon as they got out of sight of the hotel, there wasn't another living creature besides themselves to be seen except for the seabirds. The beach was wide and the sand a pale brown. Behind the tall sea grass along the edge of the beach, the sand dunes looked like impermanent pyramids. Ahead of them the strip of beach narrowed uninterruptedly till it disappeared at the horizon. She and Plum walked along silently.

She recalled the beach walks she used to take with Daddy along the heavily populated Myrtle Beach. They'd walk along in silence looking at the people they passed, and in turn being looked at by the people, feeling tanned and good-looking, commenting upon things they passed, examining together a washed-up jellyfish or an unusual shell, looking into the bucket of a fisherman to see what he'd caught. Sometimes they'd look into the far distance and set a goal for their walk—maybe a fishing pier that barely appeared on the horizon, which over the next two hours got larger as they closed the distance till they were finally there and realized they'd reached their goal, Daddy checking his watch and deciding it was time to turn around, getting back to Mother just in time for a late lunch, Mother swearing she thought she'd starve waiting for them.

Up the beach she saw the bleached wooden frame of a boat half buried in the sand

"Look, Plum," she said. "I think I see another shipwreck." She ran through the sand ahead of him. Plum walked up behind her.

"It's much too small to be a galleon," he said. "It's not even very old, either. You can see these rusty nails. They're not more than twenty-five or thirty years old, I suspect. Otherwise, they'd have rusted away. I'd guess this is just a local fishing boat. Nothing to get excited about."

"Too bad," Batty said, disappointed. "I thought I'd found another shipwreck."

"There's a very *big* shipwreck out there about a hundred and seventy-five yards," Plum said, turning toward the sea. "The *Huron* wrecked out there sometime in the eighteen seventies, and a hundred and eight lives were lost." He walked toward the shore and stood looking out to sea. She followed and stood behind him, trying to see what he was looking at.

"Did you know that the whole area out there is known as the graveyard of the Atlantic?" he asked.

"Uh-uh," Batty said. "Why's it called that?"

"Because there are treacherous shoals out there and ever since ships have been coming to America, there've been shipwrecks on those shoals. It's even worse down off Hatteras, where Diamond Shoals extends twenty-five miles out to sea."

"Do ships still wreck out there?" Batty asked.

"Sometimes," Plum said, "but not as many as did in the seventeen and eighteen hundreds. They have better instruments now." He started walking down the beach along the edge of the water. Batty fell into step beside him. "Pirates who lived on the Outer Banks used to take advantage of the shoals to plunder ships. On stormy nights, they'd tie lanterns around the necks of old nags and walk the nags up and down the beach. Ships at sea would think the lanterns were other ships and would sail toward the lights and wreck on the shoals. Then the pirates would plunder the ships. That's how Nag's Head got its name."

Batty thought the story sounded a little farfetched. If anyone other than Plum had told it, she would have thought he was teasing her or just plain lying. But Plum never teased, and he certainly didn't lie. She supposed it had to be the truth. But . . .

"How do you know that?" she asked.

"I read it somewhere," he said, walking on. He stopped and, standing on one foot, lifted the other to examine the sole. He removed a small piece of broken shell and started walking again. He was walking in the middle of the small circle of his shadow. Batty thought it must be getting close to noon. Four gulls sat on a small hummock back from the beach all facing into the breeze. A tern swept across them from behind, squawking loudly as he followed the shoreline away from them. He dived to the surface of the water and in a moment rose and continued flying away from them. Plum stopped walking and turned to her.

"Let's go skinny-dipping," he said, with a mischievous glint Batty had never seen.

"You mean you want to swim naked?"

"Yeah," Plum said, grinning now.

"Well . . . I don't know," Batty said. "I've never . . ."

"Come on," he said. "There's no one for miles. No one'll see you."

He was already taking off his clothes and making a neat little pile of them safely back from the water's edge. First he placed his hat upside down and then he took off his shirt and folded it and placed it in the bowl of his hat. Then he untied the drawstring around the waistband of his trunks and stepped out of them and laid them on top of the pile. Under his trunks he was as white as the meat of a fried flounder. His penis looked small and vulnerable. Batty wondered if he dared go into the water with nothing to protect him there. But he started into the water, waded out to where it came to his knees, and turned to wait for her.

"Take off your bathing suit and come on in," he said, grinning like a little boy.

Batty looked around her. She certainly didn't want to take any chances that there was someone behind the ridge who would appear the moment she was out of her suit.

"Just a minute," she said, and turned and ran away from the water's edge to the ridge parallel to the beach. She climbed to the top and stood among the tall dune grass and looked out over the sand and clumps of dried grass that stretched as far as she could see. A two-lane cement road several hundred yards inland ran parallel to the shoreline. Along the margin of the road was thick loose sand. She knew that anyone who drove off that concrete strip would be stuck in sand up to his axle. No one would dare try to park and get out. She stood there a moment longer. There wasn't a car to be seen in any direction. She turned and ran back to the edge of the water where Plum was waiting for her and unhooked the straps of her one-piece elasticized suit, slipped it down over her legs, stepped out of it, and tossed it on top of Plum's pile.

She looked down at herself. Her nipples were puckered in excitement at her daring. There was such contrast in the white skin under her bathing suit and the rest of her that except for her nipples and the black triangle she almost looked as though she were still wearing the bathing suit. Plum was standing there, grinning and waiting patiently for her. She started walking out to him in the water and he reached to take her hand and lead her deeper. She felt the line of the water rising on her legs, the breakers coming in splashing higher and higher, getting her body wet all over now, and then Plum moved deeper, and the water was to her waist.

"I'm afraid, Plum," she said, pulling back.

"What're you afraid of?"

I'm afraid of fish or something."

"You're not usually afraid of fish."

"I'm not usually naked in the water, either."

Plum disappeared under a breaker and came up after it had passed, his curly red hair glued straight over his face. He pushed it back.

"What's being naked got to do with it?" he asked.

She bounced with the next breaker, the ends of her hair getting wet and sticking to her back.

"It's just that I'm afraid of the little fish."

"You mean you're afraid they'll go where they shouldn't?" Plum shouted and began laughing.

"What's so funny about that?" she shouted back, hurt that he was laughing at her and making her feel foolish.

"You haven't a thing to worry about," Plum shouted over the sound of the surf. "There's not a fish in the ocean small enough or agile enough to invade that private domain."

She turned his hand loose and swam away from him. When she had swum a few feet she turned to watch him bouncing with the waves. He caught her eye and still grinning, swam to her and put his hand on top of her head and dunked her under the water. When she came up sputtering mad, he moved his body next to her and held her close and kissed her wet and salty on the mouth.

"Come on," he said and took her hand and led her out of the water onto the beach.

When they got back to the hotel the halls were filled with the smell of seafood cooking. As soon as Plum closed the door to their room and locked it behind them, he said, "Take off your bathing suit." Batty stepped out of her bathing suit and tossed it in the corner, as Plum began turning back the white chenille bedspread.

"Don't you think we ought to get the sand off us first?" Batty said.

"Okay, but hurry," Plum said.

She turned the shower on warm and stepped in and let the water rinse away the sand and salt. Then she stepped out onto the bath mat and dried herself quickly as Plum stepped into the shower. When she was dry she stretched out on the bed and waited for him. He toweled his hair quickly and with it still damp and uncombed came to bed and lay down next to her.

"Let's take our time today, okay, Batty?" he said quietly and lifted himself on his elbow and looked into her face on the pillow. He started stroking her belly. Then he moved his hand down and she opened her legs to him, and took his penis in her hand. It was already hard.

When she'd told him four days ago that she was very sore and they'd have to wait to try again, he'd been patient and understanding, and now she wasn't sore any longer. She felt the beginning of that warm singing feeling growing down there, as Plum continued to stroke her. Then he lost the place somehow and he was stroking a little too far forward. She took his hand and moved it to where it felt best. He kissed her on the neck and whispered, "Do you think you're ready now?"

"I think so," she said and moved closer to him.

He moved over on top of her again and with his weight on his knees moved closer and directed his hard penis toward her. She opened her legs wider and took a deep breath to relax. He was lowering himself now, his knees sliding away down the bed, his weight falling on her, his penis driving into her where she was lifted to him. She felt a sharp pain as he entered.

"Stop pushing just a minute now, Plum, and let me relax, okay?" She tried to relax the muscles the pain had contracted.

"Okay," she said. He pushed farther into her. She tried to concentrate on relaxing so it wouldn't hurt so much. In a few minutes she asked, "Are you all the way in?"

"Yes," he said.

For a long moment he didn't move. He just lay there with his weight resting on her, his face buried in the pillow beside her head. Then he began moving, slowly at first, pumping in and out.

So this is what it's all about, Batty thought, making love or having sex . . . or fucking. She remembered the time she and Lula Ann had looked at the dirty comic with the little drawings of Popeye fucking a naked woman with a black triangle and she'd felt warm and pleasant and tingling down there for the first time, and then she thought about the time she and Lula Ann had touched each other and had tried to fuck, and she remembered the times Paul Marley walked her home from basketball games and put his tongue in her mouth when he kissed her good night and pressed his body hard against hers, making her panties wet, and she remembered all the times when she would just think of fucking and feel herself swell into a warm cushion of desire and know that the sin of fucking had to be more fun than anything else in the world, that unmentionable act grown-ups never talked about, though you knew they did it in the privacy of their bedrooms, and you couldn't wait to be a grown-up yourself and get married so you could fuck anytime you wanted to. She thought of all those things while Plum was moving in and out. The only sensation she felt was a mild burning. At least it didn't hurt so much anymore. He moved faster and began to pant and in a minute stiffened and groaned. Then his body went limp and he died on her, a dripping and sweaty mess. He was so heavy now that she could hardly breathe.

"Roll off," she said. "I can't breathe."

He pushed himself off and lay beside her on his back, the dead weight of him making a deep valley in the mattress. She got up and went to the bathroom and sat on the toilet to let his semen drop from her.

Plum.

Everything revolved around Plum.

She was Mrs. Pelham Harding Bradley and everything and everybody conspired to let her know that *he* was the important one. People no longer asked her what *she* planned to do when she finished college. They asked only about Plum's plans. He'd draw in his breath, pull in his chin, look contemplative, and in his deepest voice begin talking about United American Chemicals and the chemical industry in general, his place in its management, his reasons for the choice of United over any other organization. Even Daddy spent a lot of time asking Plum about his plans and listening patiently and with great interest as Plum went through his lengthy response. He no longer expressed interest in Batty's plans at all. In fact, whenever she mentioned the Carolina Playmakers, or a specific play she wanted to try out for, or a course she was enjoying, his eyes glazed over as his thoughts fled elsewhere. It was as though her plans were as foreign to Daddy's interest as was quilting or canning preserves.

And Plum was the center of their home life, too. Besides studying and writing papers for her courses, Batty had to do the cooking and the cleaning, and the grocery shopping. She had to put the laundry in the drawstring bag, take it to the Laundromat and pick it up when it was finished. Plum was a real gentleman. He never turned his hand. Sometimes she got boiling mad and told him how unfair she thought he was being. He'd just draw his mouth into that tight little circle, look at her with steely eyes, and say nothing. One time she got so frustrated at his just sitting there looking at her and saying nothing that she talked more and more frantically till she knew she was practically screaming and could be heard three apartments down the line. Plum just stared at her for a while. Then, as she got louder and louder, he got up, went out the back door to the car, and drove off, leaving her standing there feeling like a crazy person yelling at nothing.

And when Plum was finished studying no matter how much more studying Batty had to do, he'd put his records on the record player and turn the volume loud and stand, his eyes closed, his hands cutting through the air, conducting to the music. Sometimes he would go on for more than an hour, while she was in the bedroom with the door closed trying to study over the noise.

The time she really knew that Plum was the center of everything was the weekend Daddy and Mother drove to Chapel Hill in Daddy's new car, which she was just *itching* to drive, the way she always drove Daddy's new cars, and Daddy offered to let Plum drive it instead. Plum, she decided, was taking up his own space in this world and was rapidly moving in to take up *hers* as well. And the worst thing was that everybody seemed to think this was just as it should be, that her space just naturally belonged to him.

And if that wasn't enough to trouble her, she learned something about Plum that she couldn't possibly respect: he lied. She'd never forget the day he told her he'd lied to his business-systems professor. He'd been too busy to finish a paper on time, and he told his professor he'd had it finished and ready to hand in and that someone stole his briefcase, with the paper in it, from the front seat of the car. The professor believed him, of course, because no one would suspect that Plum was a liar, and Plum finished the paper and handed it in a week later and got an A on it. Even though it had turned out all right, Batty thought his lying was cowardly and weak and that he should have told the truth and faced the consequences.

It was the last week of rehearsal for *The Lark*, which was the Playmakers' winter production for 1956, and tonight, Kurt Peterson, the faculty member who was directing the play, asked the cast and crew to go through every scene till he found it perfect. He wanted to make it perfect tonight, because tomorrow night the rehearsal would be uninterrupted, just like a real performance, and the night after that, it *would* be a real performance. The Playmaker Theater would be packed.

Batty was exhausted and she thought the rehearsal would never be over. The evening had been complicated by the fact that all afternoon the sky had been threatening and shortly after rehearsal had started, the wind had begun to build, and the heavens had broken loose with torrents of rain, and the lights had gone out leaving the theater in complete darkness for almost an hour. When the lights came back on, the rehearsal continued from where it had left off, but they were way behind schedule. She'd been sitting in the little room over the back of the theater with the three other members of the lighting crew and the lighting director five nights a week for the past two weeks and three nights a week for the week before that. Tonight, Kurt had asked the cast and crew to repeat every scene he felt dragged, or in which the tempo wasn't perfect, or the lighting cues not perfectly timed, or in which the dialogue didn't build to the crescendo he wanted, or in which the action wasn't properly orchestrated to create a maximum of tension. Tonight he was polishing, and when he was polishing, he treated the play like a symphony, perfecting timing, and inflection, and even melody. Batty respected his knowledge of the theater tremendously and was excited by the things she was learning from just watching him work.

She particularly liked the play they were doing. *The Lark* had immediately become one of her favorites when she first read it in preparation for tryouts. She'd wanted more than anything to play the part of Joan. How she would have loved that; to wear the mail and carry the spear, and look out over the heads of the audience and communicate with spirits, to exist for a while in that space somewhere between epiphany and insanity. She'd been called back to tryout three times, but Kurt finally gave the part to Maggie Miles, a mousy-looking girl, but loaded with talent and with a lot of experience from the Raleigh Little Theater. Batty was disappointed that she didn't get the part, but she decided if she couldn't play Joan she wanted to work on the play anyway. She wanted to learn as much as she could about every aspect of the theater, and besides she'd get credit for it in her required course on the technical aspects of the theater. She'd decided to work on the lighting crew, and though she didn't want to make a career of working on lighting crews, she knew she'd learned a lot.

"Ready cue fifty-three . . . Go cue fifty-three," the lighting director called.

Batty raised the fourth lever on the board, putting Maggie in a bright spot as the other members of the crew darkened the rest of the stage. Maggie gave the final speech of the play.

"Ready cue fifty-four . . . Go cue fifty-four . . . Bump house to full," the lighting director said.

From the auditorium, Kurt Peterson shouted, "Okay, let's do that last scene over again, beginning just after Joan is carried offstage. Don't rush it. Ladvenu, I want to see you reacting more strongly to what you're seeing offstage. You're watching Joan burning at the stake. See it! And, Joan, I want you two steps further downstage for that last speech. Okay, let's go." He cupped his hands around his mouth. "Lights," he called to the crew, "starting with Joan's exit on one-thirty-nine."

"Ready cue fifty-one . . . Go cue fifty-one, houselights out," the lighting director said.

It was very late before Kurt was satisfied with the rehearsal. The rehearsals were usually over before eleven o'clock, and Batty would get home just in time to watch the last part of the eleven-o'clock news with Plum. She looked at her watch. It was almost twelve-thirty. She was exhausted and with good reason. She'd been awake since seven o'clock this morning. And she'd be awake at seven again tomorrow morning to get to her eight-thirty class.

She grabbed her pocketbook from the floor where it rested against her stool, took her coat from one of the hooks outside the door, and made her way as swiftly as she dared down the narrow steps from the control room to the theater entrance. She pushed open the heavy wooden door with effort. Sheets of rain seemed to be blowing horizontally in the wind. She buttoned her coat to the top button, hesitated, then leaning forward, head butting into the rain, ran around the corner of the building to where her car was parked. As soon as she started the engine she turned the windshield wipers on and slowly pulled the car out of the lot and onto the street. The wipers, working frantically, weren't able to keep the windshield clear, but she was so eager to get into a tub of hot water for a few minutes before going to bed that she drove along the back streets of Chapel Hill as quickly as she dared. She was sure Plum would be asleep when she got home. She'd have to be very quiet not to wake him up. The highway was deserted. She was halfway home before she passed another car. She pulled into Glen Lennox, parked the car in the area behind the apartments, got out and ran through the wet grass to the back door.

Plum was sitting on the living-room sofa in his knee-length plaid bathrobe, leaning over his lap with his elbows on his knees. His toes were splayed where his bare feet gripped the rug.

"What on earth are you doing up, Plum?" she asked. "I thought you'd be sound asleep by now." She hung her coat over the back of a chair to dry, and he turned his head slowly to her. His eyes were sheer ice. He turned back to the television.

"What's the matter, Plum?" she asked. "Why aren't you in bed?"

Without looking at her, he said slowly, "I'm not going to bed while my wife is out God knows where."

"I haven't been God knows *where*," Batty said, "I've been at rehearsal. You *know* I've been at rehearsal."

"I don't care *where* you've been," he said. "You're a married woman, and it's not appropriate for you to be out half the night with a bunch of bohemians."

"They're not bohemians," she said defensively. "They're just theater people."

"I don't care *what* they are," Plum said. "It's wrong for a married woman to spend half the night out with *anybody*." His arms were tightly crossed in front of him and the muscles of his jaw were working furiously.

"Well . . . how can I work on plays without staying till the rehearsals are over?" Batty asked. "Tomorrow's the last dress rehearsal before . . ."

Plum got up from the sofa, walked to the television, and switched it off. He turned to Batty.

"Batty," he said in a low and controlled voice, "when are you ever going to give up this childish dream of becoming an actress?"

She felt the breath go out of her. She was too stunned and taken by surprise to answer him immediately. The room was deadly silent. He'd known all along she planned to work in the theater. He'd told her she could do whatever made her happy, and working in the theater was what made her happy.

"Being an actress isn't a foolish dream," she said.

"It is an absolutely *infantile* and *foolish* dream," Plum said, his voice louder now. "Even if you do go to New York and try for a part in a Broadway play, do you think a girl from a little hick town in North Carolina can just walk in off the street and become a *star*? If you think that, Batty, you're even more stupid than I realized."

"I'm not stupid at all," she said, her voice rising, forgetting for a moment the sleeping nurse and intern in the next apartment.

"And if you think I'm going to work hard to support you," Plum said, "while you spend your time traipsing around trying out for parts in plays, you've got another thought coming."

"I don't want you to support me," Batty said. "I want to support myself."

"Well, if you want to support yourself, you'd better start preparing for something other than *acting*," Plum said, his lip curling in distaste as he said the word.

"I'm not going to prepare myself for anything but working in the theater," Batty said. "That's what I've always wanted to do. I told you that before we were married. You didn't seem to find so much wrong with it then."

"And what were you doing all those hours?" he asked through clenched teeth.

"You know darn well I was working on the lighting board."

"And where *is* this lighting board?"

"It's in the theater," she said, confused at the meaning of his question. "In a little room over the back of the auditorium. I have to raise and lower—"

"And who *else* is in this little room?" Plum asked, advancing on her now.

"The other members of the lighting crew," Batty said, moving away from him.

"Are there boys?"

"Two are boys. Why?"

"And you, a married woman, spend five to six hours a night in a room with boys, like a common whore, while I—"

"How dare you call me a whore," she screamed. "How *dare* you!"

She hated him in that moment. In the course of ten minutes, he'd undermined her whole life and now he was impugning her honor and respectability as well. Her hatred rent the bag of angers she was storing against him and they spilled out, flooding her—all his encroachments, his stony silences, his inaccessibility to her loneliness. She wanted more than anything to hurt him as much as he was hurting her. She homed toward his weakness.

"You wouldn't have to worry about where I am every minute," she said, "if you weren't such a clod at lovemaking. We've been married for eight whole months and I've never—"

She didn't see it coming. His hand flew up and slammed into the side of her face and sent the room spinning. She fell back against the bookshelves, knocking over a vase. It shattered on the floor as she braced herself against the wall.

When she opened her eyes, Plum was standing there looking at her, his mouth pinched and his eyes bulging with anger. She grabbed her coat from the back of the chair and ran out the door into the rain. She heard him calling behind her as she ran to the end of the walk and, not knowing which way to turn, ran on across the street through the sheets of rain and turned left, heading deeper into the development. The water drenched her clothes all the way to the skin, and her wool skirt was so soaked it slapped heavily against her legs as she ran. Somewhere a dog yapped. She ran till she was exhausted and couldn't run anymore. Then she slowed down and began to walk.

Plum had literally knocked the anger out of her. She'd been angry enough to kill him, but the moment he hit her, she hadn't felt anything anymore. Her teeth began to chatter. She was chilled to the bone. The colder she got, the clearer her mind became. She wiped the water out of her eyes. She couldn't believe Plum had hit her. For a long time she tried to absorb that fact. Men didn't hit women unless they were from a family of uneducated hill people or poor white trash. Grandaddy had never hit anyone in his life, and though Daddy sometimes spoke harshly to Mother when he was angry, he would never in a million years hit her.

She was coming into that part of the development where the tall pines were thickest. She heard them swishing and creaking in the wind. In the streetlights she could see water running off the cars parked along the curb. A light burned on the porch of one of the apartments. Plum was no little shrimp against whom she had a fair chance in physical combat. When it came to hitting, she was entirely at his mercy. He was no Charlie Knipe, that was for sure. She saw the headlights of a car coming up the street and immediately ran off the sidewalk and hid behind a pine till it passed. She didn't want to have to answer questions if someone stopped. She heard the tires sucking against the wet street. When the taillights disappeared behind her, she came out from behind the tree and moved on. Suddenly she became aware of how cold she was. She was shivering violently. The wind had died, the rain was falling gently now. She turned and started back to the apartment. She would have to be very careful with Plum from now on. She'd have to reason calmly with him whenever *she* was angry, so she wouldn't make *him* angry. She couldn't take the chance of yelling at him again.

When she opened the door, Plum was standing there fully dressed.

"Where've you been?" he asked. "I've been worried to death. I've been driving all over the neighborhood, looking for you. My God, you're soaked! Take off those wet clothes." He went to the bathroom and came out with a towel and began drying her face and hair as she dropped her wet clothes on the floor around her. He rubbed her body briskly with the rough terry. When she was dry he took her in his arms.

"Batty, I'm sorry I hit you," he whispered. "I didn't mean to hit you. I'm really sorry. It's just that you provoked me. You *really* provoked me. If you hadn't provoked me so much, I'd never have hit a woman. Never."

She awakened the next morning with a terrible cold and a fever. But because there were lots of people depending on her to work lights for the last dress rehearsal and the two weekend performances of the play, she couldn't stay home and take care of herself. She got through the two performances, coughing and blowing her nose between lighting cues. She felt so miserable that she hadn't even tried to talk Plum into going to the cast party on Saturday after the final performance. At last, on Sunday, she was able to stay home and take care of herself. By then her fever had risen to a hundred and one, which was pretty high for her; she never had a fever over a hundred unless she was very sick. She slept almost all day.

Plum cooked supper that evening and offered to serve her in bed. Ever since he'd hit her, he'd been trying hard to make amends. He got out the cookbook and searched through it till he found a recipe for pot roast, and then banged around in the kitchen cooking it. When Batty put on her robe and came to the table, she was surprised at what a good dinner Plum had made. In addition to the pot roast, he'd cooked noodles, green beans, and corn bread. She only wished she'd had a better appetite. He even washed the dishes when they finished eating. It was almost worth being sick to have Plum cook and clean up.

The morning after he'd hit her, she had a big bruise at the corner of her eye. She'd covered it with a heavy coat of makeup and when a member of the lighting crew noticed it anyway and asked her about it, she said she'd run into the wall going to the bathroom at night without turning the light on. She was relieved on Sunday that she didn't have to see anyone who might notice the bruise and ask her about it. She wasn't sure the story of running into a wall was credible, and she certainly didn't want people to think she had a husband who would hit her.

On Monday morning, her fever was down to a hundred, but she still had chills and that awful acidic taste in the mouth that came with the flu. She got up, dressed with great effort, drove Plum to the campus, and then drove herself directly to the clinic connected with the medical school. It was a cold sunny day and the trees lining the roadway looked silver-gray in the sunlight. She drove to the back of the building and parked in the lot near the clinic. When she got out of the car she felt cold and vulnerable and pulled her coat tightly around her before she walked up to the waiting-room entrance. She presented her ID card to the young woman behind the reception desk, a bleached blonde wearing large gold-hoop earrings.

"What's the problem?" the woman asked.

"I think I've got the flu," Batty said.

"There's a lot of it going around," the woman said, sympathetically. "Just have a seat. It shouldn't be long."

The waiting room was nearly filled with the people who came to the clinic for the low fees. Most of them looked alien to the sophisticated academic life of Chapel Hill. A fat lady with her graying hair in a bun at the nape of her neck and wearing white ankle socks and wedge-heeled sandals sat with her chin braced in the palm of her hand, staring off into space. A frail-looking dark-haired woman wearing blue jeans rolled up above her ankles sat listlessly watching a runny-nosed little boy playing with his toy truck on the polished vinyl floor. A toothless old man wearing overalls and a shapeless straw hat sat with his large rough hands drumming on the arms of his chair as he watched with great interest the child playing on the floor. Batty decided quickly that she was the only student in the room. Picking up a magazine from the table, she sat down in one of the two empty chairs. She felt too sick to be very much interested in the magazine and was thumbing through it halfheartedly when she glanced up to see him coming through the entrance door. He was wearing a black pea jacket buttoned to the throat, the collar high on his neck. His dark hair was disheveled and his cheeks and nose were red from the cold.

"Gus," she called as she ran across the room, and then stopped abruptly and walked to him, wondering if it might be inappropriate for her, here and now, to be so glad to see him.

He stopped and looked at her, his mouth falling open. His expression went from surprise to delight, then to concern.

"My God, Batty," he said, "you look *awful*."

"I know," she said, blowing her nose in a soggy tissue. "I've got the flu, I think."

"Are you here to see a doctor?"

"Uh-huh," she said. "I didn't know you'd be here, Gus. I mean . . . what're you doing here?"

"I'm in medical school, you know that. I parked the car out back and was just taking a shortcut to class."

"Well, I knew you were *planning* to go to medical school here, but . . . "

"Mother told me you and Plum were here in school. I'm sorry I haven't called or anything. I've been very busy."

"That's all right," she said.

"Where're you living?"

"In Glen Lennox," she said, reaching into her pocket for a fresh tissue.

They were standing at the edge of the waiting-room area. The toothless old man had stopped watching the child and was watching them now.

"What happened there?" Gus asked, touching the bruise at the corner of her eye.

"I . . . I ran into a wall on the way to the bathroom one night last week," she said.

He looked at the bruise a moment. Then he looked into her face as if to read something there. "It's nice over there, isn't it?"

"Where?" she asked, thrown off the track. "Oh, you mean Glen Lennox. Yes, it's very nice. Where do you live?"

"I have an apartment in a house on Spruce Street."

"Do you still cook?"

Gus broke into a great big grin. "Yeah, that's how I relax. That is, when I have *time* to relax. Is married life treating you all right, Batty?" he asked, lowering his voice.

"Yes, just fine," she said.

He looked at her a moment. "How's Plum?"

"Fine, thank you."

"Mrs. Bradley," the woman behind the desk called.

"That's you, I guess," Gus said, smiling.

"Yes."

"Listen, Batty, we have a lot of catching up to do. I'll call you, okay? Maybe we can have lunch or something."

"Let's do, Gus," she said enthusiastically. "We'd love it."

"And for God's sake, Batty, after you've seen the doctor, go home and go to bed. You look just awful."

On Wednesday Batty was feeling much better. Her temperature was back to normal, she thought she'd be able to go to class the next day, and she planned to enjoy the luxury of this last day of rest. She'd just finished cleaning up from a late breakfast and was straightening the bed—before getting back into it to read for her course in American history—when Gus called.

"Hello, Batty," he said. "How do you feel today?"

"Much better now, thank you, Gus," she said.

"Good. I hope you *look* better, too," he said and burst out laughing.

"Some friend *you* are," she said, "and I don't look a bit better. I'm the same old runny-nosed wreck you saw on Monday."

"I'm sure you aren't," Gus said. "You certainly sound a lot better. I was worried about you."

"Were you really?" she asked. "That's nice. I like people to worry about me. I was beginning to think the only person who worried about me was me." She heard the self-pity in her words and added quickly, "Not really."

"Batty," Gus said, "listen . . . uh . . . I don't have classes this Monday and I'm just dying to make some good lamb curry. I was wondering if you could come have lunch with me?"

"We'd love to, Gus," she said, "but Monday isn't a good day. Plum has a seminar every Monday after—"

"I'm not inviting Plum," Gus said.

She didn't answer immediately. She felt herself flash hot and cold, that old familiar signal of fright. There was nothing she wanted more than to say yes, nothing she'd rather do than watch Gus cook again, and bring back the good times they'd had together. She knew it could never be the same, not anymore, but she wanted desperately to try to make it the same. Quickly she examined the possibilities. There was no *way* she could have lunch with Gus. Plum would never in a million years agree to it.

"Where?" she heard herself ask.

"At my place?"

"How would I get there?"

"It's just five short blocks from the old well. What time is your last class on Monday?"

"Ten to one."

"Where is it?"

"The scene shop."

"I'll pick you up."

"No," she said quickly, and paused a moment. "I'd better walk," she said. "Just give me the directions."

When she hung up the phone, she sat down at the dressing table and looked at herself in the mirror. Her face looked waxen, and her hair, which she hadn't washed since she got sick, was dirty. Oily strands, waving limply, fell to her shoulders. She looked terrible, but she was unmistakably herself. She wasn't looking at some stranger who'd inhabited her body long enough to make plans for a married woman to have lunch at another man's apartment. No, it was unmistakably the Batty she knew, or thought she knew until now.

She finished arranging the bed, stripped off her bathrobe and gown, went into the bathroom, turned on the shower as hot as she could stand it, and got in and began scrubbing herself vigorously all over.

She left her car in the theater parking lot where she knew Plum would never see it. He had a seminar in statistics on the other side of the campus every Monday afternoon and wouldn't be finished until four-thirty when she would pick him up. Thank God Plum hadn't asked any questions about what she was going to be doing this afternoon and she hadn't had to lie. He'd just assumed she was going home to study and do the laundry the way she usually did on Mondays. If she'd been forced to lie about Gus, she wasn't sure she could have done it. One of the things she'd always respected about herself was that she didn't lie.

She walked fast for fear someone who knew her might see her and wonder where she was going, or even *suspect* she was going someplace she shouldn't be going. She turned right onto Spruce Street, and when she got to the third house—the two-story white frame with the green shutters—she cut into the driveway and went to the back of the house and climbed the wooden steps to the second floor and stood on the little landing outside the door and knocked.

As soon as Gus opened the door, she was greeted by the delicious smell of curry cooking and felt a strange and sudden surge of joy.

"Well, come in," he said. "Don't just stand there like a ninny."

She laughed and entered a large well-lighted room filled with plants. A ceiling-high window divided into small panes overlooked a visit stretch of back lawn rimmed by huge old oak trees. A well-worn circular hooked rug formed the center of a seating area, comprised of a sofa with a fading floral-print upholstery and two stuffed chairs. Farther into the room was a Victorian table with claw feet, brightened by two place settings. Ferns, and spider plants, and wandering Jew hung in pots from the beams of the ceiling. Near the table a door led into a room Batty could see was the kitchen. Another door led into what she assumed was the bedroom.

"What a nice apartment," she said. "The plants are beautiful. Who takes care of them?"

"I do, who do you think?" Gus said, helping her take off her coat. He carried it to the bedroom and returned in a moment. "Do you really like it?"

"Oh, yes," she said. "It's so comfortable. It has a look of . . . of well-worn elegance, I guess you'd say."

"The curry should be ready in another fifteen or twenty minutes," he said. "I was just making the salad when you got here. Come on in and talk to me while I finish it."

He led the way into the kitchen. It was a small room with open shelves on which dishes, glasses, and cups and saucers were stacked upside down. There was a window with white sheer café curtains over the sink, a small refrigerator, and a gas stove that looked new. Low flames burned under a skillet and saucepan. Lettuce leaves, scallions, radishes and a tomato were draining in the dish rack.

"Pull up that stool over there," Gus said as he got down a large bowl and began breaking up the lettuce leaves.

"Are you sure there's nothing you want me to do?" Batty asked.

"No, nothing," Gus said. "Everything's under control." He

opened the oven door and Batty could see rolls browning on a baking sheet.

"Did you bake rolls just for the two of us?" she asked.

"Can you think of anybody better to bake them for?" he asked, smiling.

"No, I guess not," she said, smiling back at him. She sat watching him a minute as he sliced the scallions on the counter. She couldn't remember when she'd felt so relaxed and content. It had been a long time. "Gus," she said, "I'm awfully happy to be here."

His slicing stopped and he turned to look at her. "Good," he said, and turned back to his slicing. "How long can you stay, Batty?"

"I have to pick Plum up at four-thirty," she said. "Of course, I don't have to stay here all that time, if you have other things to do."

"*All* that time!" he said. "That's no time at all. Four-thirty'll be here before we turn around. We may not even have time for the dessert I spent all morning making."

Batty looked at her watch and laughed. "I think we'll have time for your dessert," she said.

Gus scooped rice onto each plate, then spooned the curry onto the rice, sprinkled the curry with coconut, and carried the plates to the table. He reached into the refrigerator, took out two bottles of beer, opened them on the wall can opener near the door, and carried them to the table.

"Just bring in the bread basket, Batty," he said as he poured the beer.

"I've never had beer," Batty said. "Will it make me drunk?"

"You'd have to drink an awful lot," Gus said. "You *must* have beer with curry. At least with my curry. Nothing else will do."

"It's very hot and very delicious," she said when she'd eaten the first bite.

"Have some beer," he said.

"Umm, it's good," she said.

"Just right," Gus said. "I've been longing for good curry, and the only way to get it is to make it yourself."

"I'm sure that's the only way to get curry as good as this," Batty said.

They ate for a few moments in silence. Batty hadn't realized she was so hungry . . . or thirsty, for that matter. The spicy curry made the beer delicious. Gus had been right. Beer was certainly a must with his curry.

Gus broke the silence. Suddenly, out of the blue, he asked, "Are you still planning to be an actress, Batty?"

"I . . . don't know, Gus," she said, surprised by his question. "I mean, it seems now . . . that it may not be . . . *possible* for me to work in the theater at all." She felt the tears welling up and the choke knotting in her throat. She blinked back the tears and swallowed hard. A big piece of half-chewed lamb stuck in her throat. She began choking and coughing and turned from the table and struggled to dislodge the lamb. The meat went on down and she began to breathe normally.

"Take a sip of beer," he said, holding the glass out to her. She swallowed the last of the beer, sat back, and looked at him through watering eyes.

"That must have been a disturbing question," he said.

She laughed. "I guess it was," she said.

"I didn't mean to upset you," he said. "I mean . . . I've just wondered why you decided to get married when I know how important acting was to you. I thought maybe you had some kind of an understanding with Plum."

"I guess I *thought* I did," she said. "But now it seems there's no understanding at all. Now that we're married Plum doesn't even want me to be out in the evening working on Playmaker productions which of course I *have* to do if I'm going to major in drama."

"I guess I can understand how he feels," Gus said. "I think most husbands wouldn't like the idea of their wives being out several nights a week."

He went to the kitchen and returned with two more bottles of beer. "Ready for more beer?" he asked.

"Yes, please," she said.

"And finish your curry, for heaven's sake."

He poured the beer as she ate. Then he took his plate into the kitchen and returned with it heaped with seconds. He ate in silence. Then he asked, "Why'd you marry him, Batty?"

She flicked her eyes at him and then turned her attention to cleaning up the last bite of rice. "Lots of reasons," she said. "For one thing, he's brilliant." She thought a moment. "And he's very calm and sensible, most of the time, except when I upset him terribly." She took a swallow of beer.

Gus was leaning over the table toward her now. "How on earth could you upset him terribly, Batty?" he asked. "By eating crackers in bed? Or something *equally* serious?"

The beer was beginning to make her feel warm and comfortable, and even though she feared that answering Gus's questions might somehow be a betrayal of Plum, she felt at the moment that Gus was an old friend she could talk to, and she certainly needed someone she could talk to. Gus continued looking at her with concern, waiting for her answer.

"I upset Plum by wanting to work in the theater," she said, "which he thinks is childish of me. He says I should grow up and get over this foolishness. He says I'm not committed to the marriage and if I were, I wouldn't care about acting." She began to sob. "He doesn't understand that I've wanted to work in the theater since I was twelve and taking lessons from Geraldine. He doesn't understand that I don't know another thing I'd want to do if I had to give up drama." It was all rolling out now with the tears, all the things she'd been keeping to herself for months now. "What am I going to do, Gus? I'd rather die than end up being just a housewife."

Gus was standing over her now. He put his hands under her arms and lifted her from the chair. She put her head on his shoulder and he stroked her hair gently.

"That's okay, Batty," he said. "Cry."

He led her to the sofa and sat down beside her, continuing to stroke her hair, talking to her while she sobbed. In a moment when she seemed to be calming a bit, he left her and went to the kitchen and returned with several paper napkins.

"Here, dry your face," he said, sitting beside her.

"I'm sorry I cried in the middle of your lunch," she said, blowing her nose.

"It's okay," he said, touching her hair again. His face was very close to hers now. "Batty," he said softly, "I don't think Plum makes you very happy. He's not like you at all, and he's not interested in anything that interests you. He doesn't deserve you, Batty. Whatever made you get married so early anyway?"

"In many ways, Plum's very special," she said.

"Well, I think *you're* very special," he said. "What're you going to do, Batty?" he asked, looking into her face.

"I don't know yet."

He looked at her intently a moment. Then he put his hands on either side of her face, and pulled her face to him, and kissed her forehead. He moved for her mouth then and kissed her firmly but gently. The very nearness of him gave Batty the first sense of real peace she'd known in months. He was kissing her neck now and running his hands up and down her back over her skirt and sweater. He moved his mouth to hers and kissed her, kissing her hard now, his mouth spreading over hers, his tongue pressing her lips apart and exploring inside. The feeling of peace was giving away. His hands were under her sweater, searching for her breasts. In a moment he moved away long enough to take hold of her sweater and pull it over her head. He unbuttoned her skirt.

"Take if off," he said.

She stood up and unzipped the skirt and stepped out of it.

"The slip, too," he said.

She pulled the slip over her head.

"And the rest of it."

"Not yet," she said.

He pulled her down beside him, his hand feverishly exploring her body. She knew for a lucid moment that she was about to commit adultery, and she knew that adultery was one of the worst of sins, a sin against everybody's rules. For as long as she could remember she'd played by the rules, never doing what *she* wanted to do, always doing what everybody else *expected* her to do. She'd worked hard to make good grades to please Mother and Daddy. She'd behaved herself in ways they'd be proud of because she'd heard a hundred times that her misbehavior would reflect badly on the entire family. She'd been listed among the *respectable* girls, resisting temptation right up until the day of her wedding, missing all those opportunities for hot satisfying sex when she'd wanted it so badly, waiting for the day, and then what she'd waited for so long hadn't been worth the wait. She'd been cheated. This time she was going to do what *she* wanted to do *when* she wanted to do it.

Gus's hands were on her naked buttocks. He had her panties down over her hips, and was slipping them down over her knees and feet, and lifting her from the sofa and carrying her. The ceiling revolved overhead. They were in another room. The furnishings refused to fall into place, a chest of drawers somewhere, a wall mirror, a desk littered with papers and books, he was lowering her onto sheets and was beside her. His hand was on her wetness and he was over her and moving into her. She sucked her breath in sharply and let it out in a long moan. And then he began to move slowly in and out of her and the room and its furnishings disappeared around them, and there were only she and Gus and Gus's long hard penis probing deep inside her and her vagina glowing warm and her legs spreading wider to let him in deeper, and him moving so deep as to approach the farthest wall of her, and then touching that wall of her solitude, and battering that wall of her solitude, and chipping that wall of her solitude, the pressure mounting, the glow brightening, then building into a brilliance she'd never known, her breath short and fast as Gus faded and then his cock faded and there was only the blinding light of herself filling the space she occupied, only herself for a long wonderful stretch of time, and then the wall of her solitude shattering and falling into a million pieces around them. Gus entered her aloneness, and they were there together now. She welcomed him with her kisses.

And then she cried.

"Are you crying?"

"A little."

"Why?"

"Because it was so good. Did you come?"

"Couldn't you tell?"

"I wasn't sure. Gus?"

"Uhmm?"

"That was the first time I ever had an orgasm."

He lifted himself heavily from the pillow and looked at her. "You're kidding," he said.

"No, it's true. Orgasms are nice, aren't they?"

He chuckled. Then he put his head on the pillow close to hers and kissed her neck. "I feel honored," he whispered.

During the next month, spring came to Chapel Hill. Forsythia exploded into color, and jonquils pushed through soft earth to open into blossoms clean and crisp as starched sunbonnets. Silver branches of pussy willow grew nubbly, and on maples and oaks, small buds swelled and reddened. On one particularly warm and sunny day, wide expanses of brown lawn were suddenly green.

All month long, Batty had felt a strange new lightness of spirit, a sense of power, an independence, an almost inexhaustible supply of energy. She burned through her classes and, in the afternoons when Plum was at his seminars, took long walks or drove through the countryside, pondering the things she was learning about herself. She knew that having exercised a new independence the afternoon she went to bed with Gus, she didn't want to return to the old subordination of her deep desires and wishes. She was beginning to understand that there were things she could do, things she *wanted* to do—and she wanted to do them without worrying constantly about someone else's reaction. She wanted to be a nineteen-year-old college girl and live in a dorm again, and have fun, and work on every Playmaker production, and learn everything Kurt had to teach her about the theater, and have someone—*anyone*—care about what *she* did. She was no longer convinced that going to New York to become a professional actress was a realistic goal. Maybe she'd go on to get her master's degree and teach in a college, or maybe she'd work in a good community theater in Charlotte or Atlanta. She had more than a year to figure it out exactly, but she knew she wanted to plan and control her own future.

She wanted to be Red Ryder again.

She thought about her marriage to Plum. Besides the fact that she knew as long as she was married to him his plans and dreams would always take precedence over hers and she would always have to sacrifice whatever didn't fit into Plum's life—just as it seemed she was going to have to give up her dream of working in the theater—by being unfaithful she had added what she saw as another insoluble problem to their relationship. Her infidelity was a secret she'd have to keep from him forever. If she told him, he'd never forgive her. But more than that, she was *afraid* to tell him. If he'd been angry enough to hit her for being out late at rehearsal, what would he do if he found out she'd been unfaithful? She couldn't see how a marriage with such a momentous secret between the partners could be much of a marriage at all. The secret would always be a wedge keeping them apart. It would be worse than when she was a little girl and had to keep the secret about Lula Ann from the other members of the family. For years, the secret had caused her loneliness and confusion. She didn't want a grown-up secret to cause her more years of agony. And if she kept this secret from Plum, she'd be living a lie for as long as she was married to him.

She hated lying, particularly if she was the one doing the lying. It made her feel weak and cowardly. She figured people lied only when they weren't courageous enough to handle a situation head-on, the way it should be handled. She didn't understand Plum's philosophy that sometimes, in a particular situation, the practical results of lying were better than the practical results of telling the truth, and that lying was, therefore, in some cases, not only justified, but advisable. She thought that if a superficial lie was called for, it had to be an adjustment for some profounder lie. A lie, she was convinced, was like the rings on a pool after you've thrown a pebble into the water. They multiply and expand till the whole pool is rippled. To Batty, if you wanted to keep the pool a smooth mirror of truth, you didn't throw in the pebble.

And if there *were* situations that justified lying to a college professor or to a butcher, at least in those cases the relationships were so limited that perhaps the ripples from the lie wouldn't have very far to expand. But if there was a lie between a wife and her own husband, the lie could send ripples of duplicity through the very foundations of their lives, ripples that would grow larger and multiply and confuse the mirror of truth as long as they lived.

She knew that Plum was a very special person. There was no doubt that he was brilliant and responsible and that he would love her and take care of her forever, and if she couldn't be happy simply being his wife, it was probably her own fault. She was probably too egotistical and ambitious, and her goal of working in the theater was probably too frivolous. And he was probably justified in demanding that *his* plans come first. After all, everybody knew he was the one who would have to earn a living. If she couldn't find anything wrong with him, then there had to be something wrong with her. But these days she didn't feel there *was* anything wrong with her; these days she felt that everything was *right* with her. After thinking about it for weeks, she decided that no matter what the reason for it she was unhappy in her marriage and that was that. If she'd been happy she wouldn't have been unfaithful in the first place.

She wanted a divorce.

Once she'd made the decision, she gave herself the whole month of April just to be sure of it. While she blocked *Winterset* for her directing class and wrote a term paper on Archibald MacLeish for her poetry class and a term paper on the Federalists for her American-history class, the decision percolated and settled and became firmly fixed, and by the end of the month she was more certain of it than ever.

It was the first Saturday in May when she decided it was time to tell Plum. They'd got home from lunch in the school cafeteria just in time for Plum to catch the golf tournament on television. He switched on the set.

"Plum, don't turn that on right now, please," she said. "I have something to talk to you about."

He looked at her over his shoulder, his eyebrows raised. Then he turned off the television and sat on the sofa. "What is it?" he asked, looking at her, concerned.

She thought perhaps he sensed what was coming, and hesitated a moment. Then she took a deep breath and began. "Plum," she said, "I'm not very happy being married. I want to get a divorce and live in the dormitory." She blurted it out all at once and sat stiffly looking at him, waiting for his response.

He simply stared at her, and sat not moving a muscle. She'd been wrong; he hadn't sensed what was coming at all. She continued to wait for his reaction.

"Plum?" she said finally.

He didn't respond.

In a moment he dropped his face into his hands and started sobbing. She'd never expected this, she hadn't thought Plum would cry in a million years. She felt at once a flood of pity and regret and went over to comfort him. She moved to put her hand on his shoulder and he struck out, knocking her arm away. He took a handerchief out of his pocket and quickly dried his face.

"Who is it?" he asked bitterly. "One of the drama students?"

"Of course not. It's nobody," she said. "I just don't want to be married anymore."

He sat looking at her, his arms folded across his chest, his mouth in a tight circle.

"I want to finish college and get a job," Batty said, "maybe teaching drama or working in a community theater."

He didn't move.

"Plum?" Batty said. "Don't you want to talk?"

Abruptly he got up and went into the bedroom.

"Operator, this is a person-to-person call to Robert Attwood at number forty-five in Robertson's Fort, North Carolina," she heard him say.

She froze. He was calling Daddy. He was going to *tell* on her.

She ran into the bedroom. "Plum," she begged, "please don't tell Daddy. Please don't." He was sitting on the edge of the bed. She sat on the floor at his feet. "Please, Plum, let's work this out by ourselves."

"Bob," Plum said into the phone, and began sobbing. "Batty wants a divorce. She says she's not happy married to me." He sobbed even louder now. A tear dropped from the end of his nose onto the bedspread. Then he was quiet, listening. Batty drew her knees up tight to her chest.

"Yes, she's right here," he said, and held the phone out to her, and got up and walked into the bedroom.

She took the phone and got up from the floor and sat on the edge of the bed where he'd been sitting.

"Hello," she said.

"Beatrice Louise, I'm disappointed in you," Daddy said.

"Yes, I know, Daddy, but—"

"But what?"

"But, I'm not very happy. I want—"

"You haven't been married a year yet and you've decided you're not happy. Batty, you haven't given it a chance."

"Daddy, I want to finish my education and—"

"Well, of course you're going to finish your education. That has nothing to do with giving up on your marriage. The very thought of a daughter of mine getting a divorce makes me sick," he said and took a deep breath. "Now listen, Batty, it's not like you to give up on something. You can't run away, you're the one who made the decision to marry Plum in the first place, and now you have to see it through. Your problem's always been that you're selfish. You've got to learn to think of someone other than yourself, to put yourself in the place of the other person, to empathize a little. Plum sounds almost destroyed, look what you've done to him. You've got to think about how he feels. If you always put yourself first, you'll *never* be happy . . . not with Plum, not with *anybody.*"

"Yes, Daddy."

"If you want to be happy, just start thinking about making Plum happy. That's what real happiness is all about, it's about making someone else happy. You just stop thinking about Batty all the time and start thinking about Plum, and one day you'll wake up to discover you've found true happiness, do you understand me?"

"Yes, sir."

"And don't let me hear another word about divorce. Do you understand?"

"Yes, sir."

"Now let me speak to your husband."

He was coming out of the bathroom, his eyes dry and his face freshly washed.

"Daddy wants to speak to you," she said, handing him the phone.

Glancing up occasionally from her book, Batty could see that across the lawn, Grandmother's house was dark. Thank heavens, on this night of her exhaustion, Grandmother's sleep was undisturbed. As Batty read, insects banged into the screen of her window, open to the cool evening air. She came to the end of the chapter and looked at the electric clock on the bedside table. It was almost ten-thirty. For three hours, she'd been waiting for the phone to ring. She was beginning to get a little frantic. He'd promised to call after dinner and it wasn't like him not to do what he'd said he'd do. Maybe something had happened to him— maybe he'd had an accident or something. Or maybe his day had been *such* a success, maybe he'd met so *many* scintillating people that he'd forgotten about *her* completely. Or maybe he'd met a tall, beautiful, and rich blonde looking for a good investment, and maybe he'd taken her to dinner to talk about it and maybe he was with her right now, and maybe that was why he hadn't called.

She looked at herself in the mirror across the room from the bed where she was propped against two pillows with white cases. Dressed in her favorite blue gown, high at the neck and sleeveless, her hair falling loose around her shoulders (the gray not visible from across the room), she looked small and prim, and rather young against the high, dark Victorian headboard—almost as young as she'd looked all those years ago when she went to bed every night in this same bed. She tried to evoke the image of her younger self. There was no doubt, she thought, that she looked better now that she'd lost that insipid bloom of youth, now that her face had become very definitely what it had merely been trying to become when she was sixteen, now that the candy glaze of girlhood had crazed and shattered and the promise underneath had unfolded and ripened into this woman that was herself.

She examined the small birthmark on her left hand. She remembered very well the day she'd discovered it. She didn't know exactly how old she was, only that she'd been very young and that she was sitting on the ground in the backyard and leaning against a tree trunk when her attention was captured by the small Cyrillic that her childhood eyes had seen as a tiny bird. It had faded over the years but it was still there, a small brown comma, it seemed now.

She fluffed her pillows and reached over to pick up her book again just as she heard the faint sound of the distant train whistle coming from the bottomland east of town. She put the open book, facedown, on the blanket beside her and listened. She could hear the growing roar of the engine, then the whistle again, this time nearer, and louder, and repeating over and over. If Grandaddy were here, he'd curse the engineer royally for blowing the whistle longer than necessary and waking up everybody when two or three little toots would have served as well. She heard the syncopated cadence of the wheels going over the cross-ties as the train whizzed through town and then the sound faded to an interrupted murmur as the train wound around the curves heading west and into the mountains, as though the echo of its earlier percussion were being bounced off the black forms looming against the night sky like great shadows fallen across the imagination. She sat there listening for the final wail—when it came, so faint she could hardly hear it—and then, for long moments, continued listening to the silence, and suddenly she was enveloped by the memory of all those years when her nights had been punctuated by those same train sounds while she was lying in this same bed she lay in now, and all the years in between were compressed into the tight space between those bookends. Her life had taken a long and circuitous route through that elliptical time to where she found herself at forty—at peace with herself, and, at last, fulfilled, and . . . yes, happy.

She remembered the day she gave up this room and this bed to marry Plum, and she remembered their years together at Chapel Hill. They hadn't been such bad years, she thought. They both were just so young, so *very* young. And she remembered the years in the apartment in White Plains while Plum was beginning the long hard climb up the executive ladder, and starting from the lowest rung, and she remembered him working late many days because he was ambitious, and bringing work home, and she remembered him looking tired sometimes, and getting discouraged sometimes, and thinking he'd sold his soul to the corporation sometimes, and blaming *her* for it all sometimes, and being satisfied that he was doing just what he wanted to do sometimes, because he could think of nothing in the world that he would rather be doing than working for a good company like United American Chemicals, and their both knowing that one day he would "make it" and be rewarded with money, money, money. And she remembered that while he was working his long hours, she was reading books, and doing gourmet cooking, and entertaining his friends from the company, and their wives, and taking up tennis at the company's club and she remembered Plum's continuing to insist that she couldn't go to acting school or get involved in the theater, or do anything else that would keep her away from home when he got there at the end of the day, because, of course, since he worked so hard he had every right to expect that when he finally *did* come home it was to a clean apartment, and good food and sympathetic companionship.

She tried very hard during those years to be unselfish and to think of Plum first, and to be a good wife, just as Daddy had told her back then at nineteen when she'd decided she wanted a divorce. And she might have made it, too, if she hadn't had such a sense that there was a great and meaningful void in her life, and if she hadn't suffered from a growing and undeniable restlessness, and if she hadn't decided after three years out of college that if she didn't find something worthwhile of her *own* to do, she would slowly go crazy. She decided then that if she couldn't work in the theater—which was her first love—maybe she might like to learn to paint, and she enrolled in a painting class and a drawing class at the Art Students League, taught by, of all things, a sculptor.

She remembered the first time she saw him.

It was the first day of class and he rushed in five minutes early and began arranging his materials on the large table before him. He was wearing blue corduroy pants and a white long-sleeved shirt open at the neck and with the sleeves rolled up. He was tall, but not as tall as Plum, close to six feet, she guessed, and he was very slender, almost delicately built, and his face with its delicate planes and the dark eyes slanting downward looked as though it was more at home with sadness than with joy. Yet during that first day he was almost effervescent with playfulness and volubility. Upon first sight, she knew he was unlike any man she'd ever known. There was something about him that was almost foreign, exotic. And when he introduced himself to the class as Ben Sternberger—"Call me Ben," he said—her mind groped to translate clues. She decided that maybe he was Jewish.

She remembered the first time the class drew from a live model. It was the second week of class. She recalled with pain how naive and unsophisticated she'd been at twenty-three, and how she forced herself to look at the young female body curling through a series of poses for quick gesture drawings and how she'd been afraid that her face would actually turn red when she, with a few strokes of the charcoal, suggested pubic hair, and how she furiously sketched through that series of poses hoping no one was aware of her burning humiliation—especially *him*—she certainly didn't want him to know what an unsophisticated small-town Southern dope she was, not when he was, according to the catalogue, New York born and bred, which right away meant he was a lot more worldly-wise than she, not to mention that he had to be at least thirty years old just from looking at him.

When he looked at her sketches he told her to relax her arm and make freer strokes and not to worry about distortion, because, he said, distortion is often very interesting. Just try to get the feeling, he said. And she worked on it and did as he said and the next week when there was a different model—an old woman with lots of droops and sags, bags and pouches—her sketches of the body were pretty good, she thought, until he assigned a sustained drawing and she had trouble with the feet. She sketched and erased, and sketched and erased till the paper was thin. Just as she was beginning to get very frustrated, he came up behind her and without saying a word—he didn't even ask—made three strokes on the paper that gave her everything she needed to go on from there. She looked at those foreign marks on her drawing and felt the anger rise and turned to register it with him just as he said, "Your drawing is getting much looser. Hands and feet are very difficult. You ought to spend a lot of time sketching just hands and feet. All it takes is practice, practice, practice." And she looked back at the lines that he'd drawn on her paper and it was all right now. "Thank you," she said, and smiled, and he smiled and went on to the next student as she began developing the strokes he'd given her, incorporating them, making them her own.

The next week they had lunch together. She was the last student to leave the room at the end of class because she'd got so involved in shading a modeled drawing she was working on that she didn't want to stop till she was satisfied with it. He'd puttered around the room while she was working, putting away supplies and stacking easels against the wall. Just as she was looking at her drawing one last time, before putting her supplies away and closing her sketch pad, he came up behind her.

"Think of the light as coming from only one side of the object," he said. "You almost never see light equalized on all sides of an object, certainly not natural light. Come look," he said and went to the window. "See what I mean? Everything out there—the buildings, the automobiles, the people—is lit by the sun and has a light side and a dark side. Even in the shade, when the light is reflected, one side gets more light than the other." He went back to her drawing. "You don't have to make the dark side dramatically darker, just suggest it, if you prefer. Maybe just a heavy black outline on the darker side."

With the crayon she sketched in the heavy black outline on the left side of the figure and stood back and realized that even with this small modification the drawing had taken on more dimension.

"See what I mean?" he said. "You might want to make the shading on that side a little heavier. But even without that, it's better."

"There are a lot of tricks to drawing, aren't there?" she said.

"What do you mean?" he asked.

"I mean there's not really a black line defining the edge of things, not even on the shaded side, only in drawings. Some of the drawings we've done—the contour drawings, for instance—are only black lines defining the edges. Others, like the gesture drawings, don't have black edges at all. And now you've shown me how to give a drawing more depth by giving it a black edge that the model I was drawing didn't have at all, or at least, not that I noticed," she said, laughing.

"Drawing is a combination of two things," he said, "a good eye and—you're right—a bag of tricks . . . or *symbols,* if you prefer. There are a few things you can reproduce on a flat surface just by observing them carefully, how one part relates to the others on a flat plane . . . but as soon as you move away from that flat plane you're not directly reproducing reality at all. You're beginning to use symbols that are just as abstract and as stipulated as the Phoenician alphabet." He threw his canvas bag over his shoulder. "This is an interesting topic, Batty," he said. "You want to finish the discussion over a sandwich?"

She closed her pad and put it under her arm. This was the first time in months she'd talked to anybody about anything other than organizational politics and office personnel and she felt flushed with excitement by the brief mental exertion. "Yes, thank you, I'd like to," she said.

They walked over to a delicatessen on Sixth Avenue and ate pastrami sandwiches and big juicy kosher pickles and drank cold beer, and talked with their mouths full, till they'd exhausted the subject of art and symbolism, Batty's mind stretching to comprehend more entirely things she'd begun to explore during those long hours of staying home and reading books.

"Where in the South are you from?" he asked.

"How did you know I was from the South?"

"I hadn't a clue," he said.

"I'm from North Carolina."

"What part?"

"You wouldn't have heard of it," she said. "A small town in the mountains, Robertson's Fort. It's about twenty-five miles from Asheville."

"Thomas Wolfe country."

"Yes, do you like Thomas Wolfe?"

"I read him about ten years ago," he said, "soon after I graduated from art school. I *loved* him then. I'm not sure I'd like him as much now."

"Why is that? He hasn't changed, you know," Batty said, laughing.

"No, but I probably have. I think Thomas Wolfe is more of a kindred spirit for the young who're tortured by insecurities and consumed by the search for self-identity than for older people who're more settled and more certain of who they are and what they're about."

"Maybe," Batty said, remembering how much she'd loved the emotional richness and deliciously painful sensitivity of *Look Homeward, Angel* when she'd read it a year ago. "Do you feel that way?" she asked. "I mean . . . settled and sure of who you are and what you're about?"

"Pretty much," he said simply.

"That must be wonderful," she said, smiling.

"It's not bad," he said. "What're you doing up here?"

"My husband works for United American Chemicals in White Plains."

"Is he a Southerner, too?"

"Yes."

"And he wears a white shirt to work every day?"

"Yes, how did you know?"

"Everybody knows that anybody who works for United American Chemicals wears a white shirt to work."

And then his dark eyes flashed on her face and he asked her something so unexpected that for a moment she was lost for an answer. "And do you love him?" he asked.

She looked down at her hands, folded in her lap. "Well . . . yes, of course I love him," she said, and brought her eyes up to his and waited for his next question.

He continued looking at her for a moment. She was afraid he was looking into her mind, knowing what was there before she knew. She felt awkward and at a disadvantage. Then he reached for his canvas bag and took out his wallet.

"Shall I walk you to the station?" he asked when he'd paid the bill.

"No, thank you," she said, reaching under the table for her sketch pad. "I have some things to do before I go home."

Outside the revolving door she said, "Thank you very much, Ben. I enjoyed the lunch and the conversation a lot."

He took a pipe and a tobacco pouch from his bag and—steadying himself with a hand on her shoulder—lifted a foot and tapped the ashes out of the pipe on the sole of his shoe. Then he filled the pipe and lit it, slowly sucking the match flame into the bowl. She waited. When the pipe was lit, he sucked in a mouthful and exhaled the aromatic smoke on the autumn air. He looked at her a moment, and then he smiled and said softly, "I had a good time, too, Batty. I'll see you next week." And having been released, she turned and, discovering the light was green, rushed across Sixth Avenue, heading toward Fifth. Across the street, she turned to watch him walking away from her, his jaunty duck-footed walk, his head tossing slightly from side to side with every step, puffs of smoke trailing behind him. She stood on the corner watching him till he was a block away and lost among the other pedestrians. She watched him very carefully, memorizing everything about the way he walked.

She knew already it was something she would never forget. And she'd never forget the first time he took her to see his studio. They rode the subway all the way downtown to Canal Street, and carried sandwiches and beer up three flights of stairs to enter a large room lit by three tall windows. There was a long rough worktable at one end of the room, and the inside wall was lined with shelves upon which were stored several rolls of chicken wire, a stack of iron pipes, about a dozen old cardboard boxes, two aluminum buckets, several large tin cans, and five small pieces of sculpture in a variety of materials. In the center of the room was a huge construction of iron pipes, wooden sticks, chicken wire, nuts and bolts, all bound together at the joints with what looked like huge hospital bandages. Batty looked at it a moment and turned to Ben.

"I don't know what it is," she said, "but *whatever* it is, it's been in a bad fight."

They both laughed and she felt pleased with herself for being so relaxed and open, for feeling good enough about herself to be silly, and she knew it was because of Ben, that he demanded nothing of her, that it was *herself* he liked, it was *herself* to whom he talked for hours about his sculpture, or her drawing, or a poem he'd read, or a play he'd seen, or the way he was feeling about something. And when *she* talked, it was *her* ideas he listened to so attentively and so respectfully, *her* ideas, and sometimes, she noticed, he incorporated some idea she'd shared with him into his idea so that they became one idea, and sometimes he'd change his mind about something and adopt her idea completely.

He explained that she was looking at the armature, or frame, for a piece of sculpture he was just beginning, and he showed her the small clay model for it and the drawings he'd done. It looked sort of like a big fat doughnut with the hole off-center. And then he explained that as soon as he was successful enough at selling his works and could afford the foundry costs, he would do a lot of very large pieces, and that it was the success of the show he'd had at a Madison Avenue gallery over the summer that made it possible for him to do the huge doughnut which he called "Point Blank." When she asked, he explained to her the various stages in the process of making such a piece of bronze-cast sculpture, beginning with the building of the armature and the working of the clay to the sending of the plaster mold to the foundry to be cast.

And then they ate their sandwiches on the worktable and when they had finished eating, before locking up the studio and heading uptown, he held her and kissed her gently on the eyelids, and she looked up at him with tears in her eyes because she didn't want to go.

And she would never forget the first time they made love. He called her at home, which he'd never done before, and asked her if she wanted to make love to him and she said yes so easily that she must have amazed him, and he told her to meet him at his Upper West Side apartment after class the next day, and when they were in the bedroom she took off her clothes very fast, not even waiting for him to kiss her first, not waiting for him to peel off layer by tantalizing layer, just stripped them off and left them in a pile, and he looked a little baffled by her, as though he'd been denied something. But she was dead serious about this thing and not there for childish games, and then he took off his clothes, hurrying because she was sitting on the edge of the bed, nude, waiting for him. And when he took off his pants and tried to line up the cuffs to hang them on the hanger, in his haste, he fumbled so that he couldn't get them straight and finally gave up and tossed them on the chair and gave her a weak smile of resignation, and she smiled back at him, understanding him better than she'd ever understood anyone, because he was just like her. When he'd taken off his clothes, she looked at him standing there, his delicate legs and flat belly, the fine silky hair wrapping around his body, deepening in places, her eyes flicking across him discreetly there where he stood ready for her, that part of him surprisingly substantial and solid against his delicate frame. He motioned for her to get up, and he turned back the cover and crawled in, and she slipped in beside him and wrapped her arms around him and buried her face in his neck and let her love flow over him, aware of the newness of the feel of him, his strange boniness. She remembered saying to him, "You're all corners," as she snuggled against him, and he lifted himself on one elbow and moved over her and kissed her, and she spread for him and took his cock in her hand, to guide him as he slid over her and into her. And she was so ready for him that the thick waters of her love bubbled at the edge of the moment and fell, and rose and fell, she waiting for him there, while before them the current they rode on shot into the air from the peak of their desire, a cascade, splashing and falling, bursting into spray, catching the sun, a glissando of light, and she held him and kissed his face and he joined her at the edge where before them the great white mare's tail of their passion switched in anticipation, and clinging to each other, they gave themselves to it and tumbled, weightlessly turning, slowly dropping deep into their joy. She held him inside her till the last echo of their pleasure had faded. Then he rolled away, and they lay, eyes closed and breathing heavily. He found her hand and squeezed it weakly.

"Was that all right?" he asked finally from his pillow.

"The very best," she said.

"And will you leave your husband and marry me?" he asked.

And she felt irritated that he could be frivolous enough to joke at that moment. "This is no time for jokes," she said.

"I'm not joking," he said flatly.

And she turned to look at him and knew that he was dead serious.

And she would never forget the agony of making the decision when, after a while, they *both* knew he was dead serious. And she would never forget the agony of knowing she had to tell Plum, and waiting for the right moment to tell him. And she would never forget that when she did tell him he cried a second time, but this time he didn't call Daddy, because he knew that this time Daddy was too far away to help—and *she* knew that if Daddy had been next door, he couldn't have kept her from Ben, nobody could have, now that she'd finally found him.

And so she left Plum, just moved herself out one fine spring day, and he'd been deeply hurt for an appropriate period of time and then had filled her absence with, of all things, a tall, willowy, and gorgeous redhead who was the female prototype of himself. And he'd done well over the years—not yet chairman of the board, but vice president in charge of a major division.

And for seventeen years, she'd loved Ben, and been *in* love with Ben, just as she'd promised him a long time ago when she told him she knew as long as they both lived she'd always love him, and when he'd asked, "When I'm an old man with no teeth, and rancid breath, and scrambled thoughts, will you love me then?" she'd answered, knowing it was true, "I'll always love you, Ben. Even then."

And when she knew she finally had him and that she adored him and would adore him forever, forever became too short. And so she nagged at him to quit smoking and to take care of himself, because she wanted him to live a long, long time, just as she planned to live a long, long time, because though she didn't know for sure that death was the end of everything, neither did she know it wasn't. She wanted Ben always just as he was when she met him and fell in love with him, and she wanted him as he was when they had Jennifer together—who thank God, with her brown hair and dark eyes slanted downward, looked like both of them and so was the perfect child of their love. And she wanted him the way he was before *Time* magazine did a story on him and *The New Yorker* did a profile on him and *The New York Times* put him on the cover of the Sunday Magazine Section. And she wanted him the way he was *after* his success when they bought the old sawmill in Westport so she could have a bigger studio and he could have a whole barn and the great out-of-doors to work in, and she wanted him the way she found him when at the end of the day she walked across the grass from her studio to the barn where he was working with his assistants. And she wanted him the way he was just this minute *wherever* he was that he wasn't calling her as he'd promised he'd call her after dinner and it was almost eleven o'clock already.

She thought about the opening of Ben's show today at the Pace Gallery. Over the past year and a half she'd watched the development of each of the twelve pieces, seen Ben's small models translated into the large versions, watched him move around each work with his pad, alternately examining the piece and sketching revisions and then instructing his two assistants. At times, she'd seen him struggling to find the form he wanted, the muscles of his body tensing as his mind wrestled with those huge shapes to bend them to his command.

And when the last one was finished and the patina had been applied and the twelve were lined up in the barn awaiting transportation to the gallery, she'd made dry martinis and they'd sipped them as they walked among the pieces like proud parents. She'd missed seeing them set up at the gallery for the opening, but she knew they'd still be there when she returned, and she'd have plenty of time to see the show and feel proud of Ben—which she did anyway, even without seeing it.

The phone rang. She glanced at the clock. It was eleven-fifteen. She grabbed her robe from the foot of the bed and stuck her arms in the sleeves and ran to the kitchen, pulling the robe around her.

"Hello," she said.

"Hello, Batty," Ben said.

"Oh, Ben, I've been so worried. I'm so glad to hear your voice. Is everything all right?"

"Everything is fine, darling, just fine. I'm sorry I'm so late calling. I wanted to wait till I was sure."

"Sure of what, Ben?"

"Guess who I had dinner with?"

She thought of the tall rich blonde. "I haven't the vaguest notion," she said.

"Mr. and Mrs. Hirschhorn! They're absolutely charming. And guess what! He's buying two pieces, 'Adam's Choice' and 'Medusa.' "

"Oh, that's wonderful, Ben!"

"And I told them all about you. They're dying to meet you and see your work. I told them you'd call to make arrangements when you got home. We sold nine pieces today. Isn't that incredible? And there are holds on the other three."

"I can't believe it, Ben! Oh, Ben, I'm so excited. I *wish* I could have been there."

"Me too, Batty. You would have loved it. The gallery was packed all afternoon. How's everything there?" he asked, his tone changing. "I'm sorry I couldn't be there. Is your grandmother holding up all right?"

"She's going to be fine, Ben. She just got awfully tired today. And Mother and Daddy are okay. They just went to bed a few minutes ago. There were an awful lot of people I hadn't seen in years at the funeral."

"When will you be home, Batty?"

"There's not much more I can do here. I should be able to come home Tuesday."

"Good," Ben said. "The sooner the better. I love you, Batty, and I miss you."

"I love you, too, Ben."

Jennifer stuck her head around the door just as Ben asked, "Is Jennifer still up?"

"Is that Dad?" she asked.

"She's right here, Ben."

"Let me talk to her. And Batty?"

"Yes?"

"Make it an early flight, okay?"

"The earliest," she said, smiling, and handed the phone to her daughter.